By Faye Kellerman

THE RITUAL BATH • SACRED AND PROFANE
THE QUALITY OF MERCY • MILK AND HONEY
DAY OF ATONEMENT • FALSE PROPHET
GRIEVOUS SIN • SANCTUARY • JUSTICE
PRAYERS FOR THE DEAD • SERPENT'S TOOTH
MOON MUSIC • JUPITER'S BONES
STALKER • THE FORGOTTEN
STONE KISS • STREET DREAMS
STRAIGHT INTO DARKNESS • THE BURNT HOUSE
THE MERCEDES COFFIN • BLINDMAN'S BLUFF
HANGMAN

Coming Soon in Hardcover

GUN GAMES

Short Stories

THE GARDEN OF EDEN AND
OTHER CRIMINAL DELIGHTS

With Jonathan Kellerman

DOUBLE HOMICIDE
CAPITAL CRIMES

With Eliza Kellerman

PRISM

FAYE KELLERMAN

false prophet

A DECKER/LAZARUS NOVEL

HARPER

An Imprint of HarperCollinsPublishers

HARPER

An Imprint of HarperCollins*Publishers*
10 East 53rd Street
New York, New York 10022-5299

Copyright © 1992 by Faye Kellerman
Cover photo by Steve Prezant/CORBIS
ISBN 978-0-06-199933-8

First Harper premium printing: August 2011
First Avon Books mass market printing: December 2005
First William Morrow hardcover printing: September 1992

HarperCollins ® and Harper ® are registered trademarks of Harper-Collins Publishers.

Printed in the United States of America

Visit Harper paperbacks on the World Wide Web at
www.harpercollins.com

10 9 8 7 6 5 4 3 2 1

As usual for my family

And for Liza Dawson, Leona Nevler,
and Ann Harris
—thank you

1

Working off duty meant doing the same job without pay. But since the call's location was only twelve blocks away and the case would wind up in his detail anyway, Decker figured he might as well jump the uniforms. Cordon off the scene before the blues could trample evidence, making his on-duty tasks that much easier. He unhooked the mike, answered the radio transmitting officer—and turned on the computer screen in the unmarked Plymouth. A few moments later, green LCD lines snaked across the monitor.

A female assault victim—suspected sexual trauma—no given name or age. The Party Reporting had been female and Spanish speaking. The victim had been found by the PR in a ransacked bedroom. Paramedics had been called down.

Decker made a sharp right turn and headed for the address.

The interior of the Plymouth was rich with the aroma of newly baked breads—a corn rye loaded with caraway seeds, two crisp onion boards, a dozen poppy-seeded kaiser and crescent rolls, and assorted Danishes. Goodies just pulled from the oven, so hot

the bakery lady didn't dare put them in plastic. They
sat in open white wax-lined bags, exhaling their
yeasty breath, making his mouth water.

Fresh bakery treats seemed to be Rina's only crav-
ing during the pregnancy and Decker didn't mind
indulging her. The nearest kosher bakery was a
twelve-mile round trip of peace and quiet. He enjoyed the early-morning stillness, cruising the stretch
of open freeway, witnessing the fireworks on the
eastern horizon. He reveled in the forty minutes of
solitude and resented the intrusion of the call, the
location so close he couldn't ignore it, his mind
forced to snap into work-mode.

He turned left onto Valley Canyon Drive, the
roadside cutting through wide-open areas of ranch-
land. In the distance was the renowned Valley Canyon Spa Resort—a two-story pink-stucco monolith
carved into the foothills of the San Gabriel Mountains. It looked like a giant boil on the sandy-colored
face of the rocks. The guys in the squad room had
shortened the spa's name to VALCAN, which in
turn had been bastardized to VULCAN. The running joke was that VULCAN's clientele were secret
relatives of Mr. Spock beamed down to get ear jobs.
VULCAN had hosted more stars than the sidewalks
of Hollywood Boulevard, its facilities among the
most exclusive in the United States. That, and the
fact that the place was run by Davida Eversong's
daughter, made it a national draw for rich anorexic
women wanting to exercise themselves skeletal.

Davida Eversong was one of those self-proclaimed
grandes dames of Old Hollywood. Scuttlebutt had it
that she had burrowed herself into a bungalow on

the spa's acreage. Once Decker had spotted her at a local mom-and-pop market. Her features had been hidden by sunglasses and a black turban that wrapped around her cheeks and tied under her chin. It had been her getup that had attracted his attention. Who dressed like that at night except someone wanting to be noticed? But only he had given her a second glance. To the rest of the shoppers, she had been just another L.A. eccentric.

Decker was barely old enough to remember the latter part of her long film career—the last three or four movies where she'd been thrown some bones—courtesy parts. Then came the talk-show circuit promoting the autobiography. The book had been a best seller. That had been about fifteen years ago and nothing public since. Still, the name Eversong conjured up images of studio Movie Queens and Hollywood glamour. Eversong's daughter was certainly not inhibited about using the connection. Maybe she was genuinely proud of Mama. Or maybe it just made good business sense.

Scoring the base of the spa's mountain was a single file of multicolored sweatsuits; the ladies coming back from their morning aerobic hike. From Decker's perspective, they looked like Day-Glo ants encircling a giant hill.

He reached inside one of the paper bags, broke off a piece of warm cherry Danish, and stuffed it into his mouth. Chewing, he called Rina on his radio, telling her why he wouldn't make it for breakfast. She sounded disappointed but he couldn't tell what bothered her more—his absence or the absence of her morning kaiser roll.

Not that she didn't enjoy his company, but she was more preoccupied than usual. That was to be expected. Though he kept hoping her self-absorption would pass, he'd come to realize it was wishful thinking.

El honeymoon was *finito*. Time to get down to the business of *living*.

He remembered the physical exhaustion that accompanied a newborn—long nights of interrupted sleep, the bickering, the tension. His ex-wife had looked like a zombie in the morning. Acted like one, too. He also remembered the joy of Cynthia's first smile, her first steps and words. He supposed it would be easier the second time around because he knew what to expect. But damned if he wasn't going to miss being the center of Rina's attention.

He bit off another piece of Danish, wiped crumbs off his ginger-colored mustache.

Well, that's just life in the big city, bud.

He pushed the pedal of the unmarked, the car chugalugging its way up the curvy mountain road. The address on the computer screen corresponded to a ranch adjacent to the spa. The pink blob and its next-door neighbor were separated by ten acres of undeveloped scrubland, but he couldn't find any definitive line dividing the two properties.

He found the numbers posted on a freestanding mailbox at the driveway's entrance. Turning left down a winding strip of blacktop, he parked the unmarked in front of the ranch house. It was a white, wood-sided, one-story structure sitting on a patch of newly planted rye grass. Bordering the house were rows of fruit trees—citrus on the left, apricot, plum, and peach on the right. Between the trees, he could make out crabgrass and scrub, the foliage gradually thickening to gray-green shrubs and chaparral as the land bled into the base of the mountains.

He punched his arrival into the computer—a whopping two minutes, twenty-two seconds response time. Nothing like being blocks away to skew the stats in LAPD's favor. He stepped out of the unmarked and gave the place a quick glance. Although the house was modest in size, there was something off about it.

The wood siding sparkled like sun-drenched snow—not a flake of paint dared to mar the surface. The flagstone walkway held nary a crack, and the wood shingles on the roof were ruler aligned. The porch was also freshly painted. It didn't creak and held a caned rocking chair decorated with crocheted doilies draped over curved arms. The place was a perfect ranch house. *Too* perfect. It looked like a movie set.

Decker banged on the door and identified himself in Spanish as a police officer. The woman who let him in was frazzled and babbling incoherently, evoking *Dios* between hysterical sobs. She was around forty, her soft plumpish body squeezed into a starched-white servant's uniform. Her dark eyes were full of fear and her fingers were clutching the roots of her hair. She led him into a trashed bedroom. The bed was a heap of jumbled sheets and broken glass. Drawers had been opened and emptied of their contents. But Decker's eyes focused on the center of the floor.

She lay crumpled like a discarded article of clothing, blindfolded, partially nude, her skin bruised and clay-cold. Immediately, he knelt beside her, checked her pulse and respiration. Though her breathing was shallow, her heartbeat was palpable. Quickly, Decker eyeballed the body for hemorrhage—nothing overt. Though the floor was hard and chilled, Decker didn't dare move her in case there were spinal injuries. He ordered the maid to bring him a blanket, then carefully removed the blindfold and gasped when he saw who it was.

Davida Eversong's daughter—VULCAN's owner. He'd seen her picture dozens of times in the local throwaways. Human Interest stories: the spa hosting a Save the Whales weekend extravaganza or a special two-for-one rate to benefit the homeless. Her stunning face gracing the front page of *The Deep Canyon*, *Bellringer*, arm in arm with a different star every week.

What the hell was *her* name? Everybody always called her Davida's daughter. Even the local papers constantly referred to her as so-and-so, daughter of Davida Eversong. Her name was something exotic. Lara? Not Lara, *Lilah*. That was it. Lilah. Lilah B-something. So she lived next door to her spa. That made sense.

He could make out her beauty even in her current state. Her eyelids were puffy, her lower lip swollen and cracked. Her neck was imprinted with red indentations, but there were no deep ligature marks around her throat. She had welts over her upper torso as if someone had whipped her.

Decker took out his pocket spiral and started noting the injuries he saw. If she remained unconscious, unable to give consent to be photographed, his record of specific marks would be valuable evidence of the crime.

The poor woman. Her nightdress had been hiked over her pelvis. Some sexual activity had occurred. Decker smelled the musky odor of semen in the room. He finished some cursory notes, then lowered her gown and covered her as soon as the maid returned with the comforter. Smoothing blond wisps off her clammy forehead, he gently touched her cheeks, hoping the heat from his hands would warm her face. Streams of gentle breath flowed across his hands.

He whispered "Lilah," but got no response. As the seconds passed, her cheeks seemed to take on color. Decker turned to the maid, told her not to touch anything, asked her to wait outside and direct the paramedics. In the background, he could hear approaching sirens.

Brecht! That was her name. Lilah Brecht. Her father had been an artsy German director, his name often bandied about in magazine and newspaper articles dealing with foreign films. With an actress mother and a director father, Decker briefly wondered why she hadn't pursued a career in the performing arts.

His eyes went back to Lilah's visage. At least the injuries seemed superficial, her facial bones appeared to be intact. Lucky, because her features were delicate and would have easily shattered under a well-placed blow. She had an oval face, a thin straight nose, high cheekbones leading to an angular jawline that tapered to a soft mound of chin. Making allowances for the swelling, Decker imagined her eyes to be deep-set and almond-shaped.

He heard footsteps approaching, pivoted around, and saw the paramedics cross the threshold. Two of them—a man and a woman, both wearing short-sleeved blue doctor's jackets. Decker started to rise, but something immediately jerked him back down. A hand. *Her* hand! It had shot out of nowhere, clutching his arm with surprising strength. Grimacing in pain, he knelt down again, trying to ease the pressure. She was grasping his left arm—the one still recovering from a gunshot wound. As he tried to gently pry the fingers off, she increased her vise grip, forcing him to use some muscle to pull her hand away. Then he took it and cradled it in his own.

"Do you hear me, Lilah?" he whispered.

There was no response.

The female paramedic knelt beside Decker. She was young and had short, brown curly hair that accentuated the roundness of her moon face. Her name tag said Gomez.

Decker attempted to free himself from Lilah's grip, but she wouldn't let go.

"You seem to have made a friend," Gomez said, as she shone a light on Lilah's pupils. Then she checked her pulse and respiration.

"She must be conscious at some level," Decker said. "She's just not responding verbally."

"You put the blanket over her?"

"Yeah," Decker said. "She was cold and gray when I found her."

"Shock." Gomez pocketed the light. "Her pupillary response is normal. Her pulse is weak but steady." She stared at the face. "Isn't this . . . you know . . .

the movie star's daughter? The one who runs the spa?"

"Lilah Brecht." Again, Decker tried to pull his hand away, but cold fingers had locked around his palm.

"I think she's trying to tell you something." Gomez pulled back the blanket, gave the blond woman's body a quick check-over. "Lilah, can you hear me? Squeeze . . ." She looked at Decker.

"Sergeant Decker," he said.

"Squeeze Sergeant Decker's hand if you hear me." No response.

"Maybe it's something primal," Gomez said.

Her partner—a skinny kid with sloping shoulders—came in with the stretcher.

"Can you stay with her?" Gomez said to Decker. "I'm going to help Eddie with the gurney."

"Yeah. Try not to mess things up for me."

Gomez looked around the room. "You could tell the difference?"

"It's the perp's mess, not yours." His back ached from kneeling. He sat on the floor. "Lilah, I'm Sergeant Decker. I'm here to help you. Can you hear me? Squeeze my hand if you can."

No response.

"Lilah, Miss Gomez—"

"Teresa."

"Lilah, Teresa and Eddie are going to take good care of you. They're taking you to the hospital. Everything is going to be okay."

There was no hand squeeze, but tears leaked from under closed eyes.

"Lilah, I know you can hear me, but I also know

you're too weak to talk. Don't even try. I'm going to try to find out what happened to you. When you're feeling better, I'll come to the hospital and talk to you. You just hang in. I have to take my hand away now, so the paramedics can get you to the hospital."

But as he pulled his hand away, she tightened her grip.

Eddie said, "You can hold her hand." His voice was tinny. "We can work around you."

Again, Decker tried to extricate himself. "Lilah, I'd like to look around your house. It will help me find out what happened."

Her hand remained affixed to his, fingers digging into his flesh. "Just hold her hand, Sergeant, while we load her," Teresa said. "No sense upsetting her."

Decker cooperated, but felt uncomfortable about it. Such *desperation* in her grip—and *strength*. Eerie because Lilah looked so beaten and weak. Maybe it was adrenaline reserve. He whispered, "You're safe now, Lilah. No one is going to hurt you. You're safe."

"Lilah, we're getting ready to move you," Teresa said. "I'm just bracing your neck. You're going to be okay." She turned to Decker. "As long as you're here, slip your hand under her back and help us load her."

Decker nodded.

"Count of three," Eddie said. "One . . . two . . . three, go!"

Like well-oiled machinery, the three of them loaded Lilah onto the gurney, her hand still gripping Decker's. But at least now he was able to stand, roll his shoulders to loosen his back. Again he tried to take his hand away, but Lilah wouldn't ease up.

Teresa craned her neck to look up at Decker. "From the grip she has on you, at least we know there's no spinal break . . . from the waist up, that is."

Eddie said. "Lilah, can you wiggle your toes?"

There was a slight response.

"Good, Lilah," Decker said. "That was *good*. Can you understand me? Squeeze my hand if you can."

A light squeeze.

"That's great, Lilah! The paramedics are going to take you to the hospital now. You're in excellent hands. The doctors are going to help you, run a few tests to make sure you're okay. I want them to examine you very carefully for me. Is that all right? Do you understand me?"

Another squeeze.

Decker turned to the paramedics and said, "Where are you taking her?"

"Sun Valley Memorial," Teresa said. "That okay?"

"Yeah, that's fine. Ask for Dr. Kessler or Dr. Begin and tell them it's for Detective Sergeant Peter Decker. They've both done pelvics in these types of situations and are familiar with what I need for evidence collection. The usual—all the fluids, a good pelvic- and head-hair combing, nails cleaned, the debris slided for the lab—fingernails and toenails." He stroked the hand that was clutching his. "Lilah, at the hospital, is it okay if someone takes pictures of your injuries? If I have pictures of your injuries, it will help me catch and convict the monster who did this to you. Do you understand me?"

She let out a muffled sound.

"Lilah, squeeze my hand if it's okay?"

Another squeeze.

"Good, Lilah." He faced the paramedics. "Tell the docs that I'll be sending down a police photographer. I'll also need her clothes and any other personal effects bagged. Please ask them to use *gloves*. I'll pick her stuff up myself and send it to the lab."

"You got it," Teresa said.

Decker regarded the manicured hand, long slender fingers laced around his. "Lilah, this is Sergeant Decker again. I'm going to ask you a question. Squeeze my hand if the answer is yes. Do you know who attacked you?"

No reaction.

"Okay, I'm going to ask you the same question. Squeeze if the answer is yes. Do you know who attacked you?"

Nothing.

"You *don't* know who attacked you? Squeeze if you don't know who attacked you."

Decker felt light pressure around his fingers. "Okay, that was great. I promise you, Lilah, you're safe. You're going to be all right. I have to let go now."

Her fingers tightened around his.

"Lilah, I have to let them take you to the hospital and I can't come with you." He wrenched his hand out of hers and as he did, she let out a low moan. "I'll be back, Lilah. I promise I'll come back and talk to you."

She moaned again, water trickling down her face. As they carried her out, Decker saw her hand stretching outward, reaching out to him. And those *moans*. He felt as if he were abandoning her and hoped she wouldn't hold anything against him when he came to question her . . . if she'd even remember him. Assault victims were sometimes afflicted with amnesia, especially if the ordeal was particularly vicious.

Decker stretched his long spine, then ran his thick hand through carrot-colored hair. Looking over his shoulder, he noticed the maid at the entrance to the room. She was still trembling, her hand on the doorpost for support. He told her to sit down in the kitchen and pour herself a cup of tea. He'd be with her in a minute.

From his coat pocket, he pulled out an evidence bag and slipped the blindfold inside. With a grease pencil, he roughly outlined Lilah's position on the floor. Then he unhitched his hand-held radio and asked to be patched through to Detective Marge Dunn. While waiting for her to respond, he took out a pen and his rape checklist and began to make detailed notes.

2

Tucked inside the rear corner of the bedroom's walk-in closet, the freestanding safe was open and empty. It was a waist-high, green-colored block, lined with three inches of high-grade solid steel, and contained an inner safe that was bare as well. As Benny the printman dusted the vault, Marge Dunn danced around shards of glass as she drew a layout of the bedroom and divided it into grids for evidence check.

The place had been tossed; furniture had been knocked over. Old-looking pieces: the skinny, austere stuff without curves or embellishments. Could have been replicas, but were probably antiques. Lots of embroidered pillows and doodads, doilies in garish colors, were mixed in with the mess. Lilah had a four-poster bed, the rumpled spread made out of chenille. Like the spread Granny used to have, Marge thought, white and full of little pompons. She smiled, remembering how she picked at them until the knots fell apart.

A couple of baby uniforms named Bellingham and Potter were hanging around, not really getting in the way but not doing anything productive either.

There were already a few blues outside securing the scene so the young 'uns weren't needed here. Marge called them over.

Nice-looking babies—tall and trim with well-scrubbed faces, eyes that seemed eager to work. Their enthusiasm made Marge feel old. Depressing, since she'd just turned thirty.

"Why don't you two canvass the area?" she suggested. "See if anybody or anyone heard anything?"

Bellingham rubbed a spit-polished shoe against the floor. "Sergeant Decker told us to wait here. The nearest neighbor is the spa and he didn't want us questioning anyone without him. But if you want us to go, Detective, we'll go."

Marge thought for a moment, fingering strands of blond hair. Pete was right. These kids weren't savvy enough to handle the Vulcanites.

"I noticed a stable out back," Marge said. "Why don't you check that out? See if anyone's hanging around, if anything looks suspicious. Count how many horses the stable holds."

"Sure thing, Detective," Potter said. "Should we report back to you or Sergeant Decker if we come up with anything?"

"Either one," Marge said. "And don't spend too much time on it. Just look around, jot down some notes, and report back. Then get on with your patrols. You two together?"

"Yes, ma'am . . . er, yes, Detective . . ." Bellingham blushed. "Sorry."

Marge smiled, slapped him on the back. "Get your butts out there."

After they left, she was glad to have some elbow

room. The photographer had just finished, leaving
Benny in the closet. The lab boys were checking the
doors and windows in the front section of the house,
and Pete and the maid were in the dining room.

"Detective?" Benny called out.

"Coming." Marge squeezed her large frame inside the closet. Not an easy trick with Benny occu-
pying most of the space. The man was big and blocky,
just this side of fat. Today he was dressed in a starched
white shirt and razor-pressed pants; not a spot of
dust dared sully his clothes. Definitely the neatest lab
man she'd ever worked with. "What's up?"

"We got some beauties." Benny's voice was basso
profundo. "Unfortunately, they're repeats. See right
here . . . this is a right index, it shows up twice. Here
we got a partial palm and two right thumbs on the
dial. A middle over here. On the inner dials we have
the same palm and index. You can see how small they
are. Female. I'll transfer them but I'm betting they
belong to the lady of the house."

"Anything else?"

"Not so far."

Marge shrugged off the lack of progress. Most
perps just didn't leave calling cards, but almost all
left evidence transfer. Even if she couldn't find anything else, there was the semen. Marge could smell
it as she approached the bed. She'd bag the sheets
after she sifted through the mess on top of them.

She wandered into the master bathroom. Its walls
were ceramic tiles of mint and hunter green in im-
maculate condition. The taps were old-style fixtures
but the chrome was high-polished and scratch free.
There was a beveled mirror on the back of the door.

Open glass shelving served as the medicine cabinet. The racks held pottery crocks labeled in calligraphy— witch hazel, foxglove, mint, trefoil. No over-the-counter meds, not one prescription vial. The top shelf held a bowl of cinnamon-smelling pinecones and acorns. The bathroom window was clear glass, but obscured by a curtain of dangling crystal beads. They sent prismatic rainbows onto the walls.

Whoever messed up the bedroom hadn't bothered with the bathroom.

Marge returned her attention to the bedroom. It was papered in something silky and cream-colored and dotted with a couple of dozen black-and-white photos of Lilah Brecht buddying up to celebrities. Or maybe it was the other way around. The stars looked *thrilled* to be in the snapshot. All the photos had been autographed.

To Lilah and Valley Canyon: With my fondest love, Georgina DeRafters.

To Lilah Brecht: the only woman who has seen me without makeup. Keep that cellulite off my thighs. Love, Ann Milo.

Georgina DeRafters and Ann Milo: old-timers who'd made strictly B movies. The As were probably hung on the spa's walls. How did that make the Bs feel? Did they even notice? They were bound to; all actresses are narcissistic. What did Lilah tell them after they'd paid her hundreds a day and didn't even see *their* pictures on the wall?

I keep my closest and dearest friends at home?

Marge shrugged. For every picture still on the wall, there were at least that many scattered about the room. The glass protecting the photographs had been deliberately smashed, as if someone had taken the pictures off the wall and smacked them with a hammer. One bull's-eye in the center of each picture, broken seams radiating outward. The room twinkled with glass reflecting the bright mid-morning light. The sunbeams coursed through two large windows— one on the eastern wall, one on the northern. Pete had found the bedroom windows locked: The lab men hadn't found any pry marks on their sashes.

The nightstands flanking the bed had been pushed over, the table lamps crushed to dust. The impact of the lamps falling to the floor couldn't have pulverized the ceramic bases to that extent. The table-to-floor distance was just not that great. Someone had smashed the suckers.

Someone had been *pissed*.

The dresser had been cleared of its contents, drawers pulled out and emptied, clothes tossed about carelessly.

Only Lilah's bedroom had been trashed.

Maybe the perp was expecting to find something in the safe. When it wasn't there, he'd searched the entire bedroom.

But then, why wasn't the rest of the house tossed?

Maybe he found what he wanted.

Then he raped her.

Marge carefully fingered the broken glass on the bed with her gloved hand. She'd have Benny bag the pieces. Could be someone cut himself, leaving traces of blood. The lab man came out of the closet.

"I'm done inside, Detective. You want to search it for evidence, go ahead. I'll start dusting the walls."

"Find anything other than those female prints?"

Benny shook his head.

"Detective?"

Marge turned around. Officer Bellingham had returned, a very grave look on his face.

"We finished our interview with the stable hand. I think you'd better check him out personally."

"Stable hand?"

"Yes, ma . . . Detective. He claims he lives there. There is a small hot plate inside one of the stables, some cooking utensils and work clothes. And there's a chemical toilet just outside the barn. He *could* be telling the truth. But I don't think the man has his full faculties."

"He's retarded?"

"Or very stupid, Detective. He answers in one-word sentences, won't look you in the eye. Very suspicious. Of course, he *claims* he didn't hear anything. And the stables are pretty far away from the house. But I think this man needs to be questioned. Officer Potter is with him now. Should we bring him here?"

"No, I'll go out to the stables. You make sure no one unauthorized comes in the bedroom. This stable hand have a name?"

"Carl Totes. He says he's worked for Miss Brecht for many years. Like I said, there's evidence that he does reside inside the stables but I think he could be a suspect."

"I'll check it out."

"By the way, Detective, there are six stalls and five horses inside the stable."

Marge patted him on the back. "Good job, Officer."

Bellingham tried to hold back a smile but didn't quite make it. The left corner of his mouth spasmed upward. Through crooked lips, he said, "Thank you, Detective."

It took three cups of tea and a half hour for the maid to calm down. Her name was Mercedes Casagrande, a thirty-five-year-old native of Guatemala who'd worked for Lilah Brecht for seven years. She wasn't forthcoming with the answers, but guarded as she was, Decker sensed she wanted to help. She just didn't want to jeopardize her job or the privacy of her *patrona*.

They sat at an oval dining-room table, the room furnished in early-twentieth-century pieces. The interior of the house had been done up in the style of Art Nouveau or Art Deco. Decker never could remember the difference between the two periods. As he made chitchat with the maid, she began to relax and answer his questions in halting English.

Decker slipped out his notepad and asked, "How many days a week do you work here for Missy Lilah?"

"I work all the days except Saturday and Sunday. I don' work on those days 'cause I go to church."

"What are your hours?"

"Seven to fife. But sometime I work *diferente* hours. If Missy Lilah need help in the night for the dinner. I work eleven to eight, mebbe nine o'clock. If someone take care of my kids."

Decker said, "You never sleep in?"

"No." Mercedes shook her head. "*No duermo en la casa, no.*"

Decker said, "So you weren't here yesterday?"

"I work yesterday, jes."

"But it was Sunday."

Mercedes looked confused. "I work only four hours. Missy Lilah call me and say house is a mess. So I come. That is not every week. Mebbe I work Sundays one time a month. But only if someone watch my kids."

"And what time did you leave?"

"I leave fife, fife-thurdy, mebbe. Everythin' is okay. Missy Lilah tell me she go out with her brother so I don' have to make dinner."

Decker smoothed his mustache. "Missy Lilah was going out to dinner with her brother?"

"Jes."

"Was she with her brother when you left?"

"No, he don' come yet, but she say she go to dinner with him. She go to dinner with him mebbe one or two time a week."

"What's her brother's name, Mercedes?"

"*El Doctor* Freddy."

"*El Doctor* Freddy?"

"Jes."

"Does *El Doctor* Freddy have a last name—*nom de familia?*"

"Same as Missy Lilah."

"Freddy Brecht?"

"I thin' his name is Señor Frederick."

"Frederick Brecht?"

"I thin' so."

"And he's a physician? *Un doctor de la medicina?*"

"*Sí.* He work at the spa. But he don' work there all the time."

"He has another office?"

"I thin' so."

"Do you know where his other office is? *Usted sabe donde está su otra oficina?*"

Mercedes shook her head.

Decker said, "You're doing great. *Muy bien*. You didn't see *El Doctor* Freddy come inside the house?"

"No."

"Does Doctor Freddy have a key to the house?"

Mercedes scrunched up her forehead in concentration. "I thin' . . . jes."

Decker wrote down: *No forced entry and Dr. Freddy may have a key*. "And Doctor Freddy wasn't there when you left to go home."

"No, he don' come yet."

"But Missy Lilah was home."

"Jes, she come home around four from the spa, all wet. She do very much exercise. She very, very skinny, but es okay 'cause she don't throw up like *muchas mujeres* at the spa. She tell me all the women throw up to be skinny. I thin' that's no good."

"I don't think that's good either."

"But Missy Lilah no throw up to be skinny. But she do *muchas* exercise. *Mucho tiempo corriendo. En la calle, en la montaña, todo el tiempo, ella corrió.*"

Decker wrote: *Lilah obsessive runner*. "Does she ever run at night?"

"I don' know."

If she did, it would put a new slant on the incident. After dinner with her brother, Lilah went out for a midnight run. Then someone familiar with her habits waited for her to return exhausted from her jog, and forced his way in. After she opened the safe, he attacked her, then tossed the room. That play-by-play would also be consistent with no forced entry.

Decker excused himself a moment, stood and walked around the room, wincing as pain pierced his upper body. Even though the gunshot wounds were in the left arm and shoulder, he found that stretching his spine mitigated the throbbing in his extremities. He extracted a couple of extra-strength Tylenols from his shirt pocket and popped them into his mouth, swallowing without water, the movement as reflexive as breathing. Having worked his way off codeine, then Percodan, he'd been alternating with the over-the-counter analgesics—one day Tylenol, the next Advil. Almost eight months to the day, his recovery was good but still incomplete. The OTC tablets helped take the edge off, but he knew there'd come a time when he would have to learn to live without the medicine and with the pain.

He stretched again, then sat and said, "Mercedes, when you came in this morning, did you notice anything different about the house *before* you went into Missy Lilah's bedroom?"

"No, nothing."

"Everything was in order."

"Jes."

"None of the furniture was moved or the vases put on a different table . . . anything like that?"

"No. Jus' the door to Missy Lilah's bedroom is open. She like it closed."

"But nothing different in the living room, dining room?"

She shook her head.

"The front door was locked?"

"Jes. I use my key to come in."

"You have a key?"

"Jes."

"Anyone else in your family know you have a key to her house?"

Mercedes's face flushed with fear. "*Ninguna persona!* I keep it in especial place."

"So you're positive that no one has the key to Missy Lilah's house."

"*Ninguna persona en mi familia.* Jus' me."

Decker told her he believed her, but kept the question open in his mind. "When you came in this morning, did you go straight to the bedroom? Or did you do something else first? Hang up your coat and purse, start the washing machine?"

"I hang up my coat and look around. Everythin' is okay. *Entonces*, I see the door open—"

"The bedroom door?"

"Jes, the bedroom door. I go to close it, I see Missy Lilah—"

Covering her face, she burst into sudden tears, sobbing for a full minute, Decker waiting until the crying subsided. Mercedes reached inside her purse, found wrinkled tissue and wiped her eyes. "She be okay, Missy Lilah?"

"I think so."

"I pray to *Dios*—to *Jesús*—she be okay. I go to church today to pray for Missy Lilah."

"It's good to pray," Decker said.

"Jes."

"Makes you feel better?"

Mercedes nodded. "Everyone need *ayuda*—help."

Ain't that the truth. Decker patted her hand. "Mercedes, do you clean Missy Lilah's room every day?"

"Jes."

"You clean inside her closet?"

"Jes, I vacuum every day there. She don' like the dust."

"In the closet, there's a big safe."

"Jes."

"You dust the safe?"

"Jes, every day."

"Did you dust the safe yesterday?"

"Jes, every day."

"Do you wear gloves when you dust the safe?"

"I don' wear gloves, only when I clean the toilet."

"So it's possible that your hands touched the safe. *Es posible que su mano ha tacado la puerta de la caja de seguridad?*"

"*Sí, es posible.*"

Benny had pulled some latents from the safe. The maid was going to have to be inked for print comparison. But there was a good side to her compulsive cleaning; the safe had been wiped clean every day. If some of the latents belonged to Lilah, she had to have opened the safe after Mercedes cleaned it yesterday. Had she been forced to open it? Or maybe she put something valuable inside yesterday and someone had known about it.

Decker scribbled a few notes—questions he'd bring up with Lilah. Hopefully, she'd be completely conscious by late afternoon, in good-enough shape to be interviewed briefly. "We're just about done, Mercedes. Just a few more questions. I want to talk about the man who works with the horses."

"Señor Carl?"

"Yes. He says he lives in the stables. Is that true?"

"Jes."

"How long has he lived there?"

"Four, fife years. He come after me, but he work for Missy Lilah for a long time."

"You see him a lot?"

"No."

"If something breaks in the house, who fixes it?"

Mercedes thought. "Missy Lilah send someone— different peoples. Sometimes people from her work."

"From her work? You mean the spa?"

"Jes."

"Which people?"

"*Diferentes*. I thin' sometimes a boy comes to pick the vegetables."

"A boy? A *muchacho*?"

"No. More old. His name is Mike."

"Mike," Decker repeated. "Do you know his last name?"

Mercedes shook her head.

"But he works at Lilah's spa?"

"Jes, I thin'."

"Okay," Decker said. "So Señor Carl doesn't fix things in the house."

"No. Jus' work with the horses, mebbe pick vegetables, *también*. I don' know."

"Do you ever make breakfast or lunch for Señor Carl?"

"No."

"Do you make him snacks? Give him some juice when the weather gets hot?"

"No, he stay out of the house, I stay in the house. We don' talk, mebbe jus' one or two time a year. He come to the house and ask for Missy Lilah. But he never come *in* the house."

"Does he ever use the bathroom in the house?"

"No, I thin' he have a toilet."

"You ever wash his clothes?"

Mercedes shook her head.

Decker leaned in close and whispered, "Does he scare you?"

The maid wrinkled her lips and shook her head. "No, he don' scare me. Missy Lilah say he nice. I thin' he nice, too. But I thin', he's a little . . ." With her right index finger, she made air circles next to her right temple.

"A little crazy?"

"Mebbe. But I thin' he love Missy Lilah. One time, Missy Lilah and her brother have a bad fight outside. Missy Lilah don' let her brother in the house and he get mad. Señor Carl hear it and he get *real* mad." She demonstrated his anger by wrinkling her nose and balling her fist. "He go in of the stable and get a big shobel. He show it to *El Doctor* and jell at him, and make him go away."

"It was a *bad* fight?"

"Jes, very bad."

"Does Missy Lilah fight a lot with Doctor Freddy?"

"Oh, no!" Mercedes was wide-eyed. "Missy Lilah

no fight with Doctor Freddy, never. This was *el otro doctor, su otro hermano.*"

Decker digested that. "She has two brothers?"

"Jes."

"And both are doctors?"

"Jes. *El otro doctor* come here mebbe two or three time since I work here. Missy Lilah don' like him. He come and dey fight. Señor Carl, he chase him away last time. Jell at him, shake his shobel. Say: 'Go away. Go away or I kill you.'"

"What's *el otro doctor's* name?"

"Missy Lilah don' tell me. She just call him *su otro hermano.*"

"How do you know he's a doctor?"

Mercedes was silent. "I don' remember. I jus' know he's a doctor."

"When Carl chased him away, how long ago was that?"

"I thin' mebbe two years ago."

"You haven't seen *su otro hermano* in two years?"

"No."

"Okay, let's go back to Señor Carl. You think he's a little crazy? *Un poco loco?*"

"More *estupid.*"

"You ever see him be crazy with Missy Lilah?"

Mercedes shook her head.

"Did he ever act crazy with you?"

Again a shake of the head.

Decker checked his watch. It was almost noon and his stomach was growling. But before lunch, he wanted to check out Señor Totes himself. Marge should have picked the stable hand's brain by now. He'd confer with her, then ask Totes about the fight

Lilah had with her other doctor brother. Maybe send Marge down to the spa to check out this Mike character. He pocketed his notepad and thanked the maid for her time.

3

"Be it ever so humble. . . ." Marge smiled. "May not be much, but Totes calls it home. Makes my place look pretty high-end."

Decker smiled, his eyes examining the horseless stall. The wooden floor was clean, most of it covered by a moth-eaten, hand-loomed rug. An army cot lay in the middle of the area, brown standard-issue blankets folded neatly at its foot. Against the back was a two-burner hot plate plugged into an electrical socket. Jammed into the corners were piles of canned goods, a broom, a mop, and a dustpan. Wooden wall knobs, ordinarily used to hang tack, held dirty denim overalls and dust-covered work shirts on the left side, a bath towel, a circular kitchen towel, and a heavy skillet on the right. Not a lot of living space, but then again, the horses never complained.

"A bit of a contrast from the main house," Marge said. "Notice all the antiques at her place?"

Decker nodded.

"And not just the furniture—all the vases and bowls and rugs and pillows and shit. She put a lot of money into decorating. Spa must do well."

Decker shrugged. "Is there a john here?"

"He's got a chemical toilet out back." Marge wrinkled her nose. "Why he bothered to put it outside, I don't know. Whole place smells. Lord, how in the world does he eat surrounded by this stink?"

"This ain't nothing." Decker took a deep sniff. "He's got fresh shavings in here. You should have gotten a whiff before he raked the stalls."

"Lucky me."

"Did he rake while you were interviewing him?"

"No, he just sat on the cot and answered my questions—'Yessim. Nossim.' But I think he understood everything I asked him, Pete. Claims he didn't see or hear anything. Now the stable is away from the house, but I would think that sound carries pretty well in these open spaces. There were a lot of smashed items in Lilah's bedroom. Maybe he just tuned the noise out."

"Maybe." Decker related the incident with Lilah and *el otro hermano*. "Totes was very protective of her according to the maid, threatening Lilah's nameless brother with a shovel. If he had heard something suspicious, he might have done something. He didn't mention anything about the fight to you?"

"Not a word. But with a guy like Carl, you've got to know the right questions beforehand. He doesn't volunteer a thing and I don't think it's because he's holding back. He's just too basic to improvise. I asked him if he knew anyone who didn't like Lilah. He said 'nossim.' Now if I had asked him, did Lilah have a fight with her other brother two years ago, I probably would have gotten a 'yessim.'"

"Specificity is the name of the game."

"And short questions," Marge said. "Anyway, he swore he didn't hear or see anything when he got up this morning at four-thirty."

"That's his usual rising time?"

"Yes. It was dark outside. He didn't see anything."

"You think he was being truthful?"

"I think he was, but it's hard to say. Remember that beekeeper's retarded son last year? Totes was wary in the same way when questioned. Both didn't look you in the eye."

"He's as retarded as Earl Darcy?"

"No, Carl's higher-functioning," Marge said. "He takes care of himself and the horses. Besides being the stable hand, he's the grounds keeper. Takes care of the fruit trees, maintains the huge garden out back. She's got a few acres here. Keeping it up is a lot of responsibility."

"You know, the maid mentioned that Lilah sends people from the spa to fix things in her house, pick stuff from the garden. She mentioned someone named Mike."

Marge said, "I'll check him out."

"What about Totes as a suspect? What does your gut say?"

"Gut-speaking, probably not. You told me Lilah didn't know who attacked her. I don't think Carl has enough smarts to plan an assault without being recognized."

Decker said, "How long has Carl been working out the horse?"

"He took it out maybe a half hour ago, says he tries to work out each horse for an hour. Jesus, that's six hours in the saddle every day. Guy must have nothing but a big callus for a butt."

Decker slapped his notepad against his palm. "You get used to it."

"Macho Pete."

Decker smiled, thinking that Marge wasn't so bad in the machismo department herself. At a fit five-ten, one fifty-five, she could successfully floor most men without breaking a sweat. Her most feminine feature was her eyes. Soft and doelike, they inspired trust. Everyone told Marge their secrets.

She said, "Why don't you take a look around while I organize my notes?"

Decker agreed, strolling the stables, taking in the scenery. Lilah had prime horses—well-muscled with straight backs and princely gaits. The Lippizaner was the jumper, the two Thoroughbreds were young with fine-looking legs. The Appaloosa in the middle stall looked to be about twelve—probably dead broke and a great trail rider. Aps were good range horses—fearless and surefooted. He returned to Totes's stall, sniffed the towels and bedsheet.

"His clothes are dirty, but his linens are clean. The maid said she doesn't do his laundry."

Marge said, "He's got a small empty washbasin outside. Next to the toilet."

"Who buys his food?"

"He told me Lilah gives him some canned goods—tuna, chili and beans. And then there's the garden—actually it's more like a farm. A half acre's worth of vegetables, most of the greens and herbs grown for the spa. VULCAN advertises homegrown fruits and vegetables. Guess Lilah needs something to justify those rates."

Decker smiled and rolled his shoulders.

Marge said, "Totes helps himself to the veggies. To the fruits in the orchards, too. I guess if you don't mind simple living and the smell, it's not a terrible life." She checked her watch. "How about we grab some lunch after you've spoken to Mr. Totes?"

"I want to stop off at home," Decker said. "I've got some baked goods in the car that were supposed to be Rina's breakfast. Want to come over for lunch?"

"I'm sure Rina would love that."

"I'll need you as a buffer."

"She giving you a hard time?"

"Nah," Decker said. "She's just being pregnant. Stop by with me. She likes you. Sometimes I think she likes you better than me."

"You go it alone this time." Marge stood on her tiptoes and patted his cheek. "You're a big boy, you can handle it."

Decker smiled. "You want to explain to Totes that I'm your partner? He's already had one interview today. I don't want to confuse the guy by suddenly presenting myself."

"Sure."

"While I'm talking to him, can you do me a favor?"

"Name it."

"Frederick Brecht's not at the spa and supposedly no one had his office number. The Vulcanites are very close-mouthed."

"I'll look him up. You want me to call him?"

"I don't know if he's aware of what's happened.

The maid didn't call him; the spa isn't concerned about Lilah's absence. The manager there . . . what the hell was her name?" He flipped through his notepad. "Uh . . . Kelley Ness . . . she told me that Ms. Brecht wasn't expected in today, but she didn't sound uptight."

"Did you ask Kelley about this Mike person?" Marge said.

"No. If Mike's there and involved, I don't want to spook him. I don't want to interview this Mike guy or Doctor Freddy by phone. I want to see their reactions to the news in the flesh."

"Makes sense," Marge said. "How about you talk to Totes while I break for lunch? Afterward, I'll take a peek around the spa and you check out Doctor Freddy."

"Sounds good," Decker said. "By the time I'm done with Freddy, maybe Lilah will be able to talk."

Marge said, "What should we do about Davida Eversong?"

Decker made a face and leaned backward. "What does she have to do with any of this?"

"You haven't talked to Morrison yet?"

Decker was taken aback. It was unusual for the captain to stick his nose into Decker's affairs. "Christ, what is it, Marge?"

"Just wanted to know a little about the case. Mentioned the fact that since Lilah was Davida Eversong's daughter, it could get some press." Marge sighed. "That maybe we might want to break the news to Ms. Eversong first and tell her to keep a low profile so we can do our jobs. I seemed to get the impression that he's worried that Eversong might play this for some publicity. Should I try to dig her up?"

Decker thought for a moment. "Not just yet. Let me at least try to talk to Lilah first. She may have her own method of dealing with her mother."

Plumes of dust obscured the corral's ground as the palomino kicked up cloud banks of grit. The tom-tom sound of hooves beating against the dirt, the horse rounding each bend of the fence seamlessly. In lesser hands, the stallion could have easily lost its footing, but Totes handled the animal with the combined expertise of professional cowboy and jockey.

Riding bare chested, the man was so thin he looked like an antenna. In his time, Decker had known many hands like him. Their strength was often deceptive. The guy was probably one wiry sucker.

Marge caught Totes's attention. He pulled on the reins, stopping directly in front of them, spraying them with dirt. He untied the bandanna from around his neck and wiped perspiration off his face and neck. A watery sheen had coated his chest and stomach, but he didn't bother to swab it away.

"Carl, this is my partner, Sergeant Decker," Marge said. "If you don't mind, he'd like to ask you a few questions."

There was a moment of silence. Totes's eyes were unreadable, hidden behind the shadow of his cowboy hat. He had a long face that matched his lean body. His nutmeg-colored cheeks were gaunt, hairless, and mottled with acne scars and moles.

"My partner needs to ask you a few questions, Carl," Marge said.

Totes nodded.

"How 'bout we go in the stable?" Decker said. "You can brush your horse down while we talk."

Totes nodded but made no effort to dismount. The palomino was prancing about, chafing at the bit, sweat pouring down his flanks.

Decker said, "You need to cool him off first?"

"Yes sir, I do."

"Go ahead," Decker said. "I'll wait."

Totes clicked his tongue and he and the horse trotted slowly around the corral.

"Swift, sport," Marge said.

"Like you said, you've got to know the right questions."

"I think you've got a good fix on the dude, Pete." Marge slung her purse over her shoulder. "And now if I'm no longer needed . . ."

"Give me about a half hour."

"You won't need that much time, but go ahead."

After Marge left, Decker leaned against the railing as Totes led the golden beauty through a series of cool-down exercises. The sky was clear and cloudless, the mountains studded with wild flowers. Watching Totes in the saddle, Decker felt jealous of the stable hand's freedom, of his skill, too. Totes might be blunted mentally, but he'd mastered all the subtleties of riding. Fifteen minutes passed before Totes decided it was time to call it quits. He dismounted, took off his saddle, and led the horse by the reins around the corral. After the animal had been sufficiently cooled down, Totes brought him to the stable. Decker walked abreast of the horse, admiring his stately walk.

"Miss Brecht has some beautiful animals," Decker said, once inside the stable.

Totes nodded and placed the horse in the middle stall opposite the Appaloosa. He took out a wire currycomb and brush and began to groom the beast. The comb had just made contact with the horse's skin when Totes stopped, turned around, and looked at Decker.

"You can pull up a bucket and sit if you want."

"I don't mind standing."

Totes didn't respond. He paused, then returned his attention to the horse.

"Miss Brecht a good rider?" Decker asked.

"Yessir."

"This one her favorite horse?"

"Yessir."

"What's his name?"

"Apollo."

"Apollo," Decker repeated. "After the sun god."

Again, Totes stopped what he was doing and pivoted to look at Decker. He took off his cowboy hat, wiped his forehead with his arm, and put the hat back on. His hair was cropped short—one step above a five-o'clock shadow. Eyes, pale blue. They held a vacant stare.

"Apollo's a great name," Decker said. "Lilah must be a very experienced rider to handle a stallion. She doesn't look like she has enough weight to manage him."

Totes didn't answer. He continued grooming the animal.

"How long you work for Miss Brecht, Carl?"

"Five years."

"She have the horses before you came to work for her?"

"A few."

"She have Apollo?"

"Yessir."

"How old is he? Around six?"

"Yessir."

Unimpressed.

Decker said, "Did she have the Appaloosa when you came here? He looks older, around twelve, thirteen, maybe?"

"Twelve and a half."

"He's in good shape."

"Yessir."

"Has Miss Brecht ever lived with anyone in the five years you worked here?"

No response.

"Has Miss Brecht ever lived with her brother Freddy, the doctor?"

Totes hesitated before answering. "Nossir."

"Do you see Miss Brecht's brother around here a lot?"

A pause. "Yessir."

"Was he here last night?"

Totes stopped what he was doing, but didn't turn around. "I don't remember."

"See anything strange last night?"

"Nossir. 'Ready told your lady pardner that."

"I know you did," Decker answered. "I'm just . . . you know . . . trying to figure out a few things. Did you happen to see anyone near Miss Brecht's house during the night?"

Another pause. "Nossir."

"Did you happen to see Miss Brecht last night?"

Totes continued brushing but didn't answer. Decker didn't know if he was thinking about the question or if he was just that dull. Dragging answers out of him was like wading through sludge.

"She don't ride at night so I probably didn't see her. I only see her when she rides."

"Do you pick the vegetables for her spa?"

A pause. "Nossir."

"Who does?"

"Who what?"

"Who picks the vegetables for her spa?"

"Someone from the spa."

"Do you know a guy named Mike from the spa?"

"Don't know him, nossir."

Decker waited a beat. "Carl, do you ever *see* a guy named Mike from the spa picking vegetables for Miss Lilah?"

"I see him," Totes said. "But I don't know him."

"But you know what he looks like."

" 'Course."

"Was he here yesterday?"

"Nossir."

"You're sure."

"Yessir."

Decker sighed inwardly. "Carl, does Miss Brecht ever go running at night?"

"Don't recall."

"Maybe Miss Brecht went running last night," Decker suggested. "You might have seen her?"

Totes turned slowly and faced Decker, a confused look on his face.

"Did you see Miss Brecht run last night, Carl?"

Totes shook his head.

"But she does run at night?"

Totes scratched his nose. "Don't recall."

Decker bit back frustration. "So nothing unusual happened last night?"

Totes nodded slowly.

"And you didn't see Miss Brecht's brother—Frederick Brecht—here last night."

"Nossir."

"What about Miss Brecht's other brother—the one who had the fight with her about two years ago."

Totes removed his hat. The empty expression in his eyes had been replaced by hot blue flames. "What *about* him?"

"He come around here a lot?"

"Not no more."

"You chased him away last time he was here?"

"I did do it."

"With a shovel."

"I did do it."

"Why?"

"'Cause he was yellin' at Miz Lilah something fierce."

"Did Miss Lilah ask for your help?"

Again, Totes seemed confused.

"Did she come running to you and say, 'Carl, help me chase my brother away'?"

"Nossir."

"But you figured she needed help so you chased him with the shovel."

"I just didn't like the way he was yellin'."

"Was he swearing at Miss Lilah?"

"Swearin'?"

"Yeah, swearin'. Cussin' at her."

"He was yellin'. Maybe he was cussin', too. But the yellin' was 'nuf."

"What were they yelling about?"

Totes spit. "None of my dang business."

"I know you wouldn't listen in on purpose, but maybe you overheard something?"

"None of my dang business."

Decker shifted gears. "By the way, what's Miss Lilah's brother's name?"

"Freddy."

"No, Carl, the other one. The one she was yelling at."

"*He* was yellin'."

"Okay, the one who was yelling at her. What's his name?"

Once again, the eyes became blank. "Name?"

"If you don't know it, it's okay," Decker said. "I'll get it from Miss Lilah."

The eyes filled suddenly with water. "How's Miz Lilah?"

Decker said, "I think she'll be okay."

"If King hurt her, I'm gonna kill him," Totes announced.

Decker paused to write down Totes's declaration in his notebook. "Who's King, Carl?"

"King," Totes said. "That's Lilah's brother. The one who was yellin'."

Decker let that sink in. Had to go real slow with the guy. "Lilah's other brother, the one who was yelling. Was his name King?"

"Yessir. I just remembered it."

"Is King his first or his last name?"

Totes put his cowboy hat back on and shrugged ignorance. He said, "Are we almost done? All this talk is makin' me addled. And when I'm addled, I can't work."

Decker stuffed the notepad back in his coat pocket. He patted Apollo's butt and told the stable hand they were through.

4

The smell of food in the oven awakened Decker's stomach. He placed the bags of bakery goods on his dining-room table and took off his jacket. Ginger dashed in from the other room, barking with excitement.

"Rina?"

There was no answer.

"What's Mama cooking, girl?" Decker said, petting the Irish setter. He went to the kitchen, the dog at his heels. The counters were filled with cookie sheets containing hundreds of miniature knishes—tiny bits of puff pastry filled with potato, spinach, or buckwheat. He picked up a couple and tossed them in his mouth, swallowed them down with a tall glass of orange juice.

He looked outside the window, at his own acreage, then opened the back door to let the dog out. Rina was nowhere in sight. Maybe she was inside the barn. Again, he called out her name. No answer.

The timer on the stove went off. He opened the oven door, saw the tops of the knish dough had turned golden brown and turned off the heat. With stuff left in the oven, she was bound to show up soon. Or so he told himself. But he was determined to be calm. He was getting better at not worrying about her, but as with the mending of his wounds, it was proving to be a slow process.

He opened the kitchen drawer and fished out a yarmulke stuffed between a tape measure and a hammer, then bobby-pinned the skullcap onto his hair. He filled a plate with knishes and poured himself a glass of milk. Standing, he ate while he phoned the hospital. Everyone was out to lunch. After being relegated to hold six times, then being disconnected twice, he was finally put through to Dr. Kessler's office. Kessler's secretary announced that he was in a meeting, but Decker pushed her, and a few minutes later, the OB-GYN came to the phone.

"Sergeant Decker?"

"Doctor," Decker said. "Thanks for taking time to talk to me."

"Sergeant, you rescued me from a committee meeting," Kessler said. "You did a big *mitzvah*."

Decker laughed. Imagine a Jewish doctor treating him like an MOT—a member of the tribe. Of course, he *was* Jewish. But it still took him by surprise that others could think of him as a Jew.

"Glad to be of service, Doc," he said. "Did you happen to admit Lilah Brecht this morning?"

"I sure did," Kessler said. "Isn't Lilah Brecht the one with the famous actress mother?"

"Davida Eversong," Decker said.

"Yeah, that's it. Star of late-night television. She always played vamps, didn't she?"

"I think so. Davida's a little before my time."

"Mine, too. If you can hold the line a few minutes, I'll get Lilah's chart."

"Sure. How's she doing?"

"She's doing very well, all things considered. We did a CAT scan, radiographed her orbits. Nothing showed up, but that doesn't mean anything. Takes a while for the blood to clot if there's subdural hemorrhaging, so we won't really know until after twenty-four hours. But I'm encouraged. As of an hour ago, she was still woozy, but she was oriented. Knew her name, her address."

"That's good news. She seemed pretty bad when they loaded her into the ambulance."

"Yeah, she was probably in shock. If you get to them before the body temperature sinks, they recover remarkably fast. She not only knew who she was but also why she was in the hospital."

"She knew she'd been attacked?"

"She knew she'd been *raped*. Hold on, I'll get the chart."

As Decker waited, he heard his front door slam, followed by Rina's voice calling his name.

"I'm in the kitchen."

She walked in, carrying bags of groceries, looked at Decker's plate piled with food, and placed her parcels on the counter.

"Peter, what are you doing?" She pulled his plate away. "Can't you tell these aren't for you? How can you just take without asking?"

Decker rolled his eyes. "Sorry."

Rina sighed, her shoulder sagging. "I'm sorry. I'm being ridiculous. I've got more than enough." She put the plate back in front of him. "Eat as many as you want."

"Save them. I'll grab something else."

"No, take," Rina insisted. "Take more. Take as much as you want."

"I'm fine, Rina. I'm getting full."

She piled another half-dozen knishes on his plate. "Here. Take."

"I don't want any more," Decker said.

Rina looked at him, her eyes suddenly moistening. "You don't like them?"

"No, no," Decker backtracked. "They're delicious."

"You really like them?"

"Yes."

"The spinach, too?"

"Yes."

"Really?"

"Rina, you're a fabulous cook. I like everything you make. Who are you baking for anyway?"

"I'm going to freeze them," Rina said. Then she added quickly, "It's for the *bris* . . . or the naming if it's a girl."

Decker held his temper. "I thought we *agreed* that it was too much work for you to do all that cooking. We were going to hire a cater—"

"Just a few appetizers."

"You should be resting. Isn't that what the doctor said?"

"What does a *man* know about pregnancy?"

Decker wasn't about to be suckered into *that* argument. "You're going to tire yourself out."

"Why do you say that? Do I look tired?"

"No, Rina. You look great."

She did. From the back, Decker couldn't tell she was pregnant. The front told another story: Six months gravid, but her face was as finely featured and beautiful as ever. Her milky complexion was flawless, her cerulean eyes clear and bright. Her hair had grown very long. She'd braided it and wore a tam on the crown of her head. According to Jewish law, married women had to cover their hair, but Rina had allowed the jet-black plait to escape down her back. It was thick and shiny. She simply glowed with health.

Kessler came back on the phone. Decker held up his palm.

"Okay," the doctor said. "I did all the tests you wanted, sent them to your lab. She was bruised vaginally, but there was no semen inside of her."

Decker looked at his wife. "Could you hold, Doc? I want to change phones."

"Don't bother on my account," Rina sulked. "I'll go in the other room."

"Rina—"

"No, I insist." She opened the back door and let the dog inside. "C'mon, Ginger. *You* can keep me company."

Decker knew better than to protest and waited until she was out of hearing range. Then he said, "You do a mouth and anal swab as well?"

"Everything. No one ejaculated inside any of her orifices."

"The sheets smelled like semen."

"Then he came on the linen and not inside,"

Kessler said. "I did find a trace of dried seminal fluid on her leg. I put it on a slide and sent it to the lab."

"Doc, did you happen to ask her about previous voluntary intercourse?"

"I'm on top of it, Sarge. I knew you wouldn't want your results confounded. She said no."

A premie rapist? Decker knew lots of them were. "Was there any anal or oral bruising?"

"Nothing showed up clinically."

"Any foreign hairs?"

"Nothing that looked obvious—either on the pubis or the head. She's blond all the way around, so if there was anything dark, it would have popped out at me. You comb, you're always going to pull out hairs. Whether they're hers or not, the lab will tell us. But if you have semen on the sheet, you have evidence."

"What did you do with the clothes?"

"They're bagged," Kessler said. "The ambulance driver told me you were going to pick them up yourself."

"Yeah, I'll be there in a couple of hours. Think I'll be able to talk to her?"

"Like I said, she's still woozy. But she may be able to answer a few questions. You know, come to think of it, she asked about you."

"She did?"

"Yes, she asked for you by name, matter of fact. Twice. 'Is Sergeant Deckman in?'"

"Deckman," Decker said. "Close enough. So she remembered me from this morning."

"Seems that way," Kessler said. "If her brain stays clear, she should heal up pretty quickly. She's in great shape physically—her pulse was slow, her blood pressure's nice and low. Her lungs were clear. She had an abbreviate neuro earlier in the morning, is scheduled for another one tomorrow. Her reflexes were normal, good range of vision. She checked out normal on both the fine and gross motor. Good muscle tone, too."

Decker remembered her grip. Her muscle tone had been more than good.

Kessler went on, "Her face is swollen, some subdermal bleeding below the orbits. Looks like someone belted her in the eyes. They're black and puffy. But no broken facial bones. That's good. She's a stunning woman. You can see her beauty right through the bruises and the cuts."

"Agreed. If someone can tell her I'll be down in the late afternoon, I'd appreciate it."

"Will do."

"Thanks." Decker hung up and walked into the living room. In the heat, the room seemed to sweat the scent of pine and leather. Ginger occupied one buckskin chair; Rina was in the other, feet propped up on the ottoman. She looked as if she'd swallowed a watermelon. He went over and kissed her forehead. She looped an arm around his neck and pulled him down next to her, running her fingers through thick shocks of red hair.

"I'm tired. You're right. I overdid it. But I felt so energetic this morning. I even baked cupcakes for the boys. Do you want a cupcake?"

"No, thank you."

"Did you have enough to eat?"

"I'm fine."

"You're sure?"

"Positive."

She slipped her hand underneath his shirt. Decker felt dizzy from the aroma of her skin. "You telling me something, darlin'?"

"You have time, Peter?"

He sat up and loosened his tie. "Honey, I'll make time."

"Aren't I lucky to have a man who makes his own hours."

"Good perks, huh?"

"Yes, indeed."

Decker unbuttoned his shirt. He was glad Marge hadn't come.

Stepping onto Planet VULCAN was like entering another world.

One that Marge at least had never seen before.

The lobby of the spa was a ballroom-sized rotunda, the ceiling domed and imprinted with gilt-tinged vines and flowers that trailed down the plaster walls. The floor was cut from peach-veined marble and partially covered by a thick, green-and-peach Chinese rug thirty feet in diameter. Atop the rug were several seating groups. A brocade sofa, flanked by gold-trimmed occasional tables, was occupied by three sunlamp-tanned women looking to be in their thirties. They were dressed in short shorts and T-shirts and were giggling like teenagers. They also had perfect figures—*too* perfect, not an unwanted bump or bulge anywhere. The two velvet wingbacks were taken up by leotard-clad, college-age girls. Towels draped around their necks, they sipped some tropical drink made with lots of crushed ice and examined their long red fingernails.

Three middle-aged women sat in burnt-leather club chairs around an oversized onyx backgammon table, laughing loudly, showing off white teeth. Two love seats near the fireplace held pairings of young and older women—mothers and daughters possibly. The ladies were using the marble coffee table placed between the settees as a footrest.

The hearth was set into the rear wall, the carved mantel curved to hug the circumference of the room. Against the left wall was a highly polished mahogany staircase that ended at a second-story landing. The reception desk—done in more peach-veined marble—was to the right.

A tuxedoed waiter, carrying a tray of something flesh-colored in highball glasses, walked up to Marge, eyes heavy with disapproval. But he kept a stiff upper lip.

"Your guava-passion-fruit refresher, ma'am?"

His accent was affected-English.

"Any of them laced with Stolichnaya?"

"Pardon?"

"Or just plain bar vodka will do."

"No alcohol is allowed—"

"Forget it, Jeeves."

She patted his back and strolled over to the reception desk. A bespectacled young woman—also in leotards—looked up from the cashier's desk. Her initial smile dimmed when she saw Marge.

"May I help you, madame?"

Not madam, mind you, ma-*dame*. Another little

taut body with big boobs. This one had short short hair and features sharp enough to cut meat. Her name tag identified her as Ms. F. Purcel.

"It's mademoiselle if you want to be technical," said Marge, "and yes you can help me. I'm Detective Dunn from the LAPD. I'd like to speak with Kelley Ness."

Moving her lips, Purcel studied the ID card. "May I ask what this is about?"

"Why don't you let me talk to Kelley Ness. Then if she wants you to know, she can tell you herself."

Purcel sighed. "One moment. Have a seat— No . . . maybe you could just wait in the corner."

Marge smiled but didn't move. The clerk gave up and went to the switchboard, back turned as she talked into the phone. It took about a minute before she hung up.

"I'm unable to locate Ms. Ness. May I take a message?"

Marge leaned over the desk. "Why don't you call again, ma'am."

"I'm sorry—"

"*Call again.*"

Ms. Purcel opened and closed her mouth, then about-faced and picked up the phone. Another minute passed before she returned.

"I've located Ms. Ness."

"The phantom returneth."

"Excuse me?"

"Where is she?"

Purcel became very official. "Take the staircase on the left to the second floor. Ms. Ness is in office

B on the right side." Then she added, "She's very busy."

Marge said, "Well, aren't we all, ma-*dame*."

The office was wedge-shaped. Austere-looking, especially when compared to the ornate lobby. Its walls were hung with cheap poster art. Small windows looked out to an Olympic-sized pool. The desk, piled high with loose papers, was functional and nothing more. The woman in the secretary's chair looked to be around twenty-five. Her face was pretty but angry, brown eyes smoldering. She tossed poker-straight hair over her shoulders and shuffled some papers.

Marge waited until Little Miss Irate had the decency to acknowledge her. The squaring off took about a half minute. Irate raised her eyes and waited for Marge to speak.

"You're Kelley Ness?"

"You've found me."

Marge started to pull up a chair.

"You needn't bother to sit, Detective. The civil suit was frivolous enough. Ms. Betham is just furthering her troubles by going to the police. Miss Brecht is not expected in today, but if you give me your card, I'll give it to her and she can forward your name to our lawyers. I'm sure they will educate you."

Marge sat, thought a moment before she spoke. "Do you know where Miss Brecht is?"

"She checks in with us frequently. I assure you she'll get the card."

"Did she check in with you today?"

Kelley hesitated, her eyes suddenly thoughtful. "I'll forward your card. Now if you'll excuse—"

"Was Miss Brecht *expected* to come in today?"

"What difference does it make? She won't talk to you without advice of an attorney—"

"I'm not interested in talking to Miss Brecht, Kelley. I only want to know if Miss Brecht was expected to come in today. Or did she take the day off?"

Kelley bit her lip. "You're asking strange questions."

"On the contrary, they're not strange questions. They're just not the ones you expected. So keep things simple and answer them."

Kelley paused. "Miss Brecht took the day off."

"Is that unusual?"

"Not at all. She frequently takes Wednesdays off. She experiments with new recipes for the kitchen. What's this all about, anyway?"

"She hasn't called in, has she?"

"No, she hasn't."

"Then you probably don't know."

"Know what?"

"Miss Brecht was attacked last night—"

"My God!" Kelley's hand went to her throat. "Who . . . Is she all right?"

"She's going to be okay. She was beaten. She's in the hospital now, but she's conscious. I need a guest and employee list—everyone who was on the grounds last night. Especially the men."

Kelley covered her mouth and shook her head. "This is outrag . . . God, I'm shocked. This is horrible. Does her mother—?"

"We'll take care of her mother, Kelley. I'm requesting that you don't talk to *anyone* about it."

"Of course. How about Frederick? Does he know? Frederick's her brother."

"He's being contacted."

"I don't know what to say. . . ." Kelley said. "I'm . . ."

"Were you here last night?"

"Of course. I live·on the premises."

"Then you know who else was here last night. I'll need that list as soon as possible."

"You don't suspect any of the guests—"

"We'll be as discreet as we possibly can."

"Where is Miss Brecht?" Kelley said. "Can I call her?"

"My partner is going to talk to her soon. I'll tell him you'd like to speak with Miss Brecht. Back to the list, Kelley. I'm especially interested in the men who work here—cooks, janitors, handymen, teachers. Do you have male instructors?"

"Just Eubie Jeffers and my broth— Oh, you can't possibly think they had anything to do with Lilah."

"What kind of suit is this Ms. Betham involved with?"

Kelley wrinkled her forehead. "Ms. Betham is a psychotic old witch. She actually had the audacity to claim that . . . that one of the men who works here made a pass at her."

"Which one?"

"The whole suit is ridicu—"

"Which man?" Marge pushed.

Kelley hesitated, then said, "My brother, Mike. If you knew my brother, you'd know how *inane* the suit is. I shouldn't be telling you this, but since you're not investigating that . . . she was the one who made a pass at my brother. And when he refused, *she* became vicious. We have none of that kind of nonsense in Valley Canyon Spa. Most of our clients have been referred to us by former clients. She was what we call a 'walk-in.' They're *always* the ones who give us the most problems."

"Was your brother, Mike, here last night?" Marge asked.

Kelley's eyes narrowed. "What are you saying?"

"I'm not saying anything. I'm not even *suggesting* anything, Kelley, I'm simply asking. Was your brother on the premises last night?"

"He *lives* here."

"Your brother often visits Miss Brecht's house, doesn't he?"

"No, he doesn't *often* visit Miss Brecht's house!"

"I mean to pick vegetables from the garden, maybe fix the sink . . . that kind of thing."

"Oh . . ." Kelley relaxed her shoulders. "Yes. Lilah does send him on errands for her. That should show you how much she trusts him."

Marge remained casual. "You want to start compiling that list, I'll look around the grounds, get my bearings. You don't mind, do you?"

Kelley had turned pale. "I'm not sure I should do anything without Ms. Brecht's say-so."

"Ms. Ness, why aren't you jumping to help out? Your employer was attacked, beaten. Don't you want to find who did it?"

"Of course I do! It's just such a shock— My God, this is *unbelievable*!"

Marge stood, slung her purse over her shoulder. "You know the best thing to do when you've been jolted by something like this? You do something concrete. Like make a list. The little details always bring you back to earth. Believe me, I know what I'm talking about."

"I guess—"

"I'll be wandering around," Marge said. "Page me when you have the list."

"Detective!" Kelley blurted out. "Detective, no offense, but I don't want to scare the women by having the police nose around."

"I understand completely. I guarantee you, I won't be disruptive." Marge winked. "Hey, I'll grab myself a guava juice and blend in with the crowd."

🎵 5

The group had begun the cool-down portion of the workout when Mike Ness heard his name over the loudspeaker. Towel wrapped around his neck, tank top soaked with perspiration, he told his ladies to "keep it moving" while he answered the page. The afternoon high-impact aerobics class was held in the Jazzarena, its back wall a giant mural of famous musicians. The room's phone was embedded between Dizzy Gillespie's eyes. Ness picked up the receiver.

"Mike, I just want to warn you. The police are here, poking around."

Ness couldn't answer. He felt his heart race.

"Apparently something happened to Lilah last night—"

"*What!*"

"She was attacked, Mike."

Ness felt his knees buckle. *Why did everything he touch turn to shit?* "Wha . . . what happened, Kell?"

"I only know that she's in the hospital. I don't even know which one. I'm going to do some calling around. You don't know anything about this, do you?"

"Of course not!"

Kelley paused. "Please. Just act normal. If the detective asks you where you were last night, say you were sleeping in your room, okay?"

"I *was* sleeping in my room. What the hell are you saying?"

Kelley sighed. "I'm nervous, Mike. I mean, the detective—she's a woman by the way—she was professional but pushy. All of us should just stay calm and cool, all right?"

"I am calm and cool."

"Well, *bully* for you."

"That was mature, Kell."

Kelley paused again. "Michael, I'm *scared*!"

"Have you spoken to Davida?"

"She's not in. I don't even know if she knows about it. The detective didn't want me talking to her but screw that! I can't get hold of Freddy, either. I don't know what to do, Mike."

"There's nothing to do, Kell. What are you worried about?"

"I just didn't like her attitude. She was too inquisitive."

"Correct me if I'm wrong, but aren't detectives supposed to be inquisitive?"

"No, it was more. She was like accusing everyone."

Ness felt the phone slipping out of his hand. He wiped his sweaty palm on his gym shorts. "Accusing who?"

"She wants a list of all the men who work here."

"Was Lilah raped?" Ness whispered into the phone.

"I don't know."

Ness took a deep breath. "Give her what she wants. I've got to button up this class—"

"The detective will want to talk to you."

"So?"

"So . . . is that okay?"

"Yes, it's *okay*!"

"I'm sorry, Mike, I'm just so nervous!"

Ness sighed. Little Kelley always did have a nervous tummy, always throwing up before finals. "Calm down, sis. Do some deep breathing."

"It's just that this job is so *important* to me—"

"Kell, I've got to go. We'll talk later."

Ness hung up, clapped his hands, jogged to the front of the room. Its mirrored wall was bisected horizontally by a ballet barre.

"Nice job, ladies. *Real* nice job. Now that you've burned off approximately two hundred and fifty calories and sweated off your weight in salts, you should immediately be thinking about what?"

A middle-aged woman in striped leotards yelled out, "Electrolytes!"

"Exactly," Ness said. "Your electrolytes are sorely in need of rebalancing, so we have for your dining pleasure our famous potassium-rich broth and organic veggies grown in Lilah Brecht's own garden. These comestibles are being served in the lobby from three-fifteen to three-forty-five. Be sure to partake of the feast and your body will say thank you. I'll see you all at four for yoga."

Wiping his face and neck, Ness waited in the rear as the women filed out. After the ladies left, he walked over to the video-camera stand, peered into the camera's lens, and stuck out his tongue. Then he turned off the machine.

No sense worrying about fuckups when they're out of your control.

He removed the camcorder from the stand. It was one of those tiny buggers—fitted snugly in the palm of his hand. Perfect for shooting on the sly. He'd check the tape later, see if it picked up all his body exercises, how he moved to the beat. He enjoyed watching his tapes, liked seeing his lithe body move and sweat, liked the defined muscles of his arms and legs. He knew he'd *never* be Schwarzenegger—he wasn't the buffed-up type—but at least now he felt good about the way he looked. You had to look good always or it was all over with the ladies. . . .

Out of the corner of his eye, he saw a chicka-doodle approaching him. Just what he needed—another sex-starved teenybopper. She was built, and not shy about showing it off. Her smile was too white to be natural.

"Hi, I'm Aurora," she said.

"Hi." Ness shifted his weight and folded his arms across his chest. "Have a good workout?"

"Great."

"Good to hear, Aurora."

"Really gets the endorphins going, ya know?"

"It can, that's true."

"I can feel it."

"Good." Ness started backing away. "Keep it up."

"Can I ask you a question?"

Ness looked at his watch, then at the chick. She seemed nervous, waiting for him to make his move. She was going to wait for a long time. "What's up?"

"Umm . . . I wanted to know if we should be taking salt pills?"

A good fake, Ness thought. What she really wanted to know was if he was available for fucking.

"Not necessarily, Aurora," Ness said. "Our consommé is a perfectly balanced electrolye replenisher—sodium as well as potassium." He strolled toward the door. "That's why it's so important that you take your broth break. The liquid contains everything your body needs. We sell it at our health-food store. Be sure to buy some when you leave the spa. After your home workout, your salts will be depleted same as here. If you have our broth, you won't have to worry a bit about your electrolytes." He stopped talking when he hit the threshold. "Anything else?"

"No, that's okay. I can see you're in a hurry."

"You just caught me at a bad time." Ness flashed what he hoped was a disarming smile. "I'll be here for yoga if you think of anything else."

"Thanks. I'm going in for the broth right now."

Ness waited until she was gone before he allowed the anxiety to resurface. What the hell had happened last night to bring the police out nosing around? He tossed the damp towel in the hamper and was about to lock the door. Sensing someone behind him, he turned. He knew without introduction that he had found the chick detective.

Actually, it was more like she had found him.

As he cruised the 405 Freeway south, Decker thought about the baby. It had been his idea. Not that Rina hadn't wanted children. But she would have preferred to wait a couple of years, let everyone get to know one another as a family before adding another member. Even though he was forty-two, she was only thirty and it was maternal age that was the big factor in problem pregnancies.

Rina's plan would have prevailed if he hadn't been shot. It had been an odyssey that had led him from coast to coast until he found the missing kid and the psycho who abducted him. Unfortunately, the psycho had a gun. Psychos always have guns.

After the initial recovery from the gunshot wounds, Decker had been insistent that the baby schedule be pushed ahead. After all, he wasn't a youngster and both of them had had previous fertility problems with their first spouses. What if it took a long time? What if medical intervention was needed? Why wait, only to discover a problem that could take years to fix? Rina understood his logic and agreed.

But the truth of the matter was, he'd *needed* this baby. After his brush with the other side, he'd hungered for something life-affirming. What better way to regain a sense of potency than to sire a baby?

He rolled up the window of the unmarked, shutting out noise as well as air, and turned on the air conditioner. A Freon-scented wind blasted his face.

Deliriously happy when Rina had told him the news, he had taken the whole squad room out for happy hour and actually gotten drunk. Not seriously plastered, but tipsy enough for Marge to have to drive him home.

Then reality had come knocking. Another body to feed and clothe and educate, stretching his paycheck that much further. Then there was Rina's morning sickness and moodiness, and the cold shoulder given to him by his stepsons. Both had been slow to adjust to the idea of an interloper. Lately, things had been better; all those Sundays spent in the park launching model rockets definitely helped. But Sammy and Jake were still wary critters.

Fair enough. With time, he'd prove them wrong.

What hurt most of all was the reaction of his nearly adult daughter. Cindy had seemed so independent. She'd spent last summer in Europe, was away at college this year. She rarely wrote, never called. Never stayed on long when *he* phoned. But when they did speak, the conversation had always been friendly and upbeat. She had seemed to adjust well to his marriage to Rina. In fact, Cindy and Rina had always gotten along. Great—better than he could have hoped.

It shocked him how she had responded to the news—that awful *silence*. Would it have actually hurt her to tell him congratulations when she finally did open up?

Man oh man, did she know how to *hit*.

Don't you think you're rushing things, Dad?

It had been his turn to pause.

Well, if we did rush things, Cindy, we can't exactly take it back now, can we?

That's true.

Another silence.

Well, good luck.

Snide tone. As in good luck, you're gonna need it, pal.

Cindy, I love you—

Look, Dad. I'm an adult, not a child. You don't have to reassure me. I'm well aware of the fact that you will

*love me no matter how many other children you'll have.
And I'm sure you'll have lots because Rina's young. If
that's what you want, I wish you well.*

Cindy, I'm not reassuring you—

Yes, you are. Don't lie about it.

*Okay, maybe I am. But it's not as if it's a horrible
thing for a father to say to his daughter.*

Stony silence.

Decker sighed. *I'm sorry if I upset you—*

I'm not upset.

If I upset you by trying to reassure you.

Oh. Pause. *It's okay.*

Would you like me to call you tomorrow?

Whatever.

Then I'll call you tomorrow.

Sure. She had paused a moment. *How's your arm,
Daddy?*

Don't worry about me, honey, I'm just fine.

Yeah, you're always fine. I'll talk to you later.

He had called her the next day. And the next and
the next, receiving the same frosty attitude each
time. Nothing more than a perfunctory chat, a sincere inquiry into the state of his health, and a cold
response when he told her he was okay. He knew she
wanted him to confide in her, but it simply wasn't
his style. He refused to complain to anyone, let alone
his daughter.

And so it went. Finally, Rina suggested he wait
until Cindy came to him.

Of course that conversation had led to a fight, he
accusing her of interfering with his daughter. Later,
he regretted his words but didn't feel like apologiz-

ing. Rina didn't push it; she was good about things like that.

After he cooled off, he admitted to himself that Rina's advice had been good. He knew that his constant calling was giving Cindy the message that he was insecure about their relationship. Over the months, he'd weaned himself down to a phone call a week.

And each time Cindy remained aloof.

Well, maybe she'd warm up after the baby came.

And maybe he'd win the lottery, too.

Frederick Brecht's office was in Tarzana on the western end of Ventura Boulevard—the glitzy shopping strip for the San Fernando Valley. Decker had expected a medical building, but instead, the address corresponded to a two-story mini-mall; Brecht's practice was sandwiched between a travel agency and a health-food store. Each business was allowed only two parking spaces. Brecht's spaces, marked RESERVED FOR DOCTOR, were occupied. Decker pulled into one of the health-food store's slots, hoping the owner wouldn't call and have the car towed away.

The door to the office was glass backed by an attached white curtain that prevented unwanted onlookers from peeking inside. The glass was stenciled in gold

FREDERICK R. BRECHT, M.D.
HOLISTIC AND WELL-BEING MEDICINE
ACUPUNCTURE AND NUTRITION
CONSULTATION BY APPOINTMENT ONLY

Decker went inside and halted in his tracks.

The waiting room was unoccupied and without conventional furniture. Couches and chairs were replaced with brown mats that covered the waxed wooden planks of fir. In the center of the room was a pile of specialty magazines: *Journal of Holistic Health. Annals of Eastern Medicine. The Vitamin Digest.* Hanging from the ceiling were silk-screened lanterns emitting soft, filtered light. The wallpaper was imprinted with some kind of Chinese farm scene—kimonoed men and women with one-dimensional features tilling soil and pulling some kind of root from the ground. New Age synthesizer music, along with the odor of incense, wafted through the air.

Decker pondered the reception window, then stared at the cushioned floor, unsure if he should remove his shoes. He decided to brave the trek in shod feet, but found himself tiptoeing. He knocked on the frosted glass and a middle-aged woman slid open the panel. She wore no makeup but was decked with jewelry. Dozens of bracelets, a couple of silver necklaces, and earrings that were large and beaded and hung down to her shoulders. Her brown hair had been cut short, her eyes were deep-set. Her voice was a tinkle—like wind chimes—and at odds with the mature face.

"Yes?"

"I'm Sergeant Peter Decker of the LAPD." He showed the woman his badge. "I'd like to speak with Dr. Brecht."

"Dr. Brecht is not in today. Would you like to leave a message?"

Tinkle, tinkle.

Decker said, "Where is Dr. Brecht?"

"I don't know."

"Has he checked in today?"

Suddenly the light voice was as sharp as broken glass.

"I don't know if I should answer your questions."

"Why? Are you hiding something?"

"Of course n—"

"So why wouldn't you want to answer a simple question? Has Dr. Brecht phoned in today?"

She was flustered. "Uh, I'm sure he will soon."

"But he hasn't come in yet?"

"No." She sighed. "He left a message on the machine. 'Althea, cancel all my patients today. An emergency came up.' So I canceled his patients." She played with a beaded earring. "No big deal. Today would have been a light day—three stress consultations, two deep-body massages, one biofeedback."

"What time did he leave the message?"

"It was on the machine when I arrived at eight this morning. His first appointment wasn't until ten so I had lots of time to cancel."

"Does your answering machine record the time that the call was made?"

"No."

"You're sure?"

"Yes."

"All right. Dr. Brecht has another office at his sister's spa, is that correct?"

Something malevolent clouded Althea's eyes. "It's not an official *office*. You can't make an appointment to see him there unless you're a registered guest. Freddy helps his sister out. Which is more than I can say for her."

"How often does he help out at the spa?"

"*Too* often."

"Give me an estimate."

"Maybe once or twice a week. Which may not seem like a lot to you, but it really does cut the efficiency of a practice. You know, Freddy is a *very* unique doctor. It was his treatment that cured my backaches and I really believe in him. So do a lot of people. He works very hard for his patients. I resent his jumping whenever his sister calls. He's just too nice and she takes advantage of him."

"How about his mother?" Decker asked.

"The great Davida Eversong? She and his sister are two of a kind. You think *she'd* ever help him out? To her, everything is Lilah, Lilah, Lilah. Of course whenever she needs a *massage*, she calls him and he comes running. Do you think she even *pays* him?"

"No?"

"Not a dime." Althea sighed. "Well, I've just talked too much."

"Do you think Dr. Brecht might be with his mother?"

She sighed again. "I didn't lie, but I didn't tell you the whole truth. I don't know where he is but I do know he's not at the spa. I've also called his house *and* his mother's apartments. No one answered." She suddenly blushed. "I wasn't checking up on him. It's just there are a few business matters I need to tell him about."

"Business matters?"

"It's of no concern to the police."

Decker paused a moment, letting her know that at the moment everything was of concern to the police. "Why don't you give me the addresses and phone numbers of Ms. Eversong's and Dr. Brecht's residences. I can get it myself, but you'd be saving me a few steps. And time may be of the essence here."

"Why? What do you mean?"

"There was an incident last night concerning Dr. Brecht's sister."

"An incident?"

"She was attacked."

"My God! What happ—"

"I know Dr. Brecht met her last night for supper," Decker broke in. "Now you tell me he hasn't shown up for work. I'm wondering if something might have happened to him."

"Oh, my *God!*"

"Not that I have any reason to believe that something did happen—"

"Oh, dear Lord!" Althea tugged at her earring. "*Omigod, omigod.* Of course I'll give you those numbers." She yanked on a drawer and shakily drew out a piece of paper and a pen. "Why didn't you tell me your business in the first place?"

She was scolding him. But she was giving him what he wanted so Decker let it pass.

❧ 6

A split second to decide how to handle it. Act surprised, resigned, indignant or cooperative or maybe even friendly. No, scratch friendly. Cops were wary of anyone too congenial. If she was good—*inquisitive* like Kelley had said—she'd probably heard his name paged over the loudspeaker and would wonder what that was all about. Ness knew he could probably pull off playing dumb, but now was not the time to audition for the Oscar. Keep it simple and keep her off guard. At least Kelley's call had prepared him. No weak knees or sweaty hands.

"Hi," Ness said. "I'm assuming you're the detective since you're not dressed for yoga."

Marge paused a moment, surprised he knew who she was, surprised at how *smooth* he was around her. Most people were jumpy around cops. "Did you just talk to your sister?"

"Yeah. She's totally freaked out, wasn't making a lot of sense to tell you the truth. Something about Lilah being attacked and you're here looking into it? Whenever Kelley gets freaked, she calls big brother. What happened?"

"You've got some time to talk?"

"Now?"

"Yes, now."

"I've got 'bout half an hour before my next class." Ness swallowed hard, stepped back inside the Jazz-arena, and gently placed his camcorder onto a mat. "I'm all dehydrated. You mind if I grab a cup of broth? We can talk in here. Hard to find privacy around this place."

"Your sister tells me you live on the premises. We can talk in your place."

"Nah, too far of a walk. I'll be back in a jiff. Hang tight."

He was out the door before Marge could protest. She paced around the gym. Against the side wall, there were a pile of fresh towels, a large wicker basket filled with dirty towels, and stacked blue exercise mats. In front of the mirrors was a CD player resting on the floor. With no chairs available, Marge leaned against the ballet barre.

Physically, Mike Ness wasn't at all what Marge had expected. She'd figured on a muscle man and wasn't prepared for someone on the slight side. He was sort of androgynous-looking, actually, except for the well-trimmed two-day stubble that covered his face. Shiny black hair that fell over big blue eyes. Truth be told he was almost as pretty as his sister. Though his muscles weren't over-inflated, they had been worked on. He had the wiry kind of definition in his biceps and calves.

He came back a moment later, carrying two steaming cups, and kicked the door shut with his foot. If the guy was guilty of anything, good old sister Kelley had taken away the key element of surprise.

"I brought an extra cup for you, Detective."

"Thanks, but I'll pass."

Still holding the cups, Ness sat down cross-legged without spilling a drop. "I don't know but I'd imagine there's a certain amount of tension in your job. The broth is a great stress reducer. And it's low-calorie."

Marge sat next to him, pulled out her notebook. "I'm not on a diet."

"Take it anyway. It won't kill you." Ness's lips unfolded in a half smile. "Poor choice of words, I guess."

Marge returned his expression with a half smile of her own. "Drink mine for me, bro. I've already tanked up on guava juice."

Ness broke into unexpected laughter. "I detect sarcasm. You know that cynicism is a prime toxin builder, Detective."

"So is assault."

Ness grew serious. "What happened to Lilah last night?"

"She was attacked."

"Was she raped?"

"A full report hasn't been filed yet. Do you know anything about it?"

"Me? Not a clue."

Marge studied his face. There was some concern but he wasn't overdoing it. Good eye contact. Didn't seem real fidgety. Either he wasn't worried about his ass or he was a top-notch psychopath. "How do you get along with Lilah?"

"I adore her." He smiled slowly. "As a *friend*. She's the greatest boss I've ever had. Lets me make my own hours, great about giving me time off. The pay here isn't great, I've gotta be honest. But when you factor in the perks—free room and board—the paycheck isn't as small as it looks on paper. This isn't the job I want to do all my life, but it's a great pit stop."

Mr. Sincere.

Marge asked, "How long have you worked for her?"

"I came on about eight months ago." Ness finished one cup of broth, crunched the paper cup in his hand. "My sister brought me over, actually. She's worked here close to two years and *loves* her job. Kelley's a great kid, but she worries too much about me. I was unemployed about a year ago. Didn't bother me, but it drove her crazy. She talked me into coming here. More like *dragged* me over. But I'm not sorry. Like I said, the position is okay until I figure out what I want to do."

"What do you want to do?"

"I sure as hell wouldn't mind owning a place like this," Ness said, wistfully. "But since that doesn't seem likely in the future, I'd like to have enough clients to support myself as a personal trainer. You build up lots of contacts here. I've already filled up Tuesday and Saturday evenings with people. Lilah's really good about that, she gives me the time off. But as of this moment I don't have enough of a client load—enough income—to make ends meet on my own."

"Did you meet your clients at the spa?"

"Sure, most of them. A few of the recent ones are referrals. See, that's how the ball gets rolling."

"Lilah doesn't mind you stealing business?"

"I don't *steal* business—"

"If you train women at home, who needs the spa?"

Ness slowly took a sip of his second cup of broth. "It doesn't work that way, Detective. The spa and I are *synergistic*. We *feed* off of each other. Look around. Most of the women you see here are in terrific shape. They come here for peace and quiet and want a *safe* environment to relax where they won't gain weight. Sure we have some men here—mostly husbands whose wives asked them along—but the majority of our clientele is female. They can hang out without feeling that some guy is going to hit on them."

"That how Ms. Betham felt?"

"I *knew* you were going to bring that up," Ness said. "You ever meet *Miz* Betham?"

"No."

"She's around fifty and has a face like a pineapple. Now I have nothing against ugly people except when they give me troubles. I don't know what her problem is, but she isn't going to bring *me* down. I hope the garbage she's saying isn't giving you funny ideas about me. I don't hit on women. And I certainly wouldn't ever do anything to Lilah. You haven't told me too much about that."

"Lilah will be okay," Marge said. "If she wants to tell you about it in detail, I'm sure she will."

"She know who attacked her?"

Marge was silent.

"Probably not," Ness said. "Otherwise you wouldn't be questioning me. Ask me anything you want. I'll do anything to help you find the bastard who hurt her."

"You like her a lot."

"I told you, I adore her."

"But just as a friend."

"Yep."

"Was there ever anything sexual between you and her?"

"No. Not that I'd mind, but . . ."

Marge waited.

"I guess I'm not her type."

"Who's her type?"

"Lilah's?" Ness paused. "Wouldn't know. I once heard she'd been married. I try not to delve too deeply into my boss's affairs. I think that makes a lot of sense."

"Were you here at the spa yesterday, Mike?"

"Yesterday was what? Sunday? Yep, I was here. I attended the seven o'clock lecture. Honestly, I don't even remember what it was on. They blur. Afterward, I worked out for an hour by myself. Then I drank a little herbal tea with some of the ladies." He smiled. "You know, trying to drum up a little business. I went to bed around eleven, maybe it was closer to twelve."

"Did you see Lilah anytime during the evening?"

"I don't remember."

"Was she at the lecture?"

"Was she? I don't remember. My sister, Kelley, might know. She's the one who's good with details."

"So no one can verify where you were between the hours of twelve and seven."

"Nope. No one. 'Cause I was sleeping by my little lonesome." Ness shrugged. "Is Lilah unconscious or something? Otherwise, why are you questioning me? She could tell you I didn't do anything to her."

"She's conscious."

Ness nodded. "That's good. So just ask her—"

"We intend to question her extensively when she's feeling better. In the meantime, we haven't ruled anyone out. You know anyone who might have a bone to pick with Lilah? A disgruntled employee, maybe?"

Ness shook his head. "Everyone loves her. Never heard anyone say a bad word . . . except . . . well, he didn't say anything bad about her. He didn't say *anything* about her . . . which was odd."

Marge looked at him.

"About two, three months ago, a guy *claiming* to be Lilah's brother came here," Ness said. "Actually he wanted to see Davida because it was her birthday. He had a gift. No one was around. He left the present at reception and split."

"That was it?"

"Yeah, pretty much."

"Why are you telling me this?"

"I don't know," Ness said. "I'd never seen the guy before. He hasn't been back since. I know how close Lilah is to Freddy. It just struck me as odd that this 'brother' would be such a mystery man. He was quite a bit older than her or Freddy. Looked to be in his middle forties. *Strange.*"

"What was his name?"

"I don't remember it. I do remember it was a blue-blood name, though—like Thurston Howell the Third or something."

"Does the name King ring a bell?"

He paused, then shook his head. "That wasn't his name."

There had been something in Ness's eyes—a glint of recognition. Marge said, "You're sure his name wasn't King something or something King?"

"No, that wasn't the name on the card."

"You peeked at the birthday card?"

Ness smiled. "He left his business card along with the present, too. Weird. You ever hear of someone leaving their business card with a present? Especially a family member?"

Marge didn't answer.

"I figure he's not a close family member," Ness said. "He was a doctor, by the way. I saw M.D. after his name on his card."

"You saw his card but don't remember his name."

"Sorry, no."

"What'd you do with the card?"

"I gave it to Kelley. She probably still has it unless she threw it away. I doubt she did. She's compulsive. Ask her."

"I will." Marge planted a large hand on his bony shoulder. "In the meantime, Mr. Ness, you stay close."

"No problem, Detective, I've got nowhere else to go."

Marge stood, flipped the cover over her notepad, and toed the tip of the video camera. "What do you do with this?"

Ness picked up the camera. "I tape myself working. To see how I move. I take my job seriously and don't want to look like an ass in front of the women. You want a peek?"

Marge looked at her watch. "Sure."

Ness got up. Marge followed him to the back of the Jazzarena. He opened a cupboard. Inside was a thirteen-inch TV attached to ancillary equipment. Ness opened the camera and slid the tape into a video machine. His image filled the monitor, shots of him moving with the grace of a ballet dancer. Marge asked him if he had had lessons.

"Long ago." Ness's eyes were fixed to the monitor.

"Unusual for a boy to have ballet."

"My parents were unusual people." He turned to her. "Can I eighty-six the tape?"

"Be my guest."

Ness flipped the switch and the monitor turned dark.

Marge said, "Thanks for your time, Mr. Ness." As she headed for the door, he called out her name. She turned around.

"Sure you don't want to stay for yoga? It soothes the savage spirit."

Marge smiled. "I like my spirit savage, Mr. Ness. It keeps me on my toes."

Decker leaned against a pink column near the entrance to the spa and read the business card Marge had given him.

John Reed M.D. FACOG
Obstetrics, Gynecology, Infertility

Two phone numbers were printed on the lower right corner; a medical license number was on the lower left. He flipped the card over. Nothing written on the back.

A hot, dry wind whipped through the air, the sun flashing off the chrome bumpers that spangled the parking lot. Decker loosened his tie, unbuttoned his shirt cuffs, and rolled up his sleeves.

"Is this card legitimate?"

"I called the number right before you got here." Marge checked her watch. "Must have been about four-thirty. It's a doctor's office. Apparently Reed had canceled all his afternoon appointments because he was stuck at the hospital for deliveries."

"Stuck?" Decker said.

"His secretary's word, not mine."

"Find out which hospital?"

Marge shook her head. "I asked her but she didn't answer and I didn't push it. I don't even know if he's relevant to the case. I wasn't able to get too much out of the receptionist, period, but she did tell me that yes indeed John Reed is Lilah's and Freddy's brother."

Two bikini-clad women came out of the spa, laughing loudly, arms linked together. Nubile young ladies—one blond and one brunet—tossing long damp hair over their tanned shoulders. Decker followed their sway until they disappeared inside a silver Porshe Carrera. The car zoomed off and Decker stared at the empty space for a moment.

"There's at least a couple dozen more like that inside," Marge said.

"You like that color for a Porsche? Mine could use a new paint job and I'm sick of red."

"You looking at the girls or the car, Pete?"

"At first I was looking at the girls. Then I got distracted by the car."

Marge burst into laughter. "Rina has nothing to worry about."

Decker smiled. "I could have told you that. So if this Reed is Lilah's doctor brother, who's Totes's phantom named King?"

"I asked Reed's girl about him. At that point, she started asking me questions. When I wouldn't answer hers, she refused to answer mine. But I had the feeling that this unknown King is a real person. Whether he's a brother or not, I don't know."

Decker said, "So far, Lilah has got what . . . three doctor brothers including a phantom brother named King?"

Marge shrugged.

Decker said, "I've got Hollander looking up sex offenders who live in the area. I've also asked him to punch the crime into the computer and see if it matches anything else that has gone down in the city. Until I've spoken with Lilah, we don't have too much to go on."

Marge said, "You speak with Davida Eversong yet?"

Decker frowned. "Did Morrison ask about her again?"

"I called in for messages," Marge said. "He was just curious whether we've contacted her or not. Why's he in an uproar over her?"

Decker said, "A famous actress's daughter is raped—could be big news if it got out. Lots of actresses are attention junkies. I'm sure Morrison doesn't want publicity after dealing with the fallout from the Rodney King beating."

"A new concept in Totally Hidden Video." Marge furrowed her brow. "You think you could lose it like that, Pete?"

"I think we're all just a step above apes."

Marge smiled. "You make contact with Freddy Brecht?"

"He wasn't in." Decker filled her in on his conversation with Brecht's secretary. "I don't know why he canceled his patients. Maybe he found out about Lilah and rushed over to see her. I'd like to talk to him. He supposedly saw her last night and maybe he'd remember something."

"I'll call the hospital and ask if he's been there to visit her."

"Thanks." Decker wiped his brow, damp with perspiration. Mercury must have hit the ninety-degree mark today. Poor Rina. Next couple of months were going to be hell for her. "So tell me about Kelley's brother, Mike. Is he the same guy who picks the vegetables?"

"Yeah. He gave me an *eerie* feeling. But you told me Lilah didn't know who attacked her and she knows Mike."

Decker said, "She was blindfolded, so the perp could still be someone she knows. I just shot out the question. She probably didn't even know what I was asking. I'll ask her again."

"Maybe she does know who he is and the guy has her terrorized."

"Is Ness scary?"

"No, more like wily—sly," Marge answered. "Guy

didn't flinch when he turned around and saw me staring him down. I've nothing concrete against him—he was cooperative—but I don't trust him. At first glance, he isn't physically prepossessing. Then you see him move. He tapes himself exercising."

"What?"

"Yeah, he had a video camera and I asked him what he used it for. He tapes himself. Played me the tape without hesitation. Man, the way he *moves*, maybe he's not a lion, but he's sure a jaguar. In *total* control of his body."

"Want me to look him over?"

"Let me work him over first." Marge told Decker about the Betham complaint. "I'll get back to you on that. See if the suit's legit."

"Go for it, Margie," Decker said. "I'm off to the hospital to talk to Lilah."

The entrance doors to the spa parted once again. Out came a young lass in cutoff jeans and a tank top. A way-too-small-for-her-chest tank top. And she wasn't wearing a bra. Decker felt he *had* to notice these details because noticing details honed one's skills of observation—the primary tool of detection.

Marge tapped him on the shoulder. "You want to switch assignments, Pete?"

"No." Decker's eyes shifted from the bouncing bosoms back to Marge's face. "No, Detective Dunn, that wouldn't be an efficient division of labor. You finish up your hit list. I'm off to the hospital."

7

The drive to Sun Valley Memorial was a westward stretch of freeway that had Decker riding into the late-afternoon sun. Squinting, he yanked down the unmarked's visor, which did little to mitigate the glare, then fished around in the glove compartment until he felt a pair of sunglasses. Cheapies—the lenses were gridmarked with scratches. But it was better than driving blind.

Maybe Lilah had been able to see *something* from under the blindfold. It had been made of lightweight material folded over several times, but it hadn't been form-fitting. She could have sneaked a glance or two out of an open corner.

If he got lucky.

He took the Branch Street exit, turned left, then traveled another mile on surface streets. The winds were blowing dust, little eddies of soot that looked like gold powder in the late-afternoon light.

The Foothill Substation of the LAPD patrolled the east end of the San Fernando Valley—the last bastion of rural Los Angeles filled with miles of grazing land. Slowly and steadily, commercialization was eroding the undeveloped acres, but the ranchers were a stubborn lot, often refusing to sell even if there was profit to be made. Creatures of habit, they, like Decker's father, wouldn't know what to do with the money if they didn't have their work—tasks that challenged the body and roughened the hands.

As he veered the Plymouth away from the mountains and onto Foothill Boulevard, the terrain changed. Open fields yielded to lumber- and brickyards, scrap-metal dealerships, roofing companies, wholesale nurseries, and block-long discount stores advertising everyday sale prices. The boulevard twisted and turned through large open lots until the hospital came into view.

Sun Valley Memorial—a three-story square building plastered in green stucco—shared the block with a flower farm abloom with mums and marigolds. Decker parked the car in the half-full EMERGENCY ONLY lot, stuck his OFFICIAL POLICE BUSINESS card on the dash, and took the elevator up, getting off on the second floor.

The visitors' area was small and nearly empty. To the right a woman and teenaged boy sat playing cards. On the other side of the room was a man reading a magazine and an elderly woman listening intently as a doctor, still dressed in surgical scrubs, spoke to her in hushed tones. No one was sitting at the desk marked INFORMATION.

Decker bypassed the lobby and walked down the long corridor until he found the nurses' station. He presented his badge to a young man wearing a white uniform.

"Sergeant Decker of the LAPD. I spoke with Dr.

Kessler earlier in the day and he told me I could come down and interview Lilah Brecht. She's in room two-fifty-five."

The man leaned over the counter to study the badge. "Lilah Brecht . . ."

"Yes, Lilah Brecht. She was admitted this morning, victim of an assault."

"Lilah Brecht . . ." the man repeated.

With a smile, Decker asked, "Can you page Dr. Kessler for me?"

"I know who Lilah is. I'm her floor nurse. I seem to remember Dr. Kessler saying something about you coming down. I'm sure he wrote it in her chart."

Decker waited.

"I'm not sure where the chart is now," the nurse said. He scratched a hairy forearm. "Maybe down in Neuro. But it doesn't matter. She's out of it right now."

"She's sedated?"

"No, no." The nurse frowned. "You don't sedate people with possible head injuries. She's asleep. It's been a long day for her. Her brother tried to talk to her about a half hour ago, but she was—"

"Her *brother*? You mean Dr. Brecht?"

"Yep."

"He was *here*?"

"Why is that weird? He's the patient's brother."

"I've been looking for him," Decker said. "Left messages at his office, at the hospital—"

"I never got any messages from you."

Decker let out an exasperated sigh. "Did he just get here or has he been here all day?"

"I'd say he came about a half hour ago. When he

saw she was sleeping, he said he'd be back in a half hour. But like I said, that was a half hour ago. So he should be back around . . . now."

"I'm going to take a quick peek in Lilah's room," Decker said.

"Okay," replied the nurse with hairy forearms. "But don't wake her."

Decker said he wouldn't. Her room was at the end of the hallway—one of the few privates available in the hospital. She was sleeping sitting up in the bed, glucose trailing down an IV line threaded into her arm. Her hair had been brushed off her forehead, her scrubbed face showing the bluing and swelling of her ordeal. Both eyes were puffy, with scratches and cuts above her brow. Her mouth was open; the dry air had caused her red lips to crack. Her skin tone had markedly improved. She was still pale but the cold, ashen complexion was gone. She wore the standard hospital gown backward, the split open in the front. But her modesty was protected by a bedsheet across her chest. Softly, he called out her name.

No response.

He checked his watch and decided to wait a few minutes. He pulled a chair up to the bed, about to stretch his legs when a stern voice jerked his head around, demanding to know *who the hell* he was.

The man appeared to be in his early thirties, medium height and weight, prematurely bald with just a few plugs of thin blond hair sticking up from a pink scalp. He made up for his lack of cranial hair with a full sandy-colored beard and thick eyebrows.

He had close-set, pale-blue eyes and a long beaky nose. He wore a long white coat over an embroidered work shirt and jeans. On his feet were an ancient pair of Earth sandals—the kind where the toe was higher than the heel. Decker thought those had gone the way of the Nehru jacket.

"I'm Sergeant Decker of the Los Angeles Police."

The man paused. When he spoke again, he had lowered his voice. "I don't think she's equipped to talk to the police at the moment. Maybe tomorrow."

"You're Frederick Brecht?"

"I'm Dr. Frederick Brecht, yes."

With an emphasis on the *doctor*, Decker noticed. He stood, overshooting Brecht by around six inches. He put him at about five-ten, one-seventy. Even though his coloring was similar to Lilah's, brother and sister bore little resemblance.

"I'm handling your sister's assault, Doctor. I've been trying to reach you all day."

Brecht's scalp turned a deep shade of rose. "Why is that a concern of the police?"

"You went out with your sister last night," Decker said. "Maybe you noticed something—"

"Nothing," Brecht said. "If I had, I would have contacted you. Anything else?"

Decker said, "Doctor, how about we grab a cup of coffee in the cafeteria as long as Lilah's resting? Maybe you can help me out by answering a couple of questions."

"But I have nothing to tell you," Brecht insisted.

Lilah moaned.

"Patients, even in sleep, are still receptive to their

surroundings," Brecht lectured. "I think this conversation is upsetting her. I'm afraid I must ask you to leave at once."

"Doctor, I know this is a bad time for you—"

"Bad is an egregious understatement, Sergeant. I'm in no mood to be interrogated." Brecht touched the tips of his fingers to his forehead. "I can't think clearly. Maybe tomorrow."

Decker was struck by Brecht's manner—incongruent with the informal, guru appearance. He'd expected a palsy-walsy interaction and was getting anything but.

"Sure, tomorrow's fine," Decker said. "It's just . . . you know. Well, maybe you don't. Time is really important in these kind of cases, Doc."

Brecht closed his eyes, then slowly opened them. "I suppose a few minutes . . ."

Decker walked over and looped his arm around the doctor's shoulder. Gently, he guided Brecht out the door. "You look like you could use a cup of coffee."

"I never drink caffeine," Brecht said weakly.

"Now's a good time for an exception."

"No, no." Brecht sighed. "I'm fine. Really, I'm fine. Well, that's not true at all. I'm very shaken. Who wouldn't be?"

"True."

They took the elevator down to ground level. It was after five and the cafeteria had begun to serve dinner, the special was meat loaf with mashed potatoes, peas, and coffee or soft drink for $4.99.

"Hungry?" Decker asked.

"I never eat red meat," Brecht said.

Decker picked up an apple.

"That's been sprayed," Brecht commented. "If you must eat chemically adulterated items, may I suggest an orange as opposed to an apple. Its peel, being thick, absorbs most of the pesticides, leaving only traces of the poison in the meat of the fruit."

Decker stared at him. "Maybe I'll just stick to coffee."

"Caffeine has been implicated in heart disease and infertility."

"My wife's pregnant," he said, then wondered why.

"Good God, I hope she has enough sense not to drink coffee. Caffeine's been implicated in birth defects!"

Decker was quiet. Now that he thought about it, Rina was suddenly drinking mint tea. He wondered if that had been implicated in anything, but didn't ask. He filled a Styrofoam cup with coffee and led Brecht to a corner table. He pulled out his notebook.

Brecht said, "How long have you been with the force?"

Decker held back a smile and sipped axle grease. "I've been with LAPD for seventeen years, fifteen of them wearing a gold shield."

Brecht looked at Decker, then at the tabletop. "I . . . apologize for interrogating you . . . was it Officer Decker?"

"Sergeant Decker. Detective Sergeant if you want to get technical."

"I'm usually very professional in my behavior, Sergeant. But now . . . well, surely you can understand . . ."

"Of course."

"What . . ." Brecht hesitated. "When did it happen?"

"I'm not sure of the exact time," Decker said. "I was hoping you could help me with that. You were out with her last night."

"Yes, I was. But she was fine when we parted. When did you find out about . . . ?"

"The call came through dispatch a little before seven in the morning," Decker said. "Maid phoned it in. How'd you find out?"

"I called my office."

"When?"

"Around an hour ago. My secretary was *panicked* by your visit. It took me at least five minutes to calm her down and find out what had happened. She was very worried that . . . that something had happened to me as well."

"She seems like a loyal gal."

"Althea has my interests at heart."

"Why'd you wait so long to call your office for messages?"

"I . . . it had been an unusual day. I was very busy."

"With what?"

"What does my business have to do with Lilah?"

Decker waited.

Brecht sighed. "Well, if you really must know, I was preoccupied with my mother."

"Davida Eversong."

"The Great Dame of the Silver Screen." Brecht frowned. "She can really put it on, that woman. But she *is* my mother. What can I do?"

Decker said, "You were at the spa all this time?"

"No, no, no," Brecht said. "At her beach house. In

Malibu. Mother's there at the moment. She doesn't know a thing about Lilah and I'm insisting that *you* don't tell her."

"How much do you know about the case, Doctor?" Decker asked.

Brecht stiffened. "*What* are you implying, Sergeant?"

"Take it easy," Decker said. "I was speaking in medical terms. Have you read your sister's chart?"

Brecht paused, uncoiling slowly. "Not yet. It wasn't on her door when I arrived and I haven't had the energy to go searching for it. I've put in a call to her attending physician." He looked Decker in the eye. "Is there anything I should know about?"

Decker didn't answer.

Brecht's voice turned to a whisper. "She was sexually assaulted, wasn't she?"

"I'm sorry."

"Dear *God*!" he gasped out. "Dear, dear God, I don't believe . . ." he gasped again. "Could you get me some water, please?"

Decker bolted up and retrieved a glass of water. Still trembling, Brecht clutched the glass and gulped down the water.

"Do you need another drink?" Decker asked.

Brecht held up his palm and shook his head. He took a deep breath. "No . . . no, thank you."

"You're sure?"

"Yes . . . quite. It's . . . the shock." He inhaled deeply once again. "What happened?"

"We're still putting pieces together, Doctor. I hope to have a better picture after I talk to your sister."

"I just can't *believe* . . ." Brecht buried his face in

his hands, then looked up. "Ask your questions, Detective."

Decker said, "When did your mother call you to
come down to Malibu?"

"This morning," Brecht said. "She was in terrible
pain and I rushed out to treat her."

"What time did she call?"

"Around eight-thirty, nine."

"Is that why you canceled all your appointments?"

"Yes. My appointments that day started at ten. I
knew by Mother's tone that there'd be no way that
I could get away with just a simple treatment. Once
I was out there, I just didn't feel . . . I decided to give
her the entire day."

"Your secretary said your cancellation message
was already on the machine when she arrived at
eight."

Again Brecht's scalp deepened in tone. "Well,
maybe Mother called at seven-thirty. I really don't
remember exactly."

Decker let his words hang. Forget about the phone
call for the moment. From Malibu to Tarzana was a
toll call. If Mama Eversong did dial sonny boy up,
Decker could get the *exact* time by checking phone
records. "What's wrong with your mother?"

"Age." Brecht sounded weary. "She's over seventy
with diabetes, arthritis, bursitis, osteoporosis—oh,
why bore you with the details? Conventional drugs
alone have had little success. In conjunction with my
holistic regimen, Mother does a bit better handling
the pain and skeletomuscular problems. But basically
she's just wearing out and not doing it gracefully."

"You usually treat her whenever she calls?"

Brecht sighed. "I evaluate each incident individually. If I hear a demand for attention and not genuine pain in her voice, I put her off. This time she sounded as if she really needed help."

"And you received her call around seven-thirty?"

"I suppose. Anyway, if you need her to verify my presence at the beach house, I'll have her write you a note. I'm afraid I can't give you her home number."

"That's all right," Decker said. "I have it."

There was a moment of silence.

"You have my mother's *beach house* number?"

"All of your mother's numbers. I've called all day and nobody answered."

"My mother doesn't believe in answering phones. She claims that's for secretaries."

"Does she have a secretary?"

"No."

"There were no machines answering the numbers, either."

"She claims machines are uncivilized."

"So she never answers the phone when it rings?"

"Not at the beach house. Or at her apartments. At the spa, anyone wishing to speak with her leaves a message at the desk. She does pick up her messages from time to time."

"Then why does she bother having phones?"

"To make outside calls—as she did to me this morning." Brecht blew air out of his mouth. "As I started to say, if you need her to verify my presence, I'll make sure she writes you a note."

As if a note from Davida Eversong would carry enough weight to explain anything away. The arrogance of the rich. Or maybe Brecht was used to

Mama taking care of him. A note—as in grade school. *Please excuse Dr. Freddy for being absent.*

"I'll even insist Mother have the note notarized," Brecht added.

Decker said, "I'd like to interview her."

"I'm afraid that's impossible."

"Why?"

"It just is. At least right now. I can't elaborate. Perhaps in a day or two."

Decker let it go. Brecht was being cooperative but only up to a point. Was he protecting Mama or protecting himself? Not that Decker had any reason to actually suspect Brecht. Still, Lilah's safe was wide open. What the hell was inside?

"You went out to dinner with your sister last night."

"Yes. I picked her up around . . ." Brecht stopped, stared at Decker. "Now do I have to tell you the *precise* time?"

"Do the best you can, Doctor."

"I came to her house around eight. We went out to a vegetarian restaurant in the Fairfax district. A Sikh establishment that uses only rennetless cheese. You'd be surprised how many of these vegetarian places use cheese with rennet. Rennet is—"

"I know what rennet is, Doctor. It's a chemical used as a binder in cheese making, derived from the gut of a cow."

Brecht stared at him. "Your nutrition IQ just rose a notch in my book, Sergeant."

Actually, Decker knew about rennet from keeping kosher. Rina had explained to him in great detail why ordinary cheese without certification was considered unacceptable. It didn't make a lot of sense to him for a chemical to be considered unkosher—a designation he'd thought was reserved for edible food only. But it didn't matter. Kosher cheeses were just as good and it made Rina happy. If she was happy, he was happy.

"When did you arrive back at your sister's home?" Decker asked.

"Around eleven, eleven-thirty. The restaurant is a ways from her house. There's quite a bit of traveling time."

"Did you go in the house afterward and talk?"

"No, I was fatigued from a rather stressful day and I was anxious to get my rest."

"You dropped your sister off?"

"Of course not! That would be cloddish and I am not a clod. I parked the car and walked her to the door. After she was safely inside, I drove away."

"Everything appear normal when she went inside?"

"Yes. She turned on the living-room light, told me good night and closed the door."

"Does she always leave the living-room light off when she goes out?"

Brecht stopped. "Good God, here we go again with the precise details. Next time, remind me to take my Dictaphone and video camera!"

Decker waited.

"Maybe the light was already on," Brecht said. "I don't remember."

"Was the bedroom light on?"

"I wouldn't know."

"You couldn't see?"

"I suppose I could technically see her bedroom window from my car, but I didn't pay any attention."

"Did you hear anything unusual?"

"Not at all."

"See any strange cars parked around the house?"

"No."

"You say you walked your sister to the door around eleven, eleven-thirty?"

"Yes."

"But you didn't go into the house?"

"No. Lilah asked me if I wanted to bunk down in the guest bedroom for the night, but I said I'd rather go home. Now I wish to God that I had. I'm feeling terribly guilty about it."

Decker nodded.

"Of course, I had no way of knowing . . ."

"None at all," Decker said.

"Damn, if only I had *been* there!"

"If you'd been there, maybe you'd have ended up in worse shape than Lilah."

"Better me than her!"

"All I'm saying is, it might have been both of you."

"You just don't understand." Brecht took a deep breath. "I'm not myself. Do you have any idea who did this horrible thing to my sister?"

"We're investigating every avenue right now, Doctor."

"In other words, you have no suspects."

Decker was quiet.

"Are we done, Sergeant?"

"Almost. By any chance, do you have a key to your sister's house?" Decker asked.

Brecht's voice hardened. "Yes, I have a key. Why?"

"Just checking out every avenue," Decker said. "Did you know your sister has a safe in the bedroom closet?"

Brecht shifted in his seat. "I don't like this line of questioning."

Decker waited.

"Yes, I know she has a safe in her closet! What of it?"

"Do you know what she keeps in—"

"Of course not!"

"Not even a hint?"

"*No*, Sergeant."

"Do you have the combination—"

Brecht rose from his seat. "Why would *I* have the combination to *her* safe!"

"My brother and I have the combination to *my* parents' safe," Decker said. "I don't have any idea what valuables they keep inside, but they gave us the combination in case something happened to them."

Brecht seemed suspended in midair, then he slowly sat back down.

Decker shrugged. "With you being so close to your sister—you have a key to the house—well, I thought she might have trusted you with the combination."

"She *didn't*." Brecht touched his fingers to his forehead. "May I assume the safe had been opened?"

"You can assume anything you want."

Brecht clasped his hands together. "There was a robbery in addition to the assault?"

Decker said, "Maybe."

Brecht said, "You don't say too much, do you?"

"I'm just trying to do some fact-finding. A few more questions and we can call it quits, Doctor. What did you do after you dropped Lilah off?"

"I went straight home."

"Make any calls?"

"No, not at that hour."

"Check in with your service?"

"Uh . . . no."

"Don't you usually check in with your service before you go to bed?"

"If there is an emergency, they'll page me. I believe in leaving well enough alone." Brecht folded his hands across his chest. "I think we're done now."

"Doctor, please bear with me. How many brothers do you and Lilah have?"

Brecht opened his mouth and shut it. "What?"

"How many brothers do you have? Straightforward question."

"Uh . . . two."

Decker looked at him. "You're sure, now?"

"Of *course* I'm sure. We have two other brothers—half brothers, really."

"Their names?"

Again, Brecht paused. "What do they have to do with any of this?"

Decker shrugged. "Every avenue."

"Good God," Brecht said. "No, they couldn't have. They couldn't. Could they?"

Decker didn't answer. Brecht hadn't brought up his brothers, but now he sure seemed eager to implicate them.

"It's my understanding that your sister had quite a noisy argument with King."

"The maid must have told you that." Brecht made clucking noises with his tongue. "Kingston scared the daylights out of her. If it wasn't for Carl, who knows what he might have done to Lilah. Not that I'm implying Kingston had anything to do—with Lilah." He looked at Decker. "I shouldn't be telling you this . . ."

But he was going to tell it anyway, Decker thought.

"Kingston has always been insanely jealous of Lilah, though he disguises it as being protective. The fact is, he's irate that she's the sole heir of Mother's estate. For years, he's been pressing Mother to change her will. Even though Mother slips him money from time to time."

"Slips him money?"

"Just to shut him up, I think. I really don't know much about Kingston's affairs. We've been estranged from each other for quite a while."

Decker nodded, knowing that old Freddy Brecht was no objective character witness for brother King. Still, it never hurt to listen to opinions.

"You think Kingston might have broken into his sister's safe to steal money?"

Brecht suddenly reddened. "I have no proof . . . I really don't know why I said that. Probably because Kingston's always hard up for cash. Even though he makes untold hundreds of thousands at that mill he's running."

"Mill?"

"Abortion mill." Brecht scrunched up his face. "I think he's branched out into other things—infertility is the latest rage. First women pay money to kill their babies, then they pay money to have them."

"Kingston is an OB-GYN?"

"Yes. Imagine a specialty for something as natural as childbirth."

"Excuse me, Doctor, but isn't your other brother an OB-GYN as well?"

"Indeed. But at least John seems to be a little bit more respectful of fetal life." He wagged his finger. "Not that I'm against abortion like those crazy right-to-lifers. But Kingston's mill is positively repulsive. His so-called practice is the antithesis of what we physicians profess to represent."

Decker couldn't tell if Brecht's ranting was a heartfelt opinion or yet another way of venting against his bro King.

"Are you close to John, Doctor?"

Brecht shook his head. "He's closer to Kingston. The two of them are of the same generation and in the same field, so I suppose it's natural."

"Does your mother slip John money as well?"

"I don't know," Brecht said. "John seems to mind his own business. I have little to do with him, but I harbor no animosity toward him."

"Can you spell Kingston's name for me, please?"

"Spell?"

"I want to make sure the maid gave me the right spelling."

"K-I-N-G-S-T-O-N M-E-R-R-I-T-T."

Kingston Merritt. Obviously, he and John Reed were half brothers as well.

"Do you have phone numbers for either of them?"

"No. They're both in the book. John's practice is in Huntington Beach; Kingston's is in Palos Verdes." Brecht stood. "If you don't mind, it's been a terribly long day and I'd like to check on my sister. With all these questions, I hope you haven't lost sight of the fact that there is some maniac out there who hurts people."

"I'm well aware of that." Decker stood. "I'll go up with you . . . see if Lilah's up for talking."

"And if she isn't?"

"I'll come back tomorrow."

"I'll phone the nurses' station and find out if Lilah's up," Brecht said. "Save you a trip if she's still sleeping."

Decker hesitated.

"Or you can make the call, if you'd like," Brecht suggested.

Decker pointed Brecht to the house phone in the cafeteria. Brecht made a quick call, then hung up.

"She's still sleeping."

Decker evaluated his face and felt he was telling the truth. Even if he wasn't, he couldn't get much of an interview from Lilah with Freddy standing over his shoulder. Maybe it would be better if he came back tomorrow, refreshed from a good night's sleep. He thanked Brecht for his time. Only thing left to do was running Lilah's bagged clothes over to forensics. Then his working day was *over*.

The house was deserted. Almost seven and no dinner on the table, no sons greeting him with a hug at the door, no wife taking his coat and nonexistent hat, and no dog bringing him the paper.

His fantasy of marriage—shattered in a single blow.

"Yo," he called out. "Anybody live here?"

He walked into the kitchen. Empty. Then he looked out the back window. Rina was barbecuing, tending the fire with savoir faire. She wore a denim shift under a white butcher's apron. She was laughing and her long black hair was loose and blowing in the wind. The boys were racing the horses, yarmulkes flapping as they cantered, profiles burnished by the sinking sun. Ginger was chasing after them, panting and yelping, enjoying the exercise.

Domestic bliss, except he wasn't in the picture.

He went outside.

"You made it!" Rina kissed his cheek. Her skin smelled of hickory smoke. "Go change. Dinner will be ready in about twenty minutes."

He glanced at the grill—marinated skirt steaks. Rina had also made coleslaw and macaroni salad, and had a couple of bottles of Dos Equis on ice. The patio table had been set for four so at least she'd been expecting him home. "I didn't know they made maternity aprons."

"I must look like a tent."

"A beautiful tent. I'll live inside of you any day of the year." He hugged her from behind. "How are you feeling?"

"Fine. I took a nap after you left."

"I like that. You should be babying yourself while you can."

She turned around and hugged him as best she could. "Are you okay?"

"Sure."

"You seem wound up. You're walking stiffly." She reached up and gently squeezed the nape of his neck. "Oh, you're all tight, Peter."

"Occupational hazard."

"Want a massage?"

"Later, thanks." He picked up a beer bottle, then noticed cans of soda sharing the cooler space. Coke. With *caffeine*. He shifted his weight, trying to appear casual. "You allowed to drink this stuff while you're pregnant?"

"I stay off soft drinks. Bad for the weight. Besides, Coke has caffeine and I don't drink caffeine. That's why I don't drink your coffee in the morning anymore." She smiled impishly. "Or hadn't you noticed, Peter?"

He hadn't and felt stupid because of it.

Sammy, the older of the two boys, spied his stepfather from afar and waved. "Hey, Peter, look at me."

He began racing his horse at top speed toward the edge of the mountain. Jacob, seeing his brother hogging parental attention, kicked the flanks of his horse and tried to catch up with him.

Cupping his hands, Decker yelled out, "Good going, boys. Keep it up." He turned to Rina. "They're having fun."

"You sound envious. Why don't you join them?"

Decker hesitated. His arm and shoulder were throbbing. He'd forgotten to take his afternoon dose of analgesics, but wasn't about to do it in front of Rina. "Nah, it's okay. I'll keep you company."

"Don't be silly, Peter. Go ahead."

"I said it's *okay*."

"Is your shoulder bother—"

"My shoulder's *fine*, Rina. Just *peachy*!"

Rina looked down.

Swell, he thought. She was hurt. He felt bad for

sniping at her, but he was sick of her asking, sick of telling her it was okay when it wasn't. Why didn't she stop asking?

Why didn't he stop calling his daughter?

"Cindy phone?"

"No, she didn't."

"Super."

Rina took his hand but didn't say anything. Cindy was hurting him and there wasn't a thing she could do about it. She couldn't even comfort him. As with his gunshot wound, the topic of his daughter was off limits. "Rabbi Schulman called about an hour ago. He's expecting you in his study at nine tonight."

"I'll be there."

"He also told me that he'd asked another man to join you two. A *ba'al tshuvah* who's in a lower *shiur*—"

"Someone is actually *below* me?"

Rina didn't answer, hating it when he denigrated himself. His progress in Torah studies was yet another taboo subject. Judaism was a hard religion for a newcomer. Even though Peter had made such marvelous advances, he was still uncomfortable with his newfound faith—nervous about what he didn't know instead of praising himself for what he did. He was so smart. If only he could just *relax* and enjoy his God-given brains. "Rav Schulman asked me to ask you if that's okay. He thought you'd be the perfect role model for the new kid on the block."

"Fine."

His face was impassive as he rebuffed the compliment. Rina looped her arm around his waist. "You want me to run you a hot bath?"

"Thanks, darlin', but I'll wait until after dinner to bathe."

Again, he stared longingly at the boys. Rina knew he was caught between a desire to ride and the pain the activity might inflict.

Jacob shouted to his stepfather, "Look, Peter." He took off for the mountain again.

"I wish they wouldn't ride so *fast*," Rina said.

"They're okay."

"Maybe you should go out there and supervise them. Why don't you take White Diamond, Peter? She's gentle. She shouldn't jostle you too badly."

Between clenched teeth, Decker said, "I told you I'm *fine*."

Rina sighed. "So you did. Rather forcefully, I might add."

"Okay." He ran his fingers through his hair. "Okay, I'll be honest. Maybe my arm hurts a little." With that admission, he pulled out two Advil tablets and gulped them down with a swig of beer. "I'll be fine in a few minutes, but right now I'm a tad uncomfortable. You win. I *emoted*. Are you happy?"

"I'm still in a state of shock."

Decker laughed and threw his left arm around her. "You're a good sport, know that?"

"Yes, I know that."

"I try."

The boys headed up the mountain.

"You're going too far!" Rina yelled. "Come back!"

Ignoring their mother's pleas, they rode farther on the steep trails.

"Peter, tell them to stop!"

"They're having fun."

"It's getting dark. They're going to get lost."

"They'll be fine, darlin'. Stop worrying."

"I'm not worried, I'm concerned. There's a difference."

"All right," Decker groused. "I can see you won't relax until I go after them. I won't even bother to change my clothes. Will that make you happy, Rina?"

"If your arm—" She stopped herself. "Yes, that will make me happy, Peter."

"Swell." He planted a kiss on her forehead and muttered as he walked away. But inside he was thrilled that she'd given him an excuse to saddle up. And no White Diamond for Cowboy Pete. The hell with the pain, he was going for Cobra, the biggest damn stallion in the stable. Up on the mount—man, he was *king*. But damned if he'd tell Rina how he felt. He'd emoted enough for one day.

8

What better way to start the day than with a bowl of wheat flakes and twenty-five files of registered sex offenders. As Decker scanned the rap sheets, Rina poured him a glass of orange juice. She glanced down at the table. A scowling mug shot met her eye.

"At least they're not morgue pictures."

Decker looked up. "I can do this later."

"No, I'm fine." She wrinkled her nose. "I think. Must be a big case if you're working at home."

"Nothing out of the ordinary as far as the crime goes." Decker pushed his cereal bowl away. "But the brass think there's potential for publicity. Foothill's a tad camera-shy since the King beating."

Rina sat down and picked up a spoonful of soggy flakes. "If you're going to make the world safe, you must get adequate nutrition. Open up."

Decker smiled, took the spoon, but didn't eat. He aligned the papers and placed them in his briefcase. Rina frowned.

"No one's blaming everyone in the division, Peter."

"Ah *c'mon*," Decker snapped. "The entire police force has been tarred with the same ugly brush.

109

Makes me *furious* at the guys who did it. And deep down inside, I get furious at myself, too. Because truthfully, I remember times when I felt pretty damn inhumane."

"But you didn't act like an animal. That's the difference." Rina took his hand. "Your guilt is irrational, Peter. *They* beat the guy, *you* didn't. It was horrible, it was sickening. But you had *nothing* to do with it!"

"Collective responsibility. Whole department's sinking under the weight. You know Morrison. He's not the type to get hands-on with my cases. Do you know he's called Marge and me *four* times with this current case. No *direct* pressure, just wanted to know if we've got something. Because, like I said, it's a case that could get some public attention. Before Rodney King, he wouldn't have given a hoot. A crime was a crime, no matter who was involved."

"So he's a little more hands-on," Rina said. "That's not terrible . . . as long as he's not an obstacle."

"Yeah, well, there's a fine line between being hands-on and being a stumbling block." Decker threw up his hands. "I'm just nattering. Don't pay any attention to me."

"Of course I pay attention to you," Rina said. "I love you and worry about you."

Decker smiled and patted her hand. "I'll be fine."

"That was an 'I don't want to worry Rina' smile."

"So what's wrong with that?" Decker said.

"You worry too much."

"I ain't gonna change."

"I didn't ask you to."

* * *

Decker caught Lilah just as she was about to tumble to the floor. With one hand around her tiny waist, he carefully led her back to her hospital bed and she crawled under the sheets. She seemed so frail. With a Kleenex, she wiped the cold sweat off her forehead and peered directly into his eyes.

"You seem to have made a habit of rescuing me."

Decker didn't answer. Her voice was sultry and bored at the same time, like a Tennessee Williams character. He regarded her face. The swelling below her eyes had gone down, though the skin was still black. It was the first time he'd seen her eyes open. The whites were bloodshot, the irises bright blue. Her lips were covered with something waxy, but the cuts underneath looked to be healing nicely. Her flaxen hair fell over one eye, cascading down to her bare shoulders. Her skin was pale except for a tinge of red over pronounced cheekbones.

He pulled up a chair and sat to the right of the bed. She shifted to her left until their faces were no more than a foot apart. Just like yesterday, he felt some desperation in her, a need for something to hold. But there was something unhealthy about the way she was asking for comfort. He inched back in his seat, trying to regain a margin of personal space.

"You know who I am then," Decker said.

"Sergeant Deckman, was it?"

"Decker. Very good. You must have heard a lot more than I thought. It's good to see you talking, Miss Brecht."

Her eyes glazed over. "Thank you." Her voice

was a throaty whisper. She flung hair over her shoulders. "Thank you for saving my life."

"I didn't exactly do that, but you're welcome. Everyone treating you all right?"

"This hospital is dreadful."

"Most hospitals are. Nature of the beast."

"Well, let it be a beast for some other poor soul. I'm leaving tonight."

Decker paused. "Dr. Kessler's discharging you already?"

"I'm checking out either with a discharge or against medical advice. Freddy will take care of me." Her eyes found his. "I understand you've met Freddy."

"Yesterday while you were asleep."

"He didn't like your questions. He thought you had a hidden agenda."

"Not at all. Just being thorough."

"Freddy is distrustful. It's a trait he's picked up from Mother."

"I hope you trust me enough to answer a few questions, Miss Brecht."

Lilah lowered her eyes and nodded.

"Are you in a lot of pain?" Decker asked.

"It's not the physical, but emotion . . ."

She burst into tears. Decker handed her a box of Kleenex and waited. Ordinarily, he might have patted her hand or shoulder. But something stopped him from touching this woman.

"I'm very sorry," he finally said. "I really want to find the bastard who did this to you."

"Bas*tards*," she said. "There were two of them."

"You're sure?"

"Yes."

"Only two?"

"Yes. Just two."

"Were you asleep when they came into your bedroom?"

"Yes."

"Did you hear them come in?"

"Hear them?"

"Did they wake you up?"

She looked down. "This is going to be harder than I thought."

"Take your time, Miss Brecht—"

"Lilah!" she interrupted. "I'm sorry. Just . . . please. Call me Lilah. The . . . distance . . . the formality. I need to feel close to you. To be able to tell you . . . do you understand?"

Decker nodded.

"Do you have a first name?"

"Peter."

"Peter," she repeated, then looked away. "Do you do these kinds of interviews often, Peter?"

"I've dealt with many sexual-assault cases."

"How do you *do* it?"

Decker raised his brow. "They're hard on me, but not as hard as they are for the survivors. I get a good deal of satisfaction when I apprehend a perpetrator. I like putting bad people behind bars. And that's what I'd like to do here. But to do that, I need your help."

She met his eyes, then retreated. "I woke up . . . and then . . . this . . . something was on top of me, smothering me."

"Literally?"

She shook her head. "There wasn't anything over

my face . . . just this horrible presence crushing down. And then the gun. It was . . . terrifying."

"Did you scream?"

"I was in *shock*! Should I have screamed? Did I do something wrong?"

"No, you acted perfectly—"

"I should have done *something*!"

"You *did* do something, Lilah. You *survived*. That was all you had to do and you did it."

Again her eyes moistened. "You say the most perfect things, Peter. Thank you!" She grabbed his hand. "Thank you so much!"

That familiar grip. He waited a beat, gave her a light squeeze, then wriggled out. Her eyes held his for a moment, throwing him off balance. He looked down at his notepad. "Did you happen to catch a glimpse of either of your attackers?"

She closed her eyes and seemed to enter a trance. "I see them perfectly. The first one is slight, dark-complexioned, blue eyes, black hair, thick eyebrows, a mole right under his lower lip. High cheekbones, thinnish lips, prominent chin but no cleft, birdlike neck . . ." She opened her eyes. "You're not writing. Am I talking too fast, Peter?"

Decker said, "I'm a little confused."

Lilah looked puzzled. "How so?"

"Miss Brec—Uh, Lilah, you're giving me a lot of detail—"

"Faces—as well as bodies—are my business, Peter."

"I'd like to ask a police artist to come down. I want you to describe your attackers to him."

"Certainly."

"I'd also like you to look through some mug shots I have in my briefcase. Maybe these animals have done something like this before and you can pick them out."

"As you wish."

He handed her the photos of the local sex offenders and used the hospital phone to place a call to the station. As he waited for the lines to connect, he noticed Lilah flipping through the pictures with little interest. He finally made contact with the police artist, then hung up.

"Someone will be here in about twenty minutes," Decker said. "None of these men look like—"

"No, none."

"You're sure—"

"Very." Lilah sank back into her pillow. "My God, I'm tired."

"I'm sure you must be," Decker said. "What were you doing walking around?"

"Just trying to feel . . . human again." She brushed a tear away from her eye. "I'll heal outside. I hurt, but I know I'll heal. It's the inside . . ." She regarded him, took his hand. "May I hold your hand?"

"Of course," Decker answered.

He knew that women reacted very differently to sexual assault. Some couldn't bear the sight of a man; others wanted their husbands or boyfriends to make love to them immediately after the ordeal. Some crawled into shells and never came out; others acted as if nothing of significance had happened. If the primary detective on the case was male, rape survivors often developed a kind of transference with him, either good or bad depending on the rapport.

Some women had been so grateful for Decker's sympathetic ear, they had named their babies after him. But there was something odd about Lilah.

"Are you up to answering a few more questions?" Decker asked.

Lilah brought his hand to her cheek and nodded.

"Okay. Then let me ask you this. When did you manage to make out your attackers so clearly?"

"I saw them as soon as they touched me." Her lower lip began to tremble. "I was so . . . can you hold me, Peter? Just for a brief moment."

She came to him, then abruptly pulled back and brought her hand to her mouth.

"No, forget I said that. I can see by your ring that you're married. It's just that I'm feeling so vulnerable right now. I need someone to lean on. May I take your hand again?"

She took it without waiting for a response, began to play with his wedding band. Though he had comforted many survivors, none were as overtly sexual—as *deadly* sexual—as this one. He kept his face impassive and said, "Do you have a boyfriend you want me to call?"

Lilah's eyes suddenly grew cold. "No."

"How about your bro—"

"Give me a *break*!" She jerked her hand away.

"Would *you* feel more comfortable if you were interviewed by a woman?"

"Would *you* feel more comfortable if I was interviewed by a woman?"

"Lilah, I want to nab the monsters who did this to you. Take them off the street so they can't do it to some other woman. But to do that, I need your help. I really need your help."

Again, her eyes moistened. "It's just so hard."

"I'm sorry. I really am sorry."

She grabbed his wrist before he could pull away and brought his hand to her cheek. "I connect with you."

Ignoring the impulse to tug his hand away, he said, "I'm glad you connect with me. Maybe you can connect me to your attackers."

Lilah broke into laughter and tears at the same time. Slowly, she kissed his fingers one at a time.

Despite himself, he felt a pull down below and decided to break physical contact. "Can you talk about what happened?"

She settled back. "Yes, I can. I feel strong now."

"You say you didn't hear them come in?"

"No."

"You were asleep."

"Yes."

"Do you happen to know what time you awoke?"

"No."

"You woke when you felt them on top of you."

"Actually, I sensed them. Before I felt them, before I opened my eyes. But I couldn't wake myself up fast enough. I couldn't react . . . then . . . it was too late. They were on top of me . . . slapping me . . . hitting me . . . with . . . their fists . . . beating . . ."

Decker realized she was gasping and told her to wait a moment. When Lilah regained a steady tempo of respiration, she said, "Why didn't they just break open the safe and leave? Why did they have to destroy my belongings? Why did they have to *hit* me? Why did they *hurt* me? Why did they *rape* me?"

"Because these guys are monsters and they enjoy hurting women."

"But *why*! Oh, hell, I know there aren't any simple answers. You're not like that, Peter, I can tell. I feel so safe. So . . . protected when I'm with you."

"That's what the police are for."

She locked eyes with him, not pleased with his response. He knew it, but continued anyway.

"I'm going to have to ask you some sensitive questions. Do you think you're up to answering them?"

"I don't know."

"If you start to feel panicky, stop until you're calmer. I don't care how long it takes. I want to make this as comfortable as possible for you. All right?"

She nodded.

"Did both men rape you?"

"Just . . . I . . . only one."

"You're sure?"

"Just one. I'm positive."

"Did he penetrate you vaginally?"

Her face whitened but she answered yes.

"You're sure?"

"Yes, I'm sure."

"Did he penetrate you anally?"

She shook her head.

"Did he attempt to penetrate you anally?"

"No."

"You're doing great, Lilah. Just a few more questions. Did he ejaculate inside of you?"

"I . . ." She buried her face in her hands. "I don't

remember really. While it was happening, I blanked it out."

"That's okay. That's normal, Lilah. Did either of your attackers force you to copulate orally with them?"

"No."

"All right. Did both attackers hit you?"

"I think so . . . I was hit first . . . held down . . ."

"Take your time."

"First . . . hit. Then they . . . one of them . . . went to the safe while the other . . . raped."

"Okay. One of them opened the safe while the other raped you."

"Yes."

"Then what happened? Do you remember?"

"He . . . someone started breaking things . . . I think the first one was still raping me . . . while the other broke things. It seemed to last forever."

"Did either one of them talk to you?"

"No."

"Not even at the beginning?"

"I . . . I'm sorry. Everything is such a blur. One of them might have said, 'I have a gun.' But I really don't remember."

"Do you know which one raped you?"

"I could describe his face, yes."

"Did you see a gun, Lilah?"

"He . . . at . . . I think I felt the gun at my head. I felt on my temple . . . you know. He must have been holding it. I was . . . it hurt. I thought I was . . . going to die."

There was a moment of silence.

"Do you want to take a break?" Decker asked.

"I'm . . . all right."

"It's no problem to stop."

"No . . . not yet."

"Okay. You think you were beaten before you were raped."

"Yes."

"You're doing a *great* job, Lilah. Holding up really well. Which one beat you?"

"Both . . . I think."

"Okay, they're hitting you. Then they stopped."

"Yes . . ." Her eyes focused on her lap. "Finally."

"Are you all right?"

She whispered, "It's . . . go on. I'm all right."

"You're sure?"

She nodded.

"Okay. But don't hesitate to stop if you need to. What happened after they stopped beating you?"

"One man raped me . . . the other . . ." She dabbed her eyes with a tissue. "He must have gone to the safe."

"One man raped you while the other went to the safe."

"Yes."

"Do you remember what happened after the man came out of the safe?"

"I think . . . maybe they broke more things . . ." She looked at him with urgency. "He found what he *wanted* in the safe. I don't know why he destroyed the room."

"Could he have been looking for something else?"

"Impossible."

"You're certain?"

"Yes."

"He found what he wanted in the safe."

"Yes."

"What did he want, Lilah?"

"I wish all your questions were that easy to answer. It's obvious that they were after my father's memoirs."

There was a moment of silence. Decker said, "They attacked you and trashed your bedroom for your father's memoirs?"

Lilah bristled. "You don't know who my father was?"

"He was a director—"

"Not just *any* director! He was *the* director. Hermann Brecht! As in the Brecht School of Performing Arts at Heidelberg. As in the Brecht Chair at Bonn University! He was not *just* a genius. He was *the* genius. His unsurpassed brilliance in film direction has and will be studied for years. The premier director of this century—fifteen masterpieces and all before he reached his untimely demise at twenty-eight!"

"Your father died at twenty-eight?"

"Yes." Lilah's eyes became shiny pools. "I was just a little girl so I don't remember him too clearly. That's why the memoirs are so important to me. They're *my* history!"

"Lilah, I don't mean to sound insensitive, but why would they be important to anyone else?"

Her face turned stony. "My father was a visionary of unsurpassed magnitude. About a year ago, dear *Freddy* let it slip out that Father had written his recollections and had willed them to me. Up until that time only he and I knew about them. Once Freddy let the cat out of the bag, I was suddenly deluged with calls and letters from universities asking me if I'd care to donate them. Donate! Can you imagine such gall!

"When it became clear I wouldn't donate them, they tried to buy them away. Three thousand, thirty thousand, three hundred thousand. I wouldn't have let them go for three million. Not for *thirty* million. But apparently someone else wanted them and was willing to do whatever was necessary to obtain them."

"What's in your father's papers that makes them so coveted?"

She regarded him with disgust, then softened her look. "My father never granted interviews. The memoirs are the only living record of *him* lecturing about his films—his *art*—in his *own* words. And now, I may *never* know . . ." She exploded into tears.

Decker felt a headache coming on. She wasn't making a lot of sense. Could it be a subtle sign of brain injury due to the beating? He'd ask Dr. Kessler. After she stopped crying, he said, "Why do you say you may never know? You haven't read your father's memoirs?"

"Oh, dear, why is life so complicated?"

He waited for her to continue.

"The papers were *willed* to me on the *condition* that they not be opened until the twenty-fifth anniversary of his death. That date falls two months from now. Of course I *had* to obey his wishes. Others have been after me to break my promise as soon as they found out the papers existed. But I would rather die than ignore my father's last request in his suicide note."

Suicide. Decker let that sink in. "The papers were with him when he committed suicide?"

"No, all of Father's papers were left with an old, trusted friend. I was mailed the memoirs when I reached eighteen. They were delivered into my hands, completely sealed, the wrapping untampered with. Father's wishes were recorded by the friend on a separate cover letter."

"So your father's friend knew the memoirs existed."

"Oskar died six years ago. Before Freddy opened his mouth. Poor Oskar had nothing to do with the theft of the papers if that's what you're thinking."

Decker tapped his pencil on his pad. "Was the cover letter written in English or do you read German?"

Lilah's smile held strained patience. "Both the letter and the memoirs were written in *English*. They were dedicated to *me*, Peter. Father obviously wanted me to *understand* them. Father was fluent in five languages."

"Why you and not your brother, Miss Brecht?"

"Poor Freddy . . ." Lilah sighed. "Always second-class citizen. He felt so neglected." Her face soured. "So did Mother. When she found out about the memoirs, she was absolutely *shocked*, *livid*! The witch actually insisted that I open them and disregard my father's wishes. She probably wanted to find out what was written about her. As if Father would waste his time recording their silly squabbles!"

Lilah seemed suddenly impatient.

"You never let me finish describing my attackers. Don't you want *useful* information?"

"I thought we'd wait for the police artist."

"Is your artist any *good*?"

"The best." Decker looked up from his pad. "Lilah, how long a look did you get of each man?"

"What do you mean?"

"Did you see each of them for thirty seconds? A minute?"

"I saw them as long as I wanted."

"What do you mean? You were blindfolded."

"As soon as they touched me, I was able to image their faces in my mind. That's why I'm able to recall such detail. Brain imaging gives much more resolution than does the optic nerve."

Decker hesitated a moment. "Lilah, did you see these men with your *eyes*?"

"I just told you, Peter, I *imaged* them!"

Decker paused, wondering more seriously about brain injury. "Lilah, the courts permit only *eye* witness testimony to be entered as evidence."

"Peter, I'm not about to go into court and say I imaged these men. I realize no one would believe me. But who cares about what the court allows? Once I give *you* my imaged picture, you can find these animals and get some other kind of evidence on them."

"Let me get this straight. You never actually *saw* your attackers?"

"I saw them for a moment with my eyes. But they were wearing ski masks. And then of course, they blindfolded me. As if that could stop *me* from imaging them. But then again, how could they have known I had that kind of gift?"

There was a moment of silence. Maybe the woman

had been suffering from some kind of emotional problem long before the rape.

Lilah looked down. "You don't believe me. You will learn. I have this gift, Peter, a prophetic vision of the future. And like Cassandra, I too am met with skepticism or, worse, derision. It no longer bothers me. Because unlike Cassandra's visions, eventually people do witness *my* visions."

She leaned over and took his hand.

"It is not a gift actually, it is a curse. I pray to God every day that I will wake up normal. That one day, I will see the world just as everyone else does. Perhaps I don't pray hard enough."

Decker was silent, unsure of how to answer her.

Lilah palpated his palm. "I can feel your resistance, but I can also feel your subliminal vibratory waves. Our connection makes an unusually strong field. Eventually, you will trust me, Detective. I really do have these powers."

A throat cleared, and Decker turned to the sound's source. Pad and mug books in hand, Leo, the police artist, was leaning his gut against the door frame, his cherubic face as red as cooked lobster.

Decker yanked his hand away and stood. "Will you excuse me for a moment, Lilah?"

"Certainly."

"Thank you." Decker smiled at her and led the artist out of the room, escorting him down the hospital corridor. He waited until they were out of Lilah's earshot.

"I think I dragged you out for nothing, Leo. She was giving me such detailed information about her assailants, I got excited and called you right away. Then she informed me that she never actually *saw* them with her eyes. Instead she said she did something called *imaging* with her brain. She swears she could tell me what the perps looked like after they touched her even though she was blindfolded."

Leo shifted his pad and mug books into his other hand. "You couldn't be making this up."

"I'm not creative enough."

"Was she also *imaging* you with her touch, Pete?"

Decker felt himself go hot. "She's glommed onto me."

Leo sucked in his gut and ran his tongue over his dentures. "I wouldn't mind her glomming onto me."

"She's an incomplete deck, Leo. If I'd known, Marge would be here."

"Uh-huh."

"Fuck you."

Both men laughed.

Decker said, "There is a very slight chance that she actually did see these guys with her eyes and just can't admit it . . . or is afraid to admit it. Maybe she knows them but imaging is her way of telling me she won't testify against them. So if you don't mind, indulge her and me and get some drawings."

"No problem, Sergeant, I'm an old-timer. Have seen it or heard it all." Leo peered down the hallway. "I think your deck is about to have a little company. Why don't I grab some coffee in the cafeteria? Call me when you need me."

"Fine, Leo."

Decker watched the figure approach. Tall, thin, lithe. She wore a floor-length, form-fitting, black sequined gown with slits up the sides. The dress sparkled with each movement of her legs. Her face had been powdered white, but her features—except for blood-red lips—were obscured by a black veil that fell to her shoulders. Her feet were housed in spike-heeled pumps rimmed with rhinestones. Yet her gait—her balance—was that of a young fashion model instead of an old woman. She wasn't merely walking, she was shimmying. She was sashaying.

Davida Eversong was making her *entrance*.

9

She walked past him without so much as a curious glance. Decker followed her into Lilah's room.

It was a one-sided tearful reunion.

"Dear God, what happened to my baaaaby!" Davida hugged her daughter. "My poor sweet baaaaby."

A husky voice, Decker thought. And loud. As they say in the business, it *projected*.

"My poor sweet darling little girl! How awful!"

"Mother, sit—"

"Dear God! Dear, dear, dear God!"

"Mother! Sit! Down!"

Davida ignored her, pulled out a black lace handkerchief and wiped her eyes under her veil. Lilah regarded her.

"You didn't have to dress for mourning, Mother. I didn't die."

Davida broke into a sudden smile. "Do you like my gown? It's a Vilantano. Size six. Isn't that incredible?"

Lilah looked at Decker. "I was attacked and she talks about her dress. This is so typical—"

"Oh, don't be *angry* with me, Delilah dear. Of course, I care about your welfare! When Freddy told me, I just about died."

128

"I specifically asked him not to tell you."

Davida glanced at Decker. "She didn't want to worry me. That's my daughter . . . so considerate."

Lilah closed her eyes and lowered her head to her pillow. "I'm very tired. I need rest."

"Don't be mad at Freddy, sweetheart." Davida dismissed her daughter's emotions with a wave of the hand. "I could tell he was so very bothered. I just wouldn't let him go until I wangled it out of him."

She opened a black beaded evening bag and began putting some flesh-colored bottles on the hospital bed tray.

"I brought you some makeup—a light moisturizing base, a little mascara and eye shadow, some blush and a little cover-up. Freddy told me how you were slapped around during the robbery! How awful!" She took a long appraising look. "My goodness, Lilah, you look as if they did more than slap you."

"Mother, I truly am tired."

Davida brought her hand to her chest. "Those . . . those . . . *bastards*! Are you all right, Lilah?"

"Yes."

"Truly, dear. Don't hold back."

"I don't think I'm up for my five-mile jog, but I'll recover."

"You've always had such a positive spirit! I so admire that quality, dear."

"What I need more than anything is rest, Mother."

"Darling . . . did those bastards . . . did they . . ."

Lilah looked at Decker. "No."

Davida followed her daughter's eyes, noticing Decker's presence for the first time. "Darling, who's this man?"

"He's the police, Mother."

Davida walked in measured steps over to Decker and lifted her veil. Her skin was ghostly white, but stretched tight over large cheekbones. She had broad features—a wide nose, wide-set eyes that were round and bright and very dark. Her mouth seemed to stretch from ear to ear. Her hair was pulled back over a high-set forehead and dyed blue-black. She'd need another rinse soon—a hint of white at the root line.

Up close, Decker found Davida Eversong a little simian-looking, but he could imagine that her strong features had come across well on the big screen. In the beauty department, Lilah had it over Mom hands down. But daughter's delicate features just might blur when magnified.

Decker knew Mom was studying him, her eyes boring into his without so much as a twitch of discomfort. No wonder Morrison had been pestering him on the progress of the case. Decker didn't know if it was acting or what, but Davida reeked with wealth and power. Offscreen, she was more formidable than any part she had ever played on-screen.

"So *you're* the police," Davida said.

"Yes, ma'am. Sergeant Decker."

"I'm glad you're here, Sergeant. We need to talk. Although the jewelry wasn't as valuable as the pieces I keep in the bank vault, some of the items were highly sentimental. I trust you'll do everything possible to find the criminals who took them from me."

Decker looked at Lilah. "You had jewelry in your safe?"

In a bored voice, she said, "Mother kept some jewelry there. That wasn't what they were after, Peter."

"I suppose you'll need a description, Sergeant," Davida said. "I'll give you the name of my insurance broker. He has written descriptions and Polaroids of each item. I'd like all my jewelry back but there's an emerald brooch of particular interest for me. It was a gift. Well, all the pieces were gifts . . . that's another story." She turned to Lilah. "Really, darling, you should have told me right away. Those bastards might have already fenced the larger stones."

"They weren't after your jewelry, Mother. They were after Father's memoirs."

"Lilah, dear—"

"The jewelry is garbage in comparison to the real treasure."

"Darling, a five-carat Colombian emerald isn't garbage by anyone's standards."

"Garbage!" Lilah was red-faced. "It's all *garbage*! They weren't after something as common as your jewelry. They were after Father's memoirs. Your jewelry is *GARBAGE*!"

"Dear me, Lilah, I know you've been through a terrible ordeal, but do control your temper." She turned to Decker. "Lilah was always a highly emotional child. Like me. But I directed my emotions into acting. Don't you think Lilah would have made a wonderful actress—"

"Mother, this is not a role I'm playing. This is real life. I was *hurt*, damn it—"

"Delilah Francine, do try and calm down." Davida slithered down into a seated position at her daughter's bedside and kissed her forehead. "It can't be good for you to work yourself up into a lather." She brought her hand to her chest. "Lord knows, it's not good for me." She kissed Lilah again, then looked up at Decker. "Why aren't you out looking for my jewelry?"

"I'm not done interviewing Lilah, Ms. Eversong. Would it be possible for you to step outside for a moment until I've finished up?"

"Oh, don't stop on my account. Just keep going. Pretend I'm not here."

Lilah growled, "He needs to talk to me *alone*."

"Alone?" Davida leaned in close and whispered a stage aside into her daughter's ear. "Is he trustworthy?"

Lilah closed her eyes and answered yes.

Davida patted her hand. "Well, if you think you're in good hands, I'll be on my way. I'll speak to you as soon as you've returned to the spa. Do come home soon. This place is dreadful. A little wallpaper would certainly go a long way."

"Why don't you talk to the hospital's administrator about it?"

"Girl, I don't talk to anyone unless it's a *dire* emergency. My children excepted, of course. Freddy tells me he's checking you out this afternoon."

"Yes."

"Lovely." She kissed her daughter's forehead. "I'll just leave the makeup here. Should I send more cover-up with Freddy this afternoon? After all, who knows who'll be watching?"

"Do whatever you want, Mother."

"Do try and rest, Lilah dear."

"I'm trying."

"Good-bye, dear."

"Ms. Eversong," Decker said. "I'd like to talk to you about your jewelry."

Lilah shook her head. "It wasn't what they were after, Peter. *Believe* me."

"I believe you, Lilah," Decker said, "but they took the jewelry anyway. With a good description, I might be able to track down some of the pieces and find these monsters." He turned to Davida. "Is there somewhere we can talk while Lilah's describing her assailants to the police artist?"

"You *saw* the thieves!" Davida said, clapping her hands. "Wonderful! Wonderful!"

"I didn't *see* them, Mother. I *imaged* them."

Davida stopped applauding. "Oh. That's nice, dear."

"Imaged them *very clearly*!"

Davida stood and brushed a piece of imaginary dirt off her dress. "Very good, dear." She turned to Decker. "I suppose I might be able to wait for you inside the limo in front of the hospital."

"That would be perfect."

She smiled, offered Decker her arm. "Accompany me down the hall, Sergeant."

Decker looked at Lilah.

"Go ahead."

Lilah was barely suppressing her rage. And here he was, caught between a rock and a rock. What happened when two rocks were rubbed together? Lots of friction, sometimes fire.

Decker said, "I'll be back in a minute."

Lilah didn't bother to answer.

When they were halfway down the corridor, Davida said, "Surely, you don't believe her *imaging* crap, do you?"

"I think she might be trying to tell me something and imaging is a safe way for her to do it."

Davida brushed off the suggestion. "That *child*. I do love her. But she is simply full of it—she and her brother. Although Freddy hasn't claimed to be blessed with the powers, God help us all." She let out a deep chuckle. "But I do love her so. Of my four children, she's the most like me, so I suppose it's natural for me to favor her. Such a fanciful girl. I did so want her to become an actress and follow in my footsteps. There's no predicting children, Detective."

Decker didn't answer. They walked several moments without talking.

"What a trauma!" Davida said. "For *all* of us! Sergeant, I'd really like my so-called *garbage* back. That's really what the thieves must have been after. Poor Lilah. No doubt she was in the wrong place at the wrong time. But she doesn't seem too badly hurt now, does she?"

"Not on the outside, at least."

"Outside is all that counts, let me tell you, my young man." She lowered her veil. "Shit comes and shit goes, but as long as you look good, who cares? Look at me. No one really knows how old I am. And I intend to keep it that way."

Whatever gets you through the night, lady, Decker thought. "Ms. Eversong, what do you know about your late husband's memoirs?"

"Only that Lilah has an inflated picture of her father and what his memoirs are worth. Oh, I'm sure they could fetch maybe five to ten thousand dollars on the open market—"

"Lilah felt she could sell them for three hundred thousand—"

"That's *nonsense*! But why burst her bubble? Forget about the memoirs. Concentrate on my *jewels*. As I stated, I have other pieces, but I really would like to find that brooch."

"What kind of value are we talking about?"

"Oh, maybe a million total. The brooch is the most expensive piece. That alone is worth a quarter million. The rest are dribs and drabs. Twenty thousand here, thirty there."

"Ms. Eversong, do you have the combination to Lilah's safe?"

"To the outer safe only," Davida said. "It's where the jewelry was kept."

"Anyone else know the combination to the outer safe?"

"Obviously, someone did."

"Did you *give* the combination to anyone?"

"No."

"Do you know the combination to the *inner* safe, Miss Eversong?"

"That, my young man, is exclusively Lilah's bailiwick."

"And that's where she kept the memoirs?"

"I haven't a clue as to what she squirreled away."

Decker thought a moment. The safe had been picked cleanly—a pro crack all the way. Yet there was something very amateurish about the crime. Pros didn't rape and ransack. They liked fast jobs— nothing with complications. So someone had probably hired assholes—punks—and given them the combination. Now if the punks had been hired to rob the safe of the jewels only, why bother taking the memoirs? It would have required an extra combination to break—assuming Lilah kept the memoirs in the inner safe. Logically, it would make more sense for the punks to have been hired to steal the memoirs. When they saw the jewels, they took them as a side perk. Despite Davida's insistence to the contrary, Decker wasn't ready to rule out the memoirs as the main object of the theft.

"Do you know the contents of your late husband's memoirs?"

"Not at all. As a matter of fact, I've never even *seen* them. Supposedly, they went from Oskar's estate right to Lilah's safe. Did Lilah tell you about Oskar Holtz?"

"He was your late husband's trusted friend?"

"A dear boy, little Oskar was. Now he's gone." She sighed. "They're all gone. Only I'm left. I outlived them all." She smiled. "Good genes."

"Ms. Eversong, what did you mean when you said the memoirs *supposedly* went from Oskar's estate into your daughter's hands?"

"I'm not saying they don't exist. All I'm saying is Lilah has a very active imagination. A year ago, my son suddenly told me about these supposed memoirs' existence. Perhaps she *imaged* them just like she imaged her attackers."

Decker didn't answer.

"Humor her if you want. But take my jewel theft seriously."

"I am. That's why I wanted to talk to you."

They reached the lobby, walked over to the elevators. Davida dropped Decker's arm and punched the down button.

"I'll wait for you for twenty minutes, my handsome young friend in the unpressed suit. After that, you can forget about talking to me and you'll have to deal with my insurance broker." The elevator doors opened and Davida stepped inside. As the doors closed, she said, "*Ciao.*"

"Can you believe that *woman*?"

"Are you all right, Lilah?"

"I'm furious! But I can't say that I expected anything more out of her. Or out of Freddy, either. He's just as exasperating but in a different way. So weak. I specifically tell him not to mention anything to Mother. So what happens?"

She picked up a bottle of makeup and threw it against the wall. It didn't break, merely bounced and ended up on the floor.

There was a moment of silence.

"Pick that up, Peter. I might as well use it."

He hesitated, angry at her barked orders. Then he remembered all she had gone through, complied, then sat back in his chair. "So your mother kept some jewelry in your safe."

She glared at him, panting, fire in her eyes. "They . . . weren't . . . after . . . the . . . jewelry."

"Could you just bear with me for a moment, Lilah?"

Suddenly, she dropped her gaze. "Go on. I'm listening."

"Say you're right," Decker said. "They weren't after the jewelry. They were after the memoirs. But they found your mother's jewelry. And took it. Because it's valuable. Maybe they figured there was more jewelry in your house and that's why they ransacked your place."

Lilah was quiet. "Perhaps."

"Do you have any other valuables that you don't keep in the safe?"

"Some cash—front-desk-register money. What difference does it make? If I had kept it in the safe, they would have stolen it from the safe anyway."

"True. Did you open your safe yesterday?"

"No."

"You're sure?"

"Of course I'm sure. Why?"

"We lifted your fingerprints off the dial."

"So?"

"Your maid said she dusted the safe yesterday. I would have thought she would have dusted off any prints."

Lilah said, "Mercedes is not that thorough. I think she vacuums the closet, but dusting? Forget it. I've found cobwebs in the corner. But why bother making her feel bad about it? When you asked her if she dusted the closet, you probably threatened her. So she lied."

"Okay," Decker said. "Out of curiosity, how much front-desk money are we talking about?"

"Only about a thousand dollars."

Only.

"And I keep some rainy-day money inside my bottom drawer. Five hundred or so. I could understand the ransacking of the drawers. Why did they have to destroy my room—my beautiful craftsmen furniture—pieces I've spent years looking for. Why did they smash the glass, break my lamps . . . rape me . . . *why*?"

Why? Because crime is dangerous and dangerous is *exciting*. Crime is a goddamn adrenaline fix straight into the bloodstream. Assholes get so pumped, testosterone shooting through their system, endorphins flooding their brains. They feel no pain. They rape. They kill. They destroy. And they love every minute of it. They get so friggin' *high* on their own hormones, they become addicted to crime as sure as to any drug.

Decker said, "There are a lot of sickos out there. I'm going to do my damnedest to find these bad guys." He picked up the mug sheets of the registered sex offenders. "So none of these guys fit the bill."

"No."

"You're sure you don't have . . . even an inkling as to who did this to you?"

"Positive."

"We'll keep investigating, Lilah. Just a few more questions and then I'm out of your hair."

Lilah lowered her eyes. "Why, you're not in my hair, Peter."

"Good. Let's get back to the safe. Your mother said she has the combination to your safe."

"The outer safe, yes."

"Does she use it whenever she wants to wear a piece of jewelry?"

"Usually she tells me to fetch her whatever piece she wants. But she has a key to my house. If I were out of town, she could come in and open the safe."

"What about the inner safe?"

"She doesn't know the combination to it."

"And that's where you kept the memoirs?"

"Yes."

"Anything else in the inner safe?"

"My mother's will. But that isn't exactly a collector's item. Copies all over the place. She has one, my brothers each have a copy. The lawyer has a copy."

"Do you know if your mother has made any changes in her will lately?"

"No. Why do you ask?"

"Just throwing out questions."

"I don't think she has. You've arranged a little tryst with her in the limo, why don't you ask her yourself?"

"I take it you know the contents of your mother's will?"

"I've never bothered with the specifics. I do know that the bulk of her estate is left to me."

Decker noted that her account of her mother's will was consistent with Freddy Brecht's account. Maybe Brother King was actually "insanely jealous" of his sister. He made a note to contact this Merritt guy immediately.

"Did you keep *anything* else with the memoirs?"

She shook her head.

"Okay. Can I ask the police artist to come up and take those drawings now?"

Lilah broke into an innocent smile. "You really do believe in my powers, don't you, Peter?"

"I—"

"I knew it. You *did* feel my energy."

"I believe you're trying to tell me something." Decker paused. "When you . . . imaged these men, Lilah, you're sure no one looked familiar?"

"Yes."

"Lilah, what happened after the men were done? Did you hear them leave?"

"Yes."

"Do you know what time that was?"

"No."

"Did you try to call anyone?"

"No . . . I was too scared to move."

"I understand. Were you raped on your bed?"

"Yes."

Decker paused. "Do you remember how you got on the floor?"

"He . . . pushed . . . kicked me . . . tore up my bed. I closed my eyes and tried to blank it out. Eventually, I must have passed out. The next thing I remember was your voice. Your . . . *beautiful* voice."

Decker nodded and put his pad away. "You did great."

Lilah's eyes moistened. "Thank you."

"You're welcome." Decker stood and handed her his business card. "If you think of anything else— need me for any reason—call the station house and I'll get back to you."

"This is the station house's phone number?"

"Yes."

"Don't you have another number where I could reach you?"

"No."

She looked at him. "You don't have a personal phone number, Peter?"

Intense anger had seeped into her eyes. Too bad, Decker thought. He felt bad for what had happened to her, but wasn't about to give her free rein of his personal life. He waited until she seemed to sense the finality of his decision. Then he said, "This number's better, Lilah. They can get to me twenty-four hours a day."

She nodded without enthusiasm. "You can call me at the spa if you have any other questions, Sergeant."

Sergeant. Her formality was a punishment for his refusal to relinquish his home number. Or maybe she just didn't feel the need for intimacy anymore. He said, "I have a partner—"

"A woman named Dunn?"

Decker nodded.

Lilah said, "I phoned the spa last night and my executive director told me your pal Dunn was there yesterday, asking questions. Kelley was not pleased."

"Detective Dunn is very discreet. After all, your house is right next door to the spa."

"I realize that, but I assure you no one from the spa had anything to do with this. But if she must ask questions to satisfy your superiors, I'll make sure Kelley cooperates."

"Thank you. You seem to have a great deal of trust in your staff."

She turned to him, broke into a strange smile. "As I stated before, my family's distrustful by na-

ture. I, on the other hand, can afford to trust because I can sense honesty. Look at the length of
employment of my staff. Very little turnover. I think
God gave me this power to compensate for my
overbearing mother. She doesn't believe in my powers or in me. But then again, Mother really doesn't
know me very well."

Mike Ness adjusted the dials of his video camera,
placed the instrument gingerly on the narrow wooden
bench, then opened his locker. The tap on his shoulder made him jump. Goddamn, after all these years
she could still sneak up on him. Generally, he took it
good-naturedly. Now he felt like strangling her. Instead, he took a deep breath and let it out to the count
of eight.

"Small as it is, this is the *men's* locker room, Kell."

"No one's here."

"You're getting on my nerves—"

"*I'm* getting on *your* nerves—"

"Yes, *you're* getting on *my* nerves." He slipped off
a gray T-shirt. "Everything's fine. Quit bugging me."

"Where were you last night?"

"Jesus Christ, you're worse than the police." He
pulled out a Body Glove T-shirt from the locker and
put it on. God, she could be a pain in the ass. "Ever
think about joining the Marines? You'd make a
great drill sergeant."

"Just answer me, Michael."

He turned around, placed both hands on her
shoulders. "I was giving Davida a massage. In her
room for two fucking hours listening to her prattle
on about some goddamn actor she used to ball. It

was thrilling. I left at twelve, then unplugged the phone and tried to get some goddamn sleep."

"I knocked on your door—"

"Then I didn't *hear* you."

Neither spoke. Ness sat down on the bench and began to lace his Nikes.

Kelley said, "Do you know where Eubie was last night?"

"No." He looked up. "Why?"

"The lady asked about Eubie and the rape."

Ness let out a full laugh. "Are you crazy, Kell? Eubie wouldn't *rape* Lilah. Fuck her, yes, but *rape*?" He faced his sister. "Wanna know where Jeffs was, ask Nadia. He probably bunked down with her."

"Nadia's a dyke."

"Not according to Jeffs."

Kelley bit her lip to keep it from trembling. "What did you and Davida talk about?"

"I just told you! She was talking about some weirdo she used to fuck. She was heavily into 'the good old days.'"

"Just . . ." She pushed hair off her shoulders. "Just swear to me that you were in your room all night, Mike."

He broke into a grin. "You think I raped Lilah, Kell?"

"*Stop* it, Michael."

"Then what are you saying?"

"I . . . I just want to make sure that you . . ."

"I swear I had nothing to do with Lilah." He patted her shoulder and gave her one of his assured big-brother smiles. "I swear, I swear, I swear! Now can I please have a little privacy? Or do you get a thrill out of seeing me naked?"

Kelley blushed. "You know you can be positively disgusting!"

"Then if I'm so disgusting, please leave me alone. The detective's just asking questions because that's what she's being paid to do. If the police know what's going on, they don't bother asking lots of questions."

"What *is* going on?"

"How the fuck do I know? All I know is that Davida's happy. If she's happy, I'm happy. Now relax, all right?"

Kelley bit her lower lip again. "All right, Mike. I believe you."

Ness regarded his sister. She believed him. She always believed him, God bless her.

❧10

A gracious lady, Davida accepted her chauffeur's proffered hand, resting her fingers lightly upon his wrist as if ready to dance the minuet. Carefully she stepped up from the curb, waiting until she had one foot in the limousine. Then she turned to her young driver, eyes gliding down his well-built body, and handed him twenty dollars.

"There will be a slight delay, Albert. Why don't you get yourself something to eat."

The chauffeur, whose name was Russ Donnally, thanked her and pocketed the bill in his uniform pants. After scrounging to earn a buck for years, Donnally had landed a pretty good gig. A friend of a friend had told him about the position. The old lady not only paid decently, but she had tucked away a fleet of bitchin' cars—a drop-dead Rolls Silver Cloud III, a Bentley Flying Spur, a new Bentley Turbo, and two old Packard touring sedans. And of course the limos. Cars he was *allowed* to start up and take out. He just loved to cruise the streets, girls giving him the eye. Big beauties like these machines had definite advantages. He'd fucked more than a few babes in backseats as large as a double bed.

As far as Davida went, the old broad was okay. She never asked personal questions—too busy talking about herself or checking out his crotch. Just as long as he did the old lady's bidding and tossed her compliments, she was happy as a hype in a pharmacy. Donnally didn't like being called Albert—Alberts were skinny old bald dudes with English accents—but hey, no job was perfect.

"Thank you, Miss Eversong." Donnally eased his mistress into the car and glided a palm over a crown of slicked-back black hair. "Can I get you something to eat?"

"No, Albert, I'm not due to eat again until noon. Mustn't let my girlish figure go to seed."

"That would be criminal, madam."

"Albert, you're a shameless flatterer. Keep it up." Donnally smiled. "When should I be back?"

"Thirty minutes. Don't be late."

"You got it, Miss Eversong." He waved good-bye and shut the door.

Davida sighed and studied her nails.

"That boy is a repulsive worm, Mother. Why do you keep him?"

"Because I'm whimsical." She turned to her son. "And he performs my assignments well. Which is more than I can say for *you*. Frederick, she was *beaten* up, the poor child! What *happened*?"

"I don't *know*!"

"You *should* know!" Davida opened the compartment door to a built-in nail set and pulled out an emery board. "You were the last one to see her."

"She was absolutely fine when I dropped her off.

You make horrid insinuations, Mother! I would *never* hurt her—"

"Just shut up, Freddy, and turn on the overhead light. The interior's dark and I can't see a thing."

Brecht ran his handkerchief over his face and flipped the switch. "Something must have gone wrong—"

"Damn right something went *wrong*. On top of this shit with Lilah, my jewels are gone." She filed an index finger furiously. "God, that *pisses* me off!"

"Whoever took your jewels must have hurt Lilah."

"Whole thing makes me *sick*!"

"Why are we waiting around, Mother?"

"A detective wants to talk to me about the jewels."

"The tall redheaded man?"

"Yes."

"I don't like him."

"Of course you don't. He's competent."

"Go ahead and insult me, Mother. And the next time you need an errand boy, call Kingston. See if *he* drives up to Malibu."

Davida laughed loudly and patted his knee. "Do I detect a note of fraternal competition in your voice? Now just because you're adopted doesn't mean I don't love—"

"Mother, if I hear that speech one more time, I'll throw up!"

She patted his knee again. "Poor Freddy. I do grate on your nerves. The detective should be down soon. I've made it quite clear I value my time. I'll describe my jewels to him; then we can all go home and forget about this mess."

"I'm not very comfortable about the police nosing in our affairs," Brecht said. "I'm surprised you are."

"Frederick darling, be logical. He's not nosing in our family affairs, he's trying to solve a *crime*. He's interested in *Lilah* . . . and maybe he's interested in my jewels, too. If he happens to become *sidetracked*, I'll sic some reporters on him. Last thing the police need—especially in this area—is press. In the meantime, let him look for Lilah's attacker. *I'm* not hiding anything."

"I'm not either, Mother."

Davida blew air on her nails. "Then we've both got nothing to worry about. Stop *fretting*, Freddy. If things get complicated, I'll take care of it—and you. That's what mothers are for."

"Forgive me if I don't nominate you for the Mother of the Year award."

"Freddy, don't be so mean. You don't have the knack for it." She kissed his cheek. "You know my sharp tongue. It's just an unrestrained ego talking."

Brecht flicked his wrist and checked his Rolex.

Davida said, "Pressed for time?"

"A bit."

"You mean you actually have *patients*?"

Brecht turned red. "Lilah asked me to stop by the spa and make sure things were running smoothly. And then, yes, Mother, I do have *patients*. As a matter of fact, I have an untold amount of patience for *you*."

Davida regarded him. "A pun, Frederick! How very Noel Coward of you!"

Brecht glared at her. "Mother, I think I'll take a cab back to the spa. If you'll excuse me . . ."

"Frederick, before you go, could you press back my cuticles for me. I want my nails to look nice when I shake the red-haired detective's hand."

Marge thought: Ten-thirty and the women had already been exercising for three and a half hours. Sweat streaming down their skin as they marched and kicked and squatted and made hundreds of arm circles to head-banging metal music. Enough physical activity to send a heart into overdrive. Yet, for the spa, the day was still young, four more classes scheduled in the afternoon. How did these women have the strength? The regimen seemed especially ridiculous because the gals weren't porkers. They were *skinny* women. And they paid lots of money for this torture. Hell, they could have joined the army and saved themselves beaucoup bucks.

The girl leading this class was blocky but agile. She was shouting in an accented voice over the music, with a look of grave intensity plastered to her damp face. Marge hadn't talked to her, but decided it wasn't in anyone's best interests to interrupt the class. Kelley Ness's attitude this morning had been cooperative, but she still wasn't friendly.

Marge decided to try her luck with the tennis instructor—Eubie Jeffers—maybe catch him between lessons. The spa should have his schedule mapped out at the front desk. She strolled through the ornate lobby and went over to the reception area, which was devoid of personnel. Resisting the urge to ring the little black bell, she leaned against the counter, her eyes instinctively shifting to the man at her left. He was fair and bald and looked agitated. Rocking on his feet, he rang the bell several times in quick succession.

"Where's help when you need it?" Marge said.

The man startled at the sound of Marge's voice. He wore a black silk shirt over jeans, and open-toed sandals.

"The help here is usually exemplary." He turned to Marge. "I'm Dr. Frederick Brecht—Valley Canyon's physician. Perhaps I can help you."

"Perhaps you can." Marge stuck out her hand. "Detective Dunn. Maybe we could talk a little."

Brecht looked at her hand, then finally shook it. "I've already spoken to the police. I have nothing to tell you. I really wish I did, but I don't."

Marge focused in on his face. The man dressed casually but was as tight as a bad case of constipation. "I'd like to talk about the spa and the people who work here. It's very close to your sister's house."

"No one here would hurt a hair on my sister's head. Everyone in her employ loves her. There are thousands of maniacs on the streets of Los Angeles. Why don't you start investigating them?"

Marge was about to respond when sharp-featured Ms. Purcel returned to her post behind the front desk.

"Nice of you to join us, Fern," Brecht said.

Marge smiled as Fernie-poo blushed.

"I . . . I'm terribly sorry—"

Brecht waved her away, then faced Marge. "Somewhere out there is a maniac who beats and rapes women. Go find him."

"You bet we'll keep investigating," Marge said. "But in the meantime, maybe I could speak to the men in Miss Brecht's employ. Just to be . . . thorough."

Brecht sighed forcefully. "I *suppose* it would be all right. Do try to be *discreet*, Detective. We cater to a very exclusive clientele."

"Well, well, well!" a deep baritone voice boomed. "Who emptied the gutters?"

Marge and Brecht turned to its source. He was tall and well-built. He appeared to be in his middle to late forties with icy-blue eyes, pale lips, and a Roman nose. He had a florid complexion crisscrossed with tiny spider veins throughout the nose and cheeks. His salt-and-pepper hair had been cut long enough to form a cap of curls, but the tresses were short enough to be neat. He wore a dark-blue linen blazer, a white shirt with a tab collar, a blue-silk jacquard tie, and white-and-blue-striped seersucker pants. Around his flat belly was a dyed-white lizard belt secured with a gold buckle. His feet were housed in white Cole-Haan calfskin loafers; a white-silk handkerchief fanned out from his breast pocket. Marge looked at him, then back at Brecht, whose bald head had reddened from anger.

"What the hell are *you* doing here?" Brecht spat out.

"Visiting Mother, Frederick."

"You're not welcome here," Brecht fired back. "Leave at once or I will call the authorities." He glanced at Marge. "Make yourself useful, Detective, and arrest this man. Dr. Merritt is trespassing on private property."

"I was invited down here—"

"Arrest him, Detective!"

Marge said, "Dr. Brecht—"

"Arrest him this moment!" Brecht whined.

Merritt's thin lips turned into a mirthless smile. He took a step forward; Marge blocked his advance. Merritt's eyes narrowed.

"Who the hell are you?"

"I'm the police, Dr. Merritt," Marge said. "Why don't we all sit down and try to have a civilized chat—"

"You don't know this man," Brecht said. "You can't be civilized with him."

Merritt threw him a contemptuous look, then turned to Marge. "Why are the police here?"

"Investigating your sister—" Marge said.

"What kind of *mischief* has Lilah gotten into now?" Merritt asked.

"She hasn't *gotten* into anything," Brecht said.

Merritt's eyes lost some of their self-confidence. He turned to Marge. "So why are you investigating her?"

"If she had wanted you to know, she would have told you, Kingston. Why don't you leave poor Lilah alone. She doesn't *need* you anymore."

Merritt's nostrils twitched. He sidestepped Marge until he was face-to-face with Brecht. "You little twit, don't you *dare* tell me how to treat my baby sister—"

"You can't talk to me like that!" Brecht said.

"Gentlemen—"

"I can damn well talk to you however I please!" Merritt gave Brecht a firm shove. "Now get out of my way!"

"Get your hands off me!"

"I'll put my hands wherever I please!"

Marge stepped between the men and separated them with her arms. "BACK OFF! BOTH OF YOU! BACK OFF NOW!"

They stopped, shocked by the force of her voice.

"What the *hell* is going on here!"

Marge turned to the new male voice. Mike Ness— behind him a very worried-looking Ms. Purcel. She'd called in the guard dog. Great! Another puffed-up male ego to appease!

"Dr. Brecht, are you all right?" Ness said. But he was staring at Merritt. He wore a muscle shirt and shorts and was wiping his neck with a towel. "I'm going to have to ask you to leave, sir!"

"The hell you will!" Merritt said. "My mother, Davida Eversong, called me down here and I intend to speak to her!"

"Ms. Eversong isn't in," Ness said quietly. "I'll tell her you stopped by."

"Then I'll wait for her . . . *young man*!" Merritt said.

"That wouldn't be a good idea . . . *sir*!"

"Mike," Marge broke in, "why don't you take Dr. Brecht and give him some of your stress-reducing consommé. I'll stay down here and chat with Dr. Merritt until Ms. Eversong returns. When is she due back?"

"I don't know," Brecht said. "In the meantime, this man is not *welcome* here."

"You don't own the spa, Freddy!" Merritt shouted. "*Lilah* does!"

"Lilah despises you!"

"Then let her tell me personally!"

"You are both creating quite a scene," Marge said.

She smiled and jerked her head toward a small crowd that had gathered near the marble hearth. The men followed the glance and said nothing.

Ness's eyes darted between Brecht and Merritt. Then he turned to Ms. Purcel. "It's okay, Fern, everything's under control. You can go back to work."

Ms. Purcel scurried back behind the protective shield of the reception desk.

Ness said, "Dr. Brecht, I have a couple of questions for you anyway. If you have a few minutes . . ."

Brecht brushed off his trousers, but didn't speak.

Ness gave a passing glance to Merritt. Then he said, "You know the ladies, Dr. Brecht. They ask technical questions. I just can't answer. Let's talk in your office."

Brecht nodded. Slowly, Ness led Brecht upstairs. Marge thought about the confrontation. What bothered her most was not Merritt and Brecht, but *Merritt and Ness.* They were addressing each other like strangers, yet Marge sensed that they knew each other.

". . . detest that excuse of a man," Merritt was saying.

"Pardon?" Marge said.

"Frederick," Merritt muttered. "I don't know how he has insinuated himself into Lilah's heart. She always did have a spot for the downtrodden. Probably why she married the Jew."

"The Jew?"

"Lilah's ex-husband."

"Is he a physician as well?"

"Perry? Good God, no!"

Marge smiled to herself. The one Semite in the

bunch and he wasn't a doctor. "Why don't we sit down while you wait, Dr. Merritt?"

"Fine."

Merritt parked himself in a wing chair; Marge sat in its mate. The two chairs were separated by a table piled high with VALCAN newsletters—the lead article entitled "Cellulite Reduction: Fact and Fiction." Merritt picked one up, absently scanned it, then crumpled it with disgust and threw it several feet. "Quackery passed off as medicine! If the place wasn't owned by my sister, I'd sic the Medical Board of Ethics on all of them."

"If Perry's not a doctor, what does he do?" Marge said.

"Pardon?"

"Perry. Lilah's ex. What does he do?"

"Perry?" Merritt shifted in his seat. "He's a bum—a bridge bum to be more precise. In actuality, he's a top-ranking bridge player so I suppose there is native intelligence somewhere. He plays for hire at a club in Westwood and I guess he makes enough money so he doesn't have to do honest work. Shame. Perry had a cunning mind, I'll give him that. Then again, most Jews do."

"Their break-up . . ." Marge took out her notebook. "Was it amicable?"

Merritt didn't answer.

"Were there hard feelings between Lilah and Perry, Dr. Merritt?"

Merritt shrugged. "I suppose so. Why do you ask?"

Because Marge had just found a new suspect. Lots of disgruntled exes do lots of vicious things—

if Merritt was at all credible. She asked, "How did Lilah meet him?"

"Ancient history."

"Then how about a history lesson?"

"First, young lady, please inform me what's going on with my sister!"

"You tell me, then I'll tell you."

"Quite an infantile approach, Detective. I really expected more from the LAPD."

"Dr. Merritt, what was infantile was two supposedly mature, educated men—doctors no less—squaring off like adolescents."

Merritt looked at her and smiled. "Touché, Detective, a most astute observation. Anger does turn even the most rational of men to savagery. Even those of us in the healing profession are not immune to emotion."

Marge didn't answer.

"All right," Merritt said with newfound resolve. "How did Lilah meet Perry? Unfortunately, I was the one who brought him into the house. Mother wanted to hone her skills at bridge and when I asked around, Perry's name kept coming up over and over. He was everything Lilah was taught to avoid in a man—brash, left-wing, uncontrolled, unrestrained in his opinions. A pushy Jew if you might permit me a bit of stereotype. He took pride in not caring about his appearance; his clothes were always old and out-of-date. Perry wasn't an evil boy, just not suitable for Lilah. And of course, having flirted with rebellion in her own adolescence, Lilah instantly became infatuated with him—in *love* with him. It was maddening. My beautiful, brilliant sister trailing after him. As if she were a starved mutt and his silly, do-gooder words were food. Every time he *smiled* at her, she swooned like a clay-eating Victorian gentle-woman. Later on in their so-called courtship, she would corner him in some quiet room and they'd talk for *hours*. I'd hear whispering, stifled giggling. Like children. God knows what they actually *talked* about. They had nothing in common."

Merritt sighed deeply.

"Mother blamed me, of course. Mother has to blame someone when things don't go according to her plan. Up until Perry, I'd always had a good relationship with Lilah. More than good, we'd been very close. We are not a demonstrative family, but you'd have to be an idiot not to see how much I cared about my baby sister. I was her father as well as her big brother. There's a sixteen-year difference between us. Who do you think took care of that child while Mother gallivanted around? I nurtured that little girl despite the fact that I had a full university course load. I remember teaching her to ride a bike, holding the handlebars with one hand and my biochemistry book in the other. She learned to ride a two-wheeler while I learned the Krebs cycle. How's that for dedication? When she wanted to marry Perry, I had the audacity to side with Mother, and things between Lilah and me have never been the same since.

"Of course the union was a disaster. Giggling does not a marriage make. It lasted two years. But Lilah would never admit that I was right and she was wrong. She somehow viewed her doomed relationship as my doing. Maybe Mother gave her those ideas, I wouldn't be a bit surprised. Mother has a way of turning everyone against everyone else." His eyes met Marge's. "So that's the saga of Lilah and Perry. Now it's your turn. What's going on with my sister? Whom I still care for very much despite her rejection of me."

"I'm sorry to have to tell you this, Dr. Merritt. Lilah was attacked yesterday—"

Merritt bolted upright. "Good God, no!"

Marge stood. "She'll be all right, Doctor."

"No!" Merritt began to pace. "No, it can't . . . that's *impossible*! What in God's name *happened*?"

"I don't know—"

"Who hurt her? Do you suspect Perry? Is that why you were questioning me about him? I'll kill him—"

"Doctor—"

"I'll *kill* him!"

"I don't know anything about this guy, Doctor," Marge said. "Just what you told me—"

"But you suspect—"

"No, I *don't* suspect—!"

"Where is my sister?" Merritt interrupted.

"Last I heard she was at Sun Valley Memorial."

"I must go see her right away."

"Be my guest." Marge paused then said, "What about your mother?"

"What about my *mother*?" Merritt orated. "My *mother* can damn well wait—that's what about my *mother*!"

Decker knew he shouldn't make the call under time pressure. Davida had given him twenty minutes. But the pay phone in the hospital hallway was unoccupied, begging for use. And if past be indicative of the future, the conversation wouldn't last more than a few minutes, anyway.

Go ahead, Deck. Live dangerously.

Using his phone card, he dialed the New York number by rote. As luck would have it, she was in. Her hello was breathless.

"Hi. Did I catch you at a bad time?"

"Oh, hi, Dad. I've got a final in an hour. I was just doing some last-minute cramming."

"Good luck. I'm sure you'll ace it."

"Yeah, I guess."

She sounded preoccupied. Whenever she spoke to him, she was preoccupied.

"Love you, kiddo."

"Uh, Dad?"

"What?"

"You happen to speak to Mom recently?"

"No. Why?"

"Uh, nothing. I just wondered if she . . . it's not important."

"What's not important?"

"I'd really rather not get into it right now. Regards to your family."

"Cindy, first of all, you're my family, too. Secondly, if you're going to bring things up, I'd appreciate it if you'd carry the conversation to a natural conclusion."

"Oh, that's really *great*, Dad. Push me right before a final. Thanks a heap!"

Decker exhaled forcefully. "You're right. My timing stinks. I'm sorry."

No one spoke for a moment.

"I'm sorry, too, Daddy. I know I've been difficult, lately. I'm not without insight."

"You've been fine."

"No, I haven't, but thanks for saying it anyway. Can I call you back in a few days? I'm really nervous."

"Princess, you can call me anytime you want, twenty-four hours a day. I'll be waiting."

Her voice became small. "Thank you."

"You sure you're okay, Cindy?"

"I'm fine."

Then she burst into tears.

"Is there anything I can *do* for you, honey?"

"No." She sniffed. "I should get going. I really should."

"Love you."

"I love you, too, Daddy. Bye."

The line went dead, the only thing to show for his effort, a knot in his gut. He looked at his watch. The conversation had lasted forty-eight seconds. Business as usual.

❧11

Decker was about to reach for the door when it swung open, almost clipping him in the ribs. He took a quick shuffle backward, then a seductive voice beckoned him to enter. He slid into the backseat of the limo and closed the door. Davida had removed her veil. Guess the mourning period had passed.

"May I call you Peter?" Davida asked. "Isn't that what Lilah calls you?"

Straining to keep his eyeballs from rolling back, Decker answered yes.

"Peter." Davida placed her hand on his knee. "I see you more as a Pete."

Whatever she called him, he was sorely tempted to drop her hand back in her lap. But at her age, she was harmless. Why ruin the rapport before the interview even began?

"A Pete?"

"Yes, definitely a Pete," she said. "Not in those clothes of course. What exactly are you wearing? Standard detective garb? I'd never cast you as a policeman. Yes, you're big and all that crap, but your coloring is all wrong. Redheads do *not* connote 'tough guy.' And your skin—too smooth and too fair. You're not sinister enough for a cop . . . except in the eyes. You have very piercing eyes."

Decker thought: That's 'cause you're looking in the mirror, lady. Talk about hard eyes. Hers could scratch diamonds. She'd been lifted by an excellent cosmetic surgeon. Tightened in all the right spots, yet the skin didn't look as though it would crack if she smiled. The knife work emphasized her strongest points—the great bone structure, the angular chin, the wide mouth. Her lips were still full and sensual, probably been helped along by collagen injections. Up close, she was still a nice-looking woman—discounting the eyes. There wasn't a scalpel sharp enough to excise the titanium lodged inside those irises.

"Now if *I* were to cast you," she went on, "I'd put you in some blue jeans, a plaid shirt, and a ten-gallon hat." She cocked her face. "Your face isn't weather-beaten, but makeup would take care of that." She squeezed his knee. "What do you think?"

Decker laughed. "I think it's a good idea I never went into pictures. Can I ask you a few questions? I know your time is limited."

Davida patted his leg and withdrew her hand. "I like a man who can cut to the chase. I want my jewels back, Peter."

"And I want you to get them back. Want to tell me about them?"

"You bet your derriere, I do. The first is an emerald brooch—five-carat table-cut Colombian emerald surrounded by round-cut diamonds—twenty points each—maybe four carats' worth. Three pairs of mabe-pearl earrings—one teardrop-shaped surrounded by emeralds, the other two pairs round, one surrounded by diamonds, the other surrounded by rubies—in case I was in my *red* mood."

"What are mabe pearls?"

"The big round ones that are flat on one side."

"I always thought they were costume jewelry."

"No, dear man, they are indeed *pearls*."

"Total value per pair?"

"Perhaps five to six thousand per. I also had a ruby choker—alternating rubies and diamonds, actually. A sapphire and yellow-diamond necklace—that one's worth about fifty thousand. Five strands of rose-colored pearls of varying lengths with matching pearl studs surrounded by diamond jackets. A diamond bowknot clip—antique Tiffany."

She sighed.

"God, this makes me sick! You're probably thinking the old bitch is insured anyway. What's her problem? It's not the money, it's the *pieces*. Each one told a different story in *my* life. *My* history . . . just *ripped* away. I'm furious!"

Decker nodded. Davida waved her hand in the air. "What do *you* care?"

"Believe it or not, Ms. Eversong, I understand what you're saying."

She studied him. "Maybe you do. You seem . . . sensitive."

"What else was taken from you, Ms. Eversong?"

"I also had cluster-pearl earrings woven with diamonds, emeralds, and rubies. My Christmas earrings. It makes me nauseated to think of my precious babies in the hands of some snotbucket who wouldn't know a diamond from quartz crystal."

Suddenly, the old lady's eyes moistened. She pulled out a lacy black handkerchief and dabbed her eyes. "I'm simply devastated."

"I'm sorry for your loss," Decker said. "I'm sure Lilah is devastated as well."

"Why? *She* didn't lose any jewelry." There was a momentary pause. "Oh . . . yes, that was terrible. Poor dear. But she's *young*, Peter. Youth is *resilient*. She'll get over it. It's so much harder for people like me."

"I think it would have been *very* difficult if you had been beaten," Decker said. "But you weren't, Ms. Eversong. Lilah was. And I'm going to find the perpetrator."

Davida looked up and caught his eyes. "Tell me something, Peter. Are you going to look for my jewels with as much zest as you have for Lilah's attacker?"

"We'll get to the bottom of all of it."

"You didn't answer my question."

"Let's talk some more about your jewels, Ms. Eversong. Who, besides Lilah, knew you kept your jewelry in Lilah's safe?"

"Every single one of my children. And I wouldn't put it past any of them to try to rob me blind."

The comment sparked a circuit in Decker's brain. Just as Freddy Brecht was pointing an accusing finger at Kingston Merritt, old Mom was blaming *family*. Made him awfully *curious* about the whole bunch.

"You think your children would steal from you?"

"No, not really. I'm just talking."

But Decker wasn't so sure. Her words sounded as if she were covering a slip of the tongue. But her manner was so casual. Then again, the woman was an actress.

"Does Dr. Brecht have the combination to the safe?"

"I don't think so. He's my little *messenger* boy. Brings my pieces to Lilah to lock up."

So he knew what was stored in the safe, Decker thought. He remembered how Brecht had vehemently denied knowing the contents of Lilah's safe. He jotted the inconsistency down in his notes. Family was getting more and more interesting. He decided to focus in on them.

"Do you think your children could mastermind a robbery like this one, Ms. Eversong?"

Davida laughed wickedly. "I doubt it. Not that they wouldn't mind my money. I pad their wallets from time to time, but it never seems to be enough . . . the carrion eaters."

"How much padding are we talking about?"

"A thousand or two, here and there."

"Including Lilah?"

"No, she has her own money. And why would she steal from me, knowing she's going to get the whole kit and caboodle after I move on to the next world?"

"She inherits everything?"

"Oh, I haven't given her everything. I've remembered my boys, but not as much as my little girl and that's just tough titties if they don't like it. Men have it easy in society. No one looks askance when an old frog is hooked up with a princess fifty years his junior. Women—aging women—need an extra boost and that boost is money. Lilah doesn't understand that now. She thinks her looks will last forever. Someday, when she's old and gray, she'll realize what *I've* done for her. Despite my admitted self-obsession, I do have her interests at heart."

Decker didn't answer.

Davida picked up an emery board and began to file her nails. "Not that I'm claiming to be Mother Teresa. Yes, I'm selfish. So what? Why shouldn't I take care of myself? Didn't some ancient philosopher say, 'If I'm not for myself, who'll be for me?'"

"Rabbi Hillel," Decker said.

"What?"

"Rabbi Hillel said that."

"A Jew said that?"

Decker nodded.

"That figures." Davida stopped filing and looked up at Decker. "Are you Jewish?"

"Yes."

"Did I offend you?"

"Not really."

Davida studied him. "You don't look Jewish. Sure you weren't adopted?"

Decker broke into sudden laughter.

"It wasn't that funny," Davida said.

But it was. The old lady had hit it on the nose. Born to a Jewish mother, he'd been adopted in infancy by a good Baptist family. It wasn't until he met Rina that he'd returned to the religion of his bloodline.

"Well, your Rabbi what's his face was right in this case," Davida said. "One must take care of Number One."

"You missed the next line of the quote, Ms. Eversong. Hillel also said, 'And if I'm only for myself, then who am I?'"

Davida gave him a sour expression which slowly turned into a grin. "Who am I? A bitchy, famous, rich old woman, that's who I am. Are you here to quote dead rabbis, Sergeant, or are you going to find my jewels?"

"Any other pieces inside the safe?"

"Let's see. You have the earrings, the pearls, the brooch. Did I tell you about the diamond bracelet?"

"No."

"Heavy braided gold studded with diamonds. I also have a ruby and emerald bracelet to go with my Christmas earrings. And of course, I have lesser pieces. An amethyst ring surrounded by baguettes, a peridot brooch that's identical to the emerald brooch. Sometimes I want to wear the brooch but don't feel comfortable going out in a five-carat Colombian emerald. So I had the same brooch made up with peridot and faux diamonds."

She took his hand and stroked it.

"Find my pieces, Peter. I'll make sure you're more than adequately compensated for your time."

Decker looked down at his hand in hers. Like mother, like daughter. He pulled away gently. "Doing my job well is all the compensation I need. I'd like to touch just a moment on the memoirs—"

"God, you're tedious!" She faced him. "*What!*"

"You knew about them, but you've never seen them."

"Yes, yes. I told you all this before. I don't like to repeat myself."

"Do your other children know about the memoirs?"

"How should I know? Ask them!"

"Who else do you think might know about them?"

"Don't know and don't care. Our time is up, Sergeant."

Decker inched closer to the old woman. He could smell her sweat mixed with overly sweet perfume, see the pores giving texture to her white face makeup. "Just a few more minutes? Please?"

Davida traced his jawline with a sharpened index fingernail, then let her hand fall in her lap. "Oh, go ahead! You've already ruined my morning."

"You say you haven't the faintest idea about what's contained in your late husband's memoirs."

"Correct. Hermann was a self-obsessed genius. He never spoke to me or anyone else about his art. Frankly, I wasn't interested in his *art*, I was interested in his *performance*. Which I regret to say wasn't Oscar caliber."

"Oh?"

"Yes, *oh!*" Davida stared at him. "Do you want the smarmy details?"

"Do you want to tell me details?"

"He was a drunk, which made him a *lousy* fuck. How's that for details?"

"So why'd you marry him?"

Davida shrugged. "Impulse. And . . . I was swept

away by his reputation. Even *I* wasn't immune to what others thought."

"Do you think he might have written disparaging things about you, Ms. Eversong?"

Davida pondered the question.

"I just don't see Hermann writing about his tawdry little affairs—or my tawdry little affairs, for that matter. Affairs are just something one does when one is creatively blessed. Personally, I suspect Hermann wrote exclusively about his art. I'm sure he wrote rather harshly about some of his contemporaries. Hermann was very, very *critical*. But I can't imagine some old irate compadre director breaking into Lilah's safe and stealing the memoirs just to censor what Hermann may have written about him thirty years ago." There was a pause. "Yet I've seen weirder things. Egos do abound in this business."

Decker smiled.

"We're getting off track," Davida said. "These memoirs may very well be a figment of Lilah's overactive mind. Find my jewels. Once you do, everything else will fall into place."

"Maybe." Decker noticed Davida staring at him. "Anything else you'd like to add, Ms. Eversong?"

Davida tapped her nails against the portable table. "You seem to be a very skeptical man, Peter."

Decker folded his notepad and stuffed it into his jacket. "That's why I'm a cop and not a cowboy, Ms. Eversong."

Ness sat in a lotus position on the floor and watched Freddy rant. Since Freddy couldn't handle the ladies and their medical questions, they went to Kell's office instead of Freddy's study. Man, sonny boy had a temper, but it was *nothing* compared to the old lady's. Bitch could cut metal with her tongue. Ness often wondered if she'd melt if doused with water.

"I'm talking to you!" Brecht screamed.

"I hear you, Doc," Ness said, quietly.

"Then answer me! What's he doing here?"

"I don't know—"

"Hell you don't!" Brecht screamed. "You were with Mother last night."

"She didn't mention anyone visiting her. Doc, I didn't even know this Kingston existed until today."

"That's bullshit!"

Ness didn't answer him. He watched Doc pace. Asshole just couldn't hold up well under pressure. Probably why Davida didn't trust him.

"What's he doing here?" Brecht mumbled. "He must be involved in what happened to Lilah!"

"Could be."

"Stop being so poised and *casual*! Doesn't it bother you that Lilah was beaten and . . . *raped*?"

"Of course it *bothers* me, Doc. You know how I feel about your sister. I just don't think acting like a *fool*—"

"Are you saying I was a fool?"

"C'mon, Doc, give me a break, okay?"

"It's Kingston," Brecht raved. "He brings out the worst in me." He touched his fingertips to his forehead. "I behaved very stupidly, didn't I?"

"S'right. Your sister was raped. No one expects you to behave normally."

"Mother didn't mention her son Kingston coming for a visit?"

"No."

"You're sure?"

"Yes, I'm *sure*."

"I don't believe you."

"Your prerogative."

"Why is he visiting Mother?" Brecht raged on. "At this moment! At the spa! Mother would never call him down here."

"I don't know." Ness was exasperated, but held himself in check. "Why don't you ask her?"

"I will as soon as I see her."

"Where is she?"

"Talking to the police about the theft of her jewels."

Suddenly, Ness felt the heat of Brecht's eyes. "Something on your mind, Doc?"

"You wouldn't happen to know anything about the theft, would you?"

"You think I'd steal from your mother?"

"You'd steal without a second thought."

"Sure I'd steal." Ness grinned. "But not from Davida. I'm not stupid."

Brecht didn't respond. Guy was pacing again. Ness placed splayed fingers on his knees. "Calm down, Doc, and meditate. It'll do wonders for the spirit."

But Brecht wasn't listening. Ness closed his eyes, but kept his ears open.

"Kingston's planning something, I just know it!" Brecht muttered. "He and Mother are colluding behind my back. You wouldn't know anything about that, would you?"

Ness opened his eyes. "No, I wouldn't."

"I don't believe you."

Ness stood without using his hands to rise. "What do you want me to do, Doc?" He placed his palm on Brecht's shoulder. "Huh, what should I do? Slit my wrist and sign my name in blood? Until today, I didn't even know you had a brother. And I certainly don't know what happened to Lilah!"

Brecht was quiet.

Ness patted Brecht's shoulder. "You want me to chase your brother away?"

"Can you do it without causing a scene?"

"Yeah, I can handle him."

"Then why didn't you do it before, hotshot?"

"Because you don't stick your hands in the middle of a dogfight." Ness folded his arms across his chest. "Both of you weren't receptive to suggestions." He laughed. "God, you boys really *hate* each other."

"You're very perceptive."

Ness arched his eyebrows. "Wanna tell me about it?"

Brecht sneered. "No, I don't want to *tell* you about it! If you can get him out of here, get him out of here. Tell me when he's gone. And I don't want Mother to know he was here."

"Man looked determined, Doc. You know he's gonna call her."

"I'll worry about that when the time comes. In the meantime, don't mention his visit to Mother. Give me time to figure out what those two are planning."

Ness grinned. "Secrecy's expensive, Doc."

"You're scum, Michael."

Brecht took out his wallet. Ness held out his hand.

⮞12

Another call from Morrison. Decker checked his watch—eleven-thirty. Might as well take care of the crap so he could enjoy lunch. He phoned from the unmarked and was patched through to Morrison a minute later.

"Captain," Decker said.

"What do you have on the Brecht case?"

"Lots of notes—"

"Pete—"

"Captain, we're making progress—no shortage of suspects—but there's no smoking gun." Decker filled him in on the details, hearing Morrison audibly sigh when he spoke of Lilah's imaging of her attackers.

"Lilah Brecht," Morrison said. "Is she whacked out or what?"

"She might be trying to tell us something in a roundabout way."

"You think she could give us trouble?"

"Her spa appeals to VIPs," Decker said. "I can't see where it would make sense for her to publicize her attack. Bad for business."

"But she sounds like a nut," Morrison said. "And

you know these perverse Hollywood assholes. Anything that's full of gossip—the juicier the better."

Decker said, "I think if we handle everyone with respect, they'll respect our investigation."

"What about Davida Eversong?" Morrison said. "She give a shit about her daughter?"

"Probably. It's hard to tell. She spent most of her time talking about her jewels."

"Davida Eversong knows a lot of people, Pete," Morrison said. "We're talking a seven-figure burglary on top of a rape. That's a lot of case for you, Marge, and Hollander to handle. I'll pull in a couple of dicks from Burglary."

"Fine," Decker said. "They know the fences better than I do. Just . . ."

"Spit it out, Pete."

"I want freedom to call the case as I see it. Not that I want to step on any bigwig's toes, but if that happens, I don't want to have to worry about it."

"You do your job, Pete," Morrison said, "and I'll do mine."

Business out of the way, Decker checked himself out on a Code Seven and took off for the safety and normalcy of home sweet home. Lunch at his ranch had started out as a once-a-week affair. Over the last five months he'd increased his visits to three times a week. The food was better and the amenities were terrific. And despite Rina's occasional weeping spells and flare-ups, she was wonderful company. Whether they talked or just sat around, he never felt as if he had to entertain her. Their conversations, as well as their silences, were natural. God, how he just loved to watch her putter around the house. Rina was a great putterer.

He parked the unmarked in the driveway, whistling as he walked through the door. The living room was still neo-western macho, but Rina had prettied it up with lace curtains and throw pillows on the suede couch and buckskin chairs. Throw pillows with frilly little borders. Yep, he was definitely married. He suddenly noticed that the place was eerily quiet, not even a bark from the dog. He felt a sudden rush of anxiety.

"Anyone here?"

"We're in the boys' room, Peter," Rina called out.

He breathed a sigh of relief. Ridiculous to worry, but he couldn't help himself. Then he processed the *we* part of Rina's message. *We're in the boys' room.* The boys' room had been his study.

He went inside. Sammy was dressed in his pajamas, head propped up on a pillow, covers pulled up to his waist. A slight blush tinged his cheeks, his brow was moist. His light-brown hair was mussed and crowned by a brown leather yarmulke. He smiled, but it seemed forced. Tucked under the blankets, he seemed much younger than his twelve years, much more vulnerable. He and Rina were playing cards, a discard pile set out on a bed tray. She was dressed in a cream-colored cotton maternity dress, the red scarf around her neck giving her face a splash of color. Her hair was braided and knotted and partially covered by a gold mesh net. Gold loops hung from her earlobes. How a woman could look so *beautiful* in simple clothing, without the benefit of makeup, was beyond him.

Rina was good enough to eat. But with Sammy home, the prospects of romance in the afternoon were nil. Decker walked over to his stepson and felt his forehead, then his cheeks.

"Not feeling too good?"

Sammy shrugged.

"Can I get you anything, son?"

"I'm okay."

"Do you want lunch?" Rina said. "It's a little early."

"I'll fix myself something."

"No, you sit. I'll get you a sandwich."

"Where's Ginger?"

"Being flea-bathed and groomed, poor thing. Hot weather comes and you know how she suffers. I should pick her up as long as you're here. Do you mind keeping Shmuli company?"

"Do I mind?" Decker sat on the edge of the bed. "It would be my pleasure."

Sammy smiled weakly.

"We can call this round a draw, Shmuli," Rina said. "What do you think?"

"It's fine, Eema."

Rina gathered the cards and fit them back into the box. "I'll be back. Turkey sandwich okay?"

"Perfect."

Decker smiled and patted his son's warm hand. "Just woke up like this?"

Sammy nodded.

"Well, you take care of yourself. You gotta drink, Sam. You drinking enough?"

"I'm floating away, Peter."

"Good." Decker put his arm around the boy's

shoulders. He sensed a certain amount of stiffness. "Is my arm too heavy for you?"

"I don't want you to catch anything." Sammy pulled away. "I told Eema she shouldn't get too close, either. You know, with the baby and everything."

Decker kissed his cheek. "Don't worry about me. I've got great powers of resistance."

But Sammy held his distance. Decker knew that this was normal. Stepfathers don't take the place of real fathers overnight. Or even over a period of three years. Had it been that long since he had first met Rina? He had been assigned to a rape case; Rina had been a witness. They'd both come a long way since then.

Rina then came into the room with a turkey sandwich and a mound of coleslaw on a paper plate. She was also carrying a pitcher of pale-looking orange juice.

"This is for you." She handed Decker the plate and placed the pitcher on the nightstand. "And this is for Sammy. Make sure he drinks, Peter."

"We've already been over that, Eema."

"See you boys later." She kissed her son on the forehead, then Decker on the lips, tapping his head before she went out the door. Her subtle way of reminding him to put on a yarmulke before he ate.

"Bye," Decker said. He and Sammy waited in silence, hearing Rina walking around the house. A few moments later, the door closed and Decker turned his attention to the boy.

"How's it going, kiddo?"

"You can eat, Peter. Don't let me stop you."

"I've got to wash first. Happen to have a kipah I can borrow?"

"Top drawer on the right."

"Thanks." Decker fished a Batman yarmulke out of the dresser and bobby-pinned it to his hair. He got up and washed his hands, ritually, in the kitchen sink. Then he sat back on the bed, said the blessing for breaking bread, and took a bite of his sandwich. "Hungry?"

Sammy shook his head.

"Sure?"

"Positive."

"Is the flu going around at school?"

"I don't know. I don't think so."

"Well, you and your brother've been doing okay, considering what's going on. A new baby coming around in a few months has to be a little stressful."

"I don't think that's stressful. Not for me anyway."

"It's a change."

"Yeah, I guess."

Decker took another bite of his sandwich. "I'm hoping the baby won't impact too much on you and your brother's lives. After all, there'll be a big age difference between you guys and the baby."

Sammy paused. "The same as between you and Eema."

Decker stopped chewing. A second later, he forced himself to swallow the bolus. It went down like a lead weight. "Yeah. About the same difference."

Sammy said nothing. This was *not* going to be a routine lunch.

"Our age difference bother you, Sam?"

"Not really."

"A little?"

The boy shrugged.

"It bothers me a little," Decker said.

Sammy didn't answer.

"You can't help who you fall in love with. And I'm thrilled to be in love with your mother. But sometimes our age difference bothers me. Especially since Eema doesn't seem to be aging at the same rate I am." Decker shifted his weight. "The difference is sometimes pretty noticeable. And I could see where that might embarrass you—"

"I'm not embarrassed," Sammy retorted.

"Good." Decker hesitated. "I can't say that I'm honestly not a little bit embarrassed by it sometimes. I get a lot of ribbing at the station house."

Sammy cocked his head. "They tease you?"

"It's good-natured."

"Marge teases you?"

"No, not Marge. She's decent about things like that."

"But it bothers you when the others do it?"

"Sometimes it does. As a matter of fact, I think it bothers your mother, too. She blushes a little every time someone mistakes her for my daughter instead of my wife."

And blushes a lot when someone mistakes her for Cindy's girlfriend. God, was that horrible. All three of them had felt like sinking into the ground. The *look* on Cindy's face. Not a damn thing he could have done to fix it, but that hadn't made it any easier.

"But like I said," Decker continued, "she looks young. And I look my age and then some. It's a natural error."

"Would you like it better if she was older like you? I mean not old, but closer to your age?"

"I like Eema just the way she is. And I'm glad she was young when she had you and Jakey because young mothers have a lot of energy. Sometimes, I wish I were a little younger so I'd have more energy."

"You have energy."

"Not too bad for an old guy."

"You're not that old, Peter. You know, most of the kids in my class have dads around your age. Eema was just really young. Both of them were . . . Eema and . . . you know, Abba was young, too . . . when I was born."

Decker took a deep breath and let it out slowly. "Do you wish I was as young as your abba?"

"No, no, no. Not at all. I didn't mean that."

But the boy's voice was cracking and it wasn't from hormones. The pain was palpable.

Decker said, "You know what I wish, Sammy?"

Sammy didn't answer.

"I wish . . ." Decker took his stepson's hand. "I wish that you were having this discussion with your abba right now. I swear to God, I wish that he was here instead of me."

Sammy broke into tears, folding against Decker's chest. Holding him tightly, Decker let him cry it out. The boy was developing into adolescence, a decent layer of muscle enveloping his shoulders and arms. Yet, sobbing so bitterly, he seemed so frail.

"I can't *remember* him so well anymore, Peter. I try and try, but every day the memories just get more and more . . . cloudy. I remember things I did with you, but I can't remember the things *we* used to do

together." The boy broke away, dried his red eyes
on his pajama sleeves. "Sometimes . . . sometimes . . .
you know? I think I remember things." He sniffed
and dried his eyes again. "I think I remember them
very clearly. But then I'm not sure if I remember
them because I heard Eema talk about it. Or I actually remember it 'cause it happened. And I feel terrible about it 'cause there's nothing I can do about it.
It's only *four* years ago. God, at this rate, I won't
remember *anything* by the time I'm twenty."

"Sure you will."

"No, I won't."

Okay, Decker, just back it up. "You were young
when he died." Too young. *Way* too young. "Sammy,
what do you think about this? Why don't you write
down whatever you do remember about your abba
and show it to your mother. See if she remembers it
the same way you do."

"That would upset her too much."

"No, I don't think it would."

"Yes, it would. I know it would, Peter."

Decker felt relief. It was good to see the kid arguing with him. There was nothing as scary as a pre-
teen with no spunk.

"Well, write it down anyway and show it to me.
And if I think the timing's okay, *I'll* show it to her.
How about that?"

Sammy shrugged.

"Up to you, kiddo." Decker looked down at his
partially consumed lunch. His stomach was churn-
ing, his shoulder was throbbing, and he felt a headache coming on. He fished a couple of Ecotrin from

his pocket and swallowed them dry. "Just think about it."

"Okay." Sammy paused. "It wouldn't bother you? I mean for me to . . . you know, talk about my abba?"

Truth be told, it did bother him and he felt petty because of it. But he was mature enough not to let his smallness get in the way of his stepson's well-being.

"Sammy, you and your brother talk about your abba all you want. As a matter of fact, I'd like to learn about your abba, too. But sometimes I feel funny asking your mom about him."

"I could understand that."

Decker nodded in agreement. Father-son bonding. All right!

"You know what, Peter?"

"What, big guy?"

"I feel sort of guilty that I don't call you Dad."

Oh, boy. "Do you want to call me Dad?"

"Kind of. But it doesn't . . . you know, come easy. Not that I don't think of you as my dad. I want you to know that."

"Whoa, you are really going through a lot of changes."

"Tell me about it."

"Sam, I don't care what you call me. If you want to call me Dad, *please*, go ahead and call me Dad. But certainly don't feel *guilty* if you'd rather call me Peter."

"I think Yonkie would like to call you Dad. We were discussing—I don't want you to think we talk a lot about you behind your back."

"I talked a lot about my parents behind their backs."

Sammy smiled. A genuine one this time. "Anyway, when you and Eema first got married, Yonkie was asking me, like what do we call him. And I . . . I knew I couldn't call you Abba. And I felt weird calling you Dad. So Yonkie said, if I wasn't gonna call you Dad, *he* wasn't gonna call you Dad, either. But I think he wanted to."

"Why don't you—?"

"I know, I know. Talk it over with him. Talk, talk, talk. I don't know."

Decker stroked the boy's hot cheek. "Do this. Call me Dad for a week. Better yet, call me Dad for a month. After a month, if you still feel more comfortable calling me Peter, go back to Peter. Or Akiva. My Jewish name's pretty personal to me. It could be our special name, if Dad doesn't seem to feel natural."

"Akiva. That's not bad. I didn't even think about that. Okay, I'll try Dad. If not . . . Akiva."

"Great."

Sammy looked at the half-eaten sandwich. "I ruined your appetite, didn't I?"

"Nah . . ." Decker made himself pick up the sandwich and take a bite. "See?"

"Nice save . . . Dad."

Decker laughed.

"You know?" Sammy turned serious. "Remember we were talking about how you were a little embarrassed about Eema looking so young?"

"I should remember it. The conversation took place about five minutes ago."

Sammy punched his shoulder—his good one. "Sometimes—I mean this is gonna sound real weird. But a lot of times, Eema gets mistaken for my older sister. Even when she's . . . even *now*."

Decker nodded. Apparently the word *pregnant* didn't come easy to him, either.

"I don't mean this to sound like an insult," Sammy said, "but I'm really glad you look old . . . older. When I'm around you, people know you're my *dad*. We go to the baseball game, everyone knows you're a *dad* taking his kids out to the game. I'm proud that Eema looks so young and pretty, but sometimes a kid wants his parents to look like parents, know what I mean?"

"You bet. Don't worry, Sammy, no one is *ever* going to mistake me for your brother."

"Well, I'm happy about that."

"So am I," Decker said. "Really."

"I never told you this, Pete—Dad, but most of my friends' fathers are, you know, like doctors or lawyers or businessmen."

"Uh-huh."

"The kids at school think it's real neat that you're a detective."

"Real exotic, huh?"

"Yeah, exactly. Like you do what they do in the movies we're not supposed to see. I tell them that it's not like that . . . except for that one time . . ."

"That was an *exceptional* circumstance." Chasing an errant teenager and a psycho cross-country. Do a favor for someone and get yourself shot. Still, he'd brought the teenager back to the family in one piece. That was worth it all. He shifted his weight again.

"Don't worry. It won't happen again. You're right, Sam. My job's not like the movies."

"Yeah, I tell my friends you mostly just investigate. Interview people and make a lot of phone calls . . . push pencils—"

Decker burst into laughter.

"Isn't that what you always say?"

"Word for word."

"I don't think they believe me. Maybe it's because they all know you were . . . you know, shot. *Baruch Hashem*, you're okay. You are okay, right?"

"I'm great."

"Were you scared?"

"I was scared when it was happening, sure. But I'm not scared now."

"Really?"

"Really."

"Not even a little?"

"Nope." It was the truth. His concern was saved solely for the people he loved, not for himself.

"The kids at school . . ." Sammy fingered his covers. "They ask me about the incident. I wish they'd shut up about it."

"It gets on your nerves."

"Yeah, I don't like to think about it. That's why I tell them your job isn't like that normally. But they still ask me questions. You have this kind of, I don't know, *mystic* around you."

Decker fluttered his fingers and howled like a ghost.

Sammy laughed. "*Emes*, I think it's kind of neat what you do, too. Maybe one day you can take me to work with you."

Decker felt his throat tighten. The kid was actually *proud* of him. "I'd like that, Sam. Pick a day, we'll clear it with Eema, and you can be my partner."

Impulsively, Sammy reached out and hugged Decker around the neck. Then, just as abruptly, he pushed him away. "Okay, I'm sick of talking. You want to play some cards?"

The detectives' squad room at Foothill Substation was not the location of choice when the merc climbed past ninety. With dozens of men sweating into a confined area with no air conditioning and little circulation, the room became ripe very quickly. Some took it better than others, and although Mike Hollander was fifty pounds overweight, he took it better than most.

It just wasn't his nature to get overly excited about things. Not that he was a jerk-off. But he was . . . relaxed.

Dunking his doughnut into his coffee, he had some spare time before court. He heaved his portly frame out of his wooden chair and lumbered over to Decker's desk. Resting on the scarred wooden top was a manila evidence envelope, a couple of police sketches and a list of felons who physically matched the drawings. Hollander brushed crumbs from his walrus mustache, picked up the list, and planted his butt back in his chair.

He picked up the phone and started to check out the mugs. He'd scratched two off the list by the time Decker walked in. Hollander hung up the phone and took another bite of doughnut.

"You got lab info on the Brecht case. Also, Leo dropped off the sketches and names based on your gal's description. I checked out the first two. Both are still in the cooler."

Decker took off his jacket and made a beeline for the coffeepot. "Thanks, Mike. Who'd she pick out?"

"Not guys associated with rape."

"Robbery perps?"

"Yeah, but that don't tell you squat. Most of the geniuses in the books got there by doing two-elevens."

"True."

"I marked their mug-shot pages if you want to compare them to the composites. Also, Ma Bell called you back. A call did go out from a Malibu prefix to Frederick Brecht at seven-forty-six A.M. that morning. I cross-referenced the number: It belonged to Davida Eversong."

Decker nodded. "Nice to see you doing the old work ethic, Detective Hollander."

"Don't tell anyone, but I get in these moods once in a while." Hollander extracted a pipe from his pocket and stuck it in his mouth, unlit. "What's eating you, Rabbi?"

"Nothing."

"It's Morrison, isn't it?" Hollander said. "What'd he do?"

"Nothing. He's assigning a couple of dicks from Burglary to handle the jewel theft."

"It's big bucks. They have the contacts. Let them have it."

"My sentiments exactly."

"So why're you pissed? You're thinking Morrison doesn't have faith in you or what?"

"I'm not pissed." Decker sat at his desk. "Well, I'm a little pissed. I'm pissed about all the shit we have to deal with because someone else screwed up."

Hollander shrugged. "They did it, we didn't. Fuck the nonbelievers." He chewed on the stem of his pipe. "This lady—Lilah. She seem on the level to you?"

Decker regarded the composites. "Why do you ask?"

"Take a gander at the sketches and tell me what you see, Rabbi."

"Lots of erasures. And the requisite shaggy hair and squinty eyes."

"Squinty *dark* eyes," Hollander said. "Apparently everyone in this world who squints has dark eyes."

"In answer to your question, the lady is weird."

"Leo said the lady seemed very, very fond of you."

Decker jerked his head up. "What did she tell him?"

"I don't know. Just repeating what he said. Anyway, I wouldn't worry *too* much about it. You know how rape survivors can be."

Decker looked him in the eye. "Then why'd you mention it, Mike?"

Hollander held out the palms of his hands. "No offense, Rabbi. Just that Leo placed a lot of emphasis on the *very, very* part of the *very, very* fond. If she's wacky, might be a good idea to get Marge or me involved—just to show the lady that you're not her personal public servant. Especially since she's so good-looking."

"What does good-looking have to do with it?"

"Hey, we're all human—"

"I don't believe you're telling me this shit, Hollander. I've been on the detail almost as long as you have."

"Deck, I'm not saying anything about your ability to handle Lilah Brecht or any other rape case. But you know as well as I do what a pain in the ass fruitcakes can be. Your wife is expecting and I'm just trying to save you grief. You wanna play hot dog, forget I said anything."

Hollander poured himself another cup of coffee and returned to his desk.

Decker rubbed his eyes. "Yeah, you're right. She could be grief. Both she and her mother."

"Miz Davida Eversong," Hollander said. "You ever see any of her films? Man, she was hot stuff in her heyday."

"She's still a good-looking woman. Well preserved."

"Natural or surgical?"

"I wouldn't know. Look, Mike, thanks for offering, but I can handle the case."

"Just trying to be helpful." Hollander ticked off another name on the list. "One Bobby Ray Gatten. Wonder what old Bobby Ray's been up to." He picked up the phone and dialed.

Decker sat down and broke open the seal on the Brecht evidence folder. There was a semen analysis, but it wasn't going to be useful until they had a suspect. There was also a chromosomal banding on the few foreign pubic hairs. It was interesting that none of the hairs was picked up from the combing or from her bagged clothes. All of them had been plucked from the sheet, along with half a dozen short, dark head hairs. No blood, no bits of foreign clothing. Print had come up dry as well.

Lilah's own fingernails and toenails were clean—all that meant was that she didn't or couldn't fight. Her vagina was free of semen. The envelope contained police photographs taken at the hospital. Again, Decker's wariness turned to pity when he saw her swollen eyes. There was also a picture of a splotchy bruise that ran down her right thigh.

Poor kid.

He heard Marge's voice and turned around.

"Hey there, Dunn."

"Hey there, Rabbi." She came over to him and looked down at the files he was reading. "Anything?"

"Hairs and semen. That's it."

"That's enough if we find a suspect."

"You have any luck?"

"I spoke to the kitchen help at the spa," Marge said. "They say they were home the night of the attack. Wives and friends verify it."

"And you think?"

"I think they were home. Hairs look like Hispanic hairs?"

"Head hairs were short and dark. Let's see . . ." Decker flipped through the notes. "Uh . . . under EM, they were straight hairs. Doesn't say anything else."

"Could be Hispanic." Marge pulled up a chair at Decker's desk and sat down. "But with straight hairs popping up, we're probably counting out blacks."

Decker took that in. "What do you have, Marge?"

"Eubie Jeffers, the tennis instructor at the spa, is black." Marge pulled up a chair, took off her shoes, and began to rub her feet. "He's a very light black, a very acculturated black. But he's black."

"Is he suspicious?"

"He was at the spa the night of the attack. He wasn't too keen on admitting it, either. He normally doesn't live on the premises so I asked him what he was doing there. Said he was with a patron giving her a private unscheduled lesson."

"A lesson in bedroom sports?"

"I think so."

"Don't tell me. She was married."

"So I won't tell you."

"Nice. Husband pays for his wife to get a little R and R and she goes off and boffs the hired help."

"Maybe wifey and spouse have an arrangement. I don't think Jeffers was worried about an irate husband gunning him down. I had the feeling he was more concerned about a lawsuit à la Mike Ness and Ms. Betham."

"Did you find out anything about that?"

"I went over the Betham case and it does seem frivolous. Apparently Ms. Betham has sued others for the same reason—her hairdresser, a former masseur. I don't think the suit's going anywhere. But that doesn't let Ness off the hook."

Decker nodded. "So Jeffers was doing some poking the night of the rape."

"Seems that way."

"Does he poke the guests routinely?"

"Pretty regularly, according to the other aero-

bic and weight instructor. Her name is Natanya
Frankel—a little squat thing. Claims she was once on
the Czech gymnastic team, but defected in 1985."

"Embellishing her past?" Decker asked.

"Probably, but I don't think that's significant.
What might be important was her past with Eubie
Jeffers. I think they were once an item."

"Does she seem like the vindictive type?"

"No. She was very matter of fact. Just told me that
Jeffers has a hard time keeping his pants zipped."

"That include Lilah?"

"That I don't know. Natanya was less forthcoming when it came to talking about her employer. I'll
say this—the people who work for Lilah seem to
like her. Natanya said Lilah's generous with time
and with money. Yet I never got the impression that
Lilah fraternizes with the hired help. It was clear
that Natanya was talking about her *boss*."

"Did the help have any comment on Davida Eversong?"

"Kitchen help told me she orders a lot of room
service and is a big tipper. They liked her just fine."

"What about Davida and this Jeffers guy? Get
the feeling that Jeffers's loose zipper might extend
to her?"

"Pete, Davida must be in her *seventies*."

"Margie, that don't mean a thing." Decker filled
her in on his interviews with Lilah and Davida.
"Mother and daughter are in fierce competition with
each other. If Lilah and Jeffers were getting it on, I
wouldn't put it past Davida to steal him away. Just
because the woman likes to exert power."

"What does it have to do with Lilah's rape?"

"I don't know. I'm just saying this case has the watermarks of an *inside* job for two reasons. One: We haven't turned up anyone remotely promising from the outside. And two: The family's weird."

"You said it." Marge told him about her morning encounter with Brecht and Merritt. "The boys almost came to blows. Ness and I managed to separate them. Merritt was livid until I told him what happened to Lilah. That took the starch out of his sails. He immediately left for the hospital."

"His surprise about Lilah's attack seemed genuine?"

"I think so." Marge made a face. "Are you thinking Merritt raped his own sister?"

"Maybe not directly. But how about this? According to Mom, Merritt and Brecht were always asking for handouts. Suppose one of them hired a couple of scumbags to do a jewel theft. Say the scumbags took the jewels, then they saw Lilah and decided to rape her as an afterthought."

"Then what about the memoirs?"

"Scumbags took the papers for the hell of it."

Marge shrugged. "Are Brecht and Merritt in financial straits?"

"I don't know. Let's run a check on them. And the other brother while we're at it."

"John Reed. I don't know a thing about him. For all we know, he could be a gentleman among swine."

Decker said, "Let's keep it simple for the moment, start with a bank check. See if anyone's in debt— both personal and business accounts. If one of the bros is in the hole for big bucks, a mill's worth of jewels is going to look mighty sweet."

"Agreed. I'll get to it."

"Now you said something about a first husband?"

Marge scanned her notes. "Perry Goldin. According to Merritt—who, granted, isn't exactly credible—the divorce wasn't friendly. I don't know who this Goldin is and where he was the night of the rape, but we'd better find out."

Decker nodded. "I'll do that."

Marge shook her head. "She *imaged* these guys, Pete?"

Decker shrugged helplessly.

"So the composites are bullshit," Marge stated.

Hollander piped in. "So are the IDs in the mug book. Not one of the guys she picked out was within a hundred miles of her house."

Decker nodded, wondering just what—if anything—Lilah was trying to hide. Could be just the natural confusion of the victim. Lots of victims imagined things because they were so frightened and addled.

Hollander said, "You want my unasked-for advice, forget about her *images*. Go back to good old-fashioned legwork and evidence."

"We'd better do it quickly," Decker said. "Don't want to displease Morrison."

"Did you finally talk to him?" Marge asked.

"Yep. He was all right. But the message was clear."

"Above all, no bad press," Hollander said.

"Preferably no press at all," Decker said.

🌱 13

The knock on the door was tentative, then firm.

Christ, what now?

"It's open."

Squeaking hinges followed by the door closing shut.

"You got a moment, Mike?"

Ness remained immobile, face covered by his forearm, legs stretched out, feet hanging over the side of the bed.

"Mike?"

"I hear you. I hope it's quick."

No response. Ness heard pacing. He lifted his arm from his eyes and propped himself up by his elbows. "Sit down, Jeffs. You're making me nervous."

Ness watched Eubie Jeffers drag a chair next to his bed and sit. Jeffs was still dressed in his tennis whites, his finger gripped around the handle of his racket. A thin sheen of sweat coated his café au lait face. He wiped his forehead with the back of his hand. Guy was as jumpy as griddled butter.

Ness's eyes went from Jeffs to his surroundings. The room was furnished with old leftover junk. The bedspread was torn, the dresser's paint was peeling, and the carpeting was thin. There was only one tiny window in the whole place and that looked out to the pool filter. Still, living wasn't costing him a dime. And after years of struggling, that was worth a lot.

"You gonna tell me what's bugging you or is this gonna be twenty questions?"

"You talk to the lady cop yet, Nessy?"

Ness broke into a smile. Jeffers's hazel eyes were oozing anxiety. He was biting his lower lip.

"She trip you up or something, Eubie?"

"That's bogus. I'd never hurt Lilah. I'd never hurt *anyone*. I'm a lover, not a fighter."

"You're a motherfucker, Jeffs. That's what you are."

Jeffers cast his eyes downward and moved onto the bed. "Can you say I was with you last night?"

"No."

"It's important."

Ness burst into laughter.

"Mike. *Please!*"

Ness sprang up and grabbed Jeffers's chin. "Fuck you, man! Hear what I'm saying? Fuck you!"

Jeffers felt tears in his eyes. "If it gets out, I'm gonna lose my *job*, Mike! I'm delinquent on the one credit card I have left. I'm two months behind on my rent. You gotta *help* me!"

Ness let go of Jeffers's chin with a shove. "You make me sick, know that?"

"*Please!* I swear this time will be the last."

"How many white women do you have to pork before you stop feeling black, Jeffs? Hundred's not enough? What do you need? A thousand? A mill—"

"*Mike.*"

"Jesus Christ!" Ness sat up cross-legged on the bed and shook his head. "Jeffs, I already told the lady detective that I was alone all night. Which I was. If I start changing my story, start trying to cover *your* ass, she's gonna look at me with ye olde jaundiced eye." He looked up. "Stop worrying. If you had nothing to do with Lilah, the cop'll leave you alone."

"I didn't have anything to do with Lilah, Mike. You know that. But what if the lady cop starts talking to the lady I *was* with? Mike, if that happens, the lady's gonna get mad. You know how secrecy is to the people who go here. It's part of the game. If she tells Lilah, Lilah will see it like last year all over again. This time for sure I'll lose my job—"

"How much she pay you for stud service?"

"You can have it all, Nessy."

"I didn't ask for it. I just asked how much she paid you?"

Jeffers paused. "Fifty."

"You lie like a politician, Jeffs. Try again."

"Two hundred."

"Two *hundred*?" Ness laughed. "Tell the lady I'll do her in blackface at half the price."

"*Mike*—"

"Why does the detective think you were with a lady last night?"

"I . . . she caught me off guard, Mike. I don't think as quick on my feet as you do. I knew I was coming off bad so I told her the truth. Or part of it. That I was here last night with a married woman giving her a private tennis lesson. I said I kept it secret 'cause I didn't want it getting out that I was giving the lady a discount."

"Why didn't you just say you were with Natanya?"

"I didn't think of her."

"But you thought of *me*? Christ, you're an idiot."

"Yeah, it was stupid. 'Cause immediately I saw that the detective didn't give a rat's ass about what I wanted. But she didn't press it. Then I thought . . . well, okay, I can't take back what I said. But suppose I was with you, too. Then you could cover for me and the detective wouldn't have to bother the woman."

"Exactly what do you want me to say, Jeffs?"

Jeffers took a deep breath and let it out slowly. "Thanks—"

"Hey, I didn't say I'd do it."

"I know, I know. Can you just . . . if the cop starts getting real nosy, can you just say I was with you from ten till two in the morning?"

"Too long."

"Okay, okay. Midnight till two?"

"I'll give you an hour. Midnight to one. And I didn't say anything to the detective because you were . . ." Ness sniffed several times.

"No, no, please don't mention that. I'm supposed to be clean. Lilah thinks I'm clean."

"You had a relapse. You and the woman were doping and that's why you didn't want to say her name— hey, that's why you came to *me*! You were so upset about your relapse, you had to talk to someone. And I didn't want to get you involved unless I had to. Hey, I'm a nice guy. I felt *bad* for you." Ness smiled. "After all, Jeffs, you're one sick dude and that ain't lyin'. You're an addict." He held up his fingers and began to tick them off. "A drug addict, an exercise addict, a sex addict—"

"*Mike*—"

"You've just got an addictive mentality."

Jeffers lowered his head. "Don't do this to me."

"Sob, sob, Jeffs. Betham is suing *my* butt, not yours. If you hadn't porked her in the first place, she wouldn't have gotten mad at me when I said no."

"I know, Nessy. Please don't rub it in."

"I told you she was a head case."

"You were right."

"Who'd you ball last night?"

"Patsy."

Ness smiled. "Little Patsy Levington. What is she? Five feet even?"

"They all look the same lying down."

There was a pause. Both men burst into hard laughter. They laughed until tears rolled down their eyes. Ness wiped his cheeks.

"So Patsy paid you two hundred, huh?"

"They all love to fuck a nigger, Nessy."

"You ain't much of a nigger, Jeffs."

"That's why I'm so perfect. Close enough to the real thing to be dangerous, but not so black so's I'm . . ."

"Menacing."

"That's it, man. Whitey don't like a menacing nigger."

"God, I can't believe she paid you two hundred."

"You're missing gold here. I keep telling you that."

"And I keep telling you that if you don't stop, you're gonna be out on your butt."

"I'm gonna stop—"

"Jeffs . . ."

"I am! I swear I am." Jeffers laid the racket in his lap. "I'm gonna find a rich white girl—"

"Yeah, right!"

"Hold on . . . I'm gonna find a rich white girl who *hates* her father."

"That's a possibility."

Jeffers smiled. "Get her to think of herself as real baaaad, 'cause she's fuckin' a black man."

"Go on."

"Maybe even knock her up . . ."

"There's a thing out there called abortion."

"Yeah, but I'm gonna pretend I want the baby." Jeffers smiled. "The product of our *luv*."

Ness laughed.

"Then . . ." Jeffers pointed his finger in the air. "Then I hit the old man up for cash. Bye-bye spa, bye-bye tennis. I'm outta here."

Ness grinned and patted the tennis instructor's shoulder. "Keep dreaming, Jeffs. It's good for the soul."

Jeffers gripped his racket and stood. "So we're all squared away?"

"Almost." Ness slowly rose off the bed, smiled, and unbuckled Jeffers's belt. "You owe me, you know."

"I know."

"You haven't even repaid me for Betham yet."

"I know."

"When Lilah asked, I never said a word—"

"I said I know!"

"No need to shout, Jeffs. Just setting the record straight."

"When I score big, Mike, you'll get half. I swear it. Half off the top."

"No offense, Jeffs, but I'm not holding my breath." Ness pulled Jeffers's belt from the loops. Inside the money compartment was a fold of twenties. Two hundred even. Ness counted out five bills and stuffed them in his pocket. He placed the rest of the cash, along with the belt, into Jeffers's palm. "Know what I'd do if I were you, Eub?"

"What?"

"I'd take a ten and buy a single long-stemmed red rose for Patsy. She's got another week here. Now, I'd say ten bucks on a rose is a very good investment for the future."

Jeffers relooped his belt around his waist and stowed the leftover twenties back in the compartment.

"Good idea?" Ness asked.

"Good idea," Jeffers answered.

Decker swung his legs over the bed and sat up. A bad night's sleep and it was slow going the next morning. Too bad people weren't batteries because a jump start would have been nice.

The shower helped some; so did the sting of the aftershave. As he dressed, he thought about Rina. She was always energetic, but now she'd progressed into a superhuman *industrious* phase. She hadn't only prepared a farmer-sized breakfast but had cooked the meal at five-thirty A.M., humming as she stirred and mixed and fried. At that hour, her only company had been the dog, the birds, and a few mourning doves. Half asleep, he conjured up a mental picture of her outfitted in a simple smock covered by an apron, dancing as she moved from chore to chore, talking to the animals—a pregnant Cinderella. He felt bad he wasn't more of a Prince Charming.

Towel-drying his hair, he walked into the kitchen just as the phone rang. Rina beat him to it.

"Hello," she sang into the mouthpiece.

There was a pause, followed by a husky female voice.

"May I speak to Peter, please?"

Decker saw Rina's smile fade.

The husky voice said, "This is Peter Decker's residence, isn't it?"

"Yes, it is," Rina answered. "Who is this, please?"

"Lilah Brecht."

Decker saw Rina's eyes widen.

"Who is it?" Decker asked.

"Lilah Brecht." Rina put her hand over the mouthpiece. "Why is she calling you?"

"Can I have the phone, Rina?"

Reluctantly, Rina handed him the receiver.

Decker smiled at his wife and said, "This is Decker. How'd you get my home phone number, Ms. Brecht?"

"Lilah."

"How'd you get my number?"

"Peter, I'm very sorry to bother you at home. I tried calling the station . . . I am sorry."

He rolled his tongue in his cheeks, glancing at Rina who now seemed more perplexed than angry. "What can I do for you?"

"I need to talk to you, Peter."

"Fine. I'm all ears."

"I'd like to speak with you in person."

"All right. Why don't you come to the station house around eleven."

"If it's all the same to you, could you drop by my ranch around eleven?"

Decker felt his jaw tighten as his eyes drifted back to Rina's face.

"Don't worry, I'm leaving," she said.

"Wait!" Decker called out.

"Pardon."

"Hold on, Lilah." His voice was stronger than he had intended. He placed his hand over the mouthpiece and whispered, "I didn't ask you to leave."

"You have that *look* on your face."

"What look?"

"The 'she's going to overhear something' look."

"Rina—"

"Forget it, Peter. I'm going to wake the boys." She stomped out of the room.

He glanced at the clock. Seven-oh-three and he felt a headache coming on. He returned his attention to the call. "Lilah, I hope to get a good handle on your case very soon. I realize you've been through hell—"

"I didn't sleep at all last night. I didn't dare sleep in . . . the room. It's still a mess and . . . I slept in the guest bedroom, but I kept waking up every five minutes . . . in a cold sweat. Finally, I couldn't take it anymore so I called Freddy down at four in the morning. He bunked out on the couch. I . . . I just didn't think it would be so horrible, Peter. And now . . ." She took a deep breath. "What . . . what they did was such a horrible invasion for anyone, but it's especially dreadful for me. I have a business to run, Peter. I have to face people and be healthy and happy and . . ."

She erupted into tears.

Decker waited a beat. "I know this is a terrible time for you. And I'm sorry—"

"I know you are." Her voice became soothing and seductive. "I can feel your pain through the phone wire."

Mike Hollander's words shot through Decker's throbbing head. *With an emphasis on the* very, very *part*. Point of fact was, the woman was beautiful and in pain—a dangerous combination.

"Lilah, I don't want this to sound harsh, but if we're going to work together, we need to set a few ground rules. One, you don't call me at home for any reason—"

"Afraid I'll upset the little woman?"

Above all, Deck, you're a professional.

"*If* you have to get in touch with me, you call the station house and they'll call me. Do we have an understanding here?"

"Are you coming out to the ranch or not?"

"I'll come this one time."

"Oh, Peter, thank—"

"I know it's been hard for you and I'll do it this one time. But after this one time, if you need to talk to me, if you just want to *talk* to me, you call me at the station. Call me *ten* times if you want, but call the sta—"

"You *flatter* yourself, Peter."

"Because I, like you, don't want my business intruding upon my personal life."

"Considering my circumstances, I hardly consider my call an *intrusion*."

"If you don't feel you can adhere to the ground rules, Lilah, I'll be happy to assign the case to another detective—"

Decker heard the receiver slam and then a dial tone. Slowly, he hung up the phone.

"You okay, Dad?"

Decker turned around. "Morning, Sammy." He went over and kissed the top of the boy's head. "You're looking better."

"I feel a *lot* better."

"Great." Decker gave him a hug. "Your mother made a huge breakfast. What would you like? Eggs? Toast? Pancakes and syrup?"

"Eema's ticked off."

"Yeah, I think she is."

"She's mad at you?"

"I think so."

"Anything I can do?"

"No. It will work itself out."

Jacob walked into the kitchen, his eyes still glazed with sleep. His black hair was full of cowlicks, a yarmulke resting on the left side of his head. He was wearing his school uniform, but the blue shirt was only partially tucked inside the navy slacks. Fringes from his *tzitzit*—a religious garment worn under his shirt—peeked out, fanning over his hips.

"Hi," he croaked.

"Morning, Jake." Decker put his arm around his younger stepson. "Sleep okay?"

"Yeah."

"Can I get you something to eat?"

"Just a bowl of cereal."

"I'll make it," Sammy said to Decker. "You can go talk to Eema."

"I can make my own cereal," Jacob said. "Why are you talking to Eema, Pete—uh, Dad. I can call you Dad, too, right?"

"Of course. I'm thrilled that you want to."

Jacob sloughed off the sentimentality. "Is Eema mad at you or something?"

"Something," Decker said.

"Yeah, she seemed a little uptight this morning. She sure gets mad a lot. That's 'cause of all the hormones, right?"

"Sometimes. And sometimes she has regular reasons to get mad."

"I wish she'd just have the baby already," Jacob said. "First it was the barfing. Now it's her getting mad and crying for no real reason. Is that normal?"

"Very normal," Decker assured him.

Jacob just shook his head and poured some Fruit Crunches into a bowl. "Is she gonna get upset that I'm eating sugar cereal and not the healthy stuff?"

"Why don't you take a pancake?" Decker suggested.

"Eema made pancakes on a *school* morning?" Jacob pushed the bowl aside. "That's not normal, either. But at least, that's good."

"If you boys don't need me, maybe I will have a word with your mother."

"Do we have any syrup?"

"It's on the table, Yonkel."

Jacob turned to Sam. "You ever remember Eema making pancakes on a school day?"

"I think once or twice."

"When?"

"I don't know. But I think she did."

"I don't remember it."

"Maybe it was on my birthday," Sammy said.

"I don't remember."

"Maybe it was on your birthday."

"My birthday's in the summer. There's no school in the summer."

Decker excused himself, knowing the boys were too involved in pancake conversation to hear him leave. He found Rina in the master bedroom, ripping the sheets and pillow cases off their California King.

"Need help?"

"No."

"Can you stop a moment?"

"Dirty laundry waits for no man."

"Please?"

Rina stopped moving and hugged a caseless pillow. "How did *Lilah* get our phone number?"

Decker ignored her tone. "I don't know."

"Did you tell her not to call here?"

"Of course I told her not to call here!"

"Did you also tell her not to call you Peter?"

"I can't help what she calls me."

"But you can admonish her when she does it."

"Rina, she's strictly business. She's one of my cases, for God's sake. I wouldn't give my home number to one of my cases."

"You gave it to me!"

"Wait a minute—"

"And I certainly didn't call you *Peter* right away, either." She walked out of their bedroom and started attacking the beds in the boys' room. Decker followed.

"That's not fair."

"It may not be fair, but it's accurate!"

"There's a big difference, Rina. I wasn't *married* when I gave you my number."

"Married or not, I'm sure asking out your cases is considered unprofessional!"

"I didn't ask anyone out!"

"I bet I wasn't even the *first* case where you gave out your home phone number."

"Rina—"

"Well, *was* I the first?"

The mallet inside his head was going full force. "You may not have been the first." He smiled boyishly. "But you were the last."

There was a moment of silence. Rina sank down on the bed. Decker sat beside her.

"What are we fighting about?" he said.

"We're fighting about how your cases shouldn't be calling you up at home and invading our privacy!"

"Agreed."

"And your cases shouldn't be calling you by your first name."

"She's not the only case who calls me by my first name."

"But she's no doubt the prettiest."

Bingo! Well, ain't that a kick in the head.

"Darlin', can I be honest with you?"

"Sure, Peter, break a trend."

"Rina . . ."

"Sorry."

Decker smiled. "I think you're jealous."

"*What?*"

"And I'm overjoyed about it."

"I'm not *jealous*. I'm *angry*! And you should be, too. You certainly have nothing to feel overjoyed about."

"I don't know about that." Decker paused. "Rina, I think you're the most beautiful woman on this planet—"

"I'm as fat as a cow."

"You're not fat, you're *pregnant*—"

"Oh *spare* me."

"I can tell the difference and so can everyone else. Darlin', I see *teenagers* eye you hungrily. Like you're my . . . my unwedded daughter who got herself into trouble. Man, those horny little bugs would just love to catch a piece of that trouble. As far as the guys *my* age, that's not even worth talking about. The whole squad room gets sweaty palms whenever you walk in."

"That's simply *ridiculous*."

"Except for Marge and Kate. You don't have any effect on them. Ellen I'm not so sure."

"Peter, you're talking nonsense."

"Rina, all I'm saying is that after being with you for two and a half years, always feeling like we're Beauty and the Beast, it's nice to see how much you like me."

Rina took his hand. "Somehow, I suspect I'm being manipulated."

Decker laughed.

"You told *Lilah* not to call here?"

"Yep. Matter of fact, I told her if she wasn't comfortable with that, I'd be happy to assign her to another detective."

"You told her that?"

"Yep."

"What'd she say?"

"She hung up on me."

Rina smiled. "She did?"

"Yep."

"Well . . ." She patted his hand. "I know how you feel about your unsolved cases, Peter. You can call her back and make nice."

"Nah, it's fine. She wanted to tell me something in person. I'm supposed to meet her at her ranch at eleven. I'll show up and see what kind of reception I get. If she acts inappropriate, I'll pass her to Marge."

"You're going out to her ranch? To her *home*?"

"Yes, Rina, I am."

"Fine." She withdrew her hand. "I won't tell you how to do your job."

"Thank you."

Rina checked her watch. "You'd better get going if you're going to take the boys to school."

"We're friends again?"

"I'll think about it." Rina leaned over and kissed his cheek. "Course we're friends. Go."

"Should I come home for lunch?"

"If it's late—around one, one-thirty."

"Not a problem, my dear." Decker stood. "Are you going to be home this morning?"

"No. The school called and asked if I'd sub-teach the seventh-grade girls. Why?"

"It's not urgent. But whenever you get a chance, call up the phone company and get our number changed."

"Just in case?"

"Just in case."

14

Still wearing his full-length white coat from morning rounds, Kingston Merritt checked in with his girls at the front office.

No messages from the bitch. God, how he hated that woman. Hated her and loved her at the same time. Why? Merritt wondered. Why did she have that kind of power over him? She neglected him as a young child, criticized him mercilessly the few times she was around. She was cruel and heartless. Except . . . *except* on those *rare* occasions when she showed her other side—the fun-loving woman with a laugh as light as a summer's breeze. Taking him to the circus, squeezing his hand, introducing him to the lion tamer after the show was over. He had felt so special. . . .

But this was the final straw. She could just go to hell. No doubt, it was *her* fault Lilah was hurt. It was her fault that Lilah was estranged from him in the first place.

He smiled at his ladies, made chitchat as one of them brought him coffee, another brought the day's appointments. A heavy load—forty names, roughly two-thirds routine pelvics. There was a star after

213

Mrs. Lewis's name—the cervical carcinoma *in situ* picked up on a routine Pap. She'd require extra consultation time. He'd check her into the hospital tonight, do the surgery at seven tomorrow after his six A.M. D and C. Mrs. Arlin was in for her three-month fibroid check, as was Mrs. Bennington. Three six-week postpartum checks. The rest were OB cases, five of those evals for termination. One of the candidates was already five months gravid. A termination in the second trimester, much more difficult because of the advanced development of the fetus. It was good she'd come to him.

He stuffed the schedule into his coat pocket and took the coffee into the privacy of his office. A large picture window afforded him a view of the Palos Verdes peninsula, the steely ocean a reflection of the overcast sky. He sat at his desk, extracted a bottle of bourbon from a locked drawer, and laced his drink with a single shot. Then he sat back in his chair and sipped his morning brew. The cup was half empty when his private line rang. He waited a beat, then picked it up.

"Hello, Mother. Nice of you to return my twenty calls."

"Where the hell were you yesterday?"

"Where the hell was *I*? Where the hell were *you*?"

"Talking to the police—"

"What happened to *Lilah*, Mother? I tried to see her yesterday, but she had already checked out of the hospital."

"How'd you find out about Lilah?"

"I met up with a detective at the spa—"

"You were at the *spa*?"

"Yes, I was . . . or didn't Frederick tell you."

There was a long pause over the line.

Merritt said, "I suppose Frederick didn't tell you."

Davida said, "I suppose Frederick and I are due for a little chat."

"Mother, the detective told me Lilah had been *attacked*. Tell me what happened."

"Funny, I was going to ask you that very question."

Feeling his face go hot, Merritt slammed down the receiver. A couple of beats later the private line rang again. He picked up the handpiece.

"That was a repulsive, *vile* insinuation, Mother."

"Kingston, I wasn't trying to be nasty. We're on the same side, for God's sake! I only meant that maybe you know what happened because you talked to the police."

"I don't know a thing because I left to see Lilah. And she was gone. So why don't you tell me what happened. Was Lilah attacked?"

There was a long pause. Merritt heard the drumming of fingers over the line.

"I've got a busy schedule, Mother. Is that true or not?"

"I think so."

"You *think*?"

"Well, Lilah is prone to fits of fantasy—"

"The detective told me she'd been *beaten*, for God's sake! How could she *fantasize* about that?"

"She had a few bruises. Nothing serious."

"I want to see her."

"Kingston, that's *not* a good idea—"

"Mother, I demand to see her! Despite what she

thinks, I still care for her very deeply. If she needs medical assistance, I have pull with the finest physicians in the city. God only knows how many of them owe me for discreetly getting their daughters out of sticky situations."

"Freddy's got everything under control."

"Freddy? You're letting *Freddy* handle this situation? All of a sudden, you're trusting Freddy?"

"It's not me, it's Lilah. *She* trusts—"

"Freddy?" Merritt let go a deep laugh. "Fine, Mother. You just let Freddy handle Lilah as well as *all* your situations."

"King, I know you two hate each other—"

"Of course you know. You were the one who orchestrated our hatred."

"I did not!"

"Mother, you turned Frederick against me—always comparing him to me to his detriment."

"You were smarter. I was just being honest."

"You turned him into a petty, jealous person—a shell of a human being. And as a result, he turned Lilah against me."

"I did the best I could as a mother. No one's perfect. Stop acting like a spoiled child."

"Mother, I can act however I feel like acting. At the moment, it's you who need me. Now listen closely. I'm going to see Lilah, and furthermore, you're going to arrange it. You're going to explain to Lilah how much I care about her and how much I want to help. *You*, Mother, are going to convince her to see me."

"Lilah has a mind of her own, King."

"I'm sure you can be persuasive. You're always

quite persuasive when there's something in it for you. Everything—*everything* will be put on hold until I see Lilah. Do we have an understanding?"

Again fingers drummed across the telephone wire.

"I'm hanging up, Mother."

"King, let's talk this—"

"Everything's on *hold* until I can see her. Am I making myself clear?"

"Not to worry, King. You're making yourself quite clear."

The door opened a crack, a small Spanish voice asking who was there. Decker said who it was and the door opened all the way. To Decker, the maid was still shaken. But she told him she was doing better. She led him through a spotless kitchen to the back door and told him Lilah was outside in the stable, grooming her horses. That seemed like a healthy thing for her to be doing. Painstaking tasks occupied the brain, preventing morbid thoughts from taking over. He thanked Mercedes and walked over to the stalls, but was blocked at the entrance.

"Hello, Mr. Totes," Decker said. "Lilah asked me to come down and talk to her."

"It's okay, Carl," Lilah called out. "He can come in."

The skinny man didn't move right away but stayed fixed in a military position—arms crossed, legs apart, chest extended, and brow furrowed over distrusting eyes. Totes was obliged to move out of the way. But he took his good, sweet time about it.

Decker walked inside the stable, finding Lilah with Apollo—the palomino that Totes had been riding that first day. She was combing the horse's golden mane, talking sweetly in his ear as she smoothed out the tangles. The animal had on reins and bit, but no saddle. Lilah's garb was part good ole girl, part vamp. She wore skintight jeans tucked into two-tone elephant-hide boots, and her chest was wrapped in a black tube top. Somehow she pulled the whole thing off without looking cheap. She didn't acknowledge his presence and Decker knew she was toying with him. But he wasn't bothered by the silence. There was something serene about watching one golden-haired beauty groom another. Finally, Lilah patted the horse's neck and turned to him. Her face was still bruised but healing nicely.

"I was about to go for a ride, Peter. See if I can still function. Please join me."

"A ride?"

"A ride will relax me. And when I'm relaxed, my power is more focused. In the long run, it will benefit both of us. And don't be frightened by the horses, Peter. They're very well trained."

Lilah might know his home phone number, but she certainly didn't know jack about his hobbies—all six of them sitting in his own stable. He wasn't about to tell her anything personal. Slipping his hands in his pocket, he thought: no problem, *amiga*. He could play the slick as easily as the hick.

"I'm not exactly dressed for the occasion, Miss Brecht."

She smiled seductively. "You know, Peter, I've noticed that when you get nervous, you call me Miss Brecht. Don't worry so much."

Outwardly, Decker was impassive, but internally

he was wired—angry and sexually charged at the same time. He felt like a jerk but couldn't turn around and walk away without losing face.

Just cut the losses, Deck. Ride the damn horse and get out of her way.

"I've got about forty-five minutes, Lilah. You want to spend it riding, it's fine with me. But I'm not coming out here again."

"Oh, yes, the *ground* rules." She tossed her hair over her shoulder, ran her fingers over her cheeks. "I tried to cover the . . . bruises with makeup. Can you tell?"

Decker appraised her beautiful face and told her she looked fine. Which was the truth. There was still some bluing underneath her eyes. Other than that, she appeared good enough for the cover of *Vogue* . . . or *Playboy*. He felt his face go hot. If she noticed his embarrassment, she didn't remark on it.

Lilah said, "Carl, saddle up High Time for Sergeant Decker."

"Which one's that?" Decker asked.

"The Appaloosa. The spotted horse, Peter. You'd better take your jacket off. It's hot. You can ride shirtless if you want."

"No, thanks."

"That's right, you're a redhead. You'll burn rather than tan. I don't see why Mother pictured you as a cowboy. Redheads can't be cowboys."

"Your mother told you about our little chat?"

"No. Just that she thought you'd make a marvelous cowboy. Much better than a detective. Frankly, I don't see you as either one."

Decker shrugged and looked away. He took his

jacket off and draped it over a saddle peg, watching Totes throw a western saddle on High Time. Totes's face wasn't registering any hostility; it wasn't registering much of anything. He was just doing his job with trained efficiency. When the stable hand was done, Decker walked over to the horse and eyed him carefully.

"She doesn't bite, Peter," Lilah said. "Just don't sneak up behind her." She turned to Totes. "Carl, walk High Time out and show Sergeant Decker how to mount."

His mounting was fine, thank you very much. But he followed Totes out and didn't say anything.

Totes touched the stirrup. "Put one foot in here. Then put your other leg all the way over the horse and just set up. You don't gotta do nothin' else but set. You ken hold the reins but don't go pullin' on them. Horse'll follow the Miss. You start pullin' the reins, you gonna confuse her."

"Got it," Decker said.

Totes walked away unceremoniously. Decker mounted as the horse stood passively, her tail swatting at flies. Lilah came up to his left. He noticed she seemed tight and asked her if she was in pain. She told him she was much better—at least physically—tugged on High Time's bit and the two of them were off. She rode sans saddle, sitting on some kind of Indian blanket.

Immediately, he felt the sun burning down on his scalp. Sweat filled his brow, his cheeks, and his armpits. The sky was smogless blue, the air stagnant and filled with flies and gnats and other things that buzzed. The mountaintops seemed to shimmer in the heat. About a minute into the ride, he realized he was actually grateful for this turn of events. Riding not only made him feel good, it made him feel in control.

Lilah said, "Thank you for accommodating me."

"This one time."

"Ye olde ground rules." Lilah lowered her head. "I'm sorry if I upset your wife."

Decker didn't answer her. Instead, he rolled up his sleeves and took out a pen and notepad.

"I don't believe it!" Lilah said. "You can't take *notes* and ride at the same time."

"Hey, Carl said I wasn't supposed to do anything except sit on the horse. Besides, I've got an excellent sense of balance."

"Your writing is going to look like scribbling."

"It does anyway."

"Don't you ever stop working?"

"Are you going to tell me why I'm here?" Decker said.

Lilah slowed. "Can you give me a minute to work up to it?"

Decker looked at his watch. "We're down to thirty-five minutes, Lilah."

"You're *impossible*!"

"Why aren't you riding with a saddle?"

She turned and gave him a closed-mouth smile. "I like the connection with my animals . . . the feeling of their muscles working."

Decker didn't react. He never rode bareback, believing that even the most docile of horses were still animals. Saddles gave the needed support in rare emergencies.

They rode another five minutes without speaking. Her ranch was much bigger than he had remembered. Or maybe he just hadn't seen the whole spread. Like his, it was backed by the San Gabriel Mountains, but she had much more. A dusty path divided the property into halves, the trail disappearing into a thick copse of eucalyptus trees about three hundred feet ahead. On his immediate right were the fruit groves, behind them another structure that could have been a guesthouse. On the left was the garden—at least an acre's worth of leafy vegetation.

"That's one heck of a plot," Decker said.

"I use it commercially."

"How so?"

"Every single fruit and vegetable served at the spa is grown in that garden or in one of my greenhouses. It's the only way to get quality control."

"I don't see any greenhouses."

"They're not the large prefab ones. I've several small greenhouses tucked into sunny locations. All of them are climate-controlled and pesticide-free. I grow out-of-season and exotic vegetables—just a few to tease the palate. Give my guests something memorable. I also grow tropical flowers—mainly orchids and bromeliads. They make lovely table settings for the spa's dining room."

"You've got a regular wholesale nursery here."

"My clientele has come to expect a certain style."

"It seems like an awful lot of vegetables for the spa's kitchen."

"Nothing goes to waste."

They rode in silence for a few minutes.

"Well, that was a nice diversion," Decker said. "You want to tell me what's on your mind? We're down to twenty minutes."

"Don't push me."

"Up to you—"

"Stop it!" she screamed. "Stop it! *Stop it!*"

More silence. The hum in the air suddenly seemed magnified until Apollo brayed and reared.

"What's wrong with him?" Decker asked.

"It's nothing." Lilah pulled back and forth on the reins. "My shouting upset him. He's very sensitive."

She brought the horse under control.

"What did you want to tell me, Lilah?" Decker said.

"I'm too upset."

"Lilah, I haven't got all day. If you feel I'm pushing you, I'll call it quits right now."

"Have it your way!" she said. "Call it quits!"

Peachy, he thought. What a colossal waste of time. He yanked on the reins and turned the horse in the direction of the stable. He kicked the Appaloosa's flanks and High Time broke into a canter. This time, Lilah followed him.

"You know how to *ride*!"

Decker didn't answer.

"Why did you play stupid if you knew how to ride?"

"How about if I ask the questions, Miss Brecht?" He broke away from her and with a swift set of pulls on the reins forced the animal to reverse directions, racing toward the eucalyptus grove. Galloping along the shaded trails, he wove among tree trunks as if he were barrel racing. Lilah tried to follow him.

Apollo was quick—no doubt the animal was stock palomino—but she simply wasn't skilled enough to keep up with him. He left her behind in a mist of dust. High Time rounded each bend as if she had power steering—a horse Decker wouldn't have minded owning. A few minutes later, he slowed and waited for Lilah to catch up with him. He sat back and breathed in the scent of menthol.

"You're *great*!" she said, breathlessly.

"Might as well get a decent ride out of this trip."

Apollo reared again, stretching his forelegs so high he was almost vertical.

"Lean forward, Lilah—"

"I know how to handle my own horse!"

But her voice was shaky. The palomino continued to balance on his hind legs, kicking the branches of the tall trees as he protested.

"You're still too upright. You're going to fall backward."

"I'm trying. It's not that easy bareback."

"Use your thighs," Decker instructed. "Squeeze as hard as you can."

"I'm doing that!"

"Now tighten the reins and give him a kick in the flanks. That should send him forward."

"I'm trying, dammit! He's being obstinate!"

Decker stood on his stirrups, edged High Time closer to the agitated horse, dodging steel-hooved punches. Lilah managed to maintain balance, as Decker squeezed in front of the animal. He leaned over, grabbed Apollo's bit and gave it a sharp tug, forcing the horse forward. Finally settling on all fours, Apollo kicked up dirt and leaves, then paced in circles. Lilah took the reins and once again brought him under control.

"He's really upset about something," Decker said. "Let's go back."

"I'm ready to talk to you now."

"Make it quick. I don't like the way your horse is acting."

"He senses my anxiety."

"Then let's switch horses. I'm not anxious."

"He'll be fine. Better than *I'll* be. You see, all last night and every waking minute today, I . . . I've had this dreadful sense that something terrible is going to happen. Something even more horrible than what has already happened. I'm scared out of my wits."

"Lilah, I know you're not going to believe this, but it's normal to feel that way. There'd be something wrong with you if you didn't feel frightened."

"No, no, it's not ordinary fear, Peter. I know because I feel that, too. This . . . this psychic communication is something different. A prophecy. I am a prophetess and am capable of receiving deep, underworld vibrations. They're straight out of hell. It's just horrifying!" She started to tremble. "Don't you see? It's a *warning*! Somehow, *you* must protect me against these demons!"

Had the rape terrified her to the point of hallucinations? Decker had seen assaults drive normal people literally out of their minds. Lilah was acting like one of them.

"Lilah, I'm going to work really hard to solve your case, but I can't help you ward off your individual demons. If you think someone's out to get you—and I can't say I blame you for feeling that way—hire a bodyguard. Your mother probably knows someone. If not, I'll give you a recommendation."

"You don't *understand*," she implored.

"Lilah—"

"It's bad *karma*!" Tears streamed down her cheek. "A terrifying sense of *doom*! Someone *is* out to get me, Peter. The theft was more than a desire to steal my father's memoirs. It was a desire to rip away everything dear to me. It's a personal vendetta against *me*!"

"That's why a bodyguard—"

"No, it won't help. Someone's going to come back and finish me off! My powers tell me this as fact! I'm so *frightened*!"

Apollo reared up once again, forelegs stretching toward the sun. For a moment, he did a two-foot foxtrot, flanks speckled by beams streaking through the branches, hundreds of golden dots bouncing off his honey-colored coat. Then a thousand pounds' worth of weight came crashing down—dirt, twigs, and leaves spewing in their faces.

The palomino reared and reared again. Lilah had turned ghastly white as she attempted to hold on. Decker inched closer, but powerful, flailing limbs acted as an effective barrier. Apollo's last motion was a perfect capriole as the horse leaped into the air, hind legs extended, pushing forward, forelegs tucked under.

He landed clumsily, momentarily losing his footing as his left hind leg caught on a surface tree root, stumbling but not falling. Lilah's arms encircled the animal's throat, her grip loosening with each jerk of the horse's head. She had slid up toward his neck and was sitting on the horse's withers. The blanket on his back had tumbled to the ground. Decker moved High Time closer, his extended arm within inches of Apollo's reins. Just as he was about to grab them, Apollo bolted.

Decker dug into High Time's belly and pushed forward at full speed, leaning his body horizontal to the ground, cursing as he maneuvered the Appaloosa around the trees, feeling the razor's edge of low-lying boughs abrade his back. Adrenaline shot through his body, his heart hammering against his chest, his hands shaking. But he was steady enough to guide his horse at strategic moments—a skill that avoided turning him into jelly.

Apollo was charging as if possessed, racing erratically through the trees, clearing branches and dense trunks by inches, tearing forth beyond his normal capacity. Several times, the horse jumped forward for no reason, nearly decapitating Lilah with a bough. She held tightly, hair flying through the jet stream. Decker forced High Time faster, masses of grit filling his mouth and eyes. He spit, rubbed his eyes on his shoulder, and rode harder, using every single aching muscle to urge the horse on.

The palomino had a six-foot jump on him. Pushing the Appaloosa, Decker managed to keep pace. Lilah's horse couldn't possibly continue at that heart-straining speed. Hopefully the goddamn animal would slow down before he killed her with his kamikaze mission.

High Time was galloping without so much as a

slip of the hoof. Good old Aps, nothing upset their footing. But each time the horse maneuvered a particularly difficult path, he was forced to sacrifice speed. Apollo kept widening the distance. Lilah had lost any ounce of control. The palomino was racing to his own evil drummer.

Decker cursed his sense of smugness. Lilah's evil vibrations were no longer a crazy fantasy but a terrifying reality. He could feel sweat drenching his clothes, dripping off his forehead as he pressed forward. He could feel the horror gripping his body. Yet he knew his fear couldn't possibly be as strong as Lilah's. As fast as he was riding, Decker *knew* he had control: that he could stop at any moment. Lilah had no such comfort as the palomino kept running at a maniacal pace. If only he could catch up to the sucker—a herculean task, but he was determined not to fail. He bunched his shoulders, dug deep into High Time's flanks, and drove the Appaloosa to her max.

Trees whizzed by as the horses continued at their frenetic pace. The branches above split his airstream, blowing wind onto the back of his wet neck. Swooshing sounds pounded in his ears, dirt sprayed his eyes. A kaleidoscope of nature's colors raced past him. Greens, rusts, browns, objects losing their form, relegated to a blur. Everything around him was a deadly weapon—a tree, a branch, a fence, the telephone pole that popped out of nowhere. Even a small clod of dirt could cause the horses to stumble, throwing them onto the ground at fifty miles per hour.

Ahead was a four-foot hedge running across the path—a natural hurdle, but you didn't do jumps at this kind of speed. There was no place to circumvent the shrubbery. Not that he had any choice. Where Apollo went, so did he. The palomino made the leap but shaved the bush's top with his hooves. The Appaloosa followed suit, clearing the bush completely and gaining a little distance from the leap. The palomino regained his footing and sprinted forward.

But not quite as fast as before.

Hope flooded Decker's body. He knew he was gaining ground. He could feel the palomino's tailwind in his face.

Harder!

Creeping up on the left side, inching closer and closer. Hooves clopping against the dry, dusty ground. Dirt blinding his sight. Blinking it out. Blinking and blinking!

Closer!

The clumps of trees grew thinner, the foliage turned sparse. The sun became brighter and hotter as the horses came out of the protective shade of the woodlands. A few moments later, Decker was elated to see unencumbered land straight ahead. As the palomino broke toward open space, Decker felt his head throb, hope quashed as mountains, previously obscured by the treetops, suddenly jumped into view. An indestructible wall of granite closing in on them. Lilah screamed, her wails echoing as the rocky hillside grew in height and mass. Only minutes left . . .

Harder and harder!

Inches behind Apollo's flanks, up to his flanks, up to his belly. The animals, finally neck and neck, nose and nose, the bodies so close they seemed harnessed together. Each step a choreographed death-defying dance, hooves missing each other by fractions of an inch.

Decker pulled ahead while looking backward. Lilah's complexion was gray, arms clamped around the neck of the palomino.

The mountains coming upon them with horrific clarity!

Now or never. He screamed as loud as he could:

"Lilah, jump to me on the count of three!"

"You won't catch me! You won't catch me!"

"There's no fucking choice! One! Two! Three!"

Lilah remained frozen and wide-eyed.

"Jump—"

"I can't!"

"Jump now!"

"I—"

"Goddamn it, Lilah! Jump! *Jump! JUMP!*"

She catapulted to the left as Decker's arm snaked around her waist and squeezed her tightly. He yanked the reins to the right, clearing the mountainside by at least six feet, but was still close enough to catch the blood spatter as the palomino crashed headfirst into stone.

🖎 15

It was only a horse . . .

Little comfort when looking at remains. The poor thing's head had been smashed to pulp, yet its coat was still soaked with sweat from its run.

Decker removed the camera from around his neck. He thought about calling down a police photographer but couldn't justify the expense in his mind. It wasn't a person, it was a horse. And as far as the case went, was this really an attempted murder or merely a domesticated animal going berserk? Regardless of what it was, the ordeal had to have reinforced Lilah's sense of *omniscience*. The incident began to make Decker wonder as well.

Lilah as a prophetess of doom . . . what would Rabbi Schulman say about that?

He rolled up his sleeves and snapped a full body shot, bent down and took some close-ups—the impact point of animal versus stone. He focused on the blood-spattered ground. The sun was strong and he had to shield his eyes from the glare given off by the white rocks. Heat waves shimmied up from the ground, insects hummed in his face. He batted them away and thought about Carl Totes.

The ranch hand knew Lilah's habits, knew which of the six horses she was likely to ride. He had access, he could easily obtain means—some drug to alter the horse's behavior. What could possibly be his motive? If Lilah were dead, his days at the ranch would be numbered. Decker couldn't imagine any of the clan keeping him on. He couldn't imagine any one of the greedy bunch holding the ranch, period. They impressed Decker as the "liquidate the assets just as soon as the body's buried" kind.

Maybe Totes had been hired by someone to kill his boss. But it was damn near impossible to picture Totes lifting a finger against Lilah. His affection for her was nothing short of idol worship. Decker thought about the look on Totes's face when he'd brought Lilah back to the stables. As he explained what had happened, Totes's nutmeg skin had blanched, a genuine expression of shock and fear.

Despite all that, Decker wasn't quite ready to proclaim the ranch hand innocent. He was the only one—besides Lilah—who'd been around this morning. Of course, someone could have sneaked in and done the dirty work. But Totes was never far from the stables—hell, he lived in one of the stalls. Surely he would have noticed a trespasser.

Decker checked his watch. Two hours since the horse did a kamikaze, but the heat was already doing a number on the animal's body. He took another full-body shot.

Totes and Lilah . . .

Lilah. Lilah monkeying with her own horse?

But why?

For attention . . . maybe even his attention. Maybe she'd liked being rescued the first time. Maybe this was a weak attempt to relive it.

Except that she didn't know he could ride. And she had been legitimately terrified.

Decker heard sneakers scraping against the dirt and stood. Some kid was running toward him at full speed.

Swell. Someone new to muck up the works.

The kid turned out to be a man in his twenties. He stopped short, almost crashing into the face of the mountain, not the least bit winded by a sprint in hundred-degree heat. He was sweated up but smelled minty fresh. His eyes went to the dead horse.

"My God, what *happened*?"

"Who are you?" Decker asked.

"Oh, Christ, that's right. We've never met." The guy stuck out his hand. "Mike Ness. I work at the spa—aerobics and weight training. I talked to the other one . . . Detective Dunn, was it?"

"Yeah, it was." Decker shook Ness's hand and caught his eye. They squared off. "Still is, as a matter of fact."

A slow smile spread across Ness's face. "You have a finely tuned bullshit detector. Is it from years of experience or were you born like that?"

"You're good, Mike. Clever but cocky. It's going to trip you up one day."

Ness shrugged. Decker studied Ness's face. Dots of sweat patterned his upper lip. Dark hair, blue eyes, a James Dean pout—a pretty boy except he needed a shave. But maybe that was part of his look, a deliberate attempt to make a sweet face appear more masculine. Decker touched his own cheeks. He could do with a razor himself.

"So who invited you down, Mike?"

"No one. I just popped in to do some harvesting for the kitchen. Zucchini. We've already got a couple of baseball bats growing on the vine. We'll stuff and slice those, but Lilah likes them small. Actually they're bitter when they're small, but the guests love the mini veggies. We also wilt the blossoms and toss them in our salads served with a pungent vinaigrette. That really knocks the ladies' socks off."

"Aerobics instructor, weight lifter, vegetable picker, and culinary expert. You're a regular jack-of-all-trades."

Decker pulled a cigarette out of his pocket. The kid had a light waiting before he could put the smoke in his mouth. Decker blew out the match.

"I just chew on them."

"Trying to quit? We've got a wonderful program for that at the spa."

"You're an awfully devoted employee. Anything in it for you if the boss kicks suddenly?"

Ness's eyes darkened. "Not a fucking thing."

"No need for profanity, Mike. I was just asking you a question."

"Look, you and your lady partner don't like me, it's your problem. But I didn't have anything to do with Lilah's misfortune—not with the rape, not with this—whatever it was. I *love* Lilah and not in the way *you're* thinking—"

"What am I thinking?"

"That I'm only interested in fucking her."

"Are you?"

"Yeah, I am, but I *don't*."

"Just like Ms. Betham—"

"Oh, man . . ." Ness threw his arms in the air and dropped them by his sides. "I don't fuck the clientele. That's not what *I* do, okay?"

"Who does?"

"Who says anyone does? Last I heard, Lilah runs a spa, not a stud rental."

"That's not what I hear about your good buddy, Mike. The tennis instructor . . ." Decker smiled. "Eubie Jeffers, is it?"

Ness shrugged. "What about him?"

"I hear he has a hard time keeping his pants zipped."

"Never a shortage of rumors, huh?"

"I also hear he was with a woman the night Lilah was raped."

"You'll have to ask him."

"We did. You know what else he told us, Mike?"

"That I was with him. That what you want to hear?"

Decker stopped to reappraise his questioning. The kid was very good. He took out his notebook and pencil. "How long were you with him?"

" 'Bout an hour."

"He told my partner he was with you all night."

It was Ness's turn to stop and analyze. Decker could see him thinking: Is he trying to trick me or what? The boys obviously didn't get their story straight—or someone had changed it.

Ness said, "Eubie has trouble remembering things."

"He didn't sleep over your place?" Decker asked.

"No."

"Then how long was he there?"

"I already answered that. About an hour . . . maybe it was two hours . . ."

Good old Mike giving Eubie some slack. Decker said, "What time did he arrive?"

"Late."

"How late?"

"I don't know. Probably after midnight."

"And stayed until about two?"

"Sounds about right."

"Okay." Decker's eyes were on his notebook. "Were you two fucking?"

Silence. Decker looked up. Ness had turned crimson. Guilt or anger?

Nostrils flaring, Ness whispered, "You expect me to *answer* that?"

"You have a problem answering that?"

"I wasn't *fucking* him. I don't *fuck* guys."

Decker said, "So what were you two doing?"

"Talking."

"About what?"

"Why don't you ask Eubie since we talked about his problems."

Decker tapped his pencil on his notebook. "Because I'm asking you."

Ness crossed his arms over his chest, shifting his weight from foot to foot. "Look, is this an interrogation? Do I need a lawyer?"

"Do you?"

"Oh, man, you are really messing with my head. You know, I came over here out of concern for Li-

lah. I knew something was wrong as soon as I saw
Carl. He was as white as a sheet. Somehow, I gathered that something bad happened to Lilah, but she
wasn't hurt. That's as far as I got. You ever try to get
information out of Carl? The guy isn't exactly ar-
ticulate. When I tried the ranch house to talk to the
boss, there was a cop at the door. I figured I'd check
out the scene myself."

Ness's eyes drifted to the bloody rocks, to the
dead horse now collecting fistfuls of black flies.

"God, what a mess! Is Lilah *really* okay?"

Decker regarded Ness's expression—somber.

"She's shaken up," Decker said. "But she's fine."

"What happened?"

Decker smoothed his mustache and thought:
If Ness knew what really had happened, Decker
wouldn't be revealing anything. If Ness was innocent, he was probably better off knowing the truth.

"Lilah's horse went berserk and plowed into the
mountain."

"How'd she . . . ? She must have jumped or something. Miracle she didn't break her neck. Some people
are kissed by God."

"Or lucky enough to go riding with the right person. I caught her."

Decker waited for Ness's reaction. Just surprise,
nothing else.

"You went *riding* with her? Why?"

"How about if I ask the questions?"

"Oooo, I hit upon something *official*." Ness had a
gleam in his eye. "Or personal. Talk about fucking.
Maybe the cop doth protest too much."

Decker was impassive. Ness let out a laugh.

"It's been a while since I played weeny wag with anyone. Talk about being good, Detective."

"Where were you this morning, Mike?"

Ness's smile grew flippant. "So now I'm an official suspect?"

Decker waited.

"How early are we talking about?" Ness said.

"You go first."

"Okay." He exhaled. "I woke up. I do that every morning. Then . . . let's see. Well, I made the seven o'clock hike. Had a bran muffin and tea after that. I ran the nine and ten aerobic classes. Natanya took over at eleven. I must have eaten around eleven-thirty. I was at the pool by noon." He shrugged. "There you have it. My Life by Mike Ness. Somehow, I just can't see it as a screenplay."

Decker put his notebook away.

"No more questions? Did I pass, Detective?"

Decker pulled a card from his wallet. "If you learn *anything* about this—or about the rape—give me a call."

"So, we're buddies, Detective *Sergeant*?"

Decker laid his beefy hand on Ness's shoulder. It was surprisingly bony. "I wouldn't say that, Mikey. Now, even as we speak, I hear zucchinis calling your name. Why don't you beat it before you screw up evidence?"

Ness's eyes surveyed the scene for a final time. "How fast were you two going?"

Instead of answering, Decker cocked his thumb toward the fields. Ness started to leave, then stopped. "You must ride pretty well, Detective Sergeant."

Decker picked up his camera and snapped another picture. "Yes, I must."

The Sun Valley Animal Care Center was a two-story brown and tan California bungalow in the middle of scrubland. The bottom floor was leased to Dr. James Vector, Dr. Vera Mycroft, and Dr. Skip Baker—all DMVs, none of them professional corporations. The top section of the house was the animal hospital and the labs. Behind the bungalow were the barns, the kennels, and the stables. The vets made house calls— Decker had dealt with all three of them at one time or another—but sometimes animals needed surgery, extended treatment, and convalescence away from their pals. Vector, Mycroft, and Baker—VMB—was one of the few operations in the city set up to deal with large animals.

Decker stopped the unmarked on a dirt lot with no designated parking spots. Four-by-fours, flatbeds, and pickups were scattered randomly on the grounds, spaced so no one was hemmed in. He killed the motor, opened the door, and got out. A hot wind saturated with dust assaulted his face, followed by a melee of moos, bleats, neighs, and brays. He found himself whistling "Old MacDonald."

It was after four and yet the clinic was still jammed with people. Lots of folks arriving with their animals after work. And not just dogs and cats. The place also held a skunk, a hutch full of rabbits, two newborn lambs, and a Guernsey calf. The reception area had once been the house's living room, the old wood floors replaced with the vinyl tiles already discolored from animal "accidents." The plastic chairs were mismatched and blanketed with fur and hair. The room gave off a distinct odor—antiseptics and urine. A couple of people were attempting to hold conversations over the yapping and yowling of their pets. They had to nearly scream.

The receptionist was a young, scrubbed-face blonde who wore jeans, a work shirt, and Reeboks. Her hands were squeaky clean, her nails clipped short and without polish. She held a German shepherd pup not much bigger than the hands that cupped him. She looked up when Decker walked in, kept staring at the door expecting an animal to follow on his heels. He went over to her and tickled the puppy at the scruff. The baby lifted his head and a tiny wet tongue moistened Decker's finger. Before Decker could speak, a jowly woman holding a leash attached to a bulldog jumped up.

"Excuse me, I'm next!"

Decker held up his hands in defense. "I'm not butting in, ma'am. I'm looking for the lab."

The secretary mouthed a silent O. "You're the police?"

"Yes, ma'am," Decker said.

" 'Cause of the crazy horse?"

Decker nodded.

"God, I heard Dr. Mycroft talkin' to Dr. Baker about that. She said it was awful."

"It wasn't pretty," Decker said.

"What happened?" asked the lady with the bulldog.

"Wish we could tell you, ma'am." Decker dropped his voice a notch. "But it's official business."

The woman nodded gravely.

"Is Dr. Mycroft in?" Decker asked.

"Yeah, she's up in the lab," the secretary said. "She's expecting you. Go through the back, up the stairs to the second floor. If the door's closed, just knock."

"Thank you," Decker said.

The secretary kissed the sleepy-eyed shepherd and pulled the pup to her breast. "God, you expect people to do crazy things—drive too fast and plow into a mountain." She shook her head. "But a *horse*?"

A throaty voice told Decker to come in. Vera Mycroft was at her microscope, her black and silver braid slung over her right shoulder, her knotted hands adjusting the scope's eyepiece. Her glasses, sidepieces attached to a neck chain, had been tossed over her back and were resting between her shoulder blades.

She spoke without looking up. "I already gave at the office."

"This *is* your office, Vera."

She kept turning the eyepiece. "Aha! *There* you are, you little rascal. Thought you could hide from Mama Vera. Now I ask you, Pete, when one worm is there, can others be far behind?" She looked up and squinted. "That is you, Pete, isn't it?"

Decker smiled. Vera's eyes had become slits. She claimed she was part Aztec and her features backed her up. But she never did bother to explain her Southern drawl.

"Last time I checked."

Vera returned her eyes to the scope.

"Here's number two. And here? Oh my, oh my, we

downright have a housing project. How y'all doing, little guys? Making life miserable for Pogo's gut?"

"Do you always talk to your slides, Vera?"

"Worms are animals, too." She sat back in her chair. "You ever get around to trimming the hooves of the little one, Pete?"

Decker smiled. "Now you're checking up on me?"

"Checking up on my patient." Vera stood, unbuttoned her lab coat, and fanned the sides to cool herself off. "You're going to cripple the poor thing if you don't."

"Yes, I trimmed her hooves. Ornery little sucker. When she realized I wasn't going to let her kick me, she rolled me. Just stiffened and fell on me. Took me over an hour and I was sweating like a pig by the time I was done."

Vera's laugh was deep. "You could have brought her in, Pete. Saved yourself some work."

"Macho guys like me don't do sensible things like that."

"One would have thought Rina might have sweet-talked some sense into you."

"One would have thought." Decker stuck his hands in his pockets.

Vera swung her glasses onto her chest. "Would you like some mint iced tea?"

"Very much, thanks."

"My, but it's a hot one." She opened the refrigerator, swinging the door several times, providing herself with a breeze of chilled air. Taking out a pitcher of iced tea, she poured it into a two-half-liter beaker and handed Decker some calibrated glassware. She held her container aloft, then gulped down her tea.

Decker could just imagine her tossing down some brews with the good ole boys. She had to be close to sixty, but he'd lay money that she could drink a barroom of truck drivers under the table. He finished his tea and Vera took the beaker from his hands.

"Thanks for doing a rush job for me," Decker said. "Are we in luck?"

"Yes, we are." Vera perched horn-rimmed glasses on her nose. The chain that connected to her spectacles fell down her temples like gypsy earrings. "Come on over to my desk, I'll show you my printout."

The lab wasn't Parker Center Forensics, but it seemed well equipped—a centrifuge for blood work and a half dozen microscopes. There were racks of Pyrex glassware, shelves of reagents and solvents. A waist-high table of clean white Formica provided the working area. Vera's desk was a wooden table topped with an IBM PC, a phone, and a salad bowl filled with floral potpourri. The computer's printer was spewing out data, screeching as the daisy wheel inked numbers on paper. Decker pulled a stool next to the table and sat. Vera took a folder and read its contents.

"It was an easy analysis. Your poisoner didn't go in for exotics. Does the name phencyclidine mean anything to you?"

"PCP." Decker took out a pencil and a notebook. "But that's used as an animal *tranquilizer*, isn't it?"

"Not that much anymore. We have much better drugs that don't have the side effects."

"What are the side effects in a horse?"

"Well, human and equine brain chemistries are

very different as you can well imagine. A horse's brain is less likely to self-destruct, I can tell you that."

"No argument from me."

"Yeah, we humans do the most ungodly things to ourselves." Vera scratched her head. "Anyway, most of the time, you shoot a horse with PCP, the drug'll just knock the poor thing out. But I've read more than one study where PCP can cause a paradoxical reaction even in large animals. Instead of being tranquilized, the horse metabolizes the drug as a hallucinogen. In that case, you'll get reactions similar to those observed in humans—agitation, muscle rigidity, hyperreflexia, tachycardia . . ."

"Things that would make a horse bolt."

"Things that would make a horse bolt." She put the folder down and let her glasses fall onto her bosom. "Mr. Ed notwithstanding, nobody I know has ever heard of a talking horse." She thought a moment. "Nobody who's actually lucid, that is. Once I knew a fellah who claimed to be married to his horse . . . that's another story. Since we regulars can't communicate with our equine friends, it's hard to know exactly what had transpired. But I'd be willing to bet that your suicidal palomino was seeing things that weren't there. Poor thing was probably flying while he was bolting."

Decker made a few chicken scratches on paper. "Let me ask you this. How long would it take for the drug to take effect?"

"That's an 'it depends' question. How much is given, the body weight of the horse, the stomach contents, any other potentiating drug in the bloodstream—I didn't find anything else out of the ordinary. It also depends if the drug is given intravenously, intramuscularly, or orally. Most of the time, it isn't given orally, but if someone was out to sabotage, it's conceivable that they could have mixed the powder into the horse's feed. That being the case, it might take anywhere from fifteen minutes to an hour for the drug to take effect."

Fifteen minutes to an hour, Decker thought. From ten to eleven, Mike Ness was doing aerobics. Where was Jeffers?

"That's a long-winded answer to a straightforward question." Vera played with her glasses. "I hope it helps you out."

"It sure does. Thanks a lot, Vera." Decker tapped his pencil against his pad. "PCP. Person could pick up Dust anywhere."

"Anywhere and everywhere. You'd be stunned at how many dogs and cats come in here freakin' out because they took their owner's dope." Vera looked at him. "Are you on to something?"

"Just thinking." Decker folded his notebook. "Even though PCP is everywhere . . . for a person to administer it IM to a horse . . . that person would have to be someone at ease with *large* animals. Most greeners find horses pretty intimidating because of their size."

"That's true. Horses are dumb but they are strong . . . and obstinate if you don't know how to handle them."

Decker folded his pad and nodded, thinking horses could get real obstinate. Took a firm, experienced hand to give them an injection.

An experienced hand . . . like Carl Totes.

℘16

Black coffee and corned beef with mustard on rye. Decker stared at the sandwich, enjoying the feel of his mouth watering. Leaning back in his desk chair, he took a bite, chewing with near-orgasmic pleasure. His spine and neck were sore from this morning's ordeal, his arms sunburned from exposure. But he was able to forget everything as soon as his teeth sank into the bread.

Treasure the simple things.

He took another bite and saw Marge enter the squad room, her hands shuffling little pink message slips. He whistled, she looked up, and he motioned her over. She pulled up a chair and Decker noticed his partner's longing eyes. He handed her the other half of his sandwich.

"Are you *sure*?" Marge said.

"My mother raised me with manners."

Marge bit into the bread before he could change his mind. "You know what I need?"

"You're talking with your mouth full, Detective Dunn."

"I need a wife."

"I'll tell Rina to make extra next time."

"I don't understand why her sandwiches are consistently better than mine. Why do I have such an adversarial relationship with food?"

"Lie on ze couch und vee can discuss it." Decker sipped coffee. "How's Lilah?"

"She was still freaked out. Can't say I blame her. Are you okay?"

"All in a day's work, Margie."

"I've seen mounted police," Marge said. "You're the first mounted detective so far as I know."

"That's me—a real trendsetter." Decker finished his coffee. "The whole thing happened . . . what? Six hours ago?" He shook his head. "Surreal. Anyway, did Lilah tell you anything?"

Marge said, "I couldn't get much out of her with Freddy staring over my shoulder. And when she did speak, her voice had that eerie calm that victims often have. Disbelief. She also kept asking where you were, Pete." She licked her fingers. "She wanted to know if you were all right. Do you have a tissue or a napkin? I got mustard on my hands."

Decker opened his desk, took out a short-order arrest form and handed it to her. "Did you tell her I was fine?"

Marge wiped her fingers on the stiff paper. "Sure. But it was more than just a query. She wanted *you*. She tolerated my presence but wasn't happy about it. And then when I started asking her nuts-and-bolts questions, she spaced out."

"Maybe Freddy had her sedated."

Marge shook her head. "I asked Freddy if he'd given her anything. The doctor became *offended*. Freddy doesn't believe in sedatives, tranquilizers, muscle relaxants, or anything else that artificially knocks out the body and/or mind. When I left, he was preparing a ginseng and gingerroot bath to soothe Lilah's nerves. Then they were going to meditate." Marge brushed hair away from her eyes. "Sounds rather peaceful, actually."

"Did Lilah have *any* idea who might have tampered with the horse?"

"Only that if we found the men who stole her father's memoirs, we'd find the demons who were plaguing her. Why are those damn memoirs so important to her?"

"It's her father's legacy to her. She's placed inordinate importance on them, conveniently forgetting that there was also a million dollars of ice stowed in the safe."

"But it does look like someone's out to get her."

Decker sipped coffee. "Maybe not *get* her, only scare her."

"For what reason?"

"So she won't testify against him—or them."

"She knows who did it?"

"I said from the start this looks like an inside job."

"An *inside* mill jewel heist with a rape to boot," Marge said. "Stringers are gonna *love* it. The good captain, however, won't be too pleased."

"I'm hoping to solve the damn thing before it gets into the blotters. Look how far we've come in two days."

"How far *have* we come, Pete?"

Decker thought about that and frowned. He took out his notebook. "Let's start at the path of least resistance."

Marge laughed. "Let's."

"Carl Totes," Decker said. "I've been racking my brain over him. He, more than anyone, had access to the horses. *And* he had means and experience to dope the animals up. But what would be the *motivation*? He adores Lilah and has nothing to gain if she died."

"Maybe someone was paying him to do dirty work."

"Totes as a hit man?"

"Okay, maybe the idea was to *scare* Lilah, not kill her, just like you said. Maybe someone was paying him to do . . . to pull off a little *practical joke*. Pete, look at the way Totes lives. Could be he wants more out of life than sleeping in a stable."

Decker said, "Nah, I think he *likes* living that way. Simple, uncluttered—like his mind."

"Anyone can be bought."

"You're right," Decker said. "But you have to use the right currency."

"Maybe they're buying Totes with a woman, Pete."

Decker thought about that. "Okay. Name me a woman."

Marge paused. "Kelley Ness?"

"What hat did you pull her out of?"

"Farfetched," Marge admitted.

"Stratospheric," Decker said.

Marge said, "There's something odd about her, Pete. It's not that she wasn't cooperative, just that . . . it's her *relationship* with her brother. I observed them together when they weren't looking. They meet quite a bit—minutes at a time only, but there's an intimacy. Whispering to each other, *touching* each other.

Nothing sexual, a hand on a shoulder, a pat on the back, but . . ."

"Incest?"

"I've thought about it. Or maybe she's just one of those baby sisters who adores her big brother. I don't trust Mike a bit. He has something up his proverbial sleeve. I could see him putting Kelley up to something."

Decker said, "I don't see Totes being lured by Kelley Ness but let's *assume* he was. Marge, Totes is *knowledgeable* about horses. If he were trying to scare Lilah using Apollo, he'd know better than to give the horse PCP. Totes would know it was a tranquilizer."

"So that's *perfect*, Peter," Marge said. "He was trying to *scare* Lilah, not kill her."

"What scare? Most likely, the horse would just keel over and go to sleep. It would be a little strange, but not *terrifying*."

"But it would send a message. 'You saw who stole the jewels. Keep it zipped or the next time the horse won't wake up.'"

"Okay . . . okay, you have a point." Decker doodled in his notebook. "Totes is looking pretty damn good. So someone put Totes up to spooking Lilah. Who?"

"I like Ness. I also like Kingston Merritt," Marge said. "I just got back the prelim paper on both him and John Reed. Freddy Brecht hasn't come in yet. Both Reed and Merritt are solvent, but Merritt doesn't have a lot of room for play. He's only got about five grand in savings. Not much for an OB-GYN earning three hundred fifty a year."

"No, it isn't."

Marge said, "Well, his bread is going somewhere."

"You see Merritt working directly with a guy like Carl Totes?"

Marge paused. "Maybe he used an intermediary."

"I don't know . . ." Decker exhaled forcibly. "Call it a gut feeling, but I just don't see Totes . . . fuck my gut feeling. Let's see if we can find any paper on Totes. Any sudden influx of cash."

Marge said, "I'll keep digging. God, what a mess. We got Totes, Merritt, Ness—"

"You know Ness dropped by the place today. Said he came by to pick veggies, that he had done it before. He was awfully curious about what happened. He claimed he was at the spa all morning. Now the spa and the ranch are five minutes apart?"

"About."

"Conceivably, *he* could have come down and dusted the horse's fodder and slipped away unnoticed."

"Totes was around—"

"Suppose Totes was in the corral working out one of the horses. Ness could have been in and out in five minutes. That would give him access and means for the crime."

Marge said, "And talk about motivation, as in money. Ness is definitely buyable. When I talked to him, he frothed at the mouth at the thought of owning a spa like VALCAN."

Decker asked, "Maybe Kingston Merritt was paying Ness and not Totes to drug the horse. Could those two be working together?"

Marge said, "You know, when the altercation occurred between Freddy and Kingston, Ness stepped in. He was talking to Kingston like he was a stranger . . . but in my mind, they looked like they knew each other."

"Hey, it would fit nicely with my theory that the case was an inside job."

"And I could see Ness giving a horse Angel Dust. He'd probably even think a stoned horse would be very humorous."

"A stoned horse sending a message to Lilah?"

"Well, maybe he figured the horse would go crazy—like humans on PCP do. But not *too* crazy. Except, Pete, who knew that Lilah was going to ride Apollo except *Totes*?"

Decker grimaced. "True. So we're back to Totes."

"Hell, Pete, maybe they're all in it together— used different people for different jobs. They used Totes for the horse and a bunch of lowlifes for the burglary. One of them got carried away and raped her. It's happened before. If you figure Ness to be involved, maybe he was involved in the burglary/ rape." She smiled. "Despite Lilah's *imaging*, the attackers were masked. It could have been Ness and she wouldn't have known it."

Decker said, "I don't have trouble visualizing Ness as a rapist. He admitted wanting to fuck Lilah. Let's get some tissue samples from him."

"Why single out Ness?"

"You're right. Let's ask for samples from all of the male employees of the spa. We could also get Jeffers that way."

"Jeffers the poker," Marge said. "I see him as a sneak thief, not a rapist."

"But if he was shielded behind a mask?"

"Yeah, he could do it. Once you're a scumbag, nothing's off limits. What about Totes? We should get a tissue sample on him, too."

"Absolutely," Decker said.

Marge sat back in her chair. "You know, Peter, Lilah, more than anyone, had access to her horse."

"Lilah poisoning her own horse," Decker said. "It crossed my mind. She liked being rescued the first time by me. Maybe she was hoping for a repeat. Except she didn't know I could ride."

"Maybe she didn't expect you to rescue her. Maybe she gave her horse PCP figuring Apollo would keel over in the middle of the ride, proving her point that someone was out to get her."

"Yeah, she seemed anxious to convince me that her power was real. I hate to say this, but when it was happening, I was almost convinced she did have some . . . supernatural thing."

"Prophet Lilah."

"False prophet Lilah." Decker arched his brow. "She's a strange woman. I'll tell you this much—if she did tamper with her horse, she took a big chance. She almost *died*!"

"It's still a valid thought—she's unstable."

"Agreed. Ever make contact with John Reed?"

Marge shook her head. "We've been playing phone tag. I'll try him again. I did get a call back from Burglary. None of the jewels have come through any big fences. How about you and Lilah's ex-husband . . . yet another iron in the fire."

"Perry Goldin. I called his house. His tape machine

said he was playing at the Bridge Emporium between five and seven today. If I leave now, I could
make it there by six-thirty."

Marge sat back and appraised him. "I don't see
you as a bridge player, Pete."

"Hey, they didn't call me the Slam Bammer in
the army for nothing."

Marge said, "I would have thought they called
you that for other reasons."

Decker frowned. "Maybe it was for other reasons.
Hell, it was so long ago, I've forgotten." He shook
his head. "A sad commentary on life."

Flying on the freeway when the RTO patched the
call over the line. So much for daytime reverie.
Decker picked up the mike and depressed the button, annoyed to hear his ex-wife's voice. After
Cindy turned eighteen, he felt he was finally done
with Jan.

"What's up?" he said.

"I'm sorry to call you like this, Pete. Your home
number was disconnected. Are you moving?"

"Don't worry. I'll make sure you have a current
address for sending Cindy's bills."

"Oh, God, Pete, do we have to go—?"

"Sorry, that wasn't necessary. No, we're not moving. I had our phone number changed. What can I
do for you?"

"I was just wondering if tonight was a good time
for Alan and me to drop off Cindy's car?"

Decker hesitated. "Why would I want Cindy's car?
Am I supposed to lube it or something?"

"You don't want it, Pete, but Cindy might want it over the summer."

"Hold on a sec." Decker slowed, then finally stopped the Plymouth on the right-hand shoulder of the freeway. He rolled down the windows and hot air wafted through the interior. Taking off his jacket, he picked up the mike, shouting to be heard above the traffic. "I'm missing something. Is Cindy staying with me this summer?"

"Peter Jedidiah Decker, don't you *dare* futz out on me! Do you know how long Alan and I have been planning this trip? Not to mention the expense we've already shelled out on wardrobe and luggage—"

"Hold on, Jan. I'm not futzing out on anyone. I'm just confused."

"So what else is new?"

"Do you want help or do you want to piss me off?"

Jan said, "Cindy assured me that she had arranged to stay with you this summer so Alan and I could take our *dream* vacation to Europe."

"Cindy never arranged a *damn* thing with me, Jan. But it's no problem. I can take her for the summer. I can take her anytime you want. God knows, you've done more than your fair share with her."

Nobody spoke for a moment.

"That was nice, Pete."

"Yeah, I throw you a bone every once in a while."

"She didn't clear it with you?"

"No, Jan, she didn't. But I can take her."

"We're planning on being away the entire summer—"

"It's no problem."

Decker thought: A two-month European vacation with no children. And here he was with a pregnant wife. By the time he and Rina reached the stage where Jan and Alan were, he'd be sixty-one. . . .

"Have a good time," he said.

"I can't believe Cindy didn't tell you," Jan said. "I offered to call, but she insisted she'd handle it."

Decker said, "Has she sounded upset to you lately?"

"Not any more than usual."

"Well, she's been really upset with me. That's probably the reason. What did she think? I'd say no?"

"I don't know . . . but maybe Cindy feels you don't need her anymore now that your wife is expecting—"

"That is so stupid, Jan! Totally ridiculous!"

"Fine, Pete, I'm stupid and ridiculous! Can we bring over her car or not?"

"Cindy is my *daughter*, for chrissakes! Nothing will ever change that! What are you suggesting? Sibling rivalry between an eighteen-year-old and an infant?"

"The car, Pete?" Jan sounded weary. "Around eight?"

"Yeah, bring the car over around eight."

"I'm hanging up now, Pete."

Decker heard the line go dead. He sat, hands on the wheel, listening to the sound of vehicles speeding past him. It was hot and smoggy and he was worn out. But he had a job to do. A burden being responsible. He adjusted his butt in the seat, buckled his shoulder harness, and started the engine. He was proud that he remembered to unclench his teeth before he put the car in gear.

17

There it was—the *knock*.

Mike Ness rolled onto his back and closed his eyes. "It's open, Kell."

He heard the door shut and a chair pull up next to the bed. "What is it this time?"

"The lady detective's back, Mike."

"I *know*, Kell. I just talked to her."

"You did? *When?*"

"A few minutes ago." Ness turned onto his side. "You need me to cover for you or something?"

"Stop playing games with me, Michael!" Kelley shouted. "You know how *important* this job is to me. Swear to me you had nothing to do—"

"Goddamn it, just *knock* it off!" Ness leaped up and pounded his wall. "I'm getting sick of your whining, you know that?"

The room was silent. Ness turned around and groaned. Little Kell just sitting there, eyes filled with tears, lips in that little pout. Just like old times. It was the pout that always got to him. So helpless . . .

He walked over and kissed her forehead, letting his lips rest on her cool skin. He'd always been envious of her complexion, not a single pimple or black-head even during her teenage years. He felt Kelley stroke his cheek tenderly.

"You need a shave," she said.

"Davida likes me like this." He pulled away and began to massage her shoulders. "She thinks I look *sinister*. You're tight, sis."

"I'm nervous."

"Relax."

"Feels good," Kelley purred.

"Big brother knows what's best, right?"

She didn't answer. God, she was just *impossible*. Ness said, "What's the problem, Kell?"

"What did the lady detective want?"

"She wants a couple strands of my hair!" Ness shook his head, laughed, then flopped down on the bed and faced her. "Get *this:* They want to tissue-type it against the semen sample found on Lilah's bedsheets. Can you *believe* it?"

Kelley bit her thumbnail. "What are you going to do?"

"What do you think? I'm gonna give her a sample!"

Kelley was quiet.

"Stop biting your nails." Ness took her hand and patted it. "Everything's gonna be ducky, I promise."

Kelley drew him into an embrace. He didn't re-act, then felt his hands snake around his sister's small waist.

"I love you," she said.

"I know," Ness responded. "I love you, too."

He broke away from her and lay back down. Aw, sweet slumber if only a brief catnap. In a half hour, he was scheduled to lead late-afternoon low-impact aerobics. No jogging, jumping, or bouncing, please. Just lots of marching. Hup two three four, hup two three four, all the little soldiers standing at attention. Firm bodies tar-dipped in black leotards and tights—yes, mama, *yes*!

"Are you all right, Mike?"

Ness reached out and found Kelley's hand. "Are *you* all right?"

Kelley said, "I am if you are."

"I'm fine . . . just great! And don't worry, Kell!" He felt himself grinning. "I guarantee you the sample won't *match*!"

The Bridge Emporium was located above a supermarket. Decker hunted around the building's exterior, looking for a stairway, and found the entrance in the back near the garbage—a warped door stenciled with black letters: EMPORIUM. Behind the door was a flight of steps lighted by a lone bare bulb.

The bridge club must have been a warehouse at one time—about three thousand square feet of open space floored with worn, faded tiles. Bright fluorescent fixtures lighted an expanse filled with tables and chairs and people studying the splay of cards before them. It was hot. A few fans twirled phlegmatically, pushing around stale plumes of cigarette smoke.

Decker scanned the room for someone not involved in the play. In the far right corner, two kids were engaged in a game that utilized dice. Decker could hear the muted sound of cubes tumbling over felt. He walked over and saw that the game was backgammon. The younger of the two boys had acne—not a bad-looking kid, but he obviously never bothered putting any work into his physical appearance. The older one was actually an adult, early or even mid-twenties, but the way he presented himself—his gawky face, his skinny frame in clothes a size too big, black-rimmed glasses slipping down his nose—was more reminiscent of an awkward adolescent. He pushed his glasses up and studied the game board.

"You need something?" Glasses said.

Decker said, "I'm looking for Perry Goldin."

"Still playing." Glasses rolled a pair of double sixes—one of the best tosses possible in the game. Neither player reacted. Glasses moved his men into strategic positions. "He's at his usual spot."

"What's his usual spot?"

The younger one said, "One. North."

"Table one, north position?"

"Yep." The younger one shook the dice in his cup and let them go. His roll left his men open for the pickings. He frowned and looked up. "He doesn't take appointments until after the game. You'll have to wait in line just like the rest of them."

Decker took out his gold shield. "I'm a detective."

That got their attention, but only minimally. The older one said, "What's Goldin wanted for?"

"Felonious finessing," Decker answered.

Glasses rolled the dice and said, "Ask a stupid question . . ."

Decker smiled and looked at his watch. "When's the shindig due to end?"

The younger one checked the clock. "Few minutes at most."

"Have a seat," Glasses offered. "You play?"

"Enough to know that if I was betting, I'd bet on you."

Glasses smiled and rolled another double. The younger one pushed the board aside. "If I didn't know you, Dave, I'd swear you were using loaded dice."

"It's your board, Steve," Dave said, evenly.

"This is true."

Steve looked at Decker. "You want to go a round?"

Decker shook his head. "I hear Goldin's a real bridge bum."

Dave straightened his glasses. "Perry a *bum*? He must make a hundred gees a year. His wife's pulling in another seventy, eighty gees. I reserve my tears for the needy."

"He makes a hundred gees a year playing *bridge*?"

"Private tournaments, teaching, renting himself for matches . . ." Steve shrugged. "Renting is where Perry makes most of his bread. I think his going rate's a grand a day—"

"*What?*"

"Lot of rich people out there dying to be *life* masters," Dave remarked. "Makes them feel *real* special."

Decker pulled out his notebook. "Is his wife a professional bridge player, too?"

"Nope, she's a lawyer," Steve said. "She also plays, but Wendy's strictly amateur. She's got her gold points, though. Perry made sure of that."

"And he didn't even charge her," Dave said, deadpan.

"There are other pros who play just as well," Steve said. "Perry's beauty is in his bidding. He has this uncanny ability to manipulate it to his advantage. Most of the time, he fixes it so he's declarer. That way his partner never has a chance to louse up the play. You want gold points and you want them fast, you hire Goldin."

"Gold with Goldin," Dave said.

Decker noticed some people standing up and stretching. Others were leaving the tables. The room began to hum with conversation.

"Ah, the game endeth," Steve said. "And our work beginneth. We're on scoring detail. Are you good with numbers, Detective?"

"Only if they're associated with mug shots." Decker stood. "See you boys."

Dave said, "Stick around, Detective. I guarantee you Table Number One will come in *first*."

"Don't people get resentful?" Decker asked. "Goldin winning all the time?"

"Nah," Dave said. "The Emporium is jazzed just to have him play here. It's like letting Nolan Ryan pitch on your softball team. He attracts people who pay the admission fee just to watch him. He's great for business."

"Who owns this place?" Decker asked.

Dave broke into a pleasant grin. "I do. It beats the hell out of law school."

Decker waited patiently while three expensively dressed ladies with clawish red fingernails arranged their schedules so they meshed with Goldin's. Judging by the way the bridge pro was flipping the pages of his appointment book, he was booked up far in advance.

Goldin looked to be in his forties, which would have made him quite a bit older than Lilah. Maybe he was younger, age artificially advanced by gray streaking through his shoulder-length hair and beard. He was around six feet with an ectomorphic build—long nose, high cheekbones and forehead. His emerald-green eyes were so unnatural-looking, Decker wondered if he wore contacts. He had on a black T-shirt under a black blazer, faded jeans, and Nikes. Goldin talked in a clipped, professional tone, not a moment wasted on pleasantries. When it was Decker's turn to introduce himself, Goldin spoke first.

"You're not interested in bridge."

Decker showed him his badge.

Goldin's eyes went wide. "Oh, my God! Wendy!"

Decker said, "It's not about Wendy."

"This isn't about my wife?"

"No."

At least not your current one. Decker found Goldin's reaction odd. You see a cop, you don't immediately think of your wife. Goldin seemed to sense his confusion.

"My wife . . ." He brought his hand to his chest, then dropped it slowly. "She runs a legal clinic for the indigent downtown—sitting ducks despite the fact that they're only a few blocks from the police station."

The statement seemed pointed. Decker was quiet.

Goldin said, "I can't tell you how many times the place has been burgled or robbed. Then last week a clerk was shot in the arm. . . ." He swallowed dryly. "I have no idea what you want from me. Is it a quick question or a little more?"

"It's a little more."

"Can I finish up my business first?"

"How long will that take?"

"Can you give me ten minutes?"

"That's fine. I noticed a coffee machine in the corner. I'll wait for you there."

"Thank you." Goldin exhaled slowly, then turned to the next person in line—a junior exec in a suit and tie.

Decker found the machine and sat down at an empty table. He had just finished his coffee when he saw Goldin coming his way. The bridge pro sat down, rested his head in his hands.

Decker stood and said, "Can I buy you a cup, Mr. Goldin? You look like you can use it."

"I won't refuse."

"How do you take it? Cream? Sugar?"

"Black."

Decker punched the button and brought the cup over to the table. "You look tired, Mr. Goldin. Maybe this'll wake you up."

"Perry." He sipped his coffee and checked his watch. "I've got an appointment in a half hour."

"This shouldn't take too long."

"I'm not rushing you. I'm just wondering if you want me to call and cancel. I don't mind canceling. I don't mind talking to you, either. Just don't talk about bridge."

"We talk bridge, the meter runs?"

"No . . ." Goldin shook his head. "No, that's not it at all . . . well, yeah, I like to get paid. Hell, that's the only thing I like about bridge now. God, I'm sick of it all—the backbiting, all these puny little egos vying for stupid little points."

"The disillusioned pro."

"Yeah, though I suppose it's better than the dissolute pro." Goldin smiled. "You see those women I was talking to? For them, I'm a cheap and respectable way to buy a day's worth of attention—sort of an intellectual variation on screwing the tennis instructor."

"Do you screw them?"

"Me?" Goldin laughed soundly. "Put it this way, Detective. I'd rather take thumbtacks in the scrotum."

Decker smiled. "They don't look *that* bad. Well preserved if you ask me."

"Tuck and roll no longer refers to car upholstery," Goldin said. "They've all been sucked, stuffed, and stitched many times over. In fact, Pat, the blonde, has a knock-out body. I know because one day I came to her house for her weekly bridge lesson and she greeted me stark naked. I felt like Dustin Hoffman in *The Graduate* when Anne Bancroft walks in . . . *no, no, no, this isn't what I had in mind.*" He chuckled to himself. "No, I don't do anything that jeopardizes my marriage. Other men want to louse up their lives, I wish them well and hope they're squirreling away money for alimony. We Californians live in the land of community property."

"Sounds like you've been burned."

"Not at all. I got away scot-free the first time around. I do believe my ex's family would have paid me *handsomely* to divorce her. They sure as hell offered me the moon not to *marry* her. Too bad I was after true love instead of money. I should have read the writing on the wall—wasn't too swift back then." Goldin sipped coffee. "Well, I've come down with a nasty case of verbal diarrhea. I'm sorry. What can I do for you?"

"Actually, we're on the right subject, Mr. Goldin."

"Perry. What subject is that?"

"Lilah Brecht."

Goldin's expression was pained. "Oh, man, she's come back to *haunt* me." He buried his head in his hands. "What did she do this time?"

"She didn't *do* anything," Decker said. "She was raped a couple of nights ago."

Goldin snapped his head up and placed his hands on the table. "Is she all right?"

"Yes. She's out of the hospital, her bruises seem to be fading."

"She was *beaten*, too?"

"Knocked around."

"That's terrible," Goldin whispered. "Just awful . . . I'm really sorry to hear that." He stared at Decker. "Did she ask for me or anything?"

Decker shook his head.

"Then . . . why are you telling me this?"

Decker didn't answer.

Goldin pointed to his chest. "You suspect *me*? Is *that* it? You suspect me of raping and beating my ex-wife whom I haven't seen in what? Six years?"

Decker was quiet.

"Jesus!" Goldin leaned back in his chair and crossed his arms. "Give me the exact date and time and I'll tell you where I was." He held up his appointment book.

"May I see that, Perry?"

Goldin dropped it on the table. Decker picked it up and leafed through the pages. Goldin had been at a bridge tournament on the night in question. Decker pointed to the date. "How long did the tournament last?"

"Till eleven-thirty, twelve. Then there was the postmortem with my student. I probably got home around one. Call my wife. She was home when I stumbled through the door."

Decker carefully studied the pages, looking for names: Brecht, Merritt, Reed, Eversong, Ness, Totes. Nothing. He returned the book. "Thank you."

"Anything else?" Goldin slipped the book in his jacket.

Decker said, "What went wrong with the marriage?"

"Jesus, just help yourself to my personal life."

"Mr. Goldin—"

"Perry."

"Perry, I was hoping you could help me out. I'm having a hard time getting a fix on your ex-wife."

"Detective, you are asking the *wrong* person for aid and succor. We did not part best friends. You can't reason with Lilah because she's *flipped*. The whole family is *flipped*."

Decker pulled out his notebook. "Tell me about it."

Goldin tapped his fingers on the table. "I've got to make a phone call . . . my appointment."

Decker fished a quarter out of his pocket. Goldin looked at the coin and laughed.

"That wasn't a hint, Detective."

"Take it, Perry. It's on the department."

Goldin palmed the quarter, tossed it into the air, and caught it. "Be right back."

❧18

The bungalow offered little room to pace.

Clutter, Davida thought. She pulled out a cigarette and lit it with a jewel-encrusted lighter. Goddamn room was nothing but clutter. She snapped the lighter shut, dropped it in the pocket of her silk kimono, then tapped her foot. Redone in Georgian style, most of the antique pieces picked up in Bath, the heavily wooded room now seemed ponderous—out of character with the semiarid climate that surrounded the spa. Southwestern would be more in keeping with the terrain. But *that* look was old and tiresome.

She drew nicotine into her lungs and flicked ashes into an empty Baccarat vase.

Where the hell was he?

She stared at the bar, then the clock—ten after seven. Though she needed nourishment, she knew she had to keep her head clear. Again, she surveyed the room. The John Constable landscape. The Sir Joshua Reynolds portrait—veddy English. Nice but passionless. Jimi had suggested buying into Diego Menéndez or Pedro Aguilar while Latin prices were still reasonable.

Davida thought for a moment. A hacienda look, perhaps? Hand-painted tiles, wrought-iron fixtures, textured plastered walls and polished pine frames for the windows. And of course, the mandatory furniture hunt across the border. All those handsome *hombres* with their dark mustaches, drinking tequila . . .

An idle moment of fantasy. Her eyes returned to the clock and she was back in reality.

Where was he?

She picked up the phone, then put it down when she finally heard footsteps. She drew back a maroon velvet curtain for a peek, dropped the drapery, and did a quick run to the mirror. When the door opened, she was scanning a magazine and didn't bother to look up.

"What took you so goddamn *long*?"

"And good evening to you, too, Davida." Ness tossed a sweat-soaked towel on a pink damask divan and took out two crystal tumblers from the bar. "What can I get you?"

Davida looked at the towel, then threw the magazine across the room. "I left a message for you over an hour ago!"

"I just picked it up, Davida! I don't run to my box every two min—"

"I hate to be kept waiting!"

"So I'm here—"

"Where the *hell* were you?"

"Where the *hell* was I?" Ness slammed down his glass. "I was *working*, Davida, that's where the *hell* I was. I was dodging cops, I was dodging my sister, I was trying to figure out what the fuck happened to Lilah this morning—"

"Lilah? Did something new happen to Lilah?"

Ness regarded Davida's face. She seemed genuinely baffled.

"Her favorite horse is now tomato sauce on the mountains." He plunked an ice cube in his glass and covered it with a healthy shot of Glenlivet. "It smashed headfirst into the rocks. Lilah would have been paste, too, if a big macho cop hadn't caught her—"

"*What?*"

"You don't know *anything* about this, Davida?"

"Of course not!"

"Oh, so today we're playing indignant!"

"Mike, I don't know a damn thing about this!" She tightened her kimono around her body. "Is she all right?"

Ness took a sip, then a swig. "Freddy says she'll be okay. She was badly shaken up, but not hurt."

"That's good to hear." Davida sat on the divan and folded the towel. "One less goddamn thing to worry about."

"Your level of motherly devotion is touching."

Davida threw the towel at him. "If she's all right, why should I fret?"

"The girl is raped, then nearly killed." He poured himself another shot. "I would think you'd be a *little* concerned."

"Goddamn you, don't you dare get self-righteous on me, you little *prick*!"

Ness felt his face burn. Goddamn bitch! "Apologize—"

"Mike—"

"Apologize!" he screamed.

"Easy, boy!" She strolled over to the bar and placed her hands on his shoulders. "I was just being my normal insulting self. Pour me a bourbon . . . please."

Ness forced himself to breathe slowly. "You want me to brew some coffee for it?"

"Straight bourbon is fine." She leaned against the wall. "What did the cops want?"

"You're going to love this." Ness handed her the drink and took a seat on the divan. "The police are asking for tissue samples—hair or fingernails—to match against the semen found on Lilah's sheets. I gave them a few tresses." He smiled. "I'm not exactly worried."

She didn't answer. She wasn't paying any attention. As usual she was wrapped up in her own sordid shit. He took a slow sip of booze, enjoying the feel of it burning down his throat, while he studied Davida's face.

"You're panicked. You're trying to hide it, but you're freaked. What'd you screw up this time?"

"You're very perceptive. Cheers." Davida tilted her glass, then took a long drink of bourbon.

Ness let out a bitter laugh. "Man, I should have *known* something was wrong when you asked for straight bourbon."

"It's bad, Mike."

"How bad?"

"I'm not sure, but I would think it's very bad."

Ness ran his finger over the rim of his glass. "What happened? Did Kingston screw up?"

"No, he's just being obstinate."

"More money?"

"No, he wants to see Lilah first—"

"Why didn't you let *me* handle it in the first place?"

Davida hurled her glass against the wall. It shattered instantly, raining alcohol and crystal. "Are you going to rub my nose in shit or are you going to help me?"

Ness was silent. She was *pouting*! Why do all women *pout*?

Davida said, "You will clean that up for me, won't you?"

"*Christ!*" Ness grabbed the arms of the chair and hurled his body upward. He took out a whisk broom and swept the broken pieces into a wastebasket, then held the receptacle in the air. "All done, Davida! All your garbage neatly swept away—"

"Michael—"

"If you want my help, stop power-tripping me!"

"Fair enough." Davida tapped her foot. "I made an appointment to see him. Just to talk . . . try and reason . . ."

"And?"

"I don't know and that's the problem." Davida began to pace. "I was waiting in the limo. I wasn't there. I sent a delivery boy—"

"Who?"

"It's not important." She covered her mouth with a liver-spotted hand, then dropped it to her side. "The whole thing was taking too long, so I left. I called you as soon as I got back."

"Christ! *Why* didn't you come to me in the first place?"

"Believe it or not, it was out of concern for you. I didn't want to involve—"

"A little late for that."

"Michael, after the screwup with Lilah, I was trying to *protect* you! If something broke out, I didn't want you around. I happen to *care* about you. If I were a different person, I might even *love* you." She crushed out her cigarette. "But I'm way too selfish for that."

Ness ran his hands over his face and wondered why his life sucked. "Has anyone tried to contact you?"

"No."

"No, no one *called*? Or no, you didn't pick up the phone or check for messages?"

"No calls, no one left me any messages. That's why I think it's very bad. Either he decided to shaft me . . . or something really bad happened."

"When did this take place?"

"About two hours ago. Please handle it for me, Michael. Get help if you want. Just make sure I get what I want and I'm clear. Do *whatever* you have to do."

Ness stared at the lone ice cube in his tumbler. Now she was getting all desperate on him. "I have limits."

"Michael, I'm not asking you to commit murder . . . just . . ."

Ness waited.

"If there's a . . . *problem* . . . clean up for me, please?"

"I love your euphemisms."

"I don't even know if there is a problem. Just handle what needs to be handled."

"I thought you didn't want to get me involved."

"Things *change*, dammit! I suggest if you want to keep your *job* here—"

."And here comes the mean old *threats*." Ness laughed softly. "Be my guest, Davida. Expose me. I don't care anymore."

But he did *care*! He hoped Davida wouldn't see through his bluff.

Davida said, "Kelley might—"

"Oh, *fuck* you, Davida! You want a favor, don't throw my past or my sister in my face." He stood, slowly walking over to her. Man, she was a terror, but the bitch did have her good points. And he was about to exploit one of them right this f-ing minute. He slipped his arms around her waist. "You want my help?"

"You know I do."

"Then beg me, Davida."

"Michael—"

"Fucking *beg* me!"

There was a moment of silence.

Davida whispered, "Please, Michael." She placed her hands on his chest and gently pushed him onto the divan. "Please help me."

Ness felt his breathing quicken. "Show me how much you want my help."

Davida let her kimono fall open as she dropped to her knees before him. "Please, *please* help me." She wrapped her fingers around the waistband of his gym shorts and pulled the shorts down to his ankles. "You know I *need* you."

Ness closed his eyes as she stroked his inner thigh.

"Say yes," Davida whispered. "Say yes, you'll help me."

"Yes, I'll help you."

She parted his knees and lowered her mouth between his legs. Slowly, slowly, he gave way to her, running his hands through blue-black hair thickened stiff with spray. Irony of ironies, only with this old demonic bitch could he let himself go. It was all a sick game of domination—another role for Davida but one she played well. Sometimes she'd lead, today it was his turn. But they both knew who had whom by the proverbial balls.

He moaned. If you're gonna be raped, lie back and enjoy it, man.

Goldin unwrapped a Nestlé's Crunch bar.

"One of the few vestiges of my childhood. Slowly, I've come to terms with the fact that I'm on the dark side of thirty. Things I did that I used to consider cute are now just plain pathetic."

"You're stalling, Mr. Goldin."

"Perry."

"You're stalling, Perry."

"Yes, I am." He took a bite of his candy bar. "Okay. Here we go. Take a good look at me. I was— and still am—everything that Lilah's family *didn't* want. I'm opinionated, I'm left-wing, I'm not interested in making impressions, I don't care about money, I don't care how I look, I don't do honest labor, and I won't tolerate being patronized. And in that family, I was patronized constantly and dished it back. They didn't take kindly to that."

"Lilah was rebelling when she married you."

"Obviously. Lilah's upper-crust WASP, I'm a walking Jewish stereotype. And maybe I was rebelling when I married her. But there was a hell of a lot more to it than simple rebellion. I was *crazy* about her. Lilah was a knockout—still is, I imagine."

He looked to Decker for confirmation. Decker nodded and Goldin took another bite of his candy bar.

"She was also great in bed. Absolutely sensational. It surprised me, because she was young when we started up."

"How young?"

"She told me she was nineteen, but I found out later that she wasn't even eighteen. I'm eight years older than she. But Lilah had prior experience from somewhere. Man, she bowled me over with her looks and her sexuality. I was so hot for her, I would have done *anything* to get her. I even volunteered to apply to medical school for her. She and her mother had this thing for doctors."

"I've noticed."

"Yeah, the old lady was always on some kind of drug regimen. She used her sons as candy men— legal meds of course. God forbid, I should cast aspersions on anyone's medical ethics."

"Did you go to medical school?"

"No, it wasn't necessary." He took another bite of chocolate. "Lilah took me as is. She told me I had passion, ideas, and ideals. Not to mention *character* and *warmth*."

He laughed.

"Anybody would have seemed warm compared to

those ice floes. Nobody but *nobody* in that family ever showed any affection or tenderness. Just anger and hysterics. I'll tell you, my first marriage was an excellent training ground for a career in bridge. Nothing I've ever witnessed in twenty-five years of the most heated playing has ever come close to their tantrums."

Decker said, "What pushed their buttons?"

"What didn't? They're flipped, especially the old lady. Every new moon, it was Davida enraged over treatment by a boyfriend—or a girlfriend. She'd jump anything with a heartbeat. Came on to me countless times. It was all real sick, but I put up with it, because I really wanted Lilah.

"Of course, when we announced our engagement, the old lady went off the deep end. I was great as hired help, but not marriage material, for goodness' sake! But Davida wasn't half as angry as Lilah's brother. Talk about *tantrums*! Guy popped his seams, he was so mad."

"Which brother?"

"King—oh, excuse me, Doctor Kingston Merritt, FACOG, *s'il vous plaît*." Goldin leaned back in his seat. "Dr. Pomp and Circumstance. What an overbloated stuffed shirt. Good doc, though. Had more degrees than an isobar map. More than once I heard him talking to patients over the phone. Guy could be soothing when he wanted to be. Too bad he never showed that side to any of his family members."

"Soothing?" Decker asked.

"Yeah, you know . . . 'I'll be right down, Mrs. So-and-so. You just keep breathing and everything will be just fine.' Mr. Sincere." Goldin shrugged. "Maybe his sincerity was genuine. But then he'd hang up the phone and breathe fire on me or his sister or his mother. A real Jekyll and Hyde."

Decker wrote as he spoke. "What about the other brothers?"

"I never saw too much of John . . . he kept to himself. John was also a successful doc. Lived in this big house in Palos Verdes. You know, both he and King are OB-GYNs. You don't have to be Freud to know why they both went into a profession where they could dominate women."

"Davida?"

"The great Ms. Eversong herself. Woman has *tremendous* charisma . . . a real siren. She'd turn on the anger and have me quaking in my boots. And I wasn't even a blood relative. As I look back, I think, *why* did I put up with it? My self-esteem wasn't great, but it wasn't ground level, either." He sighed. "It was *Lilah*. She had such . . . *power*."

Decker raised his brows. "Power?"

"Sexual power but also *energy*. She'd say these wacky things and I'd believe her because she radiated such force."

"What kind of wacky things?"

"Predicting the future. That kind of rot."

"Anything she say ever come true?"

"At the time I was married to her, it seemed like everything she said came true. Then one day when I was really ticked off at her, I did some mathematical computations showing her with numbers that her predictions weren't any better than the

law of averages would dictate. Man, she flew into a
rage. After that, I kept my mouth shut about her
powers."

"So it was all nonsense."

"Why?" Goldin said. "She's got you believing in
her magic? She can be pretty convincing. Don't be
fooled."

Decker remained impassive but took in Goldin's
words. Time to change the subject.

"What were your impressions of Frederick Brecht?"

"Little Freddy. He was a pathetic kid when I mar-
ried Lilah. *Totally* dominated by Davida—and
Kingston and *Lilah*. Poor guy never had a chance."
Goldin paused. "I heard he became a doctor."

Decker nodded.

"That's good. Maybe now Davida will stop tor-
menting him. She was always biased against him
because he was adopted—"

"Freddy's *adopted*?"

"Is that significant?"

"I'm not sure," Decker said. But he wrote the word
adopted in his notebook.

"The family made no secret of it," Goldin said.
"Davida was in her forties when Lilah was born. I
suppose her late husband wanted a son and Davida
just couldn't pull it off again. Hence Freddy."

He thought a moment.

"Davida wasn't nice to him, but Davida wasn't really nice to anyone. She had a real combative relationship with King, who *was* her biological son. King
was the bull seal of the family—Lilah's surrogate
father. He *despised* me, tried to buy me off. I refused

the money, and Lilah and I married, much to everyone's chagrin."

"What about John Reed? You said you didn't see too much of him."

"John was actually all right. Not that we were ever friendly. But he wasn't tangled up in Davida's little web. His words to me were: 'If you want your marriage to work, get the hell away from Mother.' I tried, but . . ."

Decker said, "Davida can be a very formidable person."

"So you know." Goldin appraised Decker. "Old lady went for you, didn't she? You're her type. You're Lilah's type, too. Despite her brief fling with Jewish intellectuals, she really likes the big macho, shoot-em-up Gentiles à la Clint Eastwood, no offense."

"I'm Jewish," Decker said.

Without missing a beat, Goldin said, "Okay, so how about you talk for a moment so I can yank my foot out of my mouth."

Decker smiled.

Goldin paused to take a breath. "You're not putting me on?"

"No, Perry, I'm not." Decker flipped a page of his notebook. "Why do you think Lilah picked you to rebel with?"

"I've often thought about that. Probably because I was handy—I was around. I was hired by King to teach Davida bridge. I wasn't intimidated by Davida's money and I think Lilah liked that. Also, Davida liked my attention and Lilah was acutely aware of that. My ex got a big thrill out of diverting my attention away from Davida. There was fierce competition between the two."

"Competition and jealousy," Decker said.

"You've got their number. Toward the end, Lilah was convinced I was sleeping with her mother. Nothing I could say or do could convince her otherwise. It was awful."

"Were there good times?"

Goldin was thoughtful. "In the beginning, it was wonderful. We'd talk a lot about solving the world's problems. The kind of thing you do when you're young and idealistic. She seemed so moved, so full of desire to do *good*. Once we even sailed with Greenpeace into the North Sea waters to prevent the Soviets from whaling. With the wind-chill factor, it was forty below on the seas. We were all freezing our butts off. Lilah *loved* it—*thrived* on it."

"Was that the extent of her altruism?"

"Not at all. We did a lot of other things on a smaller scale. Collected coats and blankets for the homeless, volunteered to serve in the hash lines at the missions. She even taught an arts and crafts class for the elderly at a recreation center. Matter of fact, one of Lilah's students became one of her best buddies for a while. Turned out the old lady was from Germany and vaguely knew Lilah's father."

That got Decker's attention. "She knew Hermann Brecht?"

"Vaguely. Lilah had a real hang-up about her father. Idolized him even though she never really knew him. We used to watch his movies together. I don't mind movies that tell life like it is. But his movies . . . *whew*! What a thoroughly depressing, debilitating view of life. I'm not the least bit surprised old Hermann committed suicide."

Decker said, "Do you remember the old woman's name?"

"Sure. Greta Millstein. Like I said, they were pretty close. Greta was different—offbeat—and I think Lilah liked that. She claimed one of her daughters was a Jewish baby given to her by neighbors right before they were sent off to Dachau. Of course the family perished, so Greta raised the child as her own. Maybe she was snowing me because I was Jewish, but I saw no reason to doubt her."

"Do you know where she lives?"

"I haven't seen her in five years. I don't even know if she's still alive. Why are you interested in her?"

"Because she knew Hermann Brecht. And like you said, Lilah is obsessed with her father." Decker looked up from his notepad. "Did Lilah ever mention her father's memoirs to you?"

"Memoirs?" Goldin played with his beard. "Did Hermann Brecht write memoirs?"

"That's what I'm trying to find out."

"If he did, this is the first I've heard about it."

"Did Lilah ever intimate she'd been willed something by her father?"

"Not to me." Goldin shrugged. "Sorry. What does this have to do with Lilah's attack?"

"I'm not sure it has anything to do with it. Do you remember where Greta Millstein was living then?"

"In the Valley—a block-long apartment complex planted with rolling lawns and trees. I doubt if it's there anymore. Some developer probably got his mitts on it and turned the space into a shopping mall."

"*Where* in the Valley, Mr. Goldin?"

"Corner of Fulton and Riverside. I never knew the exact address, but Greta's apartment number was fifty-four."

"You've got a good memory."

"Memory is my bread and butter, Detective."

"Did you see Greta often?"

"Only occasionally. But Lilah used to visit her two, even three times a week. It was sweet to see them together—this wrinkled old woman and this beautiful young princess. They had this relationship that bridged what must have been a fifty-year age span. Then, as suddenly as it started, it stopped."

"Why?"

"I don't know exactly. Frankly, that wasn't uppermost in my mind. Lilah and I were having lots of problems by that time." Goldin grew pensive. "She was on my case, nonstop. Instead of finding me enthusiastic and stimulating, now I was obnoxious and overbearing. Which I was, but I was always like that. She just didn't like me anymore. I was crushed when she served me papers. I was angry and bitter and . . ."

He threw up his hands, shook his head, and became quiet.

Decker waited a beat, then said, "You seem all right now."

Goldin smiled. "Yeah, I am. All the credit goes to my wife. Man, if Humpty Dumpty had known Wendy, he'd be sitting on the wall today. First time

I met her, I wasn't knocked off my feet like I was with Lilah, but . . ." He let out a soft chuckle. "God, I *love* that woman. She scares the hell out of me working downtown at night. But she's altruistic—genuinely altruistic." He sighed. "What can I do?"

Decker thought of Rina, how protective he felt toward her. Not that his feelings ever stopped her from doing dumb and dangerous things. "Before you leave, give me the address of the clinic."

Goldin was surprised. "Why?"

"I'll give it to the watch commanders at Central. Maybe the cruisers can beef up their passes. But that won't stop the crime, of course."

"Just like that?"

"I'm a great guy."

"Thank you." He smiled. "Thank you very much."

"You're welcome," Decker said. "Perry, you can't think of any reason why Lilah stopped seeing Greta?"

"No . . . except . . ."

"What?"

"In the beginning, Lilah and I didn't have much to do with Davida. But as we began to fall apart, she got closer to her mother. Also, around that time, Lilah stopped doing *all* her charity work. She reverted back to type, started spending lots of money. She bought the spa shortly after we divorced. I don't know. I've always felt Lilah was using Greta as a mother figure. When she started up with Davida again, it was like she didn't need Greta anymore."

Goldin furrowed his brow in concentration.

"I felt bad for Greta. I even visited her on my own once or twice. She wasn't the least bit upset by Lilah's behavior. Took it all philosophically—as if she expected it."

"Did she have any clues as to why Lilah stopped coming?"

Goldin shook his head. "I don't remember her saying anything specific. Just something about she knew it wouldn't last . . . 'it' being their relationship. Like I said, she was philosophical about Lilah's rejection. I wish I'd reacted that way. Saved me a lot of self-flagellation."

"Nah, that never gets you anywhere." Decker flipped the cover of his notebook and stuffed it in his jacket. "You've helped me out. I'll call if I have any more questions."

"That's it?"

"For now."

"Sure, call me anytime. This was kind of fun in a way—macho therapy. You missed your calling as a shrink."

Decker wondered how much money shrinks made. He said, "I'll give you my number in case you think of anything significant to add." He pulled out his business card and a picture of Rina fell out of his wallet. Goldin picked it up.

"Your daughter?"

"My wife."

Goldin moaned. "Ye olde foot back in ye olde mouth."

"She's young, Perry." Decker took the picture back. "Not as young as she looks, but young."

"Can I see that again?"

Decker paused, then handed him the snapshot.

Goldin said, "Is she this pretty in the flesh—I mean, in real life?"

Decker said, "You're asking me?"

"I'm not trying to be cute," Goldin said. "I'm asking you the question in earnest, Detective."

The guy had something on his mind. Decker said, "In earnest, she's better. She's six months pregnant and she still gets wolf whistles every time she walks down the street."

"She's pregnant?" Goldin asked.

Decker said, "It can happen."

"No, I don't mean it like that." He handed the photo back to Decker. "Don't let Lilah see her or your life'll be hell."

Decker said, "Go on."

"Lilah's competitive spirit isn't confined to Davida. She loves married men. I should know. I must have fielded dozens of calls from distraught wives. If she finds out you have a beautiful—and pregnant— wife, you'll never get rid of her." Goldin bit his lip. "Lilah can't resist a *challenge*."

Decker placed his hand on Goldin's shoulder. After all this time, the guy still sounded bruised and Decker knew that feeling. "She likes making mincemeat out of men?"

"Detective, it's what she does best."

⌘19

A full moon: the perfect topper to a freaky day. Decker stared out the window, half expecting to see werewolves or vampire bats. But instead, he played witness to a silvery disc drifting through diaphanous clouds, to silhouetted birch branches swaying in the summer wind. Transfixed by the spectacle, he hadn't even realized the rabbi had come in until he felt a gentle pat on his shoulder.

Rav Schulman was well into his seventies, and for the first time, Decker noticed a slight stooping of the old man's shoulders. The hunching had cut a couple of inches from the rav's height, putting him at around five-ten. Most of his face was covered by a beard that was more white than gray and what skin did show was creased and mottled with liver spots. But his coffee-colored eyes were as radiant as ever. As usual, he was dressed in a starched white shirt, a black suit that hung a little too loosely on his frame, a black silk tie, and an ebony homburg. The old man leaned against the windowsill, eyes focused on nature's snapshot.

"Beautiful, nu?"

"Yes, it is," Decker answered.

"Peaceful." Rabbi Schulman faced Decker. "So unlike your day from what I hear."

Decker exhaled slowly. "I must have been more affected than I realized for Rina to call you. And here I was thinking I was maintaining perfectly . . ."

The rabbi smiled. "Are you all right, Akiva?"

"Physically?"

"Physically . . . emotionally."

"I'm fine."

The old man absorbed his student's words, weighing their veracity for just a moment. Then he pointed to a chair, offering Decker a seat. Schulman eased into a leather chair, and rested his elbows on his sprawling desktop. Clasping his hands, he touched his lips to his fingers and waited.

Haltingly, Decker related the details of the morning's ordeal. As he spoke, he began to feel lighter of weight, his emotions releasing in slow steady leaks rather than sudden bursts. He was sheepish about using the rabbi as a spiritual springboard. But the old man seemed used to it.

Afterward, Schulman said, "It was a fluke, this horse going crazy?"

"No, Rabbi, the horse was drugged."

The old man pondered the statement. "Someone tried to kill this lady using a horse?"

"Maybe just frighten her. But who knows?"

"Terrible," Schulman said. "Truly terrible."

"If that's what happened, yes, it is."

The old man seemed a shade paler than before. Decker quickly added, "She's fine, Rabbi. Sure she was shaken, but she's fine."

"Did you bench *gomel*?" the old man asked.

Gomel—thanks to God for delivering a person from harm. Decker had not only said it, he had said it with feeling.

"Yes, though technically, I guess she was the one who should have done the praying." He added under his breath, "Not that I can imagine her praying."

Schulman said, "She's an atheist?"

"No, I don't think so." Decker smoothed his mustache. "She's more like a New Ager. Do you know what that is?"

"It's a person who worships chandeliers."

Decker smiled. "Crystals, Rabbi. Not chandeliers."

"There's a difference?" Schulman waved his hands in the air. "It's all *avodah zorah*—idol worship."

Easily categorized, easily dismissed. But something was gnawing at Decker's gut.

"Rabbi, the woman claims to have magical powers, says she can predict things by the miasma in the air. Of course, she's strange. But something in me can't completely disregard her. Before the horse bolted, she felt something bad was going to happen. And then the horse went crazy. I don't know what to think."

Schulman's expression was grave. "And this woman. She is beautiful, Akiva?"

Decker raised his brow. "Truthfully, she is."

"And sensual?"

"Yes."

"And seductive?"

"Very." Decker observed the old man's face. "Do you know who I'm talking about?"

"In theory only. I have met her in the Bible." Schulman adjusted his hat. "'*Mechashepha lo techaye*—do not let a sorceress live.' Not that I'm wishing harm to befall her in any way. I'm relieved that she's fine."

"I know you are, Rabbi."

"Perhaps, Akiva, this woman's feelings of power are nothing more than a wish to be special, a shout for attention."

"Could be. Although she hasn't called the press. And she could get press if she wanted to." Decker drummed his finger on the desk. "Rabbi, what made you ask if she was seductive?"

Schulman threw up his hands. "I'm not in the business of personality profiles."

"I won't hold you to anything."

"Just so we understand that I'm talking theoretically."

"Understood."

"Okay." Schulman sat up in his seat. "When one hears of predicting the future, if one is a rabbi, he thinks of false prophets or sorceresses. Makes sense, correct?"

Decker nodded.

Schulman said, "I asked about those specific characteristics because they're traits of the sorceresses and false prophetesses recounted in our history. Many of them were beautiful and seductive because they were the ones able to obtain followers. They would entice the men sexually, win them over to their profane ways, and eventually the poor wives and daughters—not wishing to be deserted—would follow the men. Many men fell prey to the lures and were sucked into lives of idol worship and sexual depravity. Insanely jealous of Hashem and His true powers, these so-called prophetesses would do anything to get Jews to abandon the Torah. That is why the biblical punishment against them is so strong."

"The Torah doesn't advocate killing prostitutes and they're pretty licentious," said Decker. "Why such harsh measures for a seductress?"

"Sorceress, not seductress, Akiva. But still it's a good question. You have a woman causing problems—who is sexually loose and is preaching false words, doing black magic—why not just exercise some other form of punishment? Perhaps a sound flogging or even banishment? Why death?"

Schulman lifted his finger in the air.

"Why? I'll tell you why. Because sexual licentiousness wasn't the sole moral problem of the false prophet. The pagan ritual practices were *barbaric*, Akiva, often full of human sacrifice and infant slaughter as offerings to their idols. If the pagans didn't kill outright, they often mortally maimed—castration, evisceration, amputation. Not to mention hideous torture to animals. Once morality is compromised like that, ethics fall by the wayside permanently. The hedonistic rituals—all of them completely contrary not only to the Torah, but to the seven Noachide laws." The old man got a gleam in his eyes. "Which are . . ."

Decker smiled.

"Always the teacher, Akiva," Schulman said. "Name them for me."

Decker listed the seven laws—the six prohibitions against blasphemy, idolatry, murder, adultery, theft, and eating or drinking blood from live animals as well as the one positive commandment to establish legal systems. Divinely revealed laws given to the world after the Great Flood.

Schulman said, "Very good. The commentaries teach us that it is not necessary to be Jewish to have a share of the world to come. But it *is* necessary to follow the Noachide laws. That is why the other religions are not an affront to Hashem—quite the contrary. There is a place for all righteous people. But *not* for pagans who torture."

Decker thought a moment about the Noachide statutes.

"You know, I'm thinking to myself, Rabbi, these laws are the polar opposites of devil worship. Satanists must have formulated their rules by doing the antithesis of the Noachide laws." He laughed. "Not exactly an earth-shattering observation."

"But a correct one, Akiva. Satan is the polar opposite of Hashem. Is your seductive lady a Satanist by any chance?"

"I don't have any indication of that, but I don't really know. Maybe she does belong to some crazy cult and some lunatic is out to make her a human sacrifice. I think that's a long shot. Still . . ."

"And as long as you're considering long shots, may I suggest something else?"

"Sure. Shoot."

"Perhaps some demented mind took the biblical words 'Don't let a sorceress live' literally. Perhaps some fanatical crazy she knows is hearing voices commanding him—or her—to do a terrible deed."

Decker thought about the suspects; none impressed

him as psychotic. But who knew what they'd concocted in the secrecy of their minds.

"It wouldn't be the first time, Rabbi. I'll think about it."

Schulman stroked his beard and nodded gravely. "Akiva, I know you have certain responsibilities to your cases. Not that I'm saying anything against this lady, I don't even know her. But a false prophetess is a tricky animal. Do use caution—physically and mentally."

"I'm always cautious in my work, Rabbi."

Schulman patted Decker's hand. "Good." He paused, looking perplexed. "These shmystal-crystals, Akiva. What do people *do* with them? Do they talk to them and wait for an answer? Do they hold them up to the sun and tan their faces? What?"

"I'm not a crystal expert, Rav Schulman, but I think they're used to communicate with the dead."

The old man shook his head with disapproval. "I will never understand the fascination with the *dead*."

"We all die."

"Yes, we do, but we all live as well. People should concentrate on bettering their lives, not trying to second-guess the other side. If they live righteously, they'll have nothing to worry about. *Boruch Hashem*, I've made it this far. Now one might even say I have one foot in the grave—"

"Rabbi—"

"Not that I'm ready to die." The old man stood and took out two shot glasses. "But if it happens, it happens. People who fear death do not fear God. Besides, Akiva, what do the sages teach us about Torah?"

"It was meant for the living not the dead."

"Correct!" Schulman filled the glasses with whiskey and handed one to Decker. "So, my friend, let us live and learn and do mitzvot as Hashem commanded us." He held his drinking glass aloft. "To life—*l'chaim*."

"*L'chaim*," Decker said.

The rabbi downed his whiskey in one gulp. Decker marveled at the way Schulman could drink rotgut without emitting fire from his nostrils. He sneaked a sidelong glance at the rav, watched him lick his lips with pleasure. What a kick to know this man— this septuagenarian chock-full of energy and spirit and humor. A relief to know the good didn't always die young.

The sharp knock woke Decker first, but Rina sat up a moment later, hand slapping onto her chest.

"Who's that?" she asked, breathlessly.

Decker swore under his breath and slipped on a robe. "Stay here, Rina."

The knocking became louder. Then the dog started barking.

"Do you want your gun?" Rina whispered.

Decker pushed hair out of his eyes. "No."

By the time he reached the living room, the banging was shaking the front door. Ginger had posted guard at the front door. Decker called out a "hold on," quieted the setter, and peeked through the peephole. But he needn't have bothered. His gut had already told him who it was. He tightened his robe, unlocked the deadbolt, and swung open the door.

Lilah was flushed and contorted with anger and fear, wet tracks streaming down her cheeks. Her arms were swinging wildly, trying to hit him and hold him at the same time—hysterical but she had taken time to dress. She wore rhinestone-studded jeans and a white T-shirt under a black blazer, the jacket collar trimmed with sequins. On her feet were black ostrich cowboy boots complete with spurs. Decker kept a careful eye on them.

"How *dare* you change your number on me especially after yesterday! How *dare* you! How *could* you!"

Ginger started growling, baring her teeth. Decker managed to shush her, but was less successful with Lilah.

"How *could* you, Peter! You know how much I depend on you, how much I need you!" She hit his chest. "How could you! *How could you!*"

Decker took another step backward. Ginger growled again. Decker held the animal by the collar and said, "Lilah, calm dow—"

She lashed out at his face with sharpened fingernails. Decker managed to get her wrist before she raked his cheek and somehow settled the dog before Ginger took a chunk out of Lilah's leg. She struggled against his grip, wriggling and hissing like a trapped cobra.

"I *hate* you!" Lilah screamed. "I hate you, you son of a *bitch*! I hate you, I *hate* you!"

The woman was skinny, but she could put up a fight. Decker was working up a sweat trying to hold her at bay without hurting her. It would have felt great to haul off and slug her. Out of the corner of his eye, he saw Rina, her hands wrapped around her chest, stroking her arms. Dressed in white, her face pale, she might have been a phantom—or an angel—except that her eyes were alert and ready for action.

"Call the station house," he said.

"You *bastard*!" Lilah shouted.

"Call the police," Decker repeated.

"How *could* you—"

"Call the police, Rina," Decker commanded.

It was as if Lilah finally comprehended his words. "Wait!" She stopped wrestling and let her arms relax. "Wait, don't do that!"

A moment passed. A small voice called out a "Mommy?"

"It's all right," Rina yelled out. "Everything's fine, I'll be there in a minute." Her eyes were on Peter. "What should I do?"

Lilah wheeled in on her. "Well, as long as you're standing there, you can make us some coffee!"

Decker dropped Lilah's wrists, his eyes, suddenly blurred with fury. "Don't speak to her like that."

Rina said, "Peter—"

"She is not one of your little gofers, Lilah, don't you *dare* speak to her like that!"

This time it was Lilah who backed away.

"She *lives* here, understand, Miss Brecht?" Decker fumed as he advanced upon her. "This is *her* house, *her* living room, and you woke *her* up at three o'clock in the morning from *her* goddamn sleep!"

"Peter—"

"You want coffee, girlie, you go home and goddamn make it yourself!"

"Peter!" Rina was holding his arm. "Peter, why don't you call Marge from the bedroom, okay?"

Panting, Decker suddenly became aware that he'd sandwiched Lilah into a corner. He took a step backward and unclenched his fists. It took him a moment to focus. Then, he turned to Rina.

"I'm sorry."

Rina smiled weakly and kissed his cheek. "Go call Marge."

Decker took another step backward and ran his hand over his face. "Okay." He felt his breath returning to normal. "Okay." He kissed Rina on the forehead and headed for the bedroom, taking the dog with him.

"Peter?" Rina called.

Decker turned around.

"Check in on the boys, please."

Decker nodded and left. Rina's eyes went from him to Lilah who was still huddled in the corner, her arms strapped across her chest protectively. But she had a strange look on her face. Like a frightened little girl who'd done something naughty—scared but nonetheless pleased with herself. Slowly, Lilah's lips formed a half smile.

"He was really angry, wasn't he?"

Rina caught the sex-hungry timbre in Lilah's voice. Or maybe she was overreacting because the woman was so beautiful. She said, "Have a seat at the dining-room table. I'll make you some coffee."

Silence.

"Come." Rina extended her arm in the direction of the table. "Sit."

"You must think I'm crazy."

There were tears in the woman's eyes. Rina said, "Not at all. Come."

Lilah extricated herself from the corner and made baby steps over to the table. Rina made a beeline for the kitchen. She took the coffee from the refrigerator and poured water into the glass carafe. Sensing another body behind her, she knew Lilah had followed her in.

"Does he get angry like that all the time?"

Rina poured the water into the coffeemaker. "Why don't you sit at the kitchen table."

"I'm very sorry," Lilah whispered. "It's just . . ." She sat down at the kitchen table. "Black coffee's fine. I'm sorry."

Rina suddenly remembered what had happened to her and softened her attitude. "It's okay. I'm very sorry about yesterday. I'm glad you're all right."

"I wouldn't have been if your husband hadn't been there."

Rina nodded.

"He's a marvelous rider."

"Yes, he is," Rina answered.

"I wouldn't mind riding with him again." Lilah brought her fingers to her lips. "I mean . . ." Lilah laughed. "I don't know what I'm saying. Please forgive me."

"Don't worry about it. Coffee'll be ready in a moment."

"Thank you."

Rina noticed Lilah's voice had turned low and sexy. Against the still of the night, it was as beckoning as an aromatic whiff from the kitchen.

"I didn't just come to wake Peter up," Lilah said.

"I really do need to talk to him. Normally, I handle stress very well, but . . ." Her eyes became wet. "But how much . . ."

She was leaking tears, but it seemed to Rina that she had a smile on her face.

"How much can one person take?" Rina said.

"*Exactly!*" Lilah wiped her eyes.

Rina picked up the carafe and said, "I made decaf. Just in case anyone's contemplating sleep."

Lilah looked up, her eyes squinting. "You're *pregnant*!"

Rina nodded and poured two cups of coffee. The telephone rang. Peter got to the line before she did. Lilah looked at the mug in front of her.

"Is this water-processed decaf?"

"Yes."

Lilah sipped, her eyes suddenly hardening. "So, is it your first—no, it can't be if you asked Peter to check on the boys. How many kids do you have anyway?" Again she squinted. "You're much younger than he is. How *old* are you?"

"Excuse me for a moment," Rina said.

She walked into the bedroom as Peter was walking out.

"I'm really sorry about this," he whispered.

"Boys are okay?"

"Yeah, they're waiting for you to kiss them good night. Rina, I'm *sorry*—"

"Don't worry about it, Peter. She's calmer now. Claims she needs to talk to you. Let her get it off her chest, then get her *out* of here." She paused. "Don't be too harsh. She's gone through a lot."

Decker thought about what Lilah had gone through.

Could be her extreme rage was a delayed reaction
from the rape. She was angry at men and taking it
out on him. If that was the case, she had the worst
case of transference *he'd* ever seen. But Lilah didn't
seem to act in moderation. Or it could be the woman
was bonkers before and the rape drove her over the
edge. Whatever the reason, no way was he going to
let this broad take it out on Rina.

"You're wonderful, Rina. The *best!*"

She shook her head knowingly. "This is true."

"I've called Marge," Decker said. "I've also called
Lilah's brother. He's coming down and picking her
up." He stuck his hands in his pants pockets. "Kiss
the boys and go back to sleep."

"Go back to *sleep*?" Rina laughed.

"Well, rest, okay?"

Rina smiled, noticing that Peter had dressed. She
held him by the arms and looked over his attire—a
pair of loose-fitting jeans, a work shirt, and sneakers.
Comfortable but not the least bit provocative. She
approved.

20

Storming through the door, Frederick Brecht was dressed in a raw-silk caftan, stone-washed black jeans, and raw-silk jacket. He wore Nike high-tops, the cuffs of his pants tucked under the oversized tongues of his shoes. His blue eyes were watery and red, his scalp and the skin around his beard pink and mottled. He'd slapped on some grassy-smelling cologne. Too much because he was in a hurry, Decker thought. Brecht's face was knotted with anger as he faced his sister. "Are you *crazy*?"

Lilah looked at Decker. "This was precisely the reason why I can't recup—"

"Are you out of your *mind*, Lilah? Waking him up at three in the morning?" Brecht was enraged. "For God's sake, why didn't you call *me*!?"

"Freddy is so jealous," Lilah said.

"Dear God, it has nothing to do with jealousy! It has to do with common sense—"

"For your information, I tried calling you, Freddy. You weren't home."

"I can be reached!" Brecht was screaming now. He pointed to Decker. "*He* reached me!"

Marge wiped a speck of dirt off her slacks. "Look,

303

I don't have kids, I'm not used to three o'clock feedings. Can we get this show on the road?"

"Why did you call *her* down?" Lilah suddenly demanded of Decker.

"You have something to report, Miss Brecht, ask for Detective Dunn. She's your new primary detective."

"*What!* You just can't *drop* me!"

"No one dropped you," Marge said evenly.

"He can't leave me in the lurch!"

"Detective Dunn is one of the most specialized people we have on the force—"

"I can't believe you're deserting me!"

"No one is deserting anyone," Marge said. "If you need my services, I'll be right there—"

"I don't want you, I want him!" Lilah pointed to Decker. "It's not that I don't trust you, Detective. I'm just used to Peter."

"Peter?" Brecht said. "You're on first-name basis with the police?"

"Frederick, stop acting so infantile."

"You're acting infantile interrupting this poor man's sleep." Brecht turned to Decker. "I'm sorry about this—"

"Stop apologizing for me as if I were your child!"

"Sometimes you act like a child!"

"If you'd stop treating me like a child—"

"Miss Brecht," Decker said, "is there something specific you wanted to talk to me about?"

Marge smiled at Pete's style. Just lay it on the line.

Lilah bit her knuckle. "It's about my brother."

"Me?" Brecht gasped.

"No, King."

"*Kingston?*" Brecht turned bright red. "What do you want with *Kingston*?"

"Freddy, you are so tiresome!"

"What does *that* jerk want?" Brecht whined. "I know he's up to something with Mother—"

"What about King, Miss Brecht?" Marge interrupted.

"I'm worried about him." Lilah bit her knuckle again. "I was supposed to meet him last night for dinner—"

"You were meeting that pompous *slimeball* for *dinner*?" Brecht held up his hands and shook them as he talked. "How could you even think about going *anywhere* after what happened to you? You need at least a few days of bed rest!"

"It was spontaneous, Freddy. Mother said he wanted to talk to me . . . after he heard about my . . . assault."

"And you agreed to talk to him?"

"I was shocked, of course, I didn't know . . ." Tears formed in her eyes. "Yes, I agreed. And he was very nice over the phone. Comforting . . . soothing. Just like when I was little. He seemed to care about me again—"

"Kingston doesn't care about anyone but himself!"

"Just because you two don't get along—"

"How'd he hear about your assault anyway?" Brecht asked.

"I told him," Marge said. "After Mike Ness took you upstairs to calm you down from your fight with Dr. Merritt."

"So how'd he find out about your *horse*?" Brecht asked.

Lilah said, "He didn't even *know* about that, Freddy. He just wanted to visit me. Isn't that so *wonderful*?"

Brecht muttered, "That ass has something on his mind—"

"Freddy, you are impossible. He *loves* me—"

"He wants something from you—"

"You don't know what you're talking about!"

Marge said, "Can we stay on a topic, people? Lilah, what about King and dinner?"

Lilah turned to her, then began to pace. "I agreed to meet him last night for dinner . . . first time in years—"

"I don't believe this!" Brecht interrupted. "How could you do that!"

"Freddy, please try and understand," Lilah said. "I know you hate him—"

"You're the one who *froths* at the mouth at the mention of his name!"

"People, please!" Marge said. "I'm tired and grumpy. Get on with it."

"I'm trying to, Detective," Lilah snorted. "I agreed to meet Kingston *if* I felt up to it. And I *did*. I called his service and left a message that dinner was on, providing we'd meet at Monique's because it was very close to the ranch. I told his service I'd be there at eight. Then I called up the spa and left a message for Mother. I wanted to borrow her limo and driver. I was still very weak—too shaky to drive my own car."

She looked to Decker for sympathy. He nodded,

remembering the genuine terror scored into her face as the horse charged toward the mountain.

"Go on," Marge said.

"I never heard from him." Lilah dropped her hand to her side. "So I called his residence. Nothing. His service hasn't been able to get hold of him, either. I *know* something has happened to him. Just as sure as I knew something was going to happen to me yesterday morning! The electricity, the vibes . . ."

Brecht said, "Why would you want to *talk* to him?"

"Freddy, for God's sake, *listen* to what I'm saying. He's *your* brother, too. Something has *happened* to him!"

"You don't know that!" Brecht said.

"Oh, God!" she screamed. "Just shut up!"

At that moment, Decker caught a glimpse of her mother in her face. "You called his house and his service. What about his office?"

"That, too. I've called all his private lines. He doesn't answer! Peter, I'm scared!"

She started to come to Decker, but he backed away. Marge stood and placed her hand on Lilah's shoulder. "Where does Dr. Merritt live, Miss Brecht?"

"Newport."

"House or apartment?"

"A condominium actually."

Marge said, "Is it an exclusive building?"

"Detective, it's very *chercher*!"

Marge looked at Decker. He shrugged. She said, "So it has maintenance, housekeeping, a doorman, maybe even a front desk."

"Of course!"

Of course, Marge thought icily. To Decker, she said, "Front desk would have a key to the place. I'll call."

Lilah gave Marge the number and they waited. Seventeen minutes later, Marge hung up the phone. "He's not there. But they told me the quarters looked fine, nothing's out of place."

"How would *they* know?" Lilah said.

Marge ignored the question and said, "Okay, that leaves his office. I'm not about to go out to Newport—"

"Palos Verdes," Lilah corrected.

"Whatever." Marge draped her parka over her shoulders. "I'm not going out on a wild-goose chase—"

"It is *not* a wild-goose chase, I can assure you! The electrical charges are very strong."

"Then maybe *you* should drive out to Palos Verdes," Marge suggested.

"In my current state of mind?" Lilah snarled. "How could you possibly think—"

"Palos Verdes will keep until the morning," Decker stated. "In the meantime, go home and sleep, Miss Brecht."

"I couldn't do that."

"Then rest," Decker said.

"Take another ginseng and gingerroot bath," Marge said.

"At last!" Brecht piped up. "Someone with good advice!"

Lilah said, "Peter—"

"Sergeant Decker," Marge corrected. "What is it, Miss Brecht?"

"My brother . . ." She let out a deep breath. "He has a little satellite office in Burbank."

"His abortion mill," Freddy Brecht clarified. "Hourly rates—"

"He's doing a service—"

"The mad butcher of Burbank—"

"No one has ever died—"

"No one *you've* heard about!"

"Hey!" Decker shouted. "Don't you two ever quit? Enough! So Dr. Merritt has the office in Burbank. Why should he be there?"

"He's not answering the phone," Lilah said, "but I know he had a few morning appointments there yesterday—he told me that. I'm sure that's one of the reasons he was coming to meet me. Burbank isn't too far from the ranch. I guess he figured as long as he was in the area . . ." She sighed. "Can't you just take a look for me?"

"What good would it do if I couldn't get in?" Marge said.

"I don't know . . ." Lilah looked down at her lap. "I'm just worried. I know something's wrong. I just know it!"

Marge checked her watch and looked at Decker. "What do you figure? Forty-five minutes tops if nothing's there?"

"That sounds about right."

Lilah peeked sheepishly at Decker. "Will you look for Kingston?"

"I'll do the honors," Marge said. She cocked a thumb toward the front door. "Now if you two could kindly make an exit?"

Brecht took Lilah's elbow and guided her to the

door. Before he left, he turned and said, "Again, I'm sorry for the intrusion."

"There you go again. Apologizing for me! I'm not sorry!"

"Lilah—"

"Don't *Lilah* me!"

Brecht steered her outside and shut the door. Decker could hear them arguing until one of the cars finally roared off. He let out a slow stream of breath. "You're sure you want to do this, Marge?"

"S'right."

"Want me to go with you?"

"Nah. A guy not answering his phone calls doesn't scream foul play. Why shouldn't at least one of us get some sleep?"

"You're making me feel guilty, Marge."

"You better believe it, Pete." Marge pushed limp blond wisps out of her eyes and smiled. "I left an empty California King. You might as well make the most out of the situation."

Decker smiled back. "Not so bad."

"Not so bad."

Rina emerged from the bedroom. "Is it safe?"

Marge laughed. "You can come out now, Mrs. Decker. Poor Rina. What did you ever do to deserve this?"

"What did *I* ever do to deserve this?" Decker said.

Marge pointed a finger at him. "Hollander warned you. He offered to take the case."

Decker glanced upward, studying the ceiling. "Is that coffee I smell?"

"I'll get you a cup, Peter," Rina said. "Marge?"

"I'll get the coffee, Rina," Marge said. "You deal

with Detective Sergeant Innocent Bystander here."
She walked into the kitchen.

"I didn't say I was an innocent bystander," Decker
called after her. But she was already out of sight. To
Rina he said, "You actually made her coffee?"

"It gave me something to do with my hands while
I dodged her questions."

"I really am sorry."

"You don't choose your cases."

"Truth be told, Marge is right. Hollander did warn
me off. But you know me. I get stubborn."

"It's called perseverance." She stood on her tiptoes and kissed his cheek. "It's what makes you a
good detective."

Decker smiled. "You can say the right things when
you want to."

"Meaning I don't always want to?"

"No, I just meant—"

"Forget it, Peter." Rina tousled his hair.

Marge returned, carrying a mug stenciled with
dinosaurs. "I'm off."

Rina looked at Peter. "You're not going?"

Marge scowled. "Who needs 'im? Good night,
folks. I'll call if something's amiss." She sipped coffee and looked at the cup. "I'll give this back to you
in the morning."

"Keep it," Decker said.

"I can't be bought off with stegosauri, Pete."

"How 'bout if I throw in a year's supply of coffee,
sugar, *and* whitener in individual packets?"

"The temptation is overwhelming." Marge wiggled
her fingers and left.

"You owe her," Rina said.

"Big." Decker raised his brow. "You want to salvage the night?" He slipped his arms around Rina's burgeoning waistline and kissed the nape of her neck. "I'll even carry you across the threshold."

Rina turned and slipped her arm around his waist. "Speaking of being turned on, your damsel in distress got quite excited when you yelled at her."

Decker dropped his arms. "She's not my anything—except my supreme pain in the ass."

"I know." Rina picked up his hands and kissed them. "I was just being . . . hostile. But what I said was true. She likes your anger."

"Okay. Thanks for telling me. I won't get angry around her anymore. But there was no friggin' way I was going to let her get away with speaking to you like that."

"I appreciated your support, Peter." She kissed his hands again. "You know, I was just thinking—"

"Uh-oh."

"Thank you, Peter."

Decker smiled. "What's on your mind?"

"It's probably stupid."

"It probably isn't. What?"

"Her getting aroused by your fury. Maybe she likes her sex rough. Maybe her rape was . . . you know . . . her partner got carried away . . . and she's trying to protect him."

Decker tapped his foot and digested her words. "A game gone too far? Then what about the burglary?"

"I don't know." She let out a laugh, took his hand, and led him to the bedroom. "*You're* the detective."

"Leave me with all the hard stuff, huh?"

But she'd made an interesting point.

He was still awake when the phone went off and he answered it before the first ring was completed, glancing at Rina. Sound asleep. That made him happy.

"Pete?"

"Yeah, go ahead, Marge," he whispered.

"I haven't gone inside yet. Just called Burbank PD and told them what I was up to, asked them if they wanted to be part of this. They're sending me a single black-and-white."

Decker hopped out of bed, tucked the receiver under his chin, and pulled on his pants. "What's tweaking your nose?"

"Empty lot, Pete, except for a lone Mercedes 450 SL. The clinic's dark, the front door closed but *unlocked*. I've banged on the door. Went around to the back, banged on that door, too. Nothing. I'm not about to go and step on anyone else's turf."

"Right."

"On top of the car and unlocked door, I shone my beam on the asphalt and found a nice trail of what could be blood drips."

Decker buttoned his shirt. "Freddy said it was an abortion mill. Women bleed after abortions."

"Yeah, in and of itself, it wouldn't have raised any hackles. But with everything else . . ."

"I'll be down."

"I'll be waiting."

* * *

Four-forty-five in the morning and there was still traffic on the freeway. The city might sleep but the roadways never did. The night was cool and clear, the moon gliding over the tops of the mountains as Decker sped along the blacktop. He pushed the gas pedal to the floor and the Plymouth shot into overdrive.

The address Marge had given him was a poorly lighted stucco and brick corner office building set behind towering eucalyptus and palm trees. There was a paved parking lot in front, spaces marked for ten cars. Decker pulled the Plymouth between Marge's Honda and a Burbank cruiser, shut off the motor, and got out. Hands on hips, he took a quick look around. Adjacent to the clinic was an empty, weed-choked lot. The three other corners of the intersection were taken up by a Taco Bell, the skeletal remains of abandoned framing, and a discount-food-chain warehouse. Marge walked over to him.

"Not exactly city central."

"Makes sense," Decker answered. "You have an abortion clinic, you want privacy. Why give the nutcases an easy target to firebomb?"

"Nutcases?" Marge smiled. "You're not sympático with the right-to-lifers?"

"I'm not sympático with firebombers."

"Hear, hear!" Marge led him to a uniform leaning against his cruiser. "Sergeant Decker, Officer Loomis."

The patrolman stuck out a spidery-fingered hand. He was tall and lean and young and Decker wondered if he'd even gone through puberty. Certainly his baby face gave no indication of needing a shave.

Decker took the proffered hand. "Thank your watch commander for indulging us."

"No problem, Sergeant." Loomis's voice still held a youthful strain. "Tell you the truth, for me, it's a break from the routine."

"Pretty quiet around here?"

"Yeah, this is an industrial area. I catch a lot of misfired alarms. Occasionally, there're legit four-fifteens. What we really get are lots of assaults from the late-night bars in the field. Assholes get tanked and we come in and mop up." He shook his head. "Same old shit."

Marge handed Decker a pair of gloves, then put on her own pair.

Decker said, "You joining us inside, Officer?"

"Sure thing."

"Don't touch and watch where you step."

"You got it."

Decker slipped on his gloves. "You wanna be point man, Detective Dunn?"

"Point person. No, I'll be backup."

Decker turned to Loomis. "You pass by here often?"

"Once, maybe twice a night."

"Ever see this car out here at this time in the morning?"

The young patrolman stared at the Mercedes and shook his head.

"Ever see any car?" Marge asked.

Again a shake of the head. "I don't *think* so. But definitely not a sleek mama like a four-fifty SL. That I'd remember."

Decker nodded. They walked up to the front

door. The flashlight's beam fell on a small splotch of
blood to the right of the threshold.

Everyone exchanged looks. Decker banged on the
door, identified them as police officers, and waited
for a response.

Nothing.

Decker stood to the side of the door frame, turned
the knob, and pushed open the door with his foot.
The hinges creaked and everyone laughed.

"Like a bad slasher flick." Loomis giggled nervously. "Hey, we're only blocks from the studios.
Maybe someone was having fun."

Decker shone his light on the brown inkblot.
"Except this ain't Karo syrup."

Loomis was about to cross the threshold, but
Decker held him back and waited.

Nothing.

Marge drew her .38 from her purse; Loomis freed
his Beretta from his holster.

Decker said, "As the cops say . . . cover me."

He stepped inside. Freon cold air. Then the smells.
Hard to single out any one in specific—a mixture of
formaldehyde, ammonia, the sweet metal of blood.
He scanned the beam along the wall until he found
the light switch, then flicked it on with latex-covered
fingers.

A ten-by-twelve waiting room lighted by fluorescent panels strung across an acoustical-tile ceiling.
High dormer windows, the tops latched shut. The
air conditioning was going strong, emitting an elec-
tronic hum. A green floral sofa, the fabric unnatu-
rally shiny—heavily Scotchgarded. Two mismatched
side chairs in shades of orange. A glass coffee table

cluttered with magazines—*Newsweek, Time, Life,* and *People* as well as *Teen, Sixteen, Seventeen, Tiger Beat,* and *Rip.* A linoleum floor in a burnt-orange brick pattern. Decker had to use the extra illumination from the flashlight to find the trail of blood on that.

Marge's eyes fell on the magazines. "Catering to a young crowd."

"Looks that way."

"What's *Rip*?" Marge asked.

"Heavy metal," Loomis said. "That's music."

Decker said, "Something for the teenage daddies."

He focused the beam onto the floor, on smears of blood that trailed up to a door punched into the back wall. Next to the door was a sliding pane of frosted glass and a ledge for writing out checks. Instructions printed on a sign resting above the frosted glass: PLEASE ANNOUNCE YOUR ARRIVAL TO THE RECEPTIONIST and PAYMENT DUE AT TIME SERVICES ARE RENDERED.

Decker tried to open the window but it was locked. Marge pushed the door with her foot and it yielded.

"Yo, police!" she shouted. "Police officers!"

Silence.

They went through the door into a hallway. Decker scanned the walls until he located the light switch.

To the right was the receptionist's office. Small affair—one desk for the secretary, one desk for the computer, and a small filing cabinet. The odor of blood was stronger, but not as powerful as the smell of formaldehyde—so overwhelming it was making all of them dizzy. Loomis coughed. Out came the handkerchiefs for nose and mouth protection. They walked down the hallway, the path of blood thickening to blotches and dried puddles.

Doors off the hallway leading to examining rooms. Long paper-coated padded tables with stirrups at the ends. A doctor's stool. Shelves of chemicals and supplies. Nothing ransacked, nothing out of place.

The formaldehyde permeated every cubic centimeter of air. Decker felt his eyes water, his nose and mouth burn. Marge let out a hacking cough.

More examining rooms. Then, three doors at the end—one in the middle, the other two on either side of the hallway. Side doors leading to the operating rooms, stapled with placards. ABSOLUTELY NO SMOKING ALLOWED. Decker entered the surgery on the left and found the lights.

Pale-green walls, crater-shaped overhead spotlights focusing down on a center steel table fitted with stirrups. Next to the table, a four-foot stand clamped with steel tubes. Gas—blue label for nitrogen, green for oxygen. Another stand to the table's right, this one bearing calibrated instruments for measuring gas levels in the blood. Strung across its top bar were a stethoscope and a blood-pressure cuff. Resting on the tile floor, at the foot of the operating table, was a tympani-sized vacuum attached to a clear five-foot hose, six inches in diameter. The plastic tubing had become discolored from repeated use.

The back wall held locked cabinets filled with bottles of IV medications and glucose. In the drawers were surgical instruments—elongated forceps, oversized scissors, hypodermics, foot-long needles, scalpels and spoon-sized curettes with sharpened edges.

Nothing appeared out of place.

The final door, blood seeping out from under the wood, the stench of formaldehyde damn near knocking Decker over. He turned the knob, then staggered backward, coughing and gagging.

Once a personal office, it was in complete disarray. Papers, notebooks, and thick medical tomes were tossed and strewn about. Drawers had been opened and dumped, shelves emptied of their contents. A large rosewood desktop was completely cleared. Walls and furniture were spattered with blood. An area rug was crumpled into a corner. Cushions from the couch were slashed open, bits of foam piling around a freestanding hat rack like snow sloughed from a Christmas tree.

Lots of broken glass, the shards intermingled with tiny doughy pale dolls. Wee, two-inch creatures with far-set eyes, extra-wide mouths, pudgy hands, and legs pushed up to the bellies.

Fetuses.

At least a dozen, maybe more, carelessly scattered through the room except for a few lucky ones who still swam unmolested in unbroken jars of formaldehyde.

In the center of the office was a contorted body resting in a pool of blood—as lifeless as the things floating in the jars.

Loomis gagged, then composed himself. "Want me to call it in, Sergeant?"

Eyes burning, Decker swallowed back the bitter taste of bile. "Yeah, do that. Use your car radio."

"Sure thing." Loomis ran out.

Decker placed his glove over his covered nose. "Shit, this is bad!"

Marge coughed, then cleared her throat. "Fucking *sick*!"

"Merritt?" Decker asked.

Marge nodded. "Yeah, it's Merritt."

21

Marge yawned and rubbed her hands together. It was still dark, dawn a good half hour away, as she sat in the passenger seat of the unmarked and listened to static coming over the squawk box. Not a lot of calls at this hour. Even perps got tired.

She stared out the windshield. The Mercedes 450 SL now had company—three cruisers flashing their blues, a meat wagon, the police photographer's Camry, a lab-tech van, and Pete's old unmarked.

"You want your dinosaur mug back?" she said to Decker. "It's in the trunk."

Decker reclined the driver's seat as far back as it could go. "Keep it."

Marge said, "Prelim hair analysis of Ness and company should be done today. Maybe between that and this scene, we'll come up with physical evidence that points a finger."

"That'd be nice." Decker put his hands behind his head. "Someone should search Merritt's premises ASAP—his main office and his condo. See if we can't find something. As far as questioning the family goes, Burbank will probably do that. It's their jurisdiction. It's a small department but they've got seven people in Crimes Against Persons who rotate into Homicide."

"Homicide's part of CAPS?"

"Yeah. The division's too small for a separate Homicide detail. Anyway, the bureau's sending out a duo. Guy I spoke to definitely wants it, but he's happy to cooperate, especially after I explained the circumstances. They should be here in a few minutes."

"What are their names?"

Decker pulled his notebook from his pocket. "I talked to a Justice Ferris."

"Justice or Justin?"

"Justice—as in blind." Decker sat up. "What a mess!"

"Should I go through all of Merritt's patient files?"

"Yeah, we should start fresh . . . even though I think the crimes are related."

"We have a robbery and rape and now a homicide."

"A *messy* homicide. Not to mention a crazy horse." Decker smoothed his mustache. "Marge, why *had* Lilah suddenly agreed to go out to dinner with Merritt after all these years?"

"Like she said, does she need an excuse to hook up with her brother? Especially after he called her in his soothing voice."

Decker let out a small laugh.

"What?"

"Soothing voice," Decker said. "When I talked to Goldin, he specifically used the word *soothing* to describe Kingston Merritt with his patients. Sounds like Merritt could be a charmer if he wanted to be."

"Think he wanted something out of Lilah?"
Marge said.

"Maybe."

"You know, Pete, when I first met Merritt, he
claimed he didn't even know about the rape. He'd
come to the spa at Davida's request."

Decker nodded. "So what kind of business could
Merritt have with Davida?"

"Who said they had any business, Rabbi? Maybe
he was just paying Ma a visit."

"Didn't Merritt say his mother called him down?"

"Yeah."

Decker said, "He had business with Davida. And
then after all these years, he suddenly wanted to
reconcile with his sister. I'm beginning to put more
credence in Freddy Brecht's words. I think Davida
and Merritt were up to something. I think Merritt
wanted something out of Lilah."

"Pete, he was genuinely upset by Lilah's attack."

"Or he just faked it well. Acting's in the genes."

Marge said, "I've seen everything, so I'll believe
anything. But my gut is telling me Kingston didn't
rape his own sister."

"But say he had something to do with the theft.
Like I said before, someone hired thugs and they
raped Lilah as an afterthought."

Marge stuck her hand in her pocket and pulled
out a stick of gum. "Okay, let's assume Merritt was
behind the burglary."

Decker said, "The only two things we know about
in the safe are the jewels and the papers, right? So
let's run with the jewels first. Assume Merritt stole the
jewels for money. He was always hard up according

to Brecht and his bank account was none too padded. Davida found out about it and that's why they
were meeting at the spa. She wanted her jewels back.
Merritt played innocent, Davida got mad and had
her own kid whacked. That would explain the robbery and Merritt's death. If Merritt hired thugs, it
could possibly explain the rape." He paused. "Only
problem with that scenario is that if Davida had
Merritt whacked, she still wouldn't get her jewels
back."

"Someone tossed his office, Pete. Maybe someone was looking for them."

"But only Merritt's office was tossed. Not the
front office, not the ORs."

Marge said, "If I were Davida and I wanted my
jewels and I suspected my *son* of lifting them, I'd
just turn him in to the police."

"She didn't want a family thing getting out."

"But she was willing to murder for it? Draw attention to herself . . ."

Decker said, "Okay, scratch whacking Kingston
for the jewels. I'm sleep-deprived and my ideas are
fucked."

Marge laughed.

"So let's run with the memoirs," Decker said.
"Keep it basic. Say Merritt stole the memoirs. We
know how Lilah felt about the papers. And I remember Lilah telling me that her mother had a fit
when Davida found out about them. Suppose Davida
wanted them, too. Merritt decided to play the two
of them against each other—very easy to do because mother and daughter are in pit-bull competition. Merritt's twiddling his thumbs, waiting for the

highest bidder, holding out for big bucks. That's why he's in sudden communication with mother and sister."

Marge considered his reasoning. "Then we'd have to assume that there's something very important in those memoirs—probably something damaging to Davida. And we'd have to assume that King *knows* there's something very damaging. How would he know what the damaging thing is if the memoirs were in Lilah's possession all these years?"

"He stole the memoirs and read them."

"But why bother stealing them unless he already knew there was something juicy in them, Pete? Something that Davida would be willing to pay money for."

Decker's brain was buzzing. Slow down. Don't have to make sense out of all of it. Just try to make sense out of *some* of it.

"How about this?" Decker said. "Merritt is hard up for cash so he has thugs steal the jewels. The thugs steal the jewels, rape Lilah, and maybe the inner safe was open so they take the memoirs, too. What the hey. Merritt reads the memoirs. Bingo, he has something more valuable than the jewels— something negotiable."

Marge said, "Okay, he knew that Davida would pay big bucks for the memoirs. Why would *Lilah* pay bucks for them?"

"Because Merritt knew that Lilah was *obsessed* with her father, Marge. You should have heard the way she talked about him. She *idolizes* him. Her first husband told me she felt the same way back when he was married to her." Decker paused. "So Merritt's setting the women against each other, one of them gets sick of the game playing and has him whacked."

Marge didn't respond.

"I'm just talking off the top of my head," Decker said. "You know, we haven't even thought about Freddy Brecht. He really *hated* Merritt."

"Brecht's hatred seems long-standing. Why would he suddenly murder now . . . focus suspicion on himself. Be pretty dumb, don't you think?"

"Maybe it was an impulsive thing. Freddy goes to Merritt, says I know you and Mom are up to something. Push comes to shove, a struggle breaks out, Freddy whacks bro."

"Then you'd have to assume that Freddy had already whacked Merritt before we saw him tonight. If that was the case, he certainly acted like a cool cookie. He was irate, but he didn't seem nervous."

Decker said, "Acting's in the genes."

"Except Freddy is adopted."

Decker smiled. "Could be Merritt's death had nothing to do with the robbery and rape. Maybe some fanatical pro-lifer didn't like Merritt pickling fetuses."

Marge grimaced. "Why *did* Merritt keep them around?"

"Because he's bizarre. He fits in perfectly with that pack of hyenas."

"Man, you said it."

"Maybe Merritt was selling embryonic tissue to some illicit lab for money. Maybe the lab was cloning . . . unborn babies to send into outer space. To attack Earth. What do you think?"

Marge tightened her parka around her chest, not

smiling. "That could be looked into . . . the selling of the tissue."

"Marge—"

"It's a possibility."

"*Anything's* possible. But is it *relevant*?"

"If it establishes a pattern of what Merritt will do for *money*. Three hundred and fifty gees a year from his practice and all he's got is five grand in the bank. That's why he runs an abortion mill, that's why he sells fetuses illegally and steals his mother's jewels—"

"Hold on—"

"All right, so we've got a tiny leap in logic," Marge confessed. "You can have fucked ideas, so can I." She paused. "You know, none of our ideas explains the crazy horse. Unless you think Merritt was behind that, too."

Decker shrugged. "I'm not saying Merritt was behind anything, although his death certainly complicates the case."

Marge said, "*If* the memoirs were the driving force behind all of this, maybe we should start finding out about Hermann Brecht."

"Maybe."

Decker thought about the old lady Lilah used to visit in her younger, do-gooder days, the one who knew Hermann Brecht in the old country. He'd pay her a visit tomorrow. If she was still alive.

And they say women yak up a storm. Marge tapped her foot with impatience. Pete and the Burbank detectives—Justice Ferris and his partner—had been talking cars for the last twenty minutes. Curly-haired

Ferris—a good-looking guy in his thirties—drove a
'67 red Vette. Ferris's partner, Don Malone, was in
good shape for a man in his fifties. *He* drove an old
Jag XKE. All three boys went on and on about different junkyards, where to find the best parts in
the city. The whole thing was mind-numbing, but
Marge knew it was Pete's way of gaining rapport with
the dudes. They finally started talking shop when the
sun came up.

The division of labor was simple. Ferris and
Malone were anxious to catch the homicide, and she
and Decker were more than anxious to let them
have it, just as long as they maintained access to all
suspects, files, and lab reports.

"No problem," Ferris said.

"One more thing," Marge said. "I'd like to be
around when you question John Reed, Merritt's other
doctor brother. We haven't connected yet."

"No problemo," Ferris said.

"And you'll leave us the paper trail," Decker added.

"*Ce n'est pas une problème, mes amis,*" Ferris said.

They all laughed.

Malone said, "You're gonna reciprocate, right?"

"Help yourself to my desk," Decker said.

"*Mi files es su files,*" Ferris said. "Or maybe I should
say: *Mi murder es su murder.*"

Malone rolled his eyes. A lab tech walked out of
the clinic, shaking her head. She was black and very
petite, her lab coat practically reaching her ankles.
She and Ferris did a high-five handshake.

"Got a problem, Sheri?" Ferris said.

"Justice, my lad, you and Donnie have your work
cut out."

"What's the bad news?" Decker said.

"Now, did I say there was any *bad* news? Just news."

"So what kind of news are we talking about?" Marge said.

"I'm glad you asked," Sheri said. "We found two completely different blood types. One matches the victim, but there's a lot of blood in there that doesn't belong to him."

"The murderer," Ferris said. "He got hurt, bled as he fled."

"He practically emptied his veins," Sheri said. "Found over two pints in the murder room alone."

Marge said, "Two *pints*?"

"Yes, sir-madam," Sheri said. "Big pool of the stuff. If I were you lads, I'd start checking out some emergency rooms. That guy—or gal—would have needed plasma, prontissimo."

"I'll start calling," Malone said.

"Shit!" Decker slapped his forehead. "That's it!"

"What, Pete?"

"The trail of blood," Decker said. "Think about it! A huge pool was found in the murder room, then there were smaller puddles and smears right outside the room, some smears in the hallway, a few more in the waiting room, then less and less blood until there was nothing but drips in the parking lot. Margie, if the murderer was bleeding as he was escaping, we'd have found *less* blood in the room, much *more* blood in the hallways, and the most in the *parking lot* as he was climbing into his car to escape!"

Marge pushed hair out of her eyes. "You're right."

Ferris said, "Unless he taped up his wounds."

"Tape up a wound that's gushed out *two* pints of blood?" Decker said.

"Okay," Malone said. "So what's your theory?"

"Simple," Decker said. "Someone was carried *out* of the murder room after sitting in his own blood for a while. He was then dragged along the floor—that's the smears—then finally lifted into a vehicle in the parking lot, dripping a little until he was safely stashed inside. Know what I think that means?"

"What?" Ferris said.

"I think it means we have another stiff somewhere."

✒ 22

Marge thought: It's better than an office of bloody fetuses, but Parker Center Crime Lab is still not the bistro of choice for breakfast. Sipping coffee and wolfing down a doughnut, she scanned the rows of tables sagging under piles of clear plastic bags filled with clothing—hundreds of pieces of evidence waiting to be analyzed. It saddened her—no matter how many times she'd seen this room—to think that these garments had once been worn by living, breathing individuals. Some of the victims were alive—recipients of assaults. But for others, what remained on the table was the only part of them that had survived the crime.

She felt a tap on the shoulder and turned around. Buck Travers was well into his sixties but still had a full head of black hair. He was stoop-shouldered, potbellied, and smiling, as usual. Marge wondered what his secret was. Maybe he was genuinely happy with his work. Travers had tried retirement once but hadn't liked it. The department, in one of its rare moments of lucidity, gave Travers back his former job. Buck was one of the best hair and fibers men around.

"Sorry I'm late," Travers grinned. "I had a date with a bloody afghan—not the canine variety. You look tired, Detective Dunn."

"Been up since three in the morning."

"Same case or a different one?"

"Two cases that are probably related. We're not sure how. We're hoping for help."

"Well, I might be able to give you a little. Come and I'll show you what we got."

Travers led Marge to his desk located between a gas chromatograph and a centrifuge lined with tubes of blood. He picked up a file and frowned. Marge caught it.

"Your expression's hinky. What's wrong, Buck?"

"What do you want first—the good news or the bad news?"

"I'm an optimist. Let's hear the cheerful stuff."

"Good news is we have a preliminary match—"

"Hallelujah!" Marge clapped her hands. "Who's the lucky man?"

"Wait a minute. You haven't heard the bad news yet."

"First let's finish with the good news. Who, Buck?"

"I think you'd better hear the bad news."

Marge bit back frustration and told herself to take her time. That's the way it was with lots of techs. They were meticulous people. "What's the bad news?"

Travers frowned again. "Who did the evidence collection?"

"I did."

"*You* did?"

"What happened? Was there a screwup?"

"Yeah, there was a screwup."

"Damn it! It wasn't me, Buck. I bagged each sample individually and marked them—"

"Now, hold on, I'm not saying it was *you*. But there was a screwup."

"How bad?"

"Well, I found this lone bag of female hairs in your evidence collection. Lord only knows which case it belongs to. Someone's going to charge in here demanding to know what the hell happened to their evidence and we're not going to have the answers. Screwups are more frequent than we'd like to think. Some staffers just pass over them. Not me." Travers pointed to his chest. "I'm not going to further the disaster and make like my results are pristine. I just want to make sure the evidence you gave me is all accounted for."

"Fine, Buck, I'm duly warned. The results?"

"I'm not stalling for the sake of stalling, Marge. I just don't want to name a person only to find out he's not the one you should be after. I'd like some more time—"

"Fine. Take as much time as you want, Buck. I'm perfectly aware that you're giving me tainted results. Who's the prelim match?"

"Well . . ." Travers opened up the file again. "After careful consideration we find consistency between the hair collection taken from sheets on Case Number REb129847563 and a hair sample collected by you. We're still waiting for DNA banding results to come in using spermatozoa as the primary marker. Banding is more conclusive but the tests take a while. So you gotta take this with a grain of salt, Margie—"

"A whole shaker full! Buck, *who* is it?"

"Carl Totes."

The stable hand was as out of place as a cow chip on china, eyes darting from one wall of the interview room to the other. Decker figured it was claustrophobia that was giving Totes the shakes, more than the situation itself. Carl had seemed baffled by the arrest but not the least bit uncooperative. He'd readily offered samples of his hair for retesting—anything to help out Miz Lilah. He'd handled the car trip over to the station house pretty well although he'd been uncomfortable riding next to Marge. But once inside the small interrogation area, Totes's nervous system began to discharge. He fidgeted and drummed the table with his hands. He took off his cowboy hat and kneaded the felt rim with calloused hands. Clearly, this was not a man used to physical boundaries.

Marge was seated closest to the door, working the tape recorder. Decker wanted to do the questioning. He had seated himself next to Totes at the other end of the table. Totes had been working out the horses when they had presented him with the warrant. The stable hand's jeans were covered with dust, his shirt had soaked up lots of sweat. Guy smelled up close, but Decker could take it. He'd spent enough of his youth on a ranch and was used to nature's perfume. After being Mirandized, Totes was given a card that stated he had been advised of his rights.

Marge asked him to read the card and sign it and he did so without reservation.

"How long this gonna take?" He wiped his face with his bandanna and stuck it in his pocket.

Decker said, "A long time, Mr. Totes."

"Don't like talking in a room." Totes's eyes were still jumpy. "Why couldn't we talk at the ranch? Like last time."

"Because you're under arrest, Mr. Totes," Decker said. "Do you understand that you're under arrest?"

"Arrest fer what? I didn't do nothin'."

Decker tapped his foot. "I think we should get him a lawyer."

"Don't need no lawyer," Totes insisted. "Jus' ask your dern questions and get this over."

Marge and Decker exchanged glances. Decker shrugged and told her to turn on the recorder. After reciting the identifying data into the mike, he began the questioning.

"Mr. Totes, do you remember last Monday, June twenty-third—"

"Don't remember no dates."

"Okay." Decker tried a different angle. "Do you remember the day after your boss, Lilah Brecht, was raped?"

"Yessir."

"Do you remember where you were the *night* Lilah Brecht was raped?"

"Yessir."

"Where were you that night, Mr. Totes?"

"Where I always were. At the ranch."

"Where?"

"Don't know the address of the place. Don't you got it?"

Decker smoothed his mustache. "In which part of the ranch were you located, Mr. Totes?"

"Oh . . . in the stable."

"What were you doing in the stable?"

"What wuz I doin'? I wuz sleepin'."

"Why were you sleeping in the stable?"

" 'Cause that's where I live."

"How long have you lived there?"

"Five years."

"And you were sleeping there the night Lilah Brecht was raped."

Totes didn't answer right away. His fingers tightened around the rim of his hat. "Yessir."

Decker assimilated Totes's pause. "You were sleeping there all night?"

"Don't *you* sleep all night, mister?"

Decker was impassive. "Were you sleeping there all night, Carl?"

Again, Totes hesitated. "Yessir."

Two pauses within a minute of each other. Was he that slow a thinker or was he formulating consistent lies?

Decker said, "What time did you go to bed that night, Carl? When did you stop working and go into the stable?"

" 'Bout eight-thirty. Gets dark 'round then."

"You went into the stable around eight-thirty?"

"Yessir."

Decker stood and leaned against the table. "Okay, Carl, you went into the stable around eight-thirty. Did you *leave* the stable the night Lilah Brecht was raped?"

Totes shook his head.

Decker said, "I need a yes or no answer, Carl. Tape recorder won't pick up a headshake. Did you ever leave the stable the night Lilah Brecht was raped?"

"Nossir, I never left the stable."

"Not once?"

"No."

Decker walked slowly from one side of the room to the other, then back again. He sat on the table, facing Totes, and frowned. "Carl, I'm confused about something. How do you explain your hair on Lilah Brecht's sheets?"

Totes was quiet.

"Carl?"

"I . . . I don't know nothin' 'bout that."

Decker sighed. "See, Carl, *your* hair was found on Lilah Brecht's sheets. How do you explain that?"

Totes shook his head, his expression was pained.

Decker said, "You don't have any idea how your hair was found on Lilah Brecht's sheets?"

"Nossir."

"Well, Carl, if you didn't visit her the night she was raped, maybe you visited her the night before . . ."

Totes looked up. "I don't get what you're asking me."

"Have you and Lilah ever had sex, Carl?"

Totes turned angry red. "That's a *turrible* question."

"I've got to ask you these questions, Carl. Have you and Lilah ever had sex?"

"Nossir!"

Decker ran his hands through his hair. "Now, you

got me confused again, Carl. If you've never had sex with Lilah, how'd *your semen* get on her sheets?"

Totes was still scarlet. "Like you said, mister, you're confused. So why should I answer your questions, if *you* don't even know what you're talkin' about?"

Totes folded his hands across his chest, his mouth hardening. Decker appraised him. Totes was the kind of guy who mistook soft-spokenness for weakness. Decker liked the good-cop approach to questioning, but it wasn't going to work here. Time to shift gears.

"Carl, you said you were in the stable the entire time on the night Lilah Brecht was raped."

"Yessir."

"The *entire* night."

"Yessir."

"You never left once?"

"Nossir."

"Not to go to the bathroom?"

"Nossir, I got a horse's bladder."

Marge tried to stifle a smile, but was only partially successful. Decker said, "So you never left the stable that night. Not even once?"

"No . . . nossir."

"Carl, how did your hairs get on Lilah Brecht's sheets?" Decker kept his voice even. "How did your *semen* get on her sheets?"

"I . . . I don't . . . I—"

"Carl, where were you the night Lilah Brecht was raped?"

"In the stable."

"C'mon, Carl, stop giving me a hard time. Tell me, how did *your* semen get on Lilah's sheets?"

Totes squeezed his hat until his knuckles turned white. "I didn't rape her."

"Okay, you didn't rape her. How'd your *hair* get on her sheets, Carl? How'd your *semen* get on the sheets?"

Totes didn't answer.

"Carl, where were you the night Lilah Brecht was raped?"

"In my stable—"

Decker pounded the table so hard, both Totes and Marge jumped. He waited a beat, then calmly resumed. "Carl, how'd your hair get on Lilah Brecht's sheets if you were in the stable the night she was raped?"

Totes looked down.

"Have you ever had sex with Lilah Brecht, Carl?"

"I already told you no!"

"So you never had sex with her—"

"Why're you repeatin' yourself?"

"'Cause you're not explaining to me how *your* semen got on Lilah Brecht's *sheets*. How'd that happen, Carl?"

Totes didn't answer.

Decker said, "Where were you the night Lilah Brecht was raped?"

"In my stable."

"The whole night?"

"The whole night."

"You didn't go out and no one came to see you?"

Totes started to speak, then turned silent. Decker picked up on it.

"Someone came to see you the night Lilah Brecht was raped, Carl?"

Again, Totes didn't answer. Decker reseated himself next to the stable hand. "Who came to see you the night Lilah Brecht was raped, Carl? Who came to your stable?"

There was a long hesitation before Totes said, "I cain't tell you that."

Decker ran his fingers through his hair. "Who came to see you, Carl?"

"I cain't . . ."

"How'd your semen get on Lilah Brecht's sheets, Carl?"

"I . . . I don't know."

Decker said, "Carl, did you see Lilah Brecht the night she was raped?"

Totes shook his head.

"Carl, answer yes or no. Did you see Lilah Brecht the night she was raped?"

"Nossir."

But Decker knew he was lying, and that made him feel like an ass. All this time he'd been sure Totes was innocent. His gut had told him that. The old gut had been wrong. The stable hand had suddenly turned pale. Decker said, "You want something to drink, Carl? You look a little funny."

Totes's expression became mulish. "I'm fine, mister. Be more fine if you'd stop confusin' me."

"Then just answer the questions one at a time, Carl. Did you see Lilah Brecht the night she was raped?"

"I told you no."

"Did you see Lilah Brecht the night she was raped, Carl?"

"Goldern it!" Totes said, "I told you I don't remember."

"No, you didn't, Carl. You told me *nossir*, you didn't see her. That's what you said. But *now*, you're telling me you don't remember—"

"'Cause you're mixin' me—"

"You're mixing yourself up. Which is it, Carl? Nossir or you don't remember? Did you see Lilah Brecht the night she was raped?"

Totes was breathing heavy. "Nossir."

"How did your semen get on her sheets, Carl?"

"I don't remember."

"Did you rape Lilah Brecht, Carl?"

"I don't . . . you're confusin' me!"

Silence.

Decker said, "Carl, how did your hair get on her sheets?"

"I . . . don't know."

"Who came to your stable the night Lilah Brecht was raped?"

"No one."

"Before, you said you couldn't tell me. Now you're telling me no one. Which is it? Who came to see you at the stable the night Lilah Brecht was raped. *Who?*"

"I . . . I . . . I cain't tell you."

"How'd your hair get on Lilah Brecht's sheets?"

"I'm mixed up."

"I know you're mixed up because you're not answering my questions. How'd *your* hairs get on Lilah Brecht's sheets? How'd they get there, Carl? *How?*"

"I don't know."

"They didn't *walk* by themselves. How'd they get on Lilah Brecht's sheets?"

"I . . . I . . . don't know."

"Carl, did you see Lilah Brecht the night she was raped?"

Silence. Decker repeated the question.

"You're confusin' me," Totes answered.

"Carl, did you see Lilah Brecht the night she was raped?"

"I . . . I'm mixed up. You're askin' too many questions."

"Just listen to them one at a time. Did you see Lilah Brecht the night she was raped?"

"I don't . . ."

"Carl, did you see Lilah Brecht the night she was raped?"

Totes was panting. "I . . . mebbe I did."

"Maybe you did," Decker repeated. "Carl, did you rape Lilah Brecht?"

"Mebbe I did."

🌿 23

The manila envelope was waiting at Marge's desk when she and Decker walked into the squad room. They exchanged quick glances. Decker lifted his eyes and said, "Please, God, let us not have made *asses* out of ourselves."

Marge smiled nervously as she ripped open the seal and pulled out the piece of paper. Then she brought her hand to her chest. "Phew!"

"It's Totes?"

Marge nodded and handed him the paper. "Travers says he passed his tests with flying colors. One down."

Mike Hollander walked into the squad room and over to the coffee urn, his fingers clutched around a paper sack. "How'd the questioning go?"

"No neat and clean confession," Decker said, flipping through pages of lab analysis.

"But we did get a confirmation from Buck Travers. I'll take that over a confession any day of the week."

"We've either got one very confused stable hand," Decker said, "or one excellent bullshit artist."

"They're all bullshit artists, Rabbi." Hollander

343

carried his mug back to his desk and sat down. "Shame on you for turnin' soft in your old age."

Marge sat down. "I vote with Pete. I think Totes is very confused . . . you know, one of those true weirdo types who gets mental blackouts when committing a crime."

"Dissociative reaction . . ." Decker said.

Marge laughed. "Oh, my, we've been hitting the books."

"Nah," Decker smiled. "Remember my weirdo friend, Abel Atwater? His shrink used to call his blackouts dissociative reactions."

"Yeah, shrinks use that kind of language so they can bilk MediCal out of big bucks." Hollander liberated a doughnut from his bag and took a bite. Crumbs sprinkled his lap. "Government ain't gonna pay for a diagnosis of blackout. Otherwise head docs would be cleaning up on drunks." He took another bite and spoke as he chewed. "Your daughter called, Rabbi. I left the number on your desk."

"Thanks, Mike." Decker crossed his arms over his chest and leaned against Marge's desk. He wasn't happy with the outcome of Totes as bad guy, and he couldn't explain why. In past cases, he'd gone to the DA with a lot less material than he had here and felt righteous about it. But it wasn't his job to pass judgment, just collect and present evidence. "Interrogation only took forty minutes; no one can charge us with tiring the suspect or police brutality. I think we have enough for the grand jury."

"I'll call the DA," Marge said.

"In the meantime, now that we have the test results, someone's got to handle the booking."

"I can do it." Hollander licked his fingers. "You want me to get him a lawyer?"

Decker said, "Court'll automatically appoint him one once he's been formally charged. I want to call Cindy first. Then I'll phone Burbank and find out where they're at with the Merritt murder. We've got Totes for Lilah's rape, but that doesn't explain the thefts or Merritt's murder."

"I'll get a warrant to search the stable," Hollander said. "Could be Totes stashed some of the goods there." He lifted his sizable buttocks out of his chair. "Glad to help just so long as the jobs don't tax my heart."

"Why don't you go on a diet?" Marge said.

"I'm on a diet, Margie."

"A *diet*?" Marge wrinkled her brow. "Mike, you just polished off a doughnut in three bites."

"I know." He licked his fingers again. "But this time I bought the kind without the jelly in the middle."

Decker made the call from the locker room because it afforded him more privacy than the squad room—everybody listening in and pretending not to. Cindy picked up on the third ring.

"Hi, princess. How did finals go?"

She burst into tears. Decker felt his stomach knot and gave her a few moments to compose herself. "Don't worry, Cindy, I'm sure you did better than you think."

"I did okay."

Decker said, "I'm sure you did very well."

"I didn't say I did *very* well." She sniffed. "I could have done *better*, but I didn't flunk or anything."

"That's good."

"Why? Did you think I'd flunk?"

"Of course not."

"I think I got an A and three Bs."

"That's terrific!"

"Aren't you cheerful."

Decker exhaled slowly. "When are you coming in to L.A., Cindy?"

"Daddy?"

"What?"

"Are you mad at me for not telling you about the summer?"

"No, sweetheart. I'm not mad at all."

"Is it okay?"

"Cindy, it's more than okay. I'm looking forward to it. We'll have a great time together if I can ever get your butt in the saddle."

She said nothing, but Decker could picture her smiling with moist eyes. Her voice was little when she returned to the line. "It's okay with Rina? I don't want to impose—"

"Cynthia, you're my *daughter*. You are never an imposition except when you get cranky and even then you're not an imposition, just a pain in the butt. You've been very cranky lately. What's bothering you? Is it Rina being pregnant? Is it me having another baby? Are you jealous?"

There was a long pause.

"Not consciously."

Decker smiled. What a college-kid answer. "Baby, I love you. I love you, love you, love you. You are my kid, you will *always* be my kid even when you're in your seventies, I'm in my nineties. It's a sentence of life without parole, Cynthia. You're stuck with me."

He heard a chuckle over the line. That made him smile again. "So just tell me when and where and I'll pick you up. Your mother already dropped off your car, so you should be all set."

"I won't get in your way—"

"Cindy, you've never gotten in my way."

"I can be a help to Rina."

Decker sighed. "For God's sake, princess, you're becoming your old man—too darn serious. Even *I* wasn't this bad at nineteen. Will you do me a favor? Will you try to have fun this summer?"

She laughed. "I'll try."

"Try hard, Cindy."

She laughed. "I'll call you after I've scheduled my flight out, Daddy. You know there's something wrong with your phone—"

"Damn!" Decker gently hit his head with his fist. "I'm working on a bizarre case and we've changed our number. I forgot to tell you."

"Thank you very much."

"I'm sorry, Cindy. Mea culpa, twenty lashes with a wet noodle, ashes and sackcloth."

"Oh, *Daddy*!"

He gave her the new number. "I love you, princess."

"I love you, too. . . . I know I've been testy. And I know you've been trying really hard. It's okay. You're really a good guy."

"'Preciate the compliment, beautiful. Thank you."

"You're welcome. Bye."

She cut the line.

Decker hung up the phone, feeling on top of the world. A good talk will do that to you. That's all she needed—a good talk, words of support from Daddy. Nothing like a father's love to make you feel good.

Then he thought: Maybe she felt better because she'd made it through her first year of college. Maybe it had nothing to do with their conversation and had a lot to do with finals being over and an A and three Bs at Columbia.

With teenagers you never could tell.

He shrugged, then laughed to himself. Of course it was their talk that had eased Cindy's mind. His understanding words, his paternal love. The hell with being a shrink. What was that famous motto? When it comes to kids, take all of the credit, none of the blame. That sounded about right to him.

It was all Ness could do to refrain from punching her lights out. Instead, he kept himself hidden, waiting until Davida opened the door to her bungalow. Then he moved in, pushing her inside with his body and shutting the door behind both of them. He latched the chain, then shoved her against the wall. Davida's expression changed from frightened to furious, then back to frightened.

"Where have you been?" Ness whispered.

Davida cast her eyes down at her pumps, then slowly inched them back to his face.

"I bought a new car, Michael. A black BMW convertible with a new Alpine stereo, DAT tape deck and CD." Her lips formed a wide smile. "I drove it off the lot. Would you like to take a ride?"

Ness closed his eyes, counted to ten, and opened them. "Do you have any idea how much *shit* you're in?"

"Me?" Davida laughed. "Why, Michael, I haven't done—"

"Remember that so-called *little* assignment you gave me yesterday, Davie?" He eased his grip on the old woman and stroked her arms, lowering his voice. "Kingston's dead."

Davida brought her hand to her mouth. "Oh, dear!" She pushed Ness away and sat on her divan. "Oh, dear, are you sure?"

"Yes, Davida, I'm sure."

Slowly, her eyes moistened. "I thought it might be bad, but I had no . . . I thought it was . . ." She choked out, "My poor baby . . ."

Ness went to the bar and poured himself a Scotch. Davida wiped her cheeks, only to have them wetted again by a fresh flow of tears. Ness sat down next to her. After downing half the shot, he held the tumbler to her lips.

"Drink."

She took the glass and sipped. "What happened?"

"I thought you could tell me."

"I told you I left." She lifted her head and faced Ness. "Was it bad?"

Ness caught her eye, then looked away. "Yes, it was very bad." He took the drink from Davida's hands. "There're going to be lots of questions. The police have been here—"

"The redheaded detective?"

"Different guys. Two clowns from Burbank—one of them couldn't take his eyes off the women's asses, the other one was clearly on a fishing expedition. They know some details, but not enough to cause damage."

"Did you get rid of them?"

"Only temporarily, Davie. They're not interested in me. I didn't even know King. But they're real interested in talking to you."

She took the tumbler back from him and finished the Scotch. "I was here all day yesterday. You know that. You were with me—"

"Davida . . ." Ness took her hand. "I can vouch that I saw you yesterday. But I was also teaching class yesterday. I was in the weight room, I was at the pool, I took the ten o'clock broth break with the ladies in the snack bar. I was with *other* people and . . ." He sighed. "And you were not there."

The old lady just sat there, tears streaming down her cheeks. Ness patted bony, liver-spotted knuckles. "Don't worry. We'll figure something out."

Davida bit her nail and blinked away tears. "I swear I don't know what happened. I wouldn't hurt my own flesh and blood. You know I . . ." She started crying again.

Ness buried his face in his hands, wondering how the bitch lied with such facility. Then he remembered what acting was all about.

Or maybe she was genuinely grief-stricken. Her son was dead. But what did she *expect*, sending in some errand boy. She *knew* King had an explosive temper! But women like Davida never thought about consequences. Just like his mom. Users. They went on their merry way, exploiting their kids as if they were property. She was talking to him.

". . . police say when they were coming back?"

"No, they never do. They just pop up when you're not expecting them."

Davida wiped her eyes. "Like audit letters from the IRS."

Ness smiled. "Freddy sent them out to Malibu—pretty clever stall on his part. You never answer the phones so the two of them are going to waste a couple of hours driving there and back. But you're going to have to talk to them eventually."

"What do I say?"

Ness shrugged. "You're the performer."

"I'm an actress, Michael, not a writer."

"Then play it simple. Act the grieving mother and keep your mouth shut."

Davida blinked her eyes in rapid succession. "I don't have to act, Michael."

"I'm sorry, Davida. But you should have known better. You should have let me handle Kingston."

Davida nodded like a chastised little girl. God, she was sick. But the bitch had a way of evoking pity. Ness sighed.

"Does Lilah know?" Davida asked.

"Yes, Davida, she knows. The cops have already talked to her—"

"What'd she say?"

"I don't know. She's been incommunicado, doing nothing but exercising—"

"*What?*"

"Leading the one o'clock class, even as we speak. She gave Natanya the afternoon off so she could take over. You know Lilah. When she's truly hysterical, she aerobicizes. She's been at it all day and hasn't eaten a thing. Freddy's really worried about her, afraid she's gonna drop dead." Ness gave her a half smile. "Or maybe that's what you want."

And then Ness felt a whack across his face. It took him a few seconds before he realized she'd actually backhanded him. He touched his burning cheek, then shook his head. Didn't know the bitch had it in her.

Davida said, "Don't you *ever*—"

"Sorry." Ness sipped his drink, then stroked his face. "Jesus, you pack a good wallop for an old broad."

She grabbed his chin, turned his head, and inspected his imprinted face. "Yes, Michael, indeed I do." She kissed his cheek. "When you were . . . *there*, did you happen to notice—"

"Davida, I was there for just a moment." He pushed hair out of his eyes. "It was so . . . so messy . . . so . . . bloody. I just got the hell out. But I took care of some details for you, Davie."

"What details?"

"Better that you don't know."

"But you didn't—"

"No papers. Your errand boy came up dry. Or King got to him before he had a chance to really look."

Davida's eyes watered. "He was my son, Michael, and I loved him. I want you to know that. I never meant for him to die."

"You don't mean a lot of things, but you screw up a lot." Ness stood and kissed her forehead. "I've got to go. Afternoon yoga with the ladies. If the cops come, I'll do the best I can. You know that."

"I know that." Davida took out a handkerchief. "Thank you. You have been a luv."

"That's me, a real luv." He took a final drink, then placed the tumbler on the bar. Reaching into his back pocket, he popped a peppermint candy into his mouth. Wouldn't do at all if the starving girlies smelled Scotch on the breath of their health-conscious aerobic guru.

Then his heart started racing. He felt around his back pockets, then his front pockets. He patted his shirt, tried his pants again. His head started spinning.

His wallet was gone.

❧ 24

Marge hung up the phone. "The best Reed can do for us is forty-five minutes at three. If we leave right now, we should make it."

Decker said, "Burbank's not going to like it—especially Malone. He wanted to be in on the interview."

"They're en route to Malibu; we can't exactly wait for them. Reed's a busy guy." Marge slung her purse over her shoulder. "We'll take the recorder and play back the interview word for word. Besides, didn't Morrison tell us to get the *lead* out?"

"If I move any faster on this case, I'm gonna turn into a sonic boom." Decker stuffed his wallet in his pants. "All right, let's do Reed . . . find out if he knows anything. I just wanted to avoid a stupid interdepartmental squabble. I have a feeling Donnie Malone might be the petty type."

"So that's his problem. He wants to field hotshot calls, let him apply to Southeast—get lowdown and funky in the pits."

Decker regarded her. "Are you still interested in working Homicide?"

Her face became animated. "Why? Is there an opening?"

"Nothing official, Margie. But scuttlebutt says Devonshire might have an opening soon."

Marge's face fell. "An opening? As in room for one: as in *white male*?"

"Maybe they could be talked into two for one."

"So what does that make me? A door prize?"

"Marjorie, you know the way the department works. If I say no, they're *not* going to ask you to apply. So either I convince them to take you as a door prize *or* we both stay put. Stop getting touchy."

There was a long silence.

"Do *you* want to work Homicide?" Marge said.

"It's a challenging detail, but it's also a lot more hours." Decker shrugged. "At this point, it's theoretical. I just wanted to sound you out, okay?"

Marge smiled. "I appreciate what you're doing. I don't mean to sound like an ingrate, but it's infuriating."

"I know it's hard being passed over because you don't have a dick. But I have one and if I can help you, why not?"

"You're a good guy, Pete."

"My daughter just told me that."

"It must be true." Marge winked. "Let's go. I'll drive."

Decker looked out the window and thought: It's good to get out of the squad room. The day was hot and clear, the freeways relatively empty. The drive was long but scenic, the unmarked trailblazing through winding canyons shaded with copses of eucalyptus, leafy maples, and gnarled California oak that shimmered in the heat. Clusters of black birds dotted the aqua summer sky.

The Plymouth was making good time until it hit Hermosa Beach at Pacific Coast Highway. Traffic immediately jammed with stalled cars and reckless motorbikes weaving in and out of lanes. The right sides of the streets were marked for bike paths and were filled with latex-coated cyclists. The sidewalks were clogged with flower-shirted tourists weighed down by cameras around their necks, and pedestrians in skin tones ranging from deep tan to lobster red. Whizzing past the walkers were the skateboarders and the Rollerbladers dressed in Day-Glo surfing shorts and muscle shirts. Gull cries and bird songs competed for air space with boom boxes or the rowdy shouts of party animals stuffed onto balconies of apartment buildings.

On the right, PCH looked down upon several streets stacked with multifamily dwellings. The buildings had been erected without much thought to architectural conformity, although most were made of stucco and wood and had lots of windows. Beyond the houses was an expanse of steely-blue undulating with the rhythmic flows of whitecaps.

With the car stopped at a congested intersection, Marge's eyes drifted from the ocean to the street scene. "Ah, to be young, single . . . and *white*. This place is Wonder bread."

Decker squinted out the window. "I think I see a couple of blacks."

"Nah, they're not real *blacks*, more like . . . chocolate-dipped surfers."

"I hear rap music."

Marge waved him off. "Rap has been coopted by whites, Pete. Look at Vanilla Ice and his Xeroxes." She laughed. "Everyone wanting what the other guy has—whites putting shit in their hair to get dreadlocks, blacks putting shit in their hair to turn it straight. No pleasing the human race."

"It's what makes us creative," Decker said. "Turning the restlessness into art. Hey, Margie, how 'bout us writing a policeman's rap:

> *"A cop's lot in life is no easy shakes.*
> *Criminals and felons and all sorts of fakes*
> *Gettin in my face every night and every day,*
> *Stalkin and waitin just to blow me away—"*

"Keep your badge and gun, Sergeant."

Decker's expression was deadpan. "I'm wounded."

Compulsively neat with a wide sweeping view of the ocean, the office looked more suited for a CEO than for a doctor. The walls were wainscoted—peach and hunter-green chintz print above the chair railing, deep-walnut paneling below. Reed's desk was an old-fashioned mahogany partner's desk, the legs carved into lions. But from the way it was positioned and the diplomas on the wall, it was clear the desk was used only by one person who demanded lots of space.

Decker made himself comfortable in one leather wing chair opposite the desk; Marge took the matching seat. Reed had seated himself erect in his desk chair, hands folded and resting on the desk, his lab coat sparkling white and stiffly starched. A man used to order. Decker bet he got anxious if things didn't go as planned.

And he was anxious now. The straight-featured, bronzed face was knitted at the brow, the chestnut eyes dancing instead of focusing. Though his fingers were constrained, he was rocking his hands on the desktop. His mocha-colored hair was thin and combed to one side, a small strand resting on his forehead. Reed glanced at his clasped hands, then looked up.

"How can I help you?" Before they could answer, Reed went on, "Perhaps I should say, how can *you* help *me*? First, Lilah, now this terrible . . . I'm . . ."

Reed's voice held the remnants of a refined British accent.

Decker said, "I'm sorry for your loss."

"I'm . . . *devastated*!" Reed said. "Simply . . ."

"Were you and your brother close?" Marge asked.

"Close?" Reed tapped his folded hands on the desk. "I wouldn't say close . . . but I was closer to him than I was to anyone else on the maternal side of my family. We had our professions in common; we used to meet for lunch and at staff meetings. We attended some of the same hospitals. We weren't exceptionally close, but Kingston was still . . . I just can't believe . . ."

He took a deep breath, got up and walked over to the water machine. "Can I offer you two any coffee or tea?"

"We're fine, Dr. Reed."

Reed played with a paper cup, then filled it with water and drank. "I . . . I don't know anything about . . ." He crumpled the corrugated container and threw it into the garbage. "I don't know how I could possibly help you. With Lilah as well. I'm . . . I'm not at all close to her. I don't . . ."

He sank back into his desk chair.

"When was the last time you saw your brother?" Decker asked.

"Saw him?" Again Reed folded his hands. "I don't remember. A few weeks ago. My girl would know. She makes my appointments. Kingston and I never met spontaneously. It was always . . . arranged. Either he'd call or I'd call. That sort of thing— Can I turn the recorder off? It's making me feel quite uneasy."

Decker turned off the machine, then pulled out his notebook and held it up. "You don't mind this?"

"Not at all," Reed said. "The recorder is just so . . . dehumanizing."

"Indeed it is," Decker said. "Were you in contact with Kingston after Lilah was attacked?"

"Contact?" Reed bit his lip. "I don't . . . oh, he . . . called me, of course. He was very upset. I was upset as well. I'm not close to my sister, but . . . I felt *terrible*!"

"Did you visit Lilah in the hospital?" Marge asked.

Reed looked down. "No, I . . . didn't. And I suppose that seems a bit callous. I did call. We spoke very briefly. I asked her if she needed anything and she said no, Mother and Freddy had everything under control. Which was the way it usually was when I spoke to Lilah. She has always . . . shut me out so . . ." He exhaled. "So, I suppose I stopped trying.

Not that my life . . . has been empty without her, without any of them. My family is . . . very difficult. I do much better when there's minimal contact."

"But you had contact with Kingston," Marge said.

"Yes, professional mostly. But personal as well."

"Do you happen to know if you talked to him just prior to Lilah's attack?" Decker asked.

"Perhaps."

Decker waited for more, but Reed wasn't forthcoming. "Did Kingston sound unusual?"

"In . . . what way?"

Decker shrugged. "Agitated, depressed, more cheerful than usual."

"Kingston was never *cheerful*," Reed said. "He was a very *driven* man."

"Did he seem unusually *driven* lately?"

"I . . . yes, to me, King did seem more driven of late." Reed sighed. "He called me about a week . . . before Lilah was attacked. He needed money."

"Why?" Marge said. "Didn't he have a thriving practice?"

"Several of them in fact," Decker added.

"You know about his place in Burbank?" Marge asked.

Reed looked up sharply. "Yes, of course. Not that I approved . . . not that I disapproved . . . of abortion, that is. Just . . . he was making money, but that was only part of it."

"Part of what?" Decker added.

"Of why he had his place in Burbank," Reed said.

"It was the fetuses," Marge said.

Reed grimaced. "So you know everything."

"It was a guess," Marge said.

A damn-good educated one, Decker thought as he wrote in his notebook.

"What was he doing with the fetuses?" Marge said.

Reed blew out air. "What he was doing wasn't legal."

"Go on," Decker said.

"He was doing research using embryonic tissue. Research has been King's passion since medical school . . . since we were young children actually. King always wanted to be a *scientist*, but Mother wanted him to be a doctor. She wanted *all* of us to become physicians."

"So I've noticed," said Marge.

"Mother was quite explicit about her wishes. And Mother has a way of getting what she wants. Not that I'm sorry I went to medical school. But afterward I wasn't about to devote my life to Mother's needs. She's an incurable hypochondriac and now poor Frederick bears the brunt of her neurosis. I've often urged him to *break* from her, but . . ." He bit his lip. "Where was I?"

"Kingston wanting to become a scientist," Decker said.

"Yes, Kingston was very adaptable. So he selected medicine as his science of choice and forged ahead with his research. Nothing could dissuade him from that."

Decker said, "I'm not familiar with Kingston's professional history. Was he affiliated with any research institution, any university?"

Reed shook his head. "No. He dropped out of academia early on—too petty, too controlled by rules and regulations, too much game playing to get proper funding."

"Your brother wasn't much of a game player, was he, Doctor?" Decker said.

"If you knew my mother, you would understand why," Reed said. "We were all pawns in Mother's games—constantly competing against each other for Mother's attention. Kingston had no tolerance for compromise. Even as a student, he used to complain how regimented the hospitals and medical schools were. He always said he was never going to rely on grants for his research. So he . . . he went into private practice and funded his own research."

Reed took a breath.

"It took *everything* out of him. He never married, never . . . never bothered with social niceties. My wife and I . . . we tried to . . . I don't know, make him realize there was another world outside, but he . . . research was his life."

"Even if it meant bending a few rules and working illegally on aborted fetal tissue," Decker said.

"Yes." Reed nodded. "Yes, he bent rules—broke rules. But that was King. Once he had a bug in his brain, he was unstoppable."

"What was he doing with the tissue?" Marge asked. "Specifically?"

"Yes," Marge said.

"He was grinding it up, running the cells through a French press to shear them open, precipitating the DNA, and protein-purifying the enzymes in an attempt to locate and isolate embryonic enzymes that might be distinctively beneficial to host-rejection of implant patients."

"I had to ask," Marge said.

"Fetal tissue—especially at the early stages of development—is nonspecific," Reed said. "The cells have the remarkable ability to grow anywhere without being rejected . . . am I making myself . . . perhaps I should give you an example."

"A short one, please, Doctor," Decker said.

"Yes, of course." Reed cleared his throat. "Let us say you need a kidney and I have a kidney to donate. But that doesn't necessarily mean your body will take my kidney."

"It has to be compatible," Marge said.

"Exactly!" Reed said. "Fetal tissue is unlike your tissue and my tissue. I can inject it anywhere in your body and . . . chances are your body will not reject it because it will not be seen as foreign material. It's nonspecific. We all start out as a single cell—a zygote. During gestation, in some sort of process we don't fully understand, cells differentiate even though they all have the same DNA complement. Cells are told to become brain cells or skin cells or kidney cells. Now, if you inject nonspecific fetal tissue into an organ system, it will become part of whatever system you inject it into. What is it about embryonic tissue that allows our bodies to accept and incorporate it? That is—was what King was working on."

Marge looked at Decker. "I understood most of that. I feel pretty smart."

Reed said, "It sounds more complicated than it is. I'll simplify—"

"Doctor Reed, it's not necessary for us to know all the medical details," Decker said. "Suffice it to say, Dr. Merritt had been working illegally with embryonic tissue. How long had he been doing his research?"

"Years. He has made some *incredible* discoveries! But he couldn't publish his findings because his research was illegal."

"So why was he more driven of late?" Decker asked. "Did he feel the heat breathing down his back? Was he getting angry letters from some right-to-lifers?"

"No, no . . . at least I don't . . . there's always some hostility when you do abortions, but . . ." Reed sat back down. "It was money. He didn't just *need* it, he was *desperate* for it. Research is expensive—the machines, the chemicals, the animals he had to buy. It was draining him. But even that was not unusual. King was always running his science on a shoestring. But he felt he was on to something very important. He needed more money to make it work. He called me up for a loan."

"And you gave him something?" Marge said.

"Yes, I did. Twenty thousand dollars to be exact. But . . . but it wasn't enough." Reed shook his head. "I will be totally honest. Money wasn't the sole reason for his call. He wanted to sound me out. Mother had a proposition for him."

"What kind of proposition, Doctor?" said Decker.

"That . . . I don't know. Frankly, as soon as I heard that it was from Mother, I advised King to stay clear of it. I have always followed that advice and found it very suitable. Mother can be quite wicked . . . playing us off against each other. King told me it could lead to quite a bit of money . . . more money than she had ever given him."

Decker said, "Your mother was giving Kingston money all this time?"

"Bits . . . a thousand here, a thousand there. But from the way Kingston was talking, I had a feeling he was expecting something more—a big payoff."

Decker remembered Davida talking about padding her sons' wallets. *But it never seemed to be enough— the carrion eaters.*

Reed continued, "I told King that if it came from Mother, it would be nothing but heartache. I don't know whether he listened to me or not."

"But you have suspicions," Decker said.

"Yes, I do." Reed clasped his hands. "As soon as King told me about Lilah . . . about the robbery, I was suspicious. Not that King would ever *hurt* Lilah, but the robbery . . . I wondered if he had . . . was . . . involved . . ."

"Did you ask him?"

"No." Reed shook his head. "No, I didn't ask him. I . . . I didn't want to know. But King was *clearly* upset. He would *never* harm Lilah. He *adored* our little sister. Lilah had always looked to him as more of a father than a brother. Certainly Mother wasn't much of a parent."

"Do you think he might have stolen something from Lilah's to please your mother?"

"I really don't know what to think."

Decker asked, "When you spoke to Kingston, did he mention anything about Hermann Brecht's memoirs?"

Reed seemed genuinely puzzled. "I wasn't even aware that Hermann Brecht compiled memoirs."

"Apparently he did."

Reed shrugged.

Decker said, "Doctor, what can you tell me about Hermann Brecht?"

"I remember Hermann as a slight, pale, morose, sullen man who took my mother away from my father. I realize my parents' marriage was probably in trouble long before Hermann came along, but I was a child and viewed Hermann as an interloper. After Mother and he married, I refused to live with them. I went back to London and lived with my father until my majority. A most wise decision."

Reed appeared lost in thought.

"My most vivid memory of Hermann was at the birth celebrations for Lilah. My mother and he were living in a prewar mansion in West Berlin—one of the few that hadn't been bombed in World War II. It was right after President Kennedy had visited and had given his famous speech—*Ich bin ein Berliner.*" Reed looked at Marge. "Before your time, Detective."

Marge smiled. "Go on, Dr. Reed."

"I was flown into Germany," Reed said. "It was the early sixties. Even though I was young, I have good recollections of the West German people because they couldn't get enough of *America* or *Americans.* And my mother was not only American, but a *famous* American. After Lilah was born, Mother was besieged with attention from the press and played it for all she was worth. It was one party after another, Mother absolutely radiant and jubilant, kissing everyone, laughing all the time, floating through the masses like a swan. I remember that image because she wore a different-color flowing peignoir every day."

Reed thought for a moment.

"Hermann, on the other hand, had balled himself into a corner drinking the entire time, refusing to talk to anyone, especially Mother's *other* children. Kingston and I absolutely were *personae non gratae* to him. Of course, Mother was too busy with her admirers to notice Hermann or her sons. I remember this nightmarish sense of being dropped into an alien world—Felliniesque, if you will."

"If your mother ignored you the whole time, why did she bother flying you in?" Marge asked.

"Because I was Davida Eversong's son," Reed said. "I *had* to be there for appearance's sake."

"So Hermann wasn't the partygoing type," Decker said.

"Not at all . . . so unlike Mother." He let out a sad laugh. "When I think of all the postpartum mothers I've attended, I can't honestly . . . recall any of them being as energetic socially as Mother had been that week. Of course, Mother was pampered from head to toe. She had a private nurse for herself. And the baby had two nurses—a wet nurse feeding Lilah and a primary nurse who did general care. Neither nurse would allow me . . . or even Kingston . . . to see our baby sister."

"Why do you say 'or even Kingston'?" Decker asked.

"I had deserted Mother for Father, but Kingston was still living with her. It was bad enough for me to be rejected, but I wasn't really part of the family, was I? Kingston, on the other hand, was *furious*. During one of Mother's many parties, Kingston became so fed up, he whisked the baby out of the nurse's arms. That enraged Hermann. The two of them became embroiled in a massive fistfight. It was broken up quickly, but not before both of them had bloody noses. King was only sixteen at the time, but was strong and *scrappy*. And Hermann was drunk, so he wasn't . . . it was horrible."

"How old were you?" Marge asked.

"Just under fourteen. Too young to endure a week in Berlin with a drunken stepfather. I kept a very low profile until I was mercifully flown back to England. When Mother had Freddy . . . or rather *adopted* Freddy, she wanted to fly me in again. I refused to go and my father, God rest his soul, respected my decision."

Marge said, "During your stay in Berlin, Doctor, did you and Hermann Brecht ever have words or come to blows?"

"No, I toed the line. Actually, I never did see Hermann Brecht again except in the open coffin at his funeral. Pity for anyone to die so young, but that didn't mitigate my hatred for the man. He was a depressive drunk who stole my mother from my father and made bloated, pretentious, cynical movies and called them art."

"You have no idea what he might have said in his memoirs?" Decker asked.

"I don't know . . . and I don't care."

25

Marge steered to the right lane and merged onto the 605 freeway. Traffic was smooth—no overturned diesels, no fender benders. The sun was strong. She could feel the heat through the rolled-up window. Pulling out a pair of bargain sunglasses, she slipped them over her eyes.

"Are you ready for Dunn's insight of the week?"

"The excitement is killing me," Decker said.

"Lilah was adopted."

"Bingo, Margie, you win the microwave."

"Your thoughts, too?"

"Yep." Decker took off his jacket and tossed it in the backseat. "I've been thinking about Davida's age. Back then, very few women over forty were even *allowed* by their doctors to continue the pregnancy."

Marge took in his words. Not that her biological clock was even close to expiring, but it was nice to have more leeway in that department. "Times do change. The wonders of medical science—fifty-year-old mothers."

"I don't know if that's a blessing or a curse."

Marge laughed and knuckled her glasses up her

nose. "You know, I didn't even consider Davida's age. I was thinking about her energy level after she supposedly just gave birth to Lilah. Hosting one party after another, gliding around like a swan with no signs of exhaustion."

"True, but we have to remember that Reed was a kid," Decker said. "Davida could have collapsed afterward and Reed wouldn't have seen it. He also wouldn't have known if his mother had faked her pregnancy. He wasn't living with her and Hermann. And even if he had been living with her, Davida still could have faked a pregnancy."

"True," Marge said. "Looks like the only one who could have told us if Ms. Eversong looked pregnant was Merritt and he isn't going to tell us anything."

They rode for several moments, making good time though it was close to rush hour.

Marge said, "If Lilah was adopted, is it important to our case?"

Decker shrugged. "Any theories?"

"Okay, how about this? For some reason, Davida didn't want it known that Lilah was adopted."

"Odd," Decker said. "Freddy's adopted and no one seems to care."

"Yeah, but let's assume Davida wanted everyone to think that Lilah was her natural daughter."

Decker stiffened. "*Biological* daughter."

Marge whipped her head around for a second, then returned her eyes to the road. "Yeah, that's what I meant. You okay, Pete?"

"I'm fine." Decker forced himself to relax, then smiled stiffly. "Go on."

Marge blew out air. What was on his mind? "Where was I?"

"Davida wanting everyone to think Lilah was her biological daughter."

"Right . . . okay. Merritt suspected Lilah was adopted all along. So he stole the memoirs, read them, and sure enough, Hermann had written about Lilah's adoption. Then Merritt contacted his mother and informed her he was going to tell Lilah the truth. Davida said, 'You have no proof.'"

Decker said, "And then King said, 'Yes, I do, Mom, I have Hermann's memoirs. So either you fork over big cash to shut me up or I tell Lilah.'"

"Exactly," Marge said. "And Davida didn't fork over, so Merritt decided to tell Lilah the truth. But Davida got to him before he had a chance."

"Sounds good, except—"

"Uh-oh, here comes the bomb."

"No bomb. Just that Reed told us that *Davida called Merritt* and offered him big cash for a favor *before* the robbery. Assume the favor was: Steal the memoirs for me. If she was worried about black-mail, why would she have asked King to pop the safe in the first place?"

"So maybe Merritt didn't even consider black-mail at first. His mother offered bucks for a theft and Merritt, being hard up for cash, agreed." Marge held up her finger. "But then Merritt got curious and read the papers . . . read about Lilah's *adoption*. Thoughts began to percolate . . . like morning coffee."

Decker smiled.

Marge said, "Merritt decided to cash in. Davida

didn't like the change of plans. She got pissed, and the rest, as they say, is history."

Decker said, "His own mother whacked him to get some twenty-year-old papers?"

"Well, maybe Davida didn't mean to whack him. Merritt's office was a mess. Maybe Davida was tossing his office and Merritt surprised her. Things got out of hand. Boom—accidents happen."

Decker aimed the air-conditioning vents at his face. "Maybe Merritt's death had nothing to do with Davida or the memoirs. Your theory about a crazed antiabortionist suddenly makes sense. Merritt was doing experiments on aborted embryos and fetuses. That could piss off a lot of people."

They fell quiet.

Marge said, "Did Burbank ever call back with the specifics on what exactly killed Merritt?"

"Yeah, I left a note on your desk while you were at Parker Center."

"I must have missed it."

"Three gunshot wounds—one to the throat, two in the chest, thirty-eight caliber S and W. Any one of them could have been lethal." Decker smoothed his mustache. "You know, as much as I like the adoption thing in theory, I see a lot of Davida in Lilah."

"They don't look alike to me."

"No, they don't. But the expression, the mannerism—"

"Environment, Pete."

"The *voice*. That's genetic."

"Lilah's a good mimic. Truthfully, I don't see much family resemblance between any of the sibs except they're all fair. Even dark-eyed Reed has light skin. To me, Lilah looks as much like her half brothers as she does like Freddy."

"Maybe." Decker pulled down the car's sun visor. "I don't know. I just see this linkage between Davida and Lilah. I can't put my finger on it."

"Try warped personalities," Marge said.

Decker thought about his own half brothers and sisters whom he'd met for the first time eight months ago. He didn't look similar to any of them, but he had taken after his biological father and his siblings were related to him through his biological mother.

His blood siblings—five religious Jews living in New York. A bizarre twist of events had thrown them all together. After it was all over, he'd maintained a relationship with the oldest, Shimon, and the youngest, Jonathan—a half-dozen letters and even a few phone calls. Shim was ultra-Orthodox and wore a long black beard and a long black coat. Jonathan was a clean-shaven Conservative rabbi, whose tastes in clothes ran toward casual. On the surface, the three of them had nothing in common—physically or otherwise. Yet there was this kinship.

His thoughts shifted to his brother Randy. They weren't blood-related, yet they had plenty in common, too. Both were cops, both were outdoorsmen, and both were devoted, loving sons and good fathers. But their personalities were completely different. Decker was the serious one, Randy, freewheeling and adventurous. Then Decker mentally examined his stepsons—genetic brothers raised in the *same* environment. They weren't at all alike.

None of it made any sense. Time to move on.

Marge said, "Maybe we should approach Davida with our little theory, Pete. Gauge her reaction."

"I don't know if the time is right for that, Marge. Davida's a damn good actress. If we bring it up casually, she could probably deny it convincingly." Decker raised his brow. "And I'll be honest. I don't want to get her riled just yet. Have her calling in the press and piss Morrison off."

"Any way for us to verify the adoption theory?"

"Short of a blood test?"

"Genetic banding . . ."

"Pull some hairs from Davida and from Lilah?" Decker shrugged. "It could be done, but I don't know how we'd justify it to the department. Not to mention the ACLU. It really is invasion of privacy."

"Evidence for a homicide?"

"Not at this point."

"You're right."

Decker said, "I'll call that old lady Perry Goldin told me about, the one who supposedly knew Hermann Brecht from Germany. Maybe she could tell me a thing or two about Davida's pregnancy."

"Maybe." Marge glanced at Decker. "You sure you're okay?"

There was a long pause.

Decker blurted: "Marge, I'm adopted."

"What?" She suddenly realized the car in front of her had slowed and slammed on the brakes. "Jesus, I'm sorry! Are you all right?"

Decker rubbed his neck. "A little whiplash never hurt anyone."

Marge inched the unmarked forward, trying to

shape her thoughts. "Peter, why didn't you tell me a long time ago?"

"I didn't think it was relevant."

"It's not, but . . ." Her mind was agog with questions. "How could you *keep* something like that from me?"

"Are you pissed at me?"

"I don't know . . ." She paused. "Maybe."

"Sorry."

"S'okay." Marge tapped her fingers on the wheel, waiting for Decker to give some details. As usual, he was playing mute. "It doesn't matter a fig to me . . . you being adopted."

"I know."

"I just think if we're gonna work together, there shouldn't be these major secrets."

"Agreed."

"I would have told you."

"I know."

"Does Rina know?"

"Yes."

Marge was silent.

"I had to tell her, Margie. In order for us to get married—"

"Hey, you don't owe me an explanation."

Decker ran his hand through his hair. "You're pissed."

"Yes, I'm pissed." Marge sighed and patted his knee. "I'm hurt, big guy. Don't you trust me?"

"I'm sorry. I should have told you a long time ago. I'm glad I told you now. It's a weight off my shoulders."

"Why do you keep things inside, Pete?"

"Because I'm macho."

Marge laughed.

Decker said, "Well, consider this. You're pissed finding out that *I'm* adopted, think how pissed Lilah would be if she found out *she* was adopted and had never been told."

"She'd be mucho pissed . . . at Davida."

"Maybe that's why Davida didn't want her to find out," Decker said. "Hiding something like that from her, it would set off more than a few fireworks."

"Why would Davida have hidden it from her in the first place?"

"Sometimes adoptive parents feel threatened by biological parents. It's silly, but . . ."

Marge said, "Are you talking from personal experience, Peter?"

"Maybe a little."

There was no listing for a Greta Millstein in the standard phone book, but there was a number for G. Millstein in the unlisted directory. Decker dialed it, let the phone ring ten times, then hung up.

He massaged his bad shoulder, popped an Advil, and looked at the clock on the squad-room wall. Four fifty-five. He'd been working nonstop for almost fourteen hours. Time to call it a day.

But instead, he grabbed a pile of Merritt's photocopied monthly Visa statements and ran down the items with the tip of a pencil. Nothing seemed unusual although Merritt had expensive tastes—Bally shoes, Neiman Marcus men's department, Scotland House of Cashmere, Gucci, Dunhill, Hermès, Aristocrats. The man needed money for research yet he was spending a pretty penny on threads.

Then he thought: A shabbily dressed OB-GYN in Palos Verdes wouldn't be a big draw.

Even with the high-ticket items, Merritt wasn't overdrawn on his bills. In fact, he'd paid off his Visa balance every month, the box marked *finance charges* always $0.00.

On to American Express. Again, nothing indicating any late fees or finance charges. And Merritt wasn't using one credit card to pay off another. Decker was halfway through the MasterCard listings when Lilah stormed into the room, her voice sending a spurt of acid into his belly. He put down the papers and looked up.

She wore a black, formfitting sleeveless dress, the hemline a good three inches above her knees. Her long legs were as tan and bare as her arms. On her feet were leather thongs, the soles slapping against the floor as she marched toward him. Her hair was loose and long and fanning over her bronze shoulders like a golden shawl.

Decker popped another Advil and saw Marge move in for the intercept. She and Lilah met about twenty feet from his desk. Lilah tried to push her way through, but Marge was taller and heavier and made a very effective brick wall. Still, everyone in the squad room was instantly aware of the standoff, ready to jump if needed. Though flushed with anger, Lilah sensed the hostility. She tugged down her dress and stood up straight.

"I'm here to talk to Sergeant Decker, please," she said *sotto voce*. "Will you kindly step aside?"

"Miss Brecht, I'm going to have to ask you to wait outside," Marge said. "I'll deliver your message—"

Lilah raised her voice and pointed. "He's right there!"

"Please wait outside, Miss Brecht. I'll be with you in a moment—"

"This is *outrageous* . . . just . . ."

Lilah burst into tears, burying her head in her hands. Marge put her arm around the sobbing woman and walked with her toward an empty interview room. She glanced over her shoulder, caught Decker's eye, and beckoned him forward with a cocked head. Decker held up two fingers—two minutes.

Marge guided Lilah inside the room and closed the door. By the time Decker arrived, Lilah had just about composed herself. Her eyes were blue pits of fire.

"I *told* you something had happened to Kingston!" She moaned. "I *told* you it was something bad! I'm *prophetic!* I *know* these things!"

"So who killed your brother?" Marge asked.

"How should *I* know!" Lilah collapsed in her chair. "Why is this *happening* to me? Why? *Why!*"

Decker waited a beat, then said, "Lilah, what did you and King talk about when he called you yesterday?"

"Yesterday . . ." She dried her eyes and sighed. "It seems like light-years ago. Maybe it was. Maybe I'm living in a different metaphysical world."

Decker and Marge exchanged glances.

"Lilah?" Decker prompted.

"What did we talk about?" Again her eyes filled with tears. "Old times. After my harrowing experiences, I was so happy to hear from him. He was my big, strong, older brother. It felt good." Her eyes slowly hardened. "Kingston was fine as long as I obeyed his every word. The trouble between us started when I began to express myself." Her face suddenly lost expression. "It's Mother. She's behind all this evil."

Marge shot Decker a look. "What do you mean?"

"Her evil is overpowering us all."

Decker said, "What kind of evil are you talking about, Lilah?"

"She's put a curse on the family. She can do those things because she's a witch."

Marge raised her brow. "Why would she curse her own family?"

"She hates me," Lilah said without emotion. "She's jealous of my youth, my beauty, my power for good—which is as strong as her power for evil. She's also jealous—jealous of the *love* my *father* had for me, jealous of the love *Kingston* has for me. It tore her apart when we all lived together. When my brother and I went our own separate ways, she was delighted. Then yesterday he came to reconcile with me. Mother couldn't take it. She had him killed."

"Lilah," Decker said, "did your mother actually make any statement to that effect—"

"Of course not! She's not *stupid*!"

"Do you have any proof of your theory?" Marge said.

"I don't need proof. I know." She faced Decker. "I just know."

Again the room fell silent.

"But that's not why I'm here," Lilah announced.

Marge said, "Why are you here?"

Lilah's face regained animation. "For Carl Totes! I heard you had the *nerve* to arrest him for my rape! I already *told* you it wasn't him."

"Lilah," Decker said, gently, "we have evidence that directly links Totes to the rape."

"That's absurd! What kind of evidence? There's some sort of error!"

Marge said, "The lab tested it twice—"

"The lab was mistaken!" Lilah insisted. "Check again!"

"We can run a retest, Miss Brecht, but it's going to come out the same," Marge said.

"We're going to the DA with Totes, Lilah," Decker said. "Unless you tell us something that will contradict the evidence we have."

"I'm telling you it's not—" Lilah paused. "What would contradict the evidence?"

"That's for you to tell us, Miss Brecht," Marge said.

"I'm telling you it wasn't him," Lilah said. "Isn't that enough?"

Decker said, "You were blindfolded—"

"It wasn't him!"

"Then how did his semen get on your sheets?" Decker stared at her.

"Why are you looking at me like that?" Lilah demanded.

"I was just wondering if maybe you and Carl had willingly . . ." Decker let the words hang in the air.

Lilah's eyes got very intense. "Me? With *Carl*? That is the most *disgusting*—"

"I just wanted to make sure—"

"—vile, fiendish insinuat—!" Lilah stood and glared at both of them. "You are all pure *evil*. Full of *evil* thoughts and *evil* deeds! Perhaps it is not Mother who is responsible for the ills which have befallen me. Perhaps *you* are the devil disguised in the name of good. A pox on both of you!" She zeroed in on Decker. "And a pox on your wife and unborn baby."

She slammed the door as she left.

Marge and Decker sat in silence for a moment. Then Decker said, "Why couldn't she have confined her curses to me? Why'd she have to drag in Rina and the kid?"

"That is one spooky lady!"

"You said it," Decker said. "I'm saying my evening prayers tonight, I can tell you that much."

"Add one for me, partner." Marge sighed. "So what do you think?"

"Well . . ." Decker straightened up in his seat. "I have to get past her craziness and ask myself if it's an act or what."

"Your conclusion?"

"At first, I thought she was trying to protect Totes. Then when I suggested that maybe he and she were screwing, she went Looney Tunes. You know, Rina suggested to me that maybe Lilah's rape was a game gone too far—"

"How'd she come up with that?"

"She said that Lilah was real turned on when I got angry at her last night. Now I'm thinking maybe that's what happened between her and Totes. They were getting it on, playing this game, and it went too far. And she's afraid now that Carl will tell all.

Faye Kellerman

So she preempted him by saying there was no possible way they were fucking. What she really was doing was protecting her own butt in case Carl said anything. She doesn't want to look like a fool."

"Sounds farfetched but who knows?" Marge shook her head. "Nothing makes any sense. The rape, the berserk horse, the theft, Merritt's murder. What vital thread am I missing?"

"Damned if I know," Decker groused.

There was a knock on the door. Hollander opened it a second later and stuck his head inside. "Pete, line three. Devonshire, Homicide."

Marge smiled. "You talked to them about me?"

Decker smiled sheepishly. "Actually, I haven't yet." He stood, punched the blinking light on the wall phone, and said, "Decker." The voice on the other end was raspy.

"Scott Oliver, Homicide, Devonshire. Are you the one who caught the rape on Lilah Brecht?"

"Yes, it's mine."

"You got anything on that?"

"Matter of fact, we have a suspect in custody. Why?"

"We picked up a DB in a charred limo early this morning. No plates and the guy was close to toast, but there was enough skin on his fingers to lift a few prints. You know about hands reflexively curling in heat, protecting the fingertips?"

"Yeah. Did you make an ID?"

"Ran the prints for a CII number and got back a nice arrest trailer. Turns out our DB was arrested several times for B and Es. He's out on parole. When

I called up his parole officer, the woman told me he was gainfully employed. Wanna know by who?"

"Who?"

"Davida Eversong. That's Lilah Brecht's mother, right?"

Decker felt his heart beating. "Right."

"Two major crimes in the same family . . . weird." Oliver cleared his throat. "I thought if you had something on your case, it might be related to this case."

"Possibly. Who was the DB?"

"Mr. Toast? Eversong's chauffeur—a Russ Donnally. I'm assuming the limo was probably hers. Does the name ring any bells?"

"No, it doesn't." He turned to Marge. "Ever hear of a guy named Russ Donnally? He was Davida Eversong's chauffeur."

Marge shook her head.

"Want to know the interesting part?" Oliver said.

"There's more?"

"Is anything in life ever simple? 'Bout five minutes ago, I get a call from the lab. There was a wallet in the car. Burned, but enough paper to make an ID on the driver's license. Not Donnally's. We ran the owner's name through CII. He's clean so far as we know. Does the name Michael Ness ring any bells?"

Decker closed his eyes and opened them. "Detective, we indeed have some mutual points of interest. Can I meet you somewhere in a couple of hours?"

"Fine. Let's shoot for seven."

"You got it."

Oliver said, "You're at Foothill. We could meet

halfway between the substations—Willy's at Roscoe and Woodman. Think the department will spring for a four-ninety-nine dinner special?"

"We could make a damn good case for it. As long as you don't get greedy and order dessert."

☙ 26

The dog barking, the television blaring, the kids talking to him at the same time. The phone rang just as Rina announced it was time for dinner. Not the kind of scene that inspired homilies for samplers, but it was Decker's chaos and don't it feel so *good.*

Rina carried a platter of grilled chicken breasts to the table. "Is someone going to catch the phone?"

"I'll get it." Jacob grabbed the receiver. "Hullo?"

The dog yapped and jumped at Decker's heels.

"Acknowledge the dog, Peter," Rina said. "Shmuli, can you help me out, please?"

"Why me?"

Rina said, "Because I asked—"

"For you, Shmuli," Jacob said.

"Call them back, Shmuel," Rina ordered. "We're actually going to try to eat dinner."

The older boy rolled his eyes and went to the phone.

"Don't look at me like that." Rina went to the kitchen and brought out a bowl of tossed salad. "Yonkie, turn off the TV. Then please bring in the pitcher of orange juice and a bottle of beer for your father."

"Pass on the beer." Decker checked the back door. Securely locked. "I've got to go back to work."

"Peter, you've been up for sixteen *hours*!"

"I'd be happy to call it a day except crime doesn't keep businessmen's hours."

"You should be raking in tons of overtime."

"Unfortunately, saying it doesn't make it so." Decker sat at the dining-room table, the cherry-wood top as shiny as the day he finished varnishing it. Rina took extra care with the furniture he'd hand-crafted. He placed a single chicken breast on each empty plate, then helped himself to two pieces. He broke a chunk of meat from the remaining breast and gave it to the dog. "How're you feeling, darlin'?"

"I'm fine." Rina set a glass dish down on a trivet. "As big as a horse, but still on two feet. Careful, this is hot."

Decker lifted the lid and a cloud of steam poured out—roasted red potatoes with jalapeño peppers and onions. He took two heaping spoonfuls.

"I chose Southwestern as our dinner theme tonight," Rina said. "*Très chic.* Or maybe it's *muy* chic. Yonkie, bring in the salsa for the chicken. Shmuli, get off the *phone*!"

"In a minute, Eema."

Decker cut a piece of chicken and popped it into his mouth. "Anyone interesting call?"

"Cindy." Rina frowned. "I think I sounded overanxious."

Decker picked his head up. No noise outside—just his imagination. "Overanxious about what?"

"About trying to make her feel welcome." Rina

speared a forkful of salad. "She was so sheepish about asking you to stay for the summer. I feel a little guilty. As if *our* relationship changed *your* relationship with her."

"That's ridiculous." Decker chewed.

"It's an adjustment for her, Peter. She's used to having you to herself. Now, she has *me* in the picture." Rina thought about her words. "I'm close to my father. I can understand her confusion."

"She's always gotten along well with you," Decker said. "Besides, her mother remarried first—takes the heat off you. She'll be okay once she's out here."

"Once she sees I'm not really a wicked stepmother." She looked over her shoulder. "Shmuli, get off the phone *now!*"

Jacob smiled. "Don't worry, Eema. I'll tell her you're not any wickeder as a stepmom than you are as a regular mom."

Rina stared at him. "Thank you, Yonkie. And wickeder isn't a word."

"More wicked." Sammy sat down. "Pass the salsa."

Decker spooned sauce over the boy's chicken, lifted his head again, then returned his attention to his potatoes.

"Are you expecting anyone, Peter?" Rina asked.

"No. Why?"

"You seem preoccupied."

Decker shrugged. "Hard to switch gears."

Rina patted his hand. "Try to relax, dear."

Sammy stuffed his mouth full of potatoes. "Yeah, we could use one calm parent around here."

"Are you suggesting I've been less than a model of patience, Shmuli?" Rina asked.

"God forbid!" Sammy smiled impishly. "You make dynamite potatoes, Eema."

Rina gave him a look of mock disapproval.

"Ginger, stop begging," Jacob said. "Can I give her some of my chicken?"

"No, you've already doused your meat with salsa," Rina said. "That's all her poor stomach would need."

"Maybe she'd like some salsa, Eema," Sammy said. "Add a little spice to her life."

Rina said, "So you're volunteering to clean up her mess if she gets indigestion?"

The boy shook his head quickly.

"Any other calls?" Decker asked.

"Nothing important."

Decker poured himself a glass of orange juice. "Like what do you mean by nothing important?"

Rina laughed. "What?"

"I mean, what calls did you get that you don't consider important?"

Rina looked at him. "What's on your mind, Peter?"

"Nothing's on my mind. I'm just asking about calls."

She continued to stare at him.

"I was just wondering if you've received any hang-ups . . . someone calling and hanging up . . . without speaking."

Rina said, "Peter, your obvious attempt to be casual is making us all nervous. What is it?"

Decker said, "Lilah—"

Rina banged down her fork. *"Again?"*

"Is she the maniac who woke us all up this morning?" Sammy said.

"Yes," Decker answered.

"Don't worry, Dad," Jacob said. "She tries anything funny, Eema'll just shoot her!"

"That's what I'm afraid of," Decker said. "Maybe it'd be a good idea if you visited your parents tonight."

Rina sat back in her chair. "Did she *threaten* me?"

"No."

"Then what did she do?"

"She . . ." Decker put down his fork. "She . . . cursed us—"

"You're upset because she used the *f-word*?" Yonkie asked.

"No, not *swearing*," Decker said. "Cursing . . . like what witches do."

"Cursing as in *klalah*," Rina clarified to the boys. "Not *nivul peh*." She mock spat several times into the air. "Pooh, pooh, pooh! That's what I think of her curses. And just *let* her try anything—incur the wrath of a grumpy, hot, pregnant woman. It's no contest, Peter."

Decker buried his head in his hands.

"I'm just *teasing* you," Rina said. "Are you really worried? If you're worried, we'll schlepp out to my parents'."

"It would make me feel better."

"Do you want us to spend the night there?"

"If I think I'll be home by nine, I'll call. If not, maybe a night at Grandma's and Grandpap's would be a good idea." Decker sighed. "This is really going to endear me to your mother. . . . 'You put my daughter in danger. . . .'"

"You do a terrible Hungarian accent." Rina turned to her sons. "Finish up, then go pack your bags. I need to talk to your father for a minute."

Jacob faced his brother. "He's gonna tell her the gory details in private."

"There are no gory details," Decker said.

"Finish up, please," Rina said.

Sammy stood. "Great grub, Eema." He kissed his mother's cheek. "Let's go, Yonkie. It's a long ride to Savta's and Saba's. If there are any gory details, we'll get them out of her."

"There are no gory details," Decker insisted.

After the boys left to pack, Rina whispered, "What are the gory details?"

"Nothing," Decker said. "Lilah Brecht is very unstable at the moment—a rape, a near-death horse ride, and now her brother's dead. She's taking it out on me and on you by extension. I don't feel comfortable leaving you home alone while I work—at least not tonight."

"What are you working on?"

"I've got an appointment with someone from Devonshire regarding a homicide that might be related to the case."

"Someone else besides the brother is dead?"

Decker nodded.

"Is that why she suddenly cursed you?"

"No. We arrested her stable hand for the rape today. We have physical evidence against him. Lilah was furious at us for arresting him—swore he wasn't the right one. Then I suggested the evidence was pretty convincing unless she and Totes had had sex that night. That pushed her button. Her reaction was so disproportionate, I immediately thought they *must* have some kind of affair. Honestly, I don't know what to think."

Rina shuddered. "Too many murders. Please be *careful*, Peter."

Decker leaned over and kissed her cheek. "I'm always careful. Especially now. Got lots of people depending on me."

"Lots of people who *love* you, Peter."

Decker regarded his wife's beautiful face, then held her hands and kissed them. *His* wife. She had actually *married* him! What the hell was he doing *right*?

The number for stolen or lost credit cards was closed for the evening. Ness slammed down the phone, then told himself to breathe deeply. Sitting on the center of his bed, he adjusted his weight until he was in a perfect lotus position. Correct posture, but an incorrect *attitude*—a goddamn spiral. The body couldn't unwind unless the mind was at peace and how the hell could you clear your mind if your body was coiled steel? He felt soft warm hands begin to rub the nape of his neck. Under his sister's touch, he allowed himself the luxury of relaxation.

"Do me a favor, Kell. Look up the twenty-four-hour number for lost or stolen credit cards."

"What bank are you with?"

"Security International." Ness banged his fist against his head. "I can't fucking believe . . . somehow . . . some way . . . it's gonna screw me up. Story of my life."

"Here's the number."

Ness copied it onto a piece of scrap paper and dialed. Busy. Gently, he placed the receiver in the cradle. "What's my chance of anything working out?"

"Michael, where do you *think* you left it?"

"I don't even know if I *left* it anywhere. Somebody might have *lifted* it from me. I think someone's trying to screw me."

"We'll think of something. *I'll* think of something."

He shrugged off her hands and patted his mattress. "Sit."

Kelley hesitated, then sat beside him, her eyes focused on her hands folded in her lap. "If only I hadn't insisted you come out here—"

"Stop flogging yourself, Kell. You know Davida. Once she wants something, she's unstoppable. Actually, I should take it as a compliment. Rich old broads like her could have hired herself a zillion studs and she wanted *me*." Ness shrugged. "Hasn't been terrible. Steady money. Regular sex—now *that's* a first. Beats blowjobs from drunken sailors—"

"Oh, Michael!"

"Or zoned-out whores."

"Mike, please let me *help* you!"

Ness kissed his sister's cheek. "You stay out of this mess. Let me take the heat."

She threw her arms around her brother's neck. "Mike, can't you just tell the cops the truth? That you had nothing to do with any of this—"

"That's not exactly true."

"You had nothing to do with the murder." She paused. "Or with Lilah's rape, right?"

Ness pivoted around, feeling a spinal chill as cold as a blustery wind. "Try to sound *convinced* when proclaiming my innocence."

Kelley whispered, "I *believe* you, Mike. I've always believed you—believed *in* you, haven't I? Unlike *others*. Was there ever a single point in our lives where *my* faith in you was destroyed?"

Ness saw it all in his sister's eyes—the pain he'd caused her—and felt the heat of shame. He held out his arms to her and she came to him, burying herself in the cocoon of his embrace.

"I'm sorry—"

"Stop—"

"No, *let* me say it, Kell." Ness cleared his throat. "I love you and I'm sorry . . . sorry for *everything*."

She didn't answer him, but he felt her tears on his shirt.

Had to be the one wearing the mirrored Porsche shades with the blue blazer slung over his arm, fingers gripping a lizard briefcase. As soon as Decker caught his eye, the man stood, removed his glasses, and held out a hand, introducing himself as Scott Oliver.

Late thirties, five-eleven, one-eighty, a broadness across the shoulders that came from weight lifting. Wavy black hair full on top but clipped short at the sides, and deep-set dark eyes under thick black eyebrows. Razor-straight nose, smooth skin stretched over high cheekbones, a white, wide smile. Marge was going to like the scenery at Devonshire. Decker took the proffered hand.

"I'm glad you called, Scott. I could use a break."

"You and me both."

Oliver winked at the peroxide-blond hostess and told her they were ready to be seated. They followed the sway of her behind to a brown Naugahyde booth in the back of the coffee shop. She handed them menus and asked if anyone would like coffee. Both said yes.

Oliver said, "I must be going senile or something. You're the guy they got slated to fill MacDougal's slot. You gonna take it?"

"It might work out. How's the climate over there?"

"Not bad. The Dee-three's a pretty good guy and the new Loo seems to be working out—doesn't play politico twenty-four hours a day. Last guy we had was a real schmuck. Left after landing police chief in some cracker town. Our garbage is now someone else's dinner. Anyway, you ever do Homicide before?"

"Six years."

"So you know the ropes. Won't be playing hot dog on the first hit." Oliver played with his napkin. "That always helps. Get some greener in, anxious to prove himself, makes everyone's life miserable."

Decker said, "If I come in, I come as a duo."

"Oh, you're one of those—you and your partner are real tight. Don't get me wrong, it works for some people. Frankly, I consider partners a pain in the ass."

"Not a good team player, Scott?"

"No, it's not that. Hey, help yourself to my files." Oliver held out his hands expansively. "I just don't

like a shadow breathing down my neck." He paused.
"I don't know. Maybe I just never had the *right* partner. Yours a good guy?"

"Gal—"

"Ah, the plot thickens."

"Strictly business."

"You fucking her, it's gonna come out, you
know."

Decker was impassive. "She's strictly business."

"She any good . . . at business, I mean."

"She's excellent."

"How old is she?"

"Thirty."

Oliver raised his brow. "Is she cute?"

"You fuck her, it's gonna come out," Decker said.

Oliver thought about that. "You married, Pete?"

"Yep."

"So am I." Oliver grinned. "What can I say?"

"Pussy file on you pretty thick, Scott?"

"Bigger than some, not as big as others." Oliver
shrugged. "I'm a curious guy. That's why I'm a detective."

Two cups of coffee were brought over by a thin-
hipped waitress. She took their orders, Oliver select-
ing the turkey dinner, Decker sticking to coffee only.
By the time Decker was done explaining the case,
Oliver was soaking up the last bits of tan-colored
gravy with a Parker House roll.

Decker said, "I've called Burbank, left a message
I was meeting you here. I was hoping they might have
found out something. But I guess they're still at the
fact-finding phase of the investigation."

"Are they the types to get bogged down with minutiae?"

"No, they seemed okay . . . eager to work."

"Good. So what do we got so far?" Oliver pushed his plate aside. "We got my stiff torched in Davida Eversong's limo."

"It was definitely her limo?"

"Can't say for sure yet, but we think so. The old lady just bought herself a new BMW, too. I gotta ask why."

Decker said, "So that's why the limo was unavailable to take Lilah Brecht out for dinner last night. Davida had other plans for it."

"I haven't been able to reach the old lady by phone, so I thought I'd drop by the spa, question her directly. But first I wanted to talk to you. From what you said, the daughter sounds as if she's crossed the other side."

"She's been through the wringer." But she still manages to dress to kill, Decker thought. "She's also a piece, Scott. You got a weakness for furry creatures, watch your ass."

"You know what you do with a seductive chick like that?"

"What?"

"You come on strong, they turn off like a light. Works every time. Bet you came on all business with an 'aw shucks' grin, flashing your wedding band in her face. Hell, with that kind of animal, a ring's like chum to a shark."

Decker sipped coffee. Guy was a sharpie.

"So . . ." Oliver ran his hand through his hair. "Do you want to talk to Ness? Ask him what his wallet was doing in a torched limo next to a DB? You know what he's gonna say."

"Yeah, Donnally lifted the wallet. Did you call up to see if there was a stop put on the credit cards?"

Oliver frowned. "No. I should have done that. Found out how far ahead Ness was thinking. And then again, maybe Donnally really did steal Ness's wallet."

"Maybe."

"So how do you figure in Donnally?"

"That's why I wish Burbank would call back. If the blood in Merritt's office was Donnally's, then you have to figure he and Merritt were whacked at the same time. Somebody carried Donnally out of the office and torched him inside the limo. Do you have an official cause on Donnally's death?"

"Hold on." Oliver pulled a folder out of his brief-case. "I just got the prelim path report 'bout five minutes before I was due to meet you. Let's see . . ." He turned pages. "Okay, official cause was two thirty-eights in the chest. I told you he was shot, didn't I?"

Decker shook his head.

"Memory's getting worse by the minute," Oliver bemoaned. "I have to write everything down now. That really bugs me 'cause I used to have a computer brain. You reach thirty-five, it's all over."

"You obviously haven't reached forty."

Oliver laughed and sipped coffee. "Got something to look forward to, Pete?"

"I prefer my future to Donnally's."

"That's for sure." Oliver returned his attention to

the path report. "Yeah, even though Donnally had been roasted, the lab made out the entry wounds. Course it was impossible to tell proximity of the discharge. Can't read powder burns off charcoal briquettes."

"What does the report say about the lungs?"

"Hold on . . ." He flipped through more paper. "Liver, kidney, spleen—"

"Backtrack," Decker said. "You're in the peritoneum."

"Yeah, I hate reading these goddamn things. Okay, lungs were clear, so the shots did him in. No smoke inhalation; he was dead before he was barbecued."

"That would be consistent with his being at Kingston Merritt's murder scene, Scott. The tech said there was a pool of blood belonging to another body. I'm betting the corpse was Donnally and some third party removed him from the scene."

"Ness."

"Or someone with Ness's wallet. Now I don't know if the third party was involved in the two shootings or if he was just a spectator while the two of them dueled it out." Decker thought a moment. "Could be Ness was just doing someone else's cleanup."

"Guess we won't know until we ask him. And maybe not even then." Oliver looked at his watch. "It's early. You want to pay a visit to Mr. Ness at the spa now?"

"Okay by me," Decker said. "I'll leave another message with Burbank. Don't want to step all over them."

"Never helps to piss off the co-investigators."

Oliver left a ten on the table. Decker figured that constituted a four-dollar tip on a six-dollar tab. No wonder Scottie was popular with the ladies.

❧ 27

The lighting was soft and recessed, the fireplace aglow with blue-white gas flames encircling fake logs. Bowls of potpourri adorned the center of each end table, emitting an apple-cinnamon scent bordering on cloying. Sitting around the hearth was a group of twenty women. Some were still dressed in exercise clothes—tights and leotards and sweatshirts. Their hair was still tied in ponytails or pulled off their foreheads by sweat bands. Others were garbed in oversized sweaters, leggings, ankle warmers, and sneakers, their faces made up, their hair blow-dried perfectly. They were listening to a young lady who stood in the center of the semicircle, waving several swatches of diaphanous cloth. She had waist-length blond hair and wore a black mini T-shirt dress that showed every curve.

Oliver leaned against the front door and looked at Decker. "You wanna flip for the broad in the center?"

Decker stuck his hands in his coat pocket. "Know what I find a real pisser?"

"Other than the fact that you can't fuck all these fine specimens at once?"

"Look what's going down here, Scottie. You got

the air conditioning running full blast so they can make it cold enough to light a fire. Jesus, it's *eighty-five degrees* outside. You want heat, open a window. Aren't they in violation of some asinine health code?"

"How 'bout this, Pete?" Oliver placed his hands on Decker's shoulders. "You look through the rule books, I'll interview the broads."

They listened to the blonde talk for a moment. She passed around the squares of cloth and a hand mirror and asked the women to hold the cloth up to their faces. Decker had caught something about ivory creams and peaches softening the rusts, when a pinch-faced girl with pink-rimmed glasses walked up to them. She wore a starched white-linen business suit, the skirt tight and short. Her legs were bare, her feet shod in backless shoes.

"Good evening, gentlemen. I'm Fern Purcel. May I help you?"

"Yeah, you can." Oliver's eyes went from Fern's legs to the circle of women. He pointed to them. "What're they *doin'* over there?"

Fern stiffened. "That's Elizabeth *Dumay*—as in *Dumay cosmetics*. She was kind enough to drop by and do *colors* for the women."

Oliver turned to Decker. "What the hell is colors?"

"Red, blue, green—"

"So this stuff is Greek to you, too."

"No, I know the letters of the Greek alphabet." Decker pulled out his badge and showed it to Fern.

"Not again!" she said. "What is it this time?—no, I don't even want to know. Just wait here until I call Ms. Ness."

Oliver's ears perked up. "Ms. *Ness?*"

"Mike's sister," said Decker. "Far as I can tell, she's the business manager here."

"You ever talk to her?"

"Not me personally. My partner did."

"If you'll excuse me, I'll call her now," Fern said.

Gently, Decker caught her by the arm, then let go of her. "I'd rather not waste your time, Fern. How about giving us a personal escort to Ms. Ness's office?" He jerked his head in the direction of the women. "Less likely to create a scene if you get us out of the lobby."

Behind the pink-rimmed glasses, dark eyes traveled from the hearth to the second-story landing off the staircase. Must be where Kelley's office is located, thought Decker. He swept his arm toward the banister. "After you, ma'am."

At first no one moved. Then, reluctantly, Fern walked across the floor of the entry and started up the steps. The men followed a half flight behind.

"What was *that* all about?" Oliver whispered.

Decker said, "In the past, sis has warned bro when the police have dropped in. I figured we, the good guys, should have the advantage of surprise."

"Definitely."

Fern led them to a pie-shaped room. In contrast to the mellow lighting of the domed lobby, the office was harsh with the white glare of fluorescence. A young woman with poker-straight brown hair had her nose inches from her desk. She pulled a long strand behind her ear, then tapped the desktop with a pencil. She didn't even bother looking up when Fern cleared her throat.

"What is it, Fern?"

"Police, Ms. Ness."

Kelley Ness snapped her head up. She wore a crew-neck red top. A thin gold choker chain showed off her long, graceful neck. Decker pulled out his badge. "Detective Sergeant Decker. This is Detective Oliver."

Kelley was silent. Not a bad-looking gal, Decker thought. Might even be pretty if she took off the scowl. She resembled her brother, but he was a better-looking boy than she was a girl. Decker wondered if that created friction between them. He thought Kelley's eyes seemed scared and wondered why. Placing his badge back in his breast pocket, he said, "We're here to talk to your brother, Mike. Is he around?"

Kelley remained quiet.

"Ms. Ness?" Oliver said.

Kelley bit her lip, her eyes jumping between the men. "I'll . . . I'll call Mike's room—"

Decker covered the phone receiver with his hand. "Why don't you just walk us over there? Heck, you're working real hard, you could use a break."

"I . . . I don't have time—"

"Make time, Ms. Ness." Oliver's smile was drop-dead charming. "Please."

Slowly, Kelley rose from her chair. The crew-neck top was actually a dress. "I'm not sure where he is."

"We've got time for a guided tour," Decker said.

Kelley suddenly toughened her demeanor. "Decker . . . *you* were the one who saved Lilah yesterday."

Yeah, that did happen just yesterday, Decker thought. Seems like weeks ago. That's what happens when you've been working forty out of the last forty-eight hours. Man, he needed *sleep*.

"Lilah told me not to permit you into the grounds."

"Now that wouldn't be very wise."

"No, not at all," Oliver agreed.

"Lilah's a little miffed at me right now," Decker said. "Anyway, I don't want to see Lilah. I want to talk to your brother."

"What about?"

Oliver scratched his head and positioned himself on Kelley's right. "This and that, Ms. Ness."

Decker flanked her left side. "Shouldn't take too long."

"In and out," Oliver said, gently guiding her to the door.

"Maybe a little longer than in and out." Decker turned off the office lights.

"Yeah, maybe a little longer." Oliver shut the door behind him. "But not too much longer."

"No, not too much longer," Decker repeated.

Kelley looked back at her office as forlorn as a kid forced off to summer camp.

"After you, Ms. Ness," Decker said.

Kelley sighed, then marched down the steps. To the left of the staircase was an open door leading to a dimly lit carpeted hallway.

Oliver whispered, "Split the sibs?"

Decker shook his head. "I want to see how they act together."

"Are they in cahoots?"

Decker shrugged.

Kelley stopped at the end of the hall, in front of room 12. She faced the door, raised her fist to knock, but didn't complete the action. Oliver knocked for her. A muffled male voice said it was open. Decker turned the knob and allowed Kelley to cross the threshold.

In a few seconds, brother and sister exchanged lots of nonverbal conversation. Neither one was pleased, but Ness looked composed. He sat cross-legged on the bed, garbed in gray sweatpants and a pink and black Body Glove muscle shirt. "Where's the lady detective? I liked her. She was cute."

Oliver stuck his hands in his pockets and said nothing. Decker looked around the spartan room and leaned against the wall. Kelley sat down on the bed and patted her brother's leg.

"Where were you yesterday, Mike?" Decker asked.

"Here."

"All day?" Decker said.

"Yes, all day. Where else would I—?" Shit! Ness told himself to slow down or he was going to trip up again. "No, of course not *all* day. I saw you at Lilah's ranch yesterday, didn't I? After the accident. I went to pick vegetables for the kitchen, remember?"

"Then you came back here?" Oliver asked.

"Yeah, I had to lead my afternoon aerobics class."

"Then where'd you go?" Decker said.

"I went on break, then came back for the final yoga class."

"Then what?"

Slowly, Ness uncoiled his legs from the lotus position and stood. "What's the point of this?"

"We don't have a hard-on for you, Mike," Decker

said. "We're just trying to retrace your day, maybe even help you out. So how about cooperating with us?"

Ness was quiet for a moment. "Sure. You want me to go over my day, I'll do the best I can. I don't remember exactly what I did after yoga, which means I probably went straight to my room. I went to my room and stayed there the entire evening. Kell visited me."

"Yes, I did," Kelley said, bobbing her head up and down.

Ness threw her a look that told her to shut up. "Kell was here, Eubie Jeffers was here. But there was lots of time I was here by my lonesome. I watched a little TV, put on some tapes. What else can I tell you?"

"What movies did you see?" Oliver asked.

"Not tapes as in movies," Ness said. "Videos of me doing exercise routines. It's not narcissism. I like to see what kind of muscles I'm working out. If I'm not getting enough triceps action, I add more tri exercises. If the hamstrings are being overworked, I reduce the stress there. Want to see them?"

Decker remembered Marge telling him about the tapes and shook his head. "Where'd you eat dinner, Mike?"

Ness eyed him for a moment. "Dinner?"

"Yeah, dinner. Simple question. Where'd you eat?"

"He had dinner with me," Kelley said.

Both detectives looked at her. Ness grimaced as if he'd sucked lemons.

"With you?" Oliver said.

"Yes, with me," Kelley said in a small voice. "Is

that so unreasonable? A brother and sister having dinner together?"

"No," Decker said.

"You have dinner with your sister last night, Mike?" Oliver said.

"Yes."

"You sure about that?"

"Of course he's sure!" Kelley said.

"You and he ate at the spa?" Decker said.

"In my office," Kelley said.

"But here at the spa," Decker said.

"Yes, my office is at the spa, Detective," Kelley said.

Decker said, "So if I asked people around the spa where you were at dinnertime, Kelley, not a soul would remember seeing you in the dining room."

Kelley's mouth dropped open, her cheeks pinkened. "Well, maybe I talked to a few women."

"But you didn't eat with them," Oliver said.

"Maybe I took a bite or two—"

"But not dinner," Decker said.

"Maybe I ordered just to be polite—"

"Kelley, shut up!" Ness growled.

Decker glared at her. "Ms. Ness, unless you're sure of exactly what you're saying, don't buy yourself a heap of trouble."

Ness said, "Leave her alone. She's trying to help me. She doesn't know squat about anything."

"What's anything, Mike?"

"Damned if I know. What's this about? Are we back with Lilah's rape? I thought you guys arrested Totes this morning for that. What do you want with me?"

"How old are you, Mike?" Decker asked.

Again, Ness eyed him warily. "Twenty-eight."

"Twenty-eight?" Decker asked. "You're sure?"

"Of course I'm sure. What? You wanna see ID or something?"

Oliver grinned at Decker. "That would be nice."

Ness closed his eyes, then opened them and smiled. "Clever. So you must have found my wallet. Why didn't you just ask me if I lost it? Why all the subterfuge?"

Nobody spoke.

"Well, that's a relief!" Ness said. "I couldn't get through to cancel my credit card. Now I'm glad I didn't keep trying. Where'd you find it?"

Casual, Decker thought, natural. The kid was good.

"Where'd you lose it?" Oliver asked.

"Hey, if I remembered where I lost it, I would have retrieved it myself."

"Funny, you being here all day and the wallet was found far, far away from here, Michael," Decker said.

Ness shrugged. "Where was it found?"

Decker shrugged. "At a murder scene."

Kelley gave an involuntary gasp. Ness stared at her, then at Decker.

"Got any answers, Mike?" Oliver asked.

"I don't know what you're *talking* about!"

"Want to hire a lawyer?" Decker said.

"A law— Why would I need . . . ?"

"Up to you," Decker said.

"Michael, don't say any more." Kelley stood. "*I'm* going to hire a lawyer."

"But I don't need a . . . I don't know how my wallet got to a murder . . . what . . . whose murder are we talking about?"

"Good question," Oliver said.

"I don't know *what* you're referring to."

Decker said, "How many murder scenes do you know about, Mike?"

"You mean Kingston Merritt?"

"Michael, shut up!" Kelley ordered.

Ness said, "Hey, everyone close to Lilah and Davida knows about Kingston being killed last night. It's terrible, but *I* didn't have anything to do with it. I don't know how my wallet got there. Jesus, I just met the man a few days ago. We had a little run-in. Hey, your lady detective was there when it happened. Maybe Merritt got mad at me and stole my wallet."

"Kingston Merritt stole your wallet?" Oliver said.

"I don't know." Ness began to pace. "I don't *know*, okay?"

Decker recognized panic in the kid's voice. The old gut told him that Ness was involved. Now it was just quibbling over the extent. "Where were you yesterday, Mike?"

"Is he being officially questioned?" demanded Kelley.

"If you'd like, ma'am, I can read him his rights," Oliver said.

Kelley said, "This is totally *absurd*!"

"No, Ms. Ness, it's the law." Oliver Mirandized Ness. "Okay, let's go down to Booking—"

"Booking?" Kelley shouted. "You're not serious!"

Ness said, "I swear I don't know a damn thing

about . . . I wasn't there . . . I mean, my wallet . . ." He buried his head in his hands. "Look, you want to book me—"

"Michael, shut up!" Kelley screamed.

"Kelley, get me a lawyer. I'll meet him at the station—"

Kelley jumped off the bed and blocked the doorway. "I won't let you go with them, Michael! You *can't*!"

"Kelley—"

They were interrupted by a knock on the door.

"Expecting anyone?" Oliver said.

Ness closed his eyes and said, "No one."

Decker opened the door, surprised to see Justice Ferris and Don Malone. The Burbank detectives were flanking a light-skinned black man with his arms drawn behind his back, secured with nylon handcuffs. Donnie was in standard-issue detective's wrinkled brown suit. Justice was garbed in black suit, black shirt, black lizard boots, and a white tie. He looked like a Hollywood producer or a pusher.

"Who're you?" Ferris asked Oliver.

Oliver said, "Devonshire—Homicide."

Again, Kelley gasped aloud, then covered her mouth as she backed into the wall.

Nice, Decker thought, she was involved too. Her hands were shaking, her forehead suddenly sheened with sweat. Decker looked at Ness. Kid's face was contorted with rage.

"You fucking *bastard*!" Ness spat. "You *set me up*!"

"It wasn't like you think, Mike!"

"Shut up, Eubie!" Kelley screamed.

Jeffers clamped his lips together. Decker made

the necessary introductions and asked what was going on.

Malone said, "Mr. Jeffers here has just been Mirandized for the murder of Kingston Merritt. He has willingly come forth with some important information. Seems he had a partner—"

"You *bastard*!" Ness repeated.

"I had to, Mike," Jeffers whined. "But it isn't like you think!"

"Eubie, shut up!" Kelley barked.

"What do you want with Mr. Ness?" Malone asked Decker.

"Murder one—" Oliver said.

"What!" Ness said. "I didn't *kill* anyone!"

"So what was your wallet doing at the murder scene?" Oliver asked.

"I wasn't there. My *wallet* was." Ness pointed a finger at Jeffers. "This fucking asshole took it and set me up!"

"I did not!" Jeffers protested.

"Wallet?" Ferris asked. "What wallet?"

"We'll swap notes later," Decker said to Malone. "You have enough to bring Ness in?"

"Enough for a twenty-four-hour hold based on Jeffers's statement."

Kelley stepped forward and proclaimed in an orator's voice, "Mike didn't kill anyone and neither did Eubie!"

"Kelley, shut up!" Ness said.

She ignored her brother and faced Malone. "I don't know what you have against Eubie, but I do know Eubie fingered Mike just to protect me—"

"What?!" Ness said.

"Michael, I'm so sorry!" Kelley said, "I was going to tell you, but . . ." She looked down at the floor, then up again. "Eubie asked me to help him remove a body from Kingston Merritt's office—"

"You got my *sister* involved in this, you *fuckhead*?" Ness shouted.

"Mike, please!" Jeffers pleaded. "I couldn't do it by myself—"

"*Shut your fucking trap! You make me fucking sick!*" Ness turned to his sister and lowered his voice. "As for *you* . . ."

"I *did* it, okay?" Kelley shouted over him.

"I'm going to read you your rights, Ms. Ness," said Oliver.

"I *removed* the body, that's *all* I did—"

"Wait until I get this out, ma'am," Oliver said, pulling a card from his pocket.

"I *can't*!" Kelley turned to Decker. "*Listen* to me, *please*! Both Dr. Merritt and Russ . . . Russ Donnally was the other body . . . both were dead when Eubie and I arrived. You must believe me! All Eubie and I did was carry Russ out of Dr. Merritt's office. He was already *dead*! *Both* of them were *dead*!"

"Why'd you gasp when we mentioned homicide, Kelley?" Decker said.

Kelley wiped tears from her eyes. "I burned Davida's limo."

"With Russ inside."

"He was already *dead*."

"Then why'd you burn him, Kelley?"

Kelley looked downcast. "Maybe someone would think it was a drug bust gone sour. Russ was a speed freak and a head." She lowered her head. "It might have been okay except I dropped my brother's wallet—"

"What were you doing with your brother's wallet?"

"I dressed myself in Michael's clothing. If anyone saw me, they'd think I was a man and be looking for two guys. Unfortunately, I had to choose the *one* jacket that had Mike's wallet. I didn't even know I had it until Mike told me it was missing."

Ness said, "For Christ's sake, why didn't—"

"Michael, please!" Kelley took a deep breath. "Look, you'd better have clear-cut evidence that links Mike to the crime other than his wallet and Eubie's say-so. Eubie was just naming Mike as his accomplice to protect *me*." She glanced at her brother, then dropped her gaze. "Eubie and I are lovers."

Ness's face lost all expression. Slowly, his mouth drew upward in an off-balance rendering of a smile. "Dead meat, Jeffers!"

"Mike, please," Jeffers begged. "I needed *help*."

"*Dead . . . dark . . . meat!*"

Ness lunged so quickly, he caught everyone off guard. The impact of his charge at Jeffers knocked Malone forward. Ferris managed to catch his partner before he hit the ground. Decker was on top of Ness within seconds, pulling Ness's hands off Jeffers's throat. After he'd freed Jeffers's neck, Decker had no trouble subduing Ness, forcing him spread-eagled on his stomach, hands across his back.

"Stop it!" Kelley yelled as she pounded Decker's back.

Oliver pulled her from Decker.

"Leave my brother alone!" shouted Kelley as she struggled in Oliver's grip.

"You wanna help your brother, just *back off*!" Oliver shouted.

The room fell still. Decker tied Ness's hands behind his back with his belt, keeping him prone on the floor. All that Kelley had spilled was inadmissible because she hadn't been advised of her rights. But at least they'd know how to question her.

Malone said, "Who're we taking in to book?"

Decker lifted Ness upward, keeping a solid hold on Ness's arm. He looked at Jeffers. "You want to press charges against him for assaulting you?"

"Leave him alone," Jeffers whispered.

"Answer the question, Eubie," Decker said. "Do you want to press charges?"

"No."

Decker jerked Ness around. "You gonna behave yourself?"

"I'll behave myself." Ness glared at Jeffers.

"I mean it, Mike," Decker said. "Don't you even fucking *look* at Eubie, 'cause if you make the wrong move, your ass is gonna be a plaything for some real big boys tonight. Get what I'm saying?"

"Yes."

Decker dropped his grip on Ness and said to Malone and Ferris, "You've got evidence against Jeffers; take him in along with the girl."

"They were both dead when I got there!" Kelley shouted. "They must have shot each other—"

"Kelley, shut up!" Ness said.

"I'm gonna read you your rights, Ms. Ness," Oliver said. "Meantime, kindly listen to your brother."

"I never admitted to a *murder*," she babbled, "just to removing a dead body and burning it—"

"Shut up, Ms. Ness and let me read you your rights."

Oliver pulled out his card once again. After she was Mirandized, Decker said, "I just have a teeny question for both of you. Who ordered the removal of the body?"

Kelley glared at Eubie, then lowered her head. "No one."

Oliver said, "We're talking about *murder*, Ms. Ness—"

"Kelley, don't *do* this!" Ness interrupted.

"Mike, I *have* to do this!" Kelley softened her voice. "I *have* to. It's okay. All I did was remove a body."

"Who asked you to do it?" Decker said.

Kelley was silent.

"You just decided to go burn a dead body, Ms. Ness?" Malone said.

Kelley said, "I went to see Dr. Merritt for a personal reason. I . . . it was horrible. I saw . . ." She paused. "The image of the spa is very important to me. Russ was a louse. No one would miss him. Why involve the spa? I did it on my own."

"You're lying," Oliver said. "Who are you protecting?"

"No one."

"Why did you go to see Dr. Merritt?" Decker asked.

"Female problems." Her eyes turned hard. "Not an abortion, I assure you."

She had returned to her old stubborn self. It must have served her well in the past. Brother and sister were exchanging glances—an unspoken language. Decker wondered just *what* those two were hiding. He looked at Jeffers. "Do you have anything to say about this?"

Jeffers whispered, "She's the boss."

Malone said, "Let's go."

Ness shouted, "Kelley, don't you or Eubie open your mouths until you've both talked to lawyers." He pivoted to Decker. "Maybe you'd like your belt back. Right now, it's not doing either one of us any good."

Decker regarded Ness's face. Pure defiance. Forged from anger or fear or both? He unknotted his belt and slipped it around his waist.

Ness rubbed his wrists. "So I'm free?"

"I wouldn't exactly call you *free*, Mikey." Decker smiled. "You're just off the hook . . . for now."

❧28

Marge's Honda resting in the driveway meant sleep was still on hold. Decker flicked his wrist; the LCD digits on his watch read twelve noon instead of midnight. He never had figured out how to change the red dot from A.M. to P.M., and after being up twenty-one hours straight, who gave a good goddamn about meridians anyway.

He parked the Plymouth, got out, and peered inside the Honda's window. Marge's head was all the way back, her mouth open, her eyes shut. She looked dead, but he'd seen her asleep before—lots of long drives at crazy hours doing their duty. He rapped on the passenger door and her head jerked forward. She yawned, stretched, then stepped out of her car. She was carrying a briefcase.

"Is it good morning or still good night?"

"We've crossed the barrier, Detective Dunn." Decker unlocked his front door, quieted the dog, and turned on one of the living-room lamps. "Come tell Uncle Pete your problems."

Marge closed the door behind her, eyes adjusting slowly to the light. She scratched Ginger's scruff.

"Coffee?" Decker asked.

"Not tonight. My stomach feels like it's swimming in acid. Maybe I'm getting an ulcer."

"Maybe you should get some sleep."

"How about some herbal tea?"

Decker tossed his jacket on the couch. "Rina might have something like that in the kitchen. I'll go check. By the way, you don't have to whisper. No one's home. C'mon, Ginger. I'll let you out."

"So the marriage lasted all of eight months." Marge flopped down on the sofa. "'Bout par for my relationships."

"Don't give Rina any ideas," Decker called from the kitchen. He came back in a moment later. "It's a testament to her good nature that she hasn't thrown me out with Lilah Brecht showing up in the middle of the night. I put some water up. Should be boiling any minute. Did you go to Totes's bail hearing?"

"Yeah," Marge said. "Five-grand bond on fifty."

"Could he post the ten percent?"

"Lilah posted for him."

"Was she at the hearing?"

"No, but I sneaked a look at the agreement." She rubbed her eyes. "She's the indemnitor. Victim posting bail for her attacker. Jury's going to have a good time with that one."

"DA's got his work cut out for him."

Marge said, "You wanna fill me in on your evening?"

"Let me get your tea first."

A minute later, Decker handed the steaming mug to Marge. She sipped as he spoke, the dog sleeping at her feet. When Decker was done, Marge looked at him with red eyes. "So Scott Oliver's a hunk, huh?"

Decker settled into one of his buckskin chairs and propped his feet on a torn leather hassock. "Don't salivate when you talk, Margie, you're not a Pavlovian dog. And recapping tonight's top story, Oliver's still married."

"Yeah, that's really too bad." She stretched out on the couch. "Does he know what he's doing from a professional standpoint?"

"He handled Kelley Ness like a pro. I mostly watched."

"It's Devonshire's homicide."

"Actually, it's Burbank's." Decker kicked off his shoes. "Donnally was dead before he was torched—his lungs were clear on the prelim. The prelim also matched the blood in Merritt's office with Donnally's although the lab still wants to run more conclusive tests."

"I was checking lab reports while you were talking to the hunk. Kingston Merritt had powder burns on his right hand. There were no firearms found at the scene."

"We asked Kelley about that. She swore she didn't remove any weapons of any kind from the scene and we couldn't trip her up. Burbank couldn't trip up Eubie Jeffers, either."

"So they're either very well rehearsed or the weapons had already been removed. Did Jeffers's and Kelley's accounts jibe well?"

"Yes, they did and in a natural way. They seemed like they were telling the truth. I don't think they did the murders, but *no one* is ruling them out yet. So they'll spend the night in jail. Tomorrow Burbank and Devonshire will bring evidence to their respective DAs. At this point, there's not enough to file a murder one, murder two, or even a manslaughter. I'd be surprised if Jeffers got anything bigger than a felony tampering and destruction of evidence. With Kelley, DA could plow her with an obstruction of justice. She refuses to tell who ordered the removal of the bodies."

"And Jeffers?" Marge asked.

"Jeffers says he doesn't know, was only following orders from Kelley."

"Help if we had the guns."

"They're probably buried under two tons of garbage by now. When we find out who ordered the removal of the bodies, we'll find out what happened to the weapons."

"Could Donnally and Merritt have killed each other?" Marge said.

"It's possible. Merritt has powder residue; he shot a gun. Could be he killed Donnally and someone else killed Merritt."

"What about Mike Ness? He's a greasy spoon."

Decker loosened his tie and unbuttoned his shirt. "Certainly a suspect. And you're right, Margie. He and his sister have a weird relationship. They're hiding something."

"Incest."

"Possibly. Except Kelley claims she and Jeffers are lovers."

"Maybe Jeffers is just a cover."

"If Jeffers knew that Mike and Kelley were screwing and was acting as a cover, he'd be *getting* favors, not *doing* favors. Remember, Kelley asked Eubie for help in removing the bodies." Decker was quiet as he fast-forwarded the night's tape in his head. "I'll tell you this, Margie. Mike went crazy when he found out Kelley was screwing Jeffers. He actually attacked him."

"Lover's jealousy?"

"Or just being a protective older brother."

"Let's assume Kelley's screwing both of them, Pete."

Again, Decker thought about Kelley's relationship with her brother, and with Eubie Jeffers. Something was off and he was just too tired to figure out what it was. "All right, assume Kelley's screwing both."

Marge said, "Now Kelley screwing Jeffers is no big deal. But Kelley fucking her own brother . . . that's heavy stuff. If *someone* found out about that, that *someone* would have a hold over both Mike and Kelley."

"Who's your someone?"

"Davida," Marge said. "She's the common link among all the victims—Lilah, Kingston, *and* Donnally. I'm betting *she* was the one who sent Russ Donnally over to Kingston Merritt's office. She was also the one who sent Kelley over to remove Russ Donnally's body. Kelley couldn't refuse, because if she did, Davida would expose her incestuous relationship with her brother."

Decker didn't speak right away. "We've got a bunch of blanks to fill in. First of all, are you assuming Davida sent Donnally over with the purpose of murdering her own son?"

"I'm not saying that. I'm saying Davida might have sent Donnally over to look for something . . . her jewels or the memoirs. A small B and E. He was on probation for B and Es, right?"

Decker nodded.

"Pete, remember how only the office was trashed? Could be that Donnally was looking for something when Kingston walked in at the wrong moment. Things got out of hand and they popped each other."

"But why would Davida send *Russ Donnally* over to talk to Merritt? Why not Mike or Kelley Ness if she has dirt on them?"

"It's possible she had dirt on Russ Donnally, also." Marge was pensive. "I'm betting Davida has dirt on a lot of people. Could be why Captain Morrison's so hinky about getting the case solved."

Decker stifled a yawn. Again, something tugged at his subconscious, but he couldn't bring it to surface. Perhaps it was because the discussion was getting far afield. "Could we pick this up tomorrow and get on with your business? I take it you're here to see me for reasons other than insomnia."

"Right about that. I'm *exhausted*!" She sat up, pulled a valise onto her lap, and clicked open the latches. "I've been going over the case—"

"*Which* case?"

"Lilah's rape."

"That's the one we *solved*, Marge." Decker closed his eyes. "You *loved* Totes as the bad guy."

"In theory, I still do. But let me play devil's advocate for a moment."

Decker opened his eyes and waited.

"Pete, I've gone over the evidence collection three times. Fibers, hair, prints—the whole thing.

The only physical stuff we have against Totes is what's on the sheets. Nothing in the room, nothing in Lilah—not under her nails or in any of her orifices."

"Nothing new."

"I know. Hollander went over the stable today. The only thing he found hidden was an old crumpled picture of Lilah that Totes keeps under his pillow. Nothing connected to the robbery—no jewels, no papers, nothing."

"Did you really expect him to find something?"

"No, I didn't. And I really don't have a problem with all the evidence being on the sheets. If he didn't climax inside of her, that's where the evidence would be."

"So what's bugging you?"

"I was thinking about the morning interview with Totes. Something's bothering me and I don't know what it is." Marge put her briefcase on the driftwood coffee table. "After listening to the tape, listening to Totes's *voice* when you asked him if he saw Lilah the night of the rape . . . I'm sure there was some kind of interaction between them."

"But you don't think he raped her."

"No, I don't, but not because of the lack of evidence. I was thinking about the rape and the incident with the horse and Lilah being nuts and all. Maybe she did orchestrate the whole thing."

"Why would she do it?"

"I don't even want to consider the why when I can't figure out the how." Marge rubbed her eyes again. "Listen, Totes swore he was in the stable the entire night. He sounded like he was telling it true.

Pete, he got tripped up when you asked him if someone came to visit *him* the night of the rape. Lilah
came to *him*. That being the case, for the life of me,
I can't explain his semen on her sheets."

"Maybe they were screwing."

"How could they be screwing in *her* bed if Carl
hadn't left the stable?"

"Maybe they screwed a couple of days before and
it was old jiz."

"Not according to the lab report. They were fresh
suckers. How could she get *his* fresh jiz on *her* sheets
unless she jacked him off in the stable or something
and hand-carried it to her bed—"

Decker hit his forehead. "Oh, shit!"

"What?"

Decker hopped up, grabbed his coat, and began
feeling the pockets for his notebook. He pulled it
out, flipped pages, and began reading. "Damn my
handwriting . . . should have practiced my loops."
He scanned his notes furiously, then clapped his
hands. "Oh, man, sometimes you get lucky! Totes's
clothes were dirty, but his sheets were *clean*, kiddo!"

"I'm not following, Pete."

"How about this, Marge? How about Lilah paying Totes a call and jacking him off? How about
Lilah taking his dirty sheets and replacing them with
clean sheets? How about Lilah using those dirty
sheets to fake the rape?"

"How about Totes just washing his sheets?"

"He washed his sheets but not his clothes?"

Marge frowned. "Why would she set Totes up,
only to bail him out?"

"Because she never thought we'd get this far,"

Decker said. "She wanted to fake a rape, not screw up her ranch hand. Hey, I'm just playing out *your* thoughts. If we accept Lilah faking a rape, we have no trouble buying that Lilah drugged her own horse. Like we said before, she, more than anyone, had access. She just miscalculated the effect the PCP would have on the animal."

"And the bruises on her body—bruises *you* saw?"

"She could have done that to herself. Some superficial cuts, whip herself a couple of times with a belt and get some nasty lacerations. Bang into a wall and that explains the lump on her forehead. Margie, we've seen women do *mutilating* things to themselves just for attention. And now that I think about it, she looked bad, but her *grip* . . . man, I had to pry a finger lock off my arm. I should've picked up on it."

"Hey, you see a rape victim, who's thinking self-inflicted wounds?" Marge said.

"My antennae should have been raised. We've seen stuff like this before. Just last month we had a lady who shot herself and blamed it on imaginary robbers. Had CAPS spinning their wheels for days."

Decker slapped his notebook against his palm.

"The lady who shot herself wanted workman's comp. Why would Lilah fake a rape and a near-fatal accident? What could she possibly get out of it?"

"Attention," Marge said.

"Lilah has never lacked for attention. Why would she want such embarrassing notoriety?"

"Beats me." Marge waited a moment before talking. "Think she might have staged the robbery, too?"

"I would say yes except Kingston Merritt and

Russ Donnally are dead. And like you said, that points to Davida."

"Maybe Lilah and Davida staged everything together."

The phone rang. Decker pounced on it, thinking, Please God, no more bad news.

"Rina?"

"No, it's Dr. Elias Kessler, Sergeant. I'm sorry if I woke you."

He caught his breath. Kessler, the doc who'd done the pelvic on Lilah. Business call. His family was okay. . . . "I was up anyway, Doc. What can I do you for?"

"I was just finishing up a midnight delivery at Sun Valley Pres when I happened to see the latest admittance sheet. Lilah Brecht—"

"Jesus, wha . . ." Decker felt his throat go dry. "Is she all right?"

"She's stable. I don't know all the details because it's not my case. A floor nurse said she ODed on Seconal—"

"Oh, *shit*!" Decker refrained from hitting the wall. "But she's okay?"

"So far as I know. Poor kid. I guess that sometimes happens with rape survivors, huh?"

"Not often, but sometimes. Doc, do you think she's too sleepy to talk right now?"

"I think you'd have much better luck in the morning. I just called because I thought you might want to know."

"Thanks, I did."

"Look, if you need any help from a forensic point of view, don't hesitate to call."

"I won't. Thanks for calling."

"You bet."

Decker hung up and leaned against the wall. "That was Kessler, the doc who did the rape swabs on Lilah. Apparently she tried to kill herself tonight."

"Oh, *Christ*!"

Decker shook his head and filled Marge in on the details. "What a mess!"

"Attempted suicide," Marge said. "That's drawing attention to yourself."

"It's also what you do if you're extremely despondent—like if you've been raped and beaten. Or if you feel guilty about your brother dying."

The quiet that followed was oppressive. Finally, Marge said, "How about if I go by the hospital tomorrow? See if I can't get something out of Lilah?"

"Fine."

"Should I run our clean-sheets theory past her?"

"Hell, it's probably stupid. Play it by ear." Decker let out a big yawn and looked at his watch again. "It's close to one. We both need sleep to think. If you want, you can bunk down here for the night . . . sleep in the guest room . . . while it's still the guest room. It's going to be the baby's room if I ever get around to putting up the wallpaper. Rina's so mad at me, she's ready to hire someone to do it."

"What's so bad about that?"

"Oh, man . . ." Decker shook his head. "You're a good cop, Margie, but you're a lousy good ole boy. You don't let some dick come into your house and charge you a fortune for something you can do yourself. That's being a wuss."

"Pete, how much is your time worth?"

"Forget it, Marge, you're sounding not only like a broad but a white-collar broad at that. The guest bed's all made up. Towels are in the bathroom. Good night."

Marge watched him trudge off to bed, muttering something about not being a wuss for any broad. It was times like these she was glad she wasn't married.

Carrying four heavy bags, Rina managed to insert the key in the front door and push it open with her feet. She was surprised to find the house so quiet. She'd noticed the Honda and had expected to see Peter and Marge conferring over coffee. The stillness stopped her from yelling out a hello. She tiptoed into the bedroom, saw her husband's form in a jumble of sheets, and left.

It must have been a long evening.

Dragging the bags to the kitchen, she put up coffee, then began to unpack groceries. A few minutes later, she heard footsteps too light to be Peter's. Marge was dressed in wrinkled clothes, her hair messy, her eyes heavy-lidded.

Rina smiled. "Coffee?"

"Thanks, I'd love a cup." Marge yawned. "What time is it?"

"Eight-thirty."

"That's not too bad." Marge stretched and rolled her neck. Rina heard the cracking sounds.

"Guest bed a little small, Margie?"

"Only 'cause I'm as big as a horse."

"No, you're not!" Rina patted her stomach. "That

honor belongs exclusively to me. Sit. You look like you could use some TLC."

"Boy, you know it." Marge sat down and leaned her elbows on the cherrywood table. "Where'd you go last night?"

"I took the kids and slept over my parents'." She pulled out a mug and filled it with black coffee. "Peter didn't want us home alone after what happened with Lilah last night."

"Yeah, he told me. Well, you won't have to worry about her tonight. She's in the hospital. Attempted suicide."

"*What?*"

"I'm going to see her today. Maybe if I'm lucky, she'll even talk to me. Find out what the heck is going on."

"That's . . ." Rina rubbed her arms. "She . . . she must be in terrible pain. I'm sorry to hear that."

"Yeah, she must be one unhappy lady."

"Poor Peter." Rina placed a cup of coffee in front of Marge. "I hope he isn't feeling guilty."

"He probably is. You know your husband. He feels guilty about everything."

"Yes, he does, doesn't he? Would you like some toast or a bran muffin? I just came back from the bakery."

"Bran muffin would be great."

The phone rang. Before Rina could answer it, Decker caught it in the bedroom. He came out ten minutes later, dressed but barefoot. His hair was wet and he'd shaved. He kissed Rina on the lips. "When did you get in?"

"About fifteen minutes ago. Who was on the phone?"

"Station house." To Marge, he said, "Perry Goldin left his number. That's Lilah's ex. I haven't the foggiest notion what he wants."

"You want some coffee, Peter?" Rina asked.

"Thanks, darlin', that would be great. How are you?"

"Fine."

"Boys in school?"

"Yes. It's a half-day today. I've got to pick them up at twelve. Some sort of teachers' conference."

"You want me to swing by and retrieve them?"

"No, that's all right. I can do it." She served Peter a cup of coffee and a plate of toast. "I was sorry to hear about Lilah. It's very sad."

"Maybe now she'll get some help." Decker took the phone from the dining-room breakfront and brought it to the table. "She sure could use some." He turned to Marge. "Are you going to see her today?"

"Right after I change my clothes."

"What time is it?" Decker asked. "What *day* is it?"

"Friday, eight-forty-eight A.M.," Rina said. "Shabbos starts at seven-twenty-six. That should give you plenty of time to finish your business."

"One can always hope," Decker said.

Marge stood and wiped crumbs from her mouth. "Thanks for breakfast, Rina." She patted Decker's shoulder. "See you, sport."

After Marge left, Rina said, "You send me away and she sleeps over? You're lucky I'm not the jealous type."

"Not to worry, my dear, the last thought on my

mind is another woman, least of all Marge. I can't even handle the one I got." Decker pulled his wife onto his lap and kissed her. "I missed you, darlin'."

Rina repositioned herself on his legs. "I can tell."

"I don't lie." Decker raised his brow. "*It* don't lie."

"Just let me get the roast in the oven," she said. "Five minutes."

"I'm setting my watch. In the meantime, I'll make my phone call."

Rina got up. "Five minutes."

Decker panted out loud as he dialed. Rina laughed as she left. A soft female voice answered the call. He asked for Perry Goldin, and after a beat, the bridge teacher came on the line.

"Hey, Sergeant, thanks for getting back to me so soon."

"No problem."

"Wendy's been telling me that there've been more police cars driving by the legal clinic. I want to thank you."

"You're welcome. I'm glad she feels safer."

"She does." He paused. "Look, do you remember I told you about an old lady Lilah used to visit?"

"Greta Millstein."

"Righto, you can be my bridge partner. Among my many bad habits is sticking my nose where it probably doesn't belong. I don't know . . . for some strange reason, I felt compelled to call Greta and tell her what had happened to Lilah. They were close a long time ago; I figured maybe she'd want to know. I touched briefly on our meeting and she expressed an interest in talking to you. I hope I wasn't out of line."

"The exact opposite. I've been wanting to talk to her."

"Great. I know she has tea every morning around ten, ten-thirty. I'll arrange a meeting if you want."

"That would be perfect."

"It might be better if I went with you . . . someone familiar. Hell, I wouldn't mind seeing her. I abandoned her along with Lilah, so even if you don't go, I'll go anyway."

"I'll meet you there at ten."

Goldin gave him directions. "I'll wait for you and we'll go in together. The apartment complex is big and you can get lost unless you know where you're going. I'll be sitting in a red Ferrari Testarossa almost trashed beyond recognition."

"Now that hurts," Decker said.

"Not for me. I picked it up for a song and a dance. And if you knew my musical talent, you'd know how cheap that was. See you later."

Decker hung up and checked his watch. "Time's up," he announced. "Are you ready?"

Rina walked into the dining room and placed her hands on her hips. "Sweep me off my feet, my darling."

Decker laughed and scooped her into his arms. "You've gained a little weight, dear."

Rina slugged his shoulder. "So have you. So what's *your* excuse?"

"Call it sympathetic pregnancy." Decker carried her over the threshold of their bedroom and lowered her onto the mattress. "I figure, why should you go it alone? I'm just that kind of guy."

𝒮 29

Dressed in clothes that didn't smell like a gym locker, Marge was ready for business. The ambulance had taken Lilah to a community hospital, but the floor nurse said in a huffy voice that Miss Brecht was in the process of being transferred to a private facility. Marge found the room and was pleased to see the door open. She took that as license to enter without asking permission.

Freddy Brecht was playing the role of chief of staff, protecting his sister as rigidly as a palace guard. Freddy blocked not only the bed, but also Marge's view of Lilah.

"She isn't up to seeing anyone, Detective," Brecht said, in a clipped tone. "Now if you'll kindly—"

"It's all right, Freddy." A pale-faced Lilah peeked around her brother's shoulders and fell back on her pillow. "Let me talk to her."

Brecht pivoted to his sister. "Lilah, you are in no condition—"

"Freddy, I know you mean well, but you're being a pain. Go away and let me talk to her."

Brecht was silent, his cheeks and bald head glowing pink. "You don't have to be rude, Lilah."

"Freddy, I'm not myself. Don't be priggish."

Brecht deepened in color. "You realize, Lilah, you're sounding more and more like Mother."

"Yes, I know that and yes, it bothers me. But we can't help who we are, can we? Now please go away." A slender hand waved in the air. "Let me talk to her alone."

Brecht was slow to leave. "Ten minutes, Detective. Despite what she says, she needs her rest."

Marge waited until Brecht was down the hallway before she closed the door. The stress of the past few days had eroded some youth from Lilah's face. Her cheeks were gaunt, her blue eyes lusterless. Marge bit back pity as she pulled up a chair by the bed.

"I was hoping you'd be Peter." Defeat was woven through Lilah's voice. "Hoping but not expecting."

Marge waited a beat. "How're you feeling?"

"I'll tell you this much." She sat up. "Frederick's constant hovering is a drain, but at least he had the decency to show up. Unlike *other* relatives I have."

"Your mother?"

"Who else?"

"Maybe she doesn't know."

"She knows. She doesn't care. Perhaps she's too busy avoiding the police—driving back and forth between Malibu and the spa. Sources say she's found another driver after knocking off Russ." Her laughter was mocking. "Good luck to anyone stupid enough to take that assignment."

Marge pulled out a notebook. "How do you know she knocked off Russ?"

"I don't know. But who else would have sent Russ over to kill Kingston?"

"You think your mother sent Russ over to kill your brother?"

"What difference does it make what I think?" Eyes watered, then overflowed with tears. "King's gone and what I think won't bring him back."

She shielded her face with her hands and cried bitterly. Marge waited, pencil poised to write. After a minute, Lilah dried her eyes and lowered her head onto a pillow.

"It's funny . . . King and I had been estranged for so long. He was overbearing, but . . ." Her voice cracked. "But deep down, I knew it was because he cared. Yesterday, when he called me, so comforting . . ." She turned to the wall.

"What did you and Kingston talk about yesterday?"

Lilah shook her head and started to cry. Softly, Marge said, "Why'd you take the pills, Lilah?"

"I don't know . . . I felt so . . . so *guilty* about King's death . . . and resentful, too. Impulses aren't often well thought out. It wasn't the first stupid thing I've ever done. I'm sure it won't be the last."

"Like taking Carl Totes's sheets?" Marge said.

Lilah jerked her head up. "He *told* you?"

Marge didn't answer. Lilah let out full laughter. "Well, I fell right into that! No, Carl wouldn't . . ." She laughed again. "Not Carl. He'd have sat in jail forever rather than . . ."

"Rather than disclose your little secret?" Marge asked.

"Something like that."

"Why'd you set him up?"

"Who said I did, Detective?"

"Carl's being brought up for rape charges, Lilah. Does he deserve that?"

Lilah waited a long time before she spoke. "That . . . it also wasn't well thought out. It . . . I . . ."

"Why'd you do it, Lilah? Why did you fake your rape?"

Lilah didn't answer.

Marge said, "We're going to get to the bottom of the whole mess, Lilah. Help us out. It'll save us a lot of energy and time, so we can concentrate on who killed your brother and why."

"I didn't have *anything* to do with King's death!" Lilah insisted. "I want you to know that."

"Go on."

Lilah twirled a strand of her hair. "I'm only telling you my part because I do care about Carl . . . and my brother."

Marge nodded encouragingly.

Lilah said, "After Freddy dropped me off from our weekly dinner, I knew instantly that my safe had been tampered with. I keep an inch of Scotch tape across the door. When I walked into my bedroom and saw that it was gone, I rushed to the safe—to the *inner safe*. The memoirs were *gone*! If I had known Kingston was in on it, I wouldn't have bothered with the rape business."

Marge sat up. "How do you *know* Kingston was in on it?"

"He intimated that he had something that was mine when he called me . . . that Mother had put him up to something. When we met for dinner, he was going to tell me more."

Lilah covered her mouth with her fist, then lowered her hand to her lap.

"But *that* evening, at *that* time, all I knew was that somehow, some way, my mother had finally gotten her paws on *my* memoirs. They've been preying on her mind for months, though she's tried to hide it. I don't know specifically what's in the papers that's driving her crazy. As I've told you before, I've respected my father's wishes and haven't read them."

Lilah's nostrils suddenly flared in anger.

"Mother took them and that is truly unforgivable. They belonged to *me*! Not *her*! *Me*! I *had* to do something! You do understand, don't you?"

Marge was impassive.

Lilah said, "So I stormed out of my house and took a late-night jog around my property! A slow jog . . . I can think when I do a slow jog. Confronting Mother was an exercise in futility. She's a marvelous actress and can lie as easily as breathe. I had to get the *police* involved. And I had to make sure the police would be just as eager to find the memoirs as I was." She drew her hospital gown tightly across her chest. "As I was jogging by the stable, I heard Carl . . ." She looked down. "I've heard him before. I knew what he was doing. He was . . . playing with himself . . . over me."

Tears formed in Lilah's eyes.

"He's in love with me, has this picture of me . . ." She looked at Marge. "I never meant to hurt him. I was just so *furious* at Mother, I couldn't think rationally. So I waited until he was done, then went in and took his sheets and towels."

"And he wasn't suspicious when you visited him in the middle of the night?"

"It wasn't the middle of the night. It was around eleven. And no, he wasn't suspicious. I told him I'd brought him *new* sheets and towels. He was pleased, more than pleased. He was ecstatic. Any attention I had ever bestowed upon Carl was greeted with unabashed, unquestioned gratitude. So I changed his sheets and towels and told him not to mention my visit to anyone. It would give certain people with filthy minds the *wrong* idea. He said he understood."

"You didn't have sex with him?"

Again, Lilah's nostrils flared. "The thought is *repugnant*!"

What Lilah was saying was consistent with what Marge and Decker had found at Totes's stable. Marge remembered Decker remarking that the linens in the stable were clean. "Then what did you do?"

"What did I do?" Lilah blinked back tears. "I . . . decided to get the police involved in a big way. I systematically destroyed my room. It wasn't hard because I was enraged. When it was close to morning, I knew I had to do something with myself to make the crime seem realistic. So I . . . hit myself at strategic places . . . squeezed myself actually. I'm very fair, I bruise easily. What didn't look swollen enough—*mean* enough—was enhanced by judicious application of the spa's astringents—special caustics we use on clients with skin problems." She wrinkled her nose. "Then before Mercedes was due to show, I took an ice-cold shower to lower my body temperature. Then the maid came . . . there you have it."

"And the horse?"

"Now, that was *truly* stupid! I loved Apollo. I was devastated when he died."

"You gave him too much PCP?"

"No, I was very careful. Apollo must have had a strange reaction. In the past when I've given a horse PCP, it simply dropped off to sleep. I give my horses tranquilizers all the time when I'm cleaning their teeth or some other such minor procedure. I was shocked . . . scared. If Peter hadn't rescued me, I'd have been dead."

"Lilah, why'd you go to all that trouble to *fake* a crime?" Marge asked. "You had a real crime—the *theft*. Why didn't you just report it?"

"*Why?*" Lilah's laugh was soft. "Detective, how much priority would you . . . or Peter . . . or *anyone* in the entire police force have given a theft of some old papers? Ah, but a rape . . . and a rape where jewels were stolen . . . now there's a *crime* worth looking into! I was hoping once you *started* investigating you wouldn't stop until you found the memoirs."

She shrugged.

"So you figured out my little subterfuge. So what? You're doing exactly as I envisioned. The case has taken on a life of its own. As far as Apollo went . . . that was to ensure that the case wouldn't stagnate, that it would be moved on. That Peter would *believe* me when I told him someone was out to get me . . . and he *did* believe me."

"We still haven't found the memoirs, Lilah."

"But now you'll *look* for them, won't you?"

Marge didn't answer. She knew that Lilah was absolutely right—the case had taken on a life of its own. And she had the police figured out as well. With all the violent crime plaguing the streets, nobody on the force would fret too much about some old lost memoirs. The woman wasn't a prophetess. But she was very clever.

"Who killed your brother?" Marge asked.

"Talk to *Mother*. Kingston implied she was involved in the theft. I'm sure she was involved in his murder."

"Who else might have been involved?"

"Mother has managed to create quite a following— Michael, Kelley, even Freddy. After all, he did take me out the night the theft occurred. Any one of them is a potential errand boy for her."

"Do you have any idea how someone broke into your inner safe?"

"No idea." Lilah suddenly looked sheepish. "You *are* going to drop the charges against Carl, aren't you?"

"Yes."

"I told you he didn't rape me."

Marge didn't answer.

"Are you going to bring charges against me?"

"That's not up to me," Marge said. "You know, in your eagerness to keep the case alive, you probably did more harm than good. We were out looking for a rapist when we should have been looking for a thief."

"At least you were out looking for *something*." Lilah regarded her hands, then smiled smugly. "No harm done if charges are brought against me. As a matter of fact, the publicity will be enormously beneficial to the spa's business. The more notorious, the better." She leaned over and whispered, "The rich just love a delicious dish of dirt!"

Marge folded the cover of her notebook and stowed the pen in her pocket. "This probably isn't the last of my visits."

"Ask whatever you want. At this point, I have nothing more to hide."

"Then let me ask you this," Marge said. "Where are your mother's jewels?"

The blue eyes suddenly set in stony hatred. "Not to worry, Detective, I have them. And I'll return them when I fucking feel like it."

Decker thought, File this one under things that make you groan: a Testarossa shaped into abstract sculpture. The passenger's side was a gray crater of primer and blood-red paint, the door held shut by electrical tape. Its nose had been blunted, both its bumpers denuded of chrome and trim.

Goldin stood on the curb and watched Decker gaze at his junk heap. He tucked his T-shirt into his jeans and stuck his hands into his back pants pockets. "You look like you're ready to deliver a eulogy."

"How can you stand driving it in that condition?"

"I'm making a statement, Sergeant."

"What kind of statement!" Decker snarled. "That it's too bourgeois to restore a thing of beauty?"

"No, actually it's more like I can't afford the thirty thousand bucks to fix her up properly."

"Do it yourself."

"Me?" Goldin laughed. "I don't know a carburetor from a radiator."

"Testarossas don't have carburetors." Decker's eyes remained on the car. "They're fuel-injected."

Goldin patted Decker's back. "It only hurts if you look. Let's go. Greta's expecting us."

Slowly, Decker turned away from the Ferrari and followed Goldin up a slight incline to an entrance to the grounds. The apartment complex was three blocks long—a series of one-story bungalows resting on yards of green hillocks shaded by wizened trees. Dozens of meandering pathways crisscrossed over the knoll, many of them diverging only to dead-end into copses of brush. But Goldin seemed to know where he was going.

Since the weather was warm and sunny, many seniors were outside visiting with their neighbors. Plump women nursing iced teas, sitting spread-kneed on lawn chairs, nylon stockings rolled down to their ankles, feet shod in orthopedic whites. Old men whose waistlines were now wider than their shoulders held green hoses, sprinkling water on the grass or flower beds. Laughing and talking. The place gave the appearance of a retirement village except the acres of complex were in the middle of prime Valley real estate.

"A real anachronism," Goldin said. "I don't know who owns all this land, but they're sitting on a gold mine. Maybe someone feels preservation of people is more important than another office building."

Decker smiled. "That's wonderfully optimistic."

"Yeah, that's me. I'm an ideological bulldog. I'll never give up. Greta lives around the corner."

He led Decker to a stucco cottage freshly painted bright yellow with white trim. The mailbox outside said G. MILLSTEIN. Without hesitation, he turned the knob and walked in. Decker remained on the threshold.

The woman who greeted Goldin had a wide, toothless smile. Her face was as wrinkled as a discarded sheet of paper, her mouth caved in, giving her a very pronounced chin. Her hair was thin and white, her eyes dark brown and holding an impish twinkle. She wiped her hands on her apron and locked Goldin to her overstuffed bosom. Her voice was musical and tinged with a German accent:

"You don't change at all, my friend!"

"You need glasses, Greta. Look at all the *gray* in my hair."

"You call dat gray, Perry, you need glasses." She took his arm and looked at Decker. "You come in, too. I don't bite." She smacked her lips together. "No teets."

"Teeth," Perry translated.

"Dat's what I said. Sit, Perry. You sit too. Your name, please?"

"Peter," Decker said.

"Ah, Peter. I have a son-in-law who's Peter. Is a real son-of-gun. I don't like him, but my daughter? She is happy. Dey married tirty-two years. I keep my mout shut and we all are happy."

She disappeared inside the kitchen. Decker took a seat on a faded green velvet couch and Goldin leaned back in a BarcaLounger, feet level with his head. The living room was hot and stuffy and dark and Decker loosened his tie. Greta came in a few minutes later with plates of strudel dusted with powdered sugar and three empty teacups.

"You bring in tea for me, Perry?"

Goldin got up and retrieved a silver tea set from the kitchen. Upon returning, he set down the tray, pulled the curtains back, and opened a window. Hot, perfumed air immediately swept away the stale smell of old age.

"You're not running a funeral home, Greta," Perry said. "Why do you keep it so stuffy in here?"

"I get scared, Perry." She poured the tea. "People walk around at night. People I don't know. I hear noises." She stopped and rubbed her arms. "I get scared." She handed a teacup to Decker.

"What kind of people?" Decker asked.

Greta shrugged. "I don't look too close. Dey hire mens to protect us, but dey are never around the same place as the noises. But . . ." She handed Goldin a cup of tea. "It is not bad here. I stay here until I die."

"Your children still visit often?" Goldin asked.

"Oh ya, dey visit me all de time. Mary comes one a week, Stephen comes one a week, Elaine come one or two a week." Greta turned to Decker. "She's married to Peter."

"The son-of-a-gun."

"But I don't say a word."

Goldin smiled. "If you had been my mother-in-law instead of Davida, I might still be married to Lilah today." He made a face. "A very disturbing thought."

"How is Lilah?"

Goldin cocked a thumb in Decker's direction. "He'd know more than I would."

Greta faced Decker. He said, "She's in the hospital—"

Greta gasped and put her hand to her chest.

"She's fine," Decker quickly added.

"I thought you said she was out of the hospital," Goldin said.

"This is separate from the first incident."

"You say rape," Greta said. "Perry tell me what happened first. What happened now?"

Decker said, "She was admitted last night after attempting suicide."

Again, Greta gasped.

"She's okay, Mrs. Millstein," Decker said, quickly. "My partner just went in to see her. If there was a problem she would have beeped me by now."

There was a long pause.

"Why?" Goldin asked.

"I don't know," Decker said.

"A cry for help?" Goldin asked.

"Maybe," Decker said.

The room was silent. Greta said, "You tink it's a cry for help?"

"I think Lilah's depressed," Decker said. "And when you're depressed, you can do irrational things."

"Someting more happened to her, ya?" Greta said.

Decker didn't answer.

Greta said, "My heart is strong. You tell us."

"Well . . ." Decker cleared his throat, repositioning himself on the couch. It didn't help. He was uncomfortable and the seat cushions had nothing to do with it. "Kingston Merritt was murdered a couple of days—"

Goldin dropped his teacup in his lap. He jumped up, swiping at his pants, the cup and saucer tumbling to the ground. Decker handed him a napkin and picked up the china.

"God, I'm sorry, Greta. I spilled tea all over your carpet."

"Don't worry—"

"At least I didn't break anything."

"Is okay, Perry." The old woman gently dabbed his wet pants leg with her apron. "I understand how you feel. I feel sick, too. Dat's horrible!"

Decker nodded. "You burn yourself, Perry?"

"Nah, I'm okay," Goldin said. "Just gotta catch my breath, that's all."

Decker turned to Greta. "Are you all right?"

"I not going to die, but I don't feel so good. It's bad news for me." Her eyes suddenly moistened. "It makes me feel very sad."

Goldin took the old woman's hand and patted it.

She gave off a teary smile and said, "So sad."

"Did you know King, Greta?" Goldin asked.

She wiped her eyes with a napkin. "Just as boy. I work for Davida when she live in Germany. I work for her tree, maybe four years. Den Hermann died and Davida go back to America. When I know him, King was unhappy boy."

Decker said, "What kind of work did you do for Hermann and Davida?"

"Not Hermann, just Davida. I make dresses for Davida . . . what you call in English?"

"Seamstress," Perry said.

"Ya, I was seamstress. I make good dresses." She pointed to her brow. "I have good eye. No one can tell difference—my dresses or de ones from Paris. Davida . . . she has lots of money, could buy the real dresses. But she says mine were just as good." Greta gave a toothless smile. "Dey were."

Decker smiled. "I'll bet. How many dresses did you make for Davida?"

"Lots. I sew fast and my daughters help me. I make lots of dresses for her 'cause she has lots of parties. Davida knows everybody. She was very nice for famous woman—famous American! Most Americans tink all Germans are Nazis."

Greta's eyes suddenly toughened, her posture turned stiff.

"I'm not Nazi. During war, I take my Jewish friend's daughter and I tell Nazis she's my niece. I keep her and raise her like mine. I tell her when she was older who she was. I save for her pictures of her parents. I love her like she is my own *blood*. I don't say a word when she marry a son-a-gun. I'm not *Nazi*!"

"Of course you're not, Greta." Goldin stood. "Let me pour you some tea."

"Dat's a good idea, Perry. You always have good ideas." She sat on the couch next to Decker. "Davida was more different den most Americans. She speak a little German and make big parties and invite *everyone*—big people, little people, me, my children. I come dere only one, maybe two times . . . lots of food, lots of *drink*—strong lager. Very, very *rich* for us. Most Germans den still very poor from the war."

Goldin handed Greta her tea. "It didn't sound as if Davida was suffering."

"She don't suffer, but she don't like Berlin. She told me dat all the time."

"So why did she live there?" Goldin asked.

"Because West Berlin is home for Hermann. It

was no good marriage. Davida likes parties, Hermann don't like any of it. He stands by himself and don't say a word to no one."

Her description of Hermann Brecht was consistent with the account John Reed had given them of Lilah's birth party. Decker thought about Reed's story: Hermann as a depressive drunk. No wonder there'd been strong lager at the parties.

"He hated parties." Greta set her teacup down on the coffee table. "He and Davida were no good together."

"Did you ever see them fight?" Decker said.

"Dey fight all de time."

"Could you hear what they fought about?"

The old woman let out a sigh. "Dey speak in English mostly, but I know what dey fight about. Hermann running wit de young girls. Why not he run wit young girls? He was a young man—twenty-one, twenty-two when dey marry. Davida was too *old* for him. She should have let him go." She began to knead her hands. "She should have let him go."

"He wanted a divorce?" Decker said.

Greta shook her head. "Davida has all de money, so Hermann don't get divorce. Davida give Hermann lots of money to make his movies. Ach . . ." Greta waved her hands in the air. "Only movies important to Hermann. Silly ass!" The old woman's eyes grew wet. "He cause himself heartbreak. He cause me more heartbreak!"

Decker waited.

"He has affair with my daughter, stupid ass!" she blurted. "My daughter . . . she was stupid, too. I tell my girls over and over, stay away from the family . . . we are only one ting above de servants. We say or do de wrong ting, Davida find some otter seamstress. My otter daughters, dey listen. Heidi don't listen. We fight all the time. That's why I don't say notting when Elaine marries son-of-gun."

"Elaine had an affair with Hermann Brecht?" Goldin asked.

"No, no, no!" Greta said. "I mean I keep my mout shut. I tried to talk to Heidi. She was so stubborn, so . . ." Greta tightened her face. "A mule!" Her eyes clouded. "A sweet mule . . . everyone take advantage of her. She believe everyone but me cause I'm her modder."

Decker said, "Is she dead, Greta?"

The old woman nodded.

"How?" Decker asked.

"Dey say suicide."

"But you don't believe them."

She bit her lip and shrugged. "I don't ask questions. Maybe yes, maybe no. First Heidi, den Hermann. Now you tell me Lilah. Maybe it runs in the family."

Runs in the family . . .

Decker said, "Your daughter was Lilah's mother, wasn't she, Greta?"

"*What?*" Goldin said.

Greta lowered her head.

Goldin said, "Are you saying Davida isn't Lilah's mother, Greta?"

"Lilah is mine," Greta whispered. "My granddotter. And Frederick is my grandson. Davida offered to take de baby and Heidi says yes because she is so young—only fifteen when Lilah was born. Davida promise to give de baby a good, rich home. I have so little 'cause I am a widow. I work and work, but de money . . . *five* children. Dey eat, dey need clothes."

She made a fist, then slowly released it.

"But den Heidi get pregnant again with Frederick. Hermann should have *married* my Heidi. He was good to us, gave us money. But he was a *weak* man. He loved my Heidi but he don't marry her, silly ass! Heidi try to take care of her little son, but it's too much. So Davida was nice and offered to take him, too. She told everyone he was adopted."

Again, the room became still. From the outside came the noise of bird songs, the sound of distant chatter.

"I don't believe . . ." Goldin shook his head. "Davida used to make this *big deal* out of Freddy being *adopted*."

Decker felt his stomach tighten.

Goldin went on. "She was so *mean* to him. And she never said a word about Lilah. I'll lay money that Lilah doesn't even know."

"No, she don't know," Greta said. "I know she don't. When we met . . . it wasn't only luck we met. One day I see her as the teacher of arts for seniors. Oh my goodness, I knew! She looks essackly like my Heidi." Her voice grew small. "I sign up for her class. Slowly, we start to talk after class. We talk and talk and it's like talking to Heidi all over again. My sweet little baby—only *eighteen* when she die."

Goldin took her hand and squeezed it gently.

"Lilah stops visiting me," she said, "I feel like I lose Heidi again. But not as bad. I know Lilah and

Frederick are still alive." She kissed Goldin's hand. "You are a good boy."

"What happened between you and Lilah, Greta?" Goldin asked. "Why'd she stop visiting you?"

"It's very hard . . ."

"Do you want some more tea, Greta?" Decker asked.

"Ya, dat's good idea."

Goldin poured her another cup of tea and wiped his damp pants with a clean napkin.

"You want to change, Perry?" Greta asked. "I put your pants outside to dry."

"Nah, I'm just a little clammy. I'll live."

Decker moved closer to the old woman. "What did happen between you and Lilah, Greta?"

"It's my fault. I rush, rush, rush and Lilah's not ready."

"You told her you were her grandmother and she didn't believe you," Goldin said.

"No, Perry, I'm not dat stupid."

Goldin blushed. "I didn't mean to imply you were."

Greta's lips formed a smile around a gaping hole. "I know. I give you a hard time because all dis is hard."

"I'm sure it's very painful," Decker said.

"Ya, painful. Painful to lose Lilah." Greta sipped tea and held the cup in her lap. "Everyone knows dat Frederick was adopted. But no one knows his parents, no?"

"Except Davida," Goldin said.

"Ya, except Davida. But she knows Hermann's

dead and Heidi's dead and there's no one to tell de trut. She tink I'm dead or in Germany. I come to America maybe twenty year ago. I'm very happy I come. Dey let me in because I have sister in St. Louis, Missouri."

"It's nice to have family," Decker said.

"Ya, she tell dem she will give me job. So dey let me come. I move to California because it's warm here and I like warm. But Davida . . . she never knows I'm here."

Decker nodded and waited.

"So I talk and talk to Lilah. Den one day, I tell her maybe I know who Frederick's parents are. And she says, who? And den I say, maybe Frederick is my grandson." She placed the cup and saucer on the table. "Oooo, dat is bad ting to say! She gets so mad at me. She says I was only being nice to her to see Frederick. Not *true*! She is *mine too*. I just *test* her with Frederick. But it's too late! She goes out of my house and will never talk to me again. She says I betry her."

"Betray," Goldin said.

"Ya, betray her. She never gives me chance to tell her whole trut."

"Maybe you should tell her the truth now, Greta," Goldin said. "Maybe she'd want to know."

"Maybe I tell her and she tries anodder suicide." Greta shook her head. "No . . . I don't open my mout no more. You don't tell her, Perry. You promise me. You have big mout."

"Yes, I do. And I promise to respect your wishes."
Silence.

"I still don't get it," Goldin said. "All these years,

Davida was a you-know-what on wheels to Freddy and *doted* on Lilah. What makes people so selectively cruel?"

"Maybe it was because Lilah was a girl," Decker said.

"I tink no," Greta said. "She closer to Lilah because she was hers."

Goldin frowned. "I thought you said Lilah was *your* granddaughter."

Greta said, "Ya, she was."

"Then I don't get—"

"Oh, I confuse you," Greta said. "I tink Davida was mean to Frederick because she was very mad at Hermann. She mean to Frederick to get back at her husband, you see."

Decker sat up in his seat. Suddenly, it all made sense.

Goldin said, "No, I don't—"

"Different fathers," Decker interrupted. "Hermann Brecht was Frederick's father, but not Lilah's."

"Ya," Greta said. "Essackly."

Goldin said, "So who was Lilah's father?"

Decker's own words ran through his brain.

. . . *linkage between Davida and Lilah* . . .

"Kingston Merritt." Decker looked at Greta. "It was Kingston, wasn't it."

"Ya, it was Kingston," Greta said. "He had eye out for her. I tell Heidi not to talk to family." She shook her head. "She don't listen. She get into trouble . . . twice. Stupid girl. Stupid, stupid girl!"

And then the old woman broke into woeful tears.

❧ 30

Decker adjusted his weight in the driver's seat of the parked Plymouth and pulled a cold meat-loaf sandwich out of his paper bag. He felt the stare as strong as a blast of heat and regarded the body in the passenger's seat . . . Marge's waifish eyes upon him. He gave her half.

"Ah, Pete, you don't have to."

"I'm going to have a big dinner tonight anyway." He checked his watch—one o'clock. Dinner was still *seven* hours away. Oh, what the hey. He'd fill up on coffee. "Don't worry about it. So what's up, Doc?"

"Which doc?" Marge bit into the sandwich. "How about we start with Kingston Merritt."

"Shoot."

"I'm wondering if Lilah knew King was her daddy and that's why she felt so guilty over his death."

"Did she imply that Kingston might be her father?"

"Well, she called him overbearing, but also said he acted that way out of *love*. Doesn't that sound like something a kid would say about her father rather than her brother?"

"Yeah, Marge, but we've got to remember that Merritt was *functionally* her father. And it's not just from what *he* told you. Goldin and Reed painted us the same picture." Decker sipped coffee from a thermos. "At this moment, I see no point in asking Lilah what she knows. She's heavily invested in being Hermann Brecht's daughter. I don't want to tell her something that may shove her into the deep end again."

"Pete, I don't think the lady's ever swum in the shallow."

Decker capped his thermos. "Good point."

"So what exactly took place in the Rhineland?" Marge asked. "King knocked up this woman's daughter and the daughter gave Lilah to Davida to raise as her own?"

"Yep. Greta was Davida's personal dressmaker. The job involved a lot of housecalls—fittings. Greta brought along her daughters as assistants. She tried to keep a tight rein on her girls, but hormones won out. Heidi caught King's eye and nature took its course. They were both fifteen at the time. According to Greta, Davida was more than happy to take the baby. And Hermann seemed willing, too. With Davida being over forty, a healthy pregnancy looked remote. Herm wanted someone to bear his name. The only one who was *not* happy about the arrangement was Kingston. Not that he wanted Heidi, but he was furious about Hermann co-opting *his* baby."

Marge said, "Remember John Reed telling us about Lilah's birth party. How Merritt and Hermann came to blows?" She licked her fingers. "All makes sense now."

"Yes, it sure does. Greta remembered a lot of hatred and fierce competition between the two of them. They were only seven years apart. When Hermann knocked up Heidi, Kingston was *crazed* with anger. First, Hermann stole his baby, then his *girl*. Hermann had been a big pussy hound to begin with. He and Davida used to fight about his roving eye. Old Herm scored a big coup when he knocked up Heidi, managing to piss off his wife *and* his stepson. What I can't understand is why Kingston—who *hated* Hermann—played along with the charade of older brother."

"I'll use your words, Pete," Marge said. "After Brecht died, King was functionally Lilah's father. Why stir up dirt when you have what you want? Or maybe King didn't say anything out of consideration for Davida."

Decker thought a moment. "Maybe that was the secret in the memoirs. Davida didn't want it coming out that King was Lilah's father."

"Or that Hermann was Freddy's father. Speaking of which, why were the memoirs sent to *Lilah* and not Freddy—Hermann's true blood son?"

"Maintaining the sham, I guess," Decker said. "Lilah was acknowledged blood offspring of Hermann and Davida. Freddy was the outcast—the adopted child."

"Just a good old family with old bones in the closets," Marge said.

Decker said, "A good old family that's not big on natural deaths. Both Heidi and Hermann committed suicide. Heidi's may have been accidental. Greta told

me the official line was alcohol and drug intoxication—
Seconal. I can't imagine a reputable doctor prescrib-
ing barbiturates to a sixteen-year-old back then.
Maybe they were Hermann's."

Marge considered his words. "Or maybe they
were Davida's. Maybe Davida *gave* them to Heidi . . .
supposedly out of the kindness of her heart. Pete,
Hermann was a big *drinker.* Suppose Davida knew
Herm and Heidi used to drink together and she
hoped that pills and booze wouldn't mix." She became animated. "Pete, maybe it wasn't King's pater-
nity thing that scared Davida. Maybe Hermann
somehow implicated Davida in Heidi's *death*! That
would be something worth murdering over."

"Murdering who?" Decker asked.

"Kingston," Marge said. "Davida thought Her
mann wrote about Heidi's death in his memoirs. And
Davida also knew that Lilah was getting ready to read
them—the twenty-five years were just about up. So
Davida decided to steal the memoirs. Suppose she
asked *King* to steal them."

"And he agreed to do it for money."

"Right. So he lifted the papers, then began to
have second thoughts about forking them over to
Mama."

"Why the second thoughts?" Decker asked. "Why
didn't he just take the money and run?"

"Maybe something was more important to King
than money. Maybe, when he read the memoirs, all
his latent paternal feelings came out. He became
furious not only at *Hermann* but at *Davida* for deny-
ing him his true role as Lilah's father. And he knew

the truth was in the papers. And he suddenly wanted Lilah to know, too. Heidi *was* her birth mother after all. So old King did a U-turn and told his mother he was going to give Lilah her memoirs back."

"And Davida became so enraged she had him whacked?"

"Hey, I have no trouble believing she'd do it if she thought it was a toss-up between her skin and his. Or like I said before, maybe King's death was *un-planned*. Davida sent Russ Donnally to look for the memoirs, King walked in at the wrong time, and things got out of hand. Plausible?"

"Plausible," Decker said. "But this is all speculation."

"Of course it's speculative." Marge finished her coffee and threw the cup in an overflowing garbage box. "That's our job. When we don't have evidence, we speculate. And we certainly don't have evidence against Davida."

"You think it's Davida?"

"She's the common link among the victims. If we could only get . . . get some *ammunition* against her." Marge frowned. "Unfortunately, Kingston Merritt and Russ Donnally are dead. And Kelley, Eubie, and Mike have gone the way of bivalves. Of course, there is Lilah . . ."

"I ain't about to confront her right now," Decker said. "She probably doesn't know anything and I don't want her death on my conscience."

"Neither do I," Marge said. "So who's left?"

"Who's left?" Decker started the Plymouth's engine. "Marge, we've got Hermann Brecht's *son*, that's who's left."

* * *

The spaces marked RESERVED FOR DOCTOR were once again occupied, so Decker stowed the unmarked in a slot reserved for the health-food store. He turned to Marge and said, "Remind me to pick up some wheat germ on the way out. I'm always parking in their spaces, might as well give them a little business."

"Wheat germ?"

"Maybe I meant oat bran—you know what I'm talking about. The stuff that tastes like sawdust. Any questions?"

Marge shook her head. They got out of the car and walked up to Brecht's clinic. Decker opened the glass door, a small tinkle of bells announcing their arrival. Place still looked like an ashram. Formless synthesizer music whined from a wall speaker. Not a soul in sight. Decker walked across the mats and knocked on the receptionist's window. Althea slid the window open, her wrist bedecked in jewelry just like the last time.

"Do we have to take out our badges or can we dispense with the formalities?"

Althea folded her silver-bangled arms across her chest, bracelets jingling in the swift movement. "I remember you."

Marge said, "We *know* Dr. Brecht is in. We just spent the last half hour tracking him down. We need to see him."

Althea nodded. "I'll buzz him."

Marge's hand covered the intercom. "Why don't you open the door and *we'll* let him know we're here."

Althea eyed her, then stood and opened the

connecting door. She blocked the threshold with her body. "He's been under terrible stress, you know. You're bothering him on his lunch hour."

Decker sidestepped around her into the hallway of the suite. "We'll try to be quick."

"His office is in the back."

"Thank you," Marge said.

They walked down the hallway. On impulse, Decker opened the door to a patient examining room. In gross contrast to Merritt's surgical offices, Brecht's rooms seemed more suited for love-ins than medical practice. The area was furnished with beanbag chairs, stuffed pillows, and a floral-sheeted mattress. Wood-framed glass-door cupboards held old-fashioned apothecary crocks, each one labeled with a different herb—witch hazel, foxglove, taro root, belladonna, hyssop, sage, peppermint, juniper berries, thistle, trefoil. In the corner was a brass incense holder.

Marge and he exchanged glances. She shrugged and said, "Hey, all things being equal, I'd rather take peppermint and juniper berries than bitter-tasting pills and shots."

"All things being equal . . ." Decker winked. "That's the catch."

He found Brecht's office and opened the door. The doctor was at his desk, phone cradled in one hand, a pita sandwich in the other. His face was a mask of confusion. He told the party on the other end of the line he'd call back, hung up, then stood, palms placed flat on his desk.

"Do you make it a habit of barging into people's private space?"

"Not a habit," Decker said. "Sorry about our manners but we need to talk to you, Doctor. It's about your adoption."

Brecht's face compacted with rage. "How dare you intrude upon my *private* life! Who *I* am and the circumstances of my birth are none of your *damn* business!"

"I don't blame you for being mad," Decker said, "I know how you feel—"

"You don't *know* a goddamn thing! Now kindly leave here—"

"I *do* know," Decker blurted, "because I'm adopted, too."

The room fell quiet. Decker observed Brecht. Angry? Confused? Maybe wary was the best description.

"Ever wonder about your birth parents, Doc?" Decker stuck his hands in his pockets. "I did . . . still do. I think that's normal. Everyone wants to know where they come from. Know what I'm talking about?"

The glint in Brecht's eyes—now it was *curiosity*. The man was *hooked*.

Brecht shifted his focus from Decker to Marge and then back again to Decker. "It's obvious you have something to tell me. You might as well make yourselves comfortable."

Marge thanked him and rooted herself in an office chair across from Brecht's desk. Decker remained standing, studying Brecht's place of work. No hoo-hah mystics for Dr. Freddy, just a conventional physician's office, maybe even nicer than most. Parquet floor, Chinese area rugs, wood paneling, rosewood desk and matching credenza, their tops displaying miniature ceramic vases and glass figurines. Floor-to-ceiling bookcases held medical tomes, the top four rows devoted to basic texts, nothing to indicate any conventional specialization. But the last two shelves were books on New Age and Organic Medicine. Thick texts labeled Herbology, Nutrition, Acupuncture, Biofeedback. A series of books on the Art of Healing—Quantum Healing, Healing Through Light, Healing Through Wu Chi, Healing Through Meditation, Healing Through Aerobics, Healing Through Water.

On the walls were photographs of sunsets interspersed with professional degrees. Decker read the certificates.

Brecht said, "Do my credentials meet with your approval, Sergeant?"

"Looks good to me, Doctor," Decker said. "But frankly, I wouldn't know a bogus diploma from the real thing."

"Yes, that's usually the case. The degrees are there to satisfy my clientele, not for service of the ego." Brecht fidgeted with his hands. "Do sit, Sergeant, you're making me nervous."

Decker turned a chair around and straddled the seat, resting his arms against the chair's back. "Dr. Brecht, there might be a connection between Hermann Brecht's memoirs and Kingston Merritt's death."

Brecht shook his head vigorously. "I don't see how they could possibly be related. And what does that have to do with my adoption?"

Decker kept his face blank. Brecht was still on

adoption. Had him hook, line, *and* sinker. "I'm getting to your adoption," Decker said. "But first, let's go back to the memoirs. Did you ever *see* them, Doctor?"

"*See* them? Don't you mean *read* them?"

"No, *see* them," Marge said. "Physically *touch* them."

Brecht paused. "Are you after verification of their existence?"

Decker said, "Yes."

"Yes, they exist. I've seen them. I was with Lilah when they arrived at her house. I never read them of course, but I saw them and a cover letter."

"Did you read the cover letter?" Decker asked.

"No. It was addressed to Lilah."

Marge said, "Did Lilah tell you not to mention the memoirs to anyone?"

"Yes. Lilah wanted their existence kept private until twenty-five years after Hermann's death had passed. That was one of Hermann's requests spelled out in the cover letter."

"Which you never read," Decker said.

"Which I never read. Lilah told me the specifics of the letter."

"Then how do you know the cover letter was addressed to Lilah?" Decker asked.

"Well, I saw . . ." Brecht twitched. "I noticed the box the memoirs came in. It had been addressed to Lilah . . . to the child of Hermann Brecht, actually . . . *Kinder de Hermann Brecht*. Something like that. Only the address was in German. The cover letter was in English. I don't understand how the memoirs are relevant to Kingston's death or my adoption."

Decker said, "Doctor, what do you know about your biological parents' backgrounds?"

Brecht shook his head. "Sergeant, either be forthcoming or kindly leave. I have three clients this afternoon and then I must rush back to the hospital. Lilah's not very psychologically sound. I don't want either of you disrupting her healing arena."

"Nah, I'm not interested in talking to her," Decker said. "Just you."

Brecht looked stupefied. "Very well. Talk."

"Doctor," said Marge, "we've discovered some interesting things about you—by accident. I don't want anything we say to come as a shock—"

"Nothing could shock me." Brecht was suddenly impatient. "I know my background, Detective. Mother was always very open about it. Get on with it."

"Doctor, I'm not stalling," Decker said. "It's just . . . well, I don't think your mother has been completely . . . honest about your background. That's why I want to hear what *you* know."

"Oh, very well! I see the only way to rid myself of you two is to talk." Brecht picked up a pyramidal crystal from his desk and began to rub the base. "It's not a background of which I'm particularly proud. I was the product of a union between a simpleton mother and a felonious father. They never married, of course. My biological mother had been simply a vessel for my father's lust. Mother—Davida Eversong, that is—took pity on me and rescued me from that impoverished environment. Mother has told me innumerable times how fortunate I was to have the wealth that allowed me to exploit my inferior genetic capacity to its fullest."

Decker thought: Greta Millstein—an impoverished environment. At that moment, he felt sorry for Brecht and for Greta. She had sacrificed her heart, mistakenly thinking she'd done her grandchildren an immense act of kindness.

Brecht placed the crystal back on his desk with a thump. "Not that Mother has been much of a mother. Both Lilah and I were raised by nannies and governesses and nurses and chauffeurs and cooks and— good Lord, you think the woman would have been a bit interested in our development."

"The price of fame," Decker said.

"No price for my mother," Brecht said, "but for me . . . *especially* for me. Kingston hated me from the day I was born. I don't know what I did to deserve his hatred. I know Mother loved him more than me . . . and yes, I was a bit jealous, but who wouldn't be? I tried to please them all. Kingston just never accepted me. As fond as he was of Lilah, that's how much he despised me. John was a decent man, but he was never around. Mostly, it was Lilah and me and the hired help. And Kingston being horrible to me."

Brecht rubbed moisture from his eyes.

"It is despicable to talk ill of the dead, but I can't grieve over a brother I never had."

Decker nodded, wanting to tell Brecht he hadn't *done* anything to deserve Merritt's hatred. And maybe he would do just that. Try to make him understand that Merritt didn't hate him per se but just his parents—the girlfriend who jilted him for his drunken stepfather. Jealousy. Rabbi Schulman once said it rots the flesh off the bone. And that's what the family was now. Nothing but bones. He saw Brecht flash him a sickly smile.

"Now it's your turn," Brecht said.

Marge said, "This is what your mother told you?"

"Yes. Do you have information to the contrary?"

Decker said, "Yes, we have some information that . . . *conflicts* with your mother's account."

Brecht perched forward. "Tell me what you know."

Decker said, "Before I tell you, I want some information from you in exchange. I want you to tell me how your mother planned the theft of the memoirs."

"*What!? Mother* was behind the theft?"

Marge said, "Doctor, you knew she was behind the theft all along. In fact, maybe you were in on it yourself."

Brecht turned ashen. "I know *nothing!*"

"She's been *using* you, Doctor," Decker said. "She's always *used* you as her *errand* boy. But you took it from her because you thought she'd rescued you from an impoverished life. She's been telling you that she was your savior all these years. In fact, she's been *lying* to you. The story she's been feeding you is a bunch of bull."

Decker noticed Brecht's breathing had quickened. The expectant look in his eyes . . . as if he'd always known.

"Then who am I?" Brecht panted.

Marge said, "Doctor, we need your help—"

"Who *am* I?" Brecht's voice rose a notch.

Decker said, "If Davida did rope you into some kind of a scheme, we can make a deal."

"*Who am I, damn you?*" Brecht jumped up and pounded his desk. "*Who!*"

"You are the *sole* offspring of Hermann Brecht," Decker said, softly. "*He* was your biological father."

Brecht stood motionless for a long time. Finally, Decker stood, placed a firm hand on Brecht's shoulder and physically pushed him back into his desk chair. Even then, Brecht didn't move except to breathe and blink.

Eventually, Brecht whispered, "You're certain?"

Marge said, "We'll start from the beginning, if you'll tell us what you know about the theft of the memoirs."

Brecht licked his lips. "I . . . I want you to know I had *nothing* to do with Kingston's death."

"But you do know something about the theft of the memoirs," Marge said.

Brecht's eyes were still glazed. "How can I be Hermann Brecht's *sole* offspring? What about Lilah?"

Decker smoothed his mustache. "Lilah's another long story. Let's take it one story at a time."

Brecht spoke as if hypnotized. "I always knew it . . . deep down, I knew I couldn't be what Mother had said I was. I just couldn't be. . . ." He covered his mouth with a fist, then exhaled. "All these years of her lying to me . . . making me feel as if I were the scum of the earth. What a scheming *witch*!" He looked at Decker. "*Who* was my *real* mother?"

"All in due time, Doc," Decker said. "First you tell me about how your mother—"

"*Davida Eversong* is no longer my *mother*!" Brecht

screamed. "You want to know about Davida, ask about *Davida*. Never use the words *mother* and *Davida* interchangeably!"

"Fine, Doctor," Marge said. "How did Davida entangle you in the burglary of the memoirs?"

"You expect me to *admit* my involvement in a crime?" Brecht said.

"It's the only way we can gather evidence against your moth—against Davida. Hell, it's a simple theft. We could probably cut you a decent deal—"

"Deal?" Brecht's laugh was high-pitched and hysterical. "Why would *I* need a *deal*? If what you are saying is true, I wasn't involved in any theft! I was simply reclaiming . . . what was rightfully *mine* in the first place."

"Bravo, Doc, you're right about that!" Marge pulled out her notebook. "The memoirs belonged to you all along. Tell us what Davida put you up to."

Brecht nodded. "Yes, I'll tell you what she put me up to." He held out his hands. "Now, how should I begin?"

❧31

Davida's bungalow was sited about a hundred yards behind the spa's main hotel, elevated, fenced, and hidden from view by overgrown flowering brush. Decker felt as if he were on safari as he and Marge hiked the rising stone pathway to the gated entrance. An intercom was perched on a fence post. Marge depressed the red button and a scratchy voice asked who it was. Decker identified himself and they were buzzed inside the grounds—green hillside shaded by towering oak. Davida's hangout lay on the knoll's pinnacle. He and Marge started up the fieldstone steps.

Marge said, "I'm working up a sweat."

"It's the afternoon heat," Decker said. "Saps your energy."

"This case is sapping my energy."

"Tell me about it."

"What did Morrison say when you mentioned the warrant?"

"He wasn't happy," Decker said. "But he's a good cop. Told me to go for it *first*, then added—if possible—to keep it from the press."

"So what happens if we bring Davida in for questioning?"

Decker made a sour face. "Let's worry about it if the time comes. We'll search first, then I'll wing it . . . work my way into the questioning . . . throw her off guard."

"We don't have much against her, do we?"

"Not yet."

Davida was waiting for them at her door, her smile as welcoming as ice water in the face.

"We finally caught up with you," Marge stated.

Davida's smile widened. "Caught up with me? That sounds ominous."

Decker presented her with the search warrant for her bungalow. Davida gave it a cursory glance, then stepped aside. "Do come in."

They entered the cluttered but expensively furnished living room. Decker noticed the artwork— English painters, famous names. Millions of dollars hanging on the walls.

"Would you like some coffee?" Davida purred.

Davida in her hostess mode, Decker thought. Actresses. Do they ever play themselves? Do they even know how? "No, thanks." He checked his watch. A little after two, still five hours to go before Sabbath. To Marge he said, "I'll take the living room, you take the bedroom."

"You've got it, Pete."

Davida said, "May I ask what you're looking for?"

Decker regarded the old woman. She was amused. He peeled a seat cushion from the pink divan. "We'll try to be as quick and neat as possible."

"Am I under arrest for anything?" Davida asked.

"Not at the moment." Decker felt inside the seam

along the back of the couch. Not even a crumb, let alone papers or a weapon. He picked up the cushion, squeezed it inch by inch, then unzipped the upholstery cover and peered inside. "But don't go anywhere. We need to ask you a few questions."

"What kind of questions?"

"First, let me finish up with the search, Ms. Eversong. I find it hard to concentrate on two things at one time."

Davida marched over to the bar and poured herself a shot of Wild Turkey. "If I'm not under arrest, why are you searching my *residence*?"

Decker flashed her an enigmatic smile, thinking: I'm tearing up the place 'cause I've always liked treasure hunts. But in reality it was a valid question. He wasn't about to tell her they were searching for evidence.

The case had reached a frustrating impasse. He had learned from Frederick Brecht that Davida had bribed both him and Kingston to do the old lady's dirty work. Brecht was to occupy Lilah for the evening so Kingston could do a neat little B and E, removing Hermann Brecht's memoirs. The original plan was for Kingston to fork over the papers in exchange for money to keep his research going. But old King had a sudden change of heart when he spoke to Lilah. Suddenly King wanted something more than money. He wanted his relationship with his sister/daughter back. Attachments weren't something Davida had planned on because attachments were a foreign concept to her.

The rest was Brecht's conjecture. He thought his

mother probably sent Russ Donnally over to Merritt's office. *Why* was the big question. Did Davida want Donnally to filch the memoirs?—the tossed office certainly seemed to suggest that. But just *maybe* she wanted Donnally to do something more.

Decker remained stoic as he hunted, concealing his frustration.

Freddy Brecht's account was Decker's sole source. He had no concrete *proof*—just Davida's word against Freddy's. Barely enough of a story to persuade a judge to sign a search warrant to look for the damn papers and the weapons that murdered King and/or Russ Donnally. Where the memoirs were was anyone's guess. Decker knew he would probably come up empty-handed. But let's hear it for the old college try.

His eyes drifted to Davida, housed in a flamingo-pink silk robe secured by a wide sash. White feet in fur slippers—probably dyed mink. Her face had been carefully made up. Clear, bagless eyes topped by feathery lashes. A slight blush to her cheeks. Lips glossed and painted in a heart shape. Hair recently done, short black tresses framing her jawline. She looked in her mid-fifties, a *good-looking* mid-fifties. She seemed to notice the positive appraisal and batted her lashes.

"If you'd just tell me what you're looking for, perhaps I could save you some trouble."

Decker returned his attention to the couch, flipped it over and began to check out the bottom. No signs of tampering.

"It's those fictitious memoirs," Davida said. "Am I not correct?"

Decker didn't answer.

"Peter, for God's sake, stop wasting your time on some silly old papers and get out and look for my jewels. You haven't made a damn bit of progress on that front, have you?"

"Actually, we have. If I were you, I'd talk to Lilah."

"Lilah? *Lilah* has them? She actually stole my precious babies?" Fingers clutched into fists. "I'll *kill* that little ingrate!"

"If she doesn't kill herself first," Decker added.

"That silly gesture?" Lilah dropped into an armchair. "*Please!* Lilah's a very competent woman and a *wonderful* actress. She really missed her calling in the theater. If she had wanted to plug herself, she would have succeeded. It was nothing but an attempt to get some attention. Oscar-level attempt to be sure, but *I* can see through it. Now you march right over to her, Peter, and *demand* that she give you my jewels!"

"Would you like us to formally arrest your daughter for the theft?"

"Arre . . . just tell her to give them back to me."

"Would you like to file a—"

"Oh, *cut* it!" Davida said, sharply. "Your dialogue is like a bad movie."

Decker didn't answer and continued to search. Now it boiled down to who could psych whom. Odds in favor of Davida because she had years of experience dealing in Hollyweird. But don't rule out Rabbi Pete . . . all those years of interviewing felons . . .

Decker said, "If you want your jewels, Davida, it might be easier to talk to Lilah yourself. But it's up to you. I'm just a paid public servant. Personally, I'm not interested in your jewels. But I *am* interested in Hermann's papers. And I think you are, too."

The old woman laughed derisively. A real scornful chuckle. Strike a point for the actress.

"See what I think," Decker went on, "what I *know*, is that King pinched the papers for you. But at the last minute, he decided to keep them instead of turning them over to you for research money."

Davida ambled over to the bar and poured herself another bourbon. "Where'd you come up with that little beauty?"

Again the sarcastic tone of voice. But without the fire. Score one for the detective.

"Dr. Brecht," Decker said.

"Freddy?" Davida frowned. "What's *he* up to now? That boy's the bane of my existence. That's what happens when one adopts children from *dubious* lineage."

Decker moved on to a wing-back chair. He could hear Davida tapping her foot. She said, "If Freddy concocted such an outlandish story that puts me at odds with the law, why aren't I under arrest?"

Decker grinned. "At odds with the law. I like that."

"You didn't answer my question."

Decker knelt and looked under the couch—nothing, not even any dust balls. Woman paid well to have a clean house.

"You don't have any evidence against me, do you?" Davida asserted. *"That's* what you're looking for! Evidence against *me*! Well, Peter, I'm going to do you a great favor. You're wasting your time. You won't find anything here—no memoirs . . . no *anything*. If you think Kingston took the papers, search his place."

Decker didn't answer. Burbank had already combed his places . . . nothing.

"Peter, I swear to you, I never even *saw* any memoirs."

Decker regarded the old woman. She was nervous, biting her thumbnail. She ran her fingertips along her jawline. "If you do happen to find these so-called papers, just what do you plan to do with them?"

"Give them to their rightful owner."

"It's not in Lilah's best interests to read them."

"It might be in Dr. Brecht's best interests. That's who they were intended for in the first place. Because Hermann Brecht was Frederick's father, wasn't he?"

Davida was motionless for a moment. Then she downed her drink. "You speak poppycock, my friend. That's a euphemism for *shit*! You want to spend your time making groundless assumptions, go ahead. But if I were you, I wouldn't say too much. I've got a very good lawyer on retainer for slander hounds like you. I'd advise you to tread lightly, Peter."

"Where were you on Wednesday between the hours of three and six, Davida?"

"Oh, so now I'm being *officially* questioned? Do I need a *lawyer*, Detective?"

"Hey, why not, Davida? He's on retainer anyway."

"Oh, go to *hell*!"

"Temper." Decker called Marge in from the other

room, then took out a pocket-sized card and Mirandized the old lady. He took out a pocket tape recorder and turned it on.

"Do you mind?"

"Be my guest." Davida studied her nails. "Is your
little henchwoman going to cuff me now?"

"No, she isn't going to cuff you," Decker said.
"You're not under arrest."

"Then why did you read me my rights?"

Marge said, "I'll be in the bedroom. Call me if
you need me, Pete."

Decker nodded. Davida said, "What do you *want*
from me?"

"Why'd you have Kingston whacked?"

"Are you out of your mind, Peter?" Davida threw
back her head. "I didn't have him *whacked*."

"So how did he die?"

"How the hell should I know? *I* wasn't there!"

"So, if you weren't there, where were you last
Wednesday between the hours of three and six?"

"I don't have to answer your questions."

"No, you don't."

There was a moment of silence.

"If you must know, I was probably driving up to
Malibu."

Decker sat on the sofa. "Took the old limo to
Malibu, did you?"

"I always travel in high style."

"Funny how you and the limo can be driving
to Malibu at the same time Russ Donnally and the
limo were in Kingston Merritt's parking lot."

The old woman leaned against the wall and closed
her eyes. "You're very good."

Decker said, "You sicced Donnally onto Kingston—"

"I didn't *sic* Albert on anyone!"

"Albert?"

"Russ." Davida smiled. "I used to call him Albert. I thought Albert was a far more appropriate name for a chauffeur." Again, she fluttered her lashes. "Don't you agree?"

Decker rolled his eyes.

Davida said, "So Albert decided to drop by Kingston's office. So Albert had a run-in with Kingston. That's not my fault."

"Russ Donnally was in your employ, Davida. We're talking possible solicitation for murder—"

"That's absurd! I want to talk to my lawyer."

Decker said, "You know where the phone is."

"Oh, fuck off!" Davida began to pace. "Okay, maybe Albert did drop by Kingston's office. Just to talk to him . . . talk some *bloody* sense into him. Goddamn Kingston anyway. He was opening up a Pandora's box. I didn't want to have to deal with shit at such a late date. You're getting on in years. Surely you can understand that."

Decker was silent.

"I don't know . . ." Davida took a deep breath. "I don't know what happened. If Albert acted on his own accord, went to King's office and acted like an enforcer for the mob, that's not my fault."

Davida's hand went to her throat.

"My son kept a gun in his office. And Albert . . . he . . . always packed. Made him feel like a hotshot, the little shit. Maybe Albert made demands on Kingston. And King did have a terrible temper.

Things probably got out of hand. Probably they . . . pulled the guns on each other . . . like a bad western."

"King's office was ransacked, Davida," Decker said.

"There was probably a terrible . . . struggle." Again, she bit her thumbnail. "I don't know what happened because I wasn't inside. I left when I heard—"

She stopped herself. Decker said, "You left when you heard gunshots?"

The room was silent. The old woman slid down onto the divan. Pink robe against pink upholstery, she seemed to meld into the couch—a woman with dimension but no contrast. Like a bas-relief. But her voice still had control—not a waver or a whimper.

"Russ merely wanted to *talk* to Kingston, Sergeant."

"Talk to him about what?"

"Kingston claimed he had the memoirs."

"And you wanted them, didn't you?" Decker said. She was silent.

"Why?" Decker asked.

"None of your damn business."

Decker said, "You asked Kingston to steal them—"

"I did not!" Davida seemed offended. "I *blurt* things out—things like 'God, I wish I had those papers.' It's not my fault if my son loves me so much, he tries to grant me my every wish."

Decker said, "So why'd he change his mind and keep the papers himself, Davida?"

"I don't know. I tried calling him to ask him just that. He wouldn't talk to me over the phone. And I wasn't about to go into his office when he was butchering his fetuses. His *research* made me sick!"

"What'd you do with the gun you gave Donnally?"

Her eyes hardened. "What *gun*? I don't own a gun. I told you Albert packed. Not me. I don't have any guns. Your search will verify that."

Meaning that if there were guns at the scene, she probably had Kelley and Eubie ditch them when they took Russ's body. Yet . . . they swore they didn't see any guns. Worry about that one later.

Decker said, "So King never did tell you *why* he changed his mind and decided to keep the memoirs?"

Davida fell silent.

"Know a woman named Greta Millstein, Davida?"

She snapped her head upward, then let out a peal of mirthless laughter. "My God, where did you dig up *that* senile kraut? She must be a hundred years old."

"Nah, she's not that old. Not much older than yourself, as a matter of fact."

The hit was dead-center. Again, she threw her empty glass across the room, the tumbler smashing into pieces.

"That wrinkled old Nazi, just *what* kind of fairy tales did she tell you?"

Decker said, "Those memoirs must have posed a big problem for you, Davida. After all these years of trying to convince Freddy he was adopted . . . now he might learn his true biological heritage. And then of course, there was *Lilah*. Plus there were other things in those papers that you didn't want coming out—other things you've done."

Davida looked up, confused. "What *other* things?"

"Heidi Millstein's murder."

"Heidi's mur—did that old bitch say I was responsible for her daughter's death?" Davida began to pace. "Well, let me tell you something, *Sergeant*. It was Heidi's choice to *fuck* my husband. It was Heidi's choice to *drink* with my husband. And it was Heidi's choice to *pop pills* while she was drinking and fucking with my husband. *My* husband, do you understand? *MY* husband! So if she made a series of stupid choices, I have no tears for the little tramp. I'm *glad* she died. And if Hermann with his overly sodden emotions has written it any other way, he's not only a shithead, he's a liar!"

Winded, she stopped walking and flopped onto her settee. "Pour me a drink, Peter."

"Not part of my job description, Davida."

"Do it for me anyway . . . please?"

Decker glanced at her face—old and defeated. He got up and poured her a finger's worth of bourbon. Davida held the glass with shaking hands and swallowed quickly.

"Good old Freddy. He must despise me."

She sounded sad. More self-pity than regret. Decker said, "Yes, I think he does."

"I had to . . . to hide the truth. It would have resulted in too many questions."

"Truth might have been simpler, Davida. Deception's hard work."

"I had my reasons."

"Must have been good ones for you to go to all that trouble—keeping secrets and stealing papers.

What would it have hurt to tell Freddy that he was Hermann's son?"

The old woman stared at him, her eyes filled with tears. "It wasn't Freddy. It was *Lilah*! I couldn't have her learn the truth!"

Decker thought about Lilah, how she worshiped Hermann Brecht. How it might have destroyed her, if she learned that Brecht wasn't her biological father. Maybe even an egocentric woman like Davida had seen that as well. Decker felt strong fingers grip his arms. Davida was shaking him.

"Don't you *understand*, Peter? I would have done *anything* to prevent Lilah from . . ." The old woman closed her eyes, cheeks wet and shiny. "I couldn't bear the thought of it!"

She lowered her chin onto her chest and sobbed openly.

Decker patted her shoulder. "You couldn't bear the thought of *what*, Davida?"

"I couldn't . . ." She looked up at him with puffy eyes. "I wouldn't have been able . . . to look Lilah in the eye. Because . . . I'd know that every time . . . she looked at me . . . that she'd be thinking: There goes my *grandmother*."

❧ 32

It would make the five o'clock news. And talk about *images:* The captain himself personally escorting the great *grande dame* of the late-night one-checker, pushing her head down as she slid into the transport so she wouldn't bump it on the cruiser's ceiling. The black Mercedes that housed Davida's silk-suited lawyer. For the crowd scene, there were young nubile wide-eyed things in bikinis, their color-coordinated lips forming smoke-ringed Os of surprise. The uniforms dispersed the gathering as the black-and-whites drove away. Hands in pocket, Decker watched without comment.

The reporters eventually gave up on him and went to Marge. She smiled at the cameras and offered a "Hi, Mom" as her sole statement. Eventually, the hordes moved on, the reporters packed up their camerapeople, and he and Margie were left alone to finish up their job of searching Davida's bungalow.

Decker looked at his watch. The Sabbath was three hours away. What he should do was go home and take a long hot shower. What he was going to do was work until the last minute because they *still* didn't have anything to take to the DA. The more Marge talked about the case, the more he realized that sad fact. Without the memoirs, they were hogtied. Merritt had probably stowed the papers in a good, *safe* place—a place they'd never locate.

"But Davida admitted being on the scene," Marge said.

"She admitted being in the *car*," Decker corrected. "That's a far cry from being at the scene. If she paid Russ, I'm sure she did it in cash. Nothing exceptional went in and out of Donnally's bank accounts. Who knows? Maybe Donnally did act on his own . . . trying to gain brownie points with his employer."

"Like Kelley Ness," Marge said. "Didn't she swear she did it on her own?"

"Yep," Decker said. "Claimed she found Russ by accident and was trying to protect the spa's image. She refused to implicate anyone."

"How could she do it on her *own*? Davida *had* to have *mentioned* something to her."

Decker held out his arms and shrugged.

"God, that *pisses* me off," Marge said. "Woman's literally getting away with murder! We're never gonna find the papers, Pete."

"I know." Decker paused. "Do you really think she paid Donnally to kill Merritt?"

Marge thought about that. "Maybe it was like Davida stated—that Merritt and Donnally did kill each other. But I'm not going to let this go until *I'm* convinced that the shooting was just another *stupid* accident by two hotheaded people. To be continued . . ."

Decker nodded. "Yeah, we'll do some follow-up."

"You bet we will. . . ." Marge sighed. "Even though our caseloads are already bursting at the seams."

"A cop's work is never done."

Marge smiled.

Decker said, "Morrison looked pretty good, don't you think?"

"Not too bad considering he was swearing under his breath."

"This kind of PR isn't all bad—a famous woman being hauled in for questioning." Decker shifted his feet. "The law is money-blind and all that rot. Too bad they won't be able to hold her more than a couple of hours."

"She'll sue, Pete. False arrest."

"She wasn't arrested, just brought in for questioning—"

"Pete—"

"She can sue, but it won't stick. No one's going to bag her for anything because we don't have enough evidence." Decker turned to Marge and noticed she was holding a large book under her arm. "What do you have?"

"A high-school yearbook." Marge flipped through the pages. "Ten years old. Kelley Ness was in tenth grade."

"It's Kelley's?"

"Yeah, all the little inscriptions written on the cover are made out to her. Ordinarily I wouldn't have thought a thing about it except it was hidden under a floorboard in Davida's bedroom."

"Really. Find anything else there?"

"Nope. So far as I can tell, there's nothing unusual in the album. But the mere fact that Davida has it squirreled away must mean I missed something significant." She handed it to Decker. "You try your luck."

Decker took the yearbook and looked at the cover—Jackson High, Fountainville, California. A picture of Old Hickory in sepia tones.

"Let's go inside."

"Good idea," Marge said. She closed the door and sat on a wingback. Decker sat on Davida's pink settee and opened the album.

> *It's been fun being in history with you. See ya next year. Have a rad summer—Heather*
>
> *Don't get all gnarly about geometry, Kell. You always were good with squares—Ryan*

Gnarly. Ten years old.

More adolescent wisdom. Decker flipped another page—an inscription that took up half the space. This one seemed personal. Decker read silently, then began again out loud:

My dearest Kelley,

> *I know this has been the most trying of trying times for you and for Mitchy too. But you have to remember that we all must do what we all must do. That drums beat differently for each and every individual and we must all go at our own pace. I will always be there for you. You know how much I care about you and we will always be friends no matter what people will say or do. And people do say and do nasty things. But this kind of thing only serves to*

make us strong. Alone, we fall, together we can stand tall. There will always be jerks who try to bring you down. Don't listen to them. Listen to your heart and know that I care about you and luv you with all my heart. I only want the best for you. You know that.

Luv 4-ever,
Denise

"Denise?" Marge said. "Sure that doesn't say Dennis, Pete?"

"No, it says Denise." Decker showed her the page. "See. She even dotted her *i* with a little heart."

Marge suddenly sat up. "You know, Pete. Not that it matters much, but maybe that's the secret Kelley and Mike were trying to *hide*."

"What secret?"

"Maybe Kelley's a lesbian."

Decker frowned. "I don't see being gay as blackmail material in this day and age. And besides, Marge, I've seen my daughter's album inscriptions. Cindy's yearbook was full of mush—using words like *love* and *friendship* interchangeably. Denise was probably Kelley's best friend."

"Maybe it was friendship that turned to sex."

"Doesn't spell blackmail to me."

"Then why does Davida have the yearbook, Pete?"

"I don't know."

He turned to the tenth-grade class pictures, found Kelley Ness's small black-and-white. Hair cut very short, showing off dangling earrings. Hard to tell if she was wearing makeup. One thing she wasn't wearing was a smile. The girl looked downright grim. Like old Denise had said, it must have been a hard year for Kelley.

Then he scanned the class for Denise. He found her easily, because underneath her picture was a tag line: *Luv from me. Denise Dillon*. Cute little thing. Short curly hair and dangling earrings. Decker flipped from her picture to Kelley's. The earrings matched. He looked at Denise again. She was smiling—a broad, toothy smile.

Decker showed Marge the pictures. "Look, they're wearing identical earrings."

"I'm telling you, that's the hold Davida has over Kelley," Marge said. "*That's* why Kelley was willing to remove the bodies for her. And that's why Kelley isn't implicating Davida. She didn't want it getting out that she was a lesbian! Pete, we *can* use Kelley to get to Davida!"

Decker shut the book and drummed his fingers. "You know what's bothering me? Kelley doing dirty work for Davida when Mike was around. Marge, he's very protective of his sister. I have a feeling he watches her like a hawk. I don't think he'd permit Kelley to move a body for Davida when he could have done it himself."

"I'm not following."

"I'm not making myself real clear." Decker paused a moment. "Suppose Davida had something on Kelley."

"She was a lesbian."

"Whatever. Suppose Davida told Kelley she knew her dirty secrets. First thing Kelley would do would be what? Tell her brother, right?"

"Yeah, maybe."

"Not maybe. *Definitely!* Now Ness is a punk, but look at the way he acted when he found out Eubie was getting it on with his sister. He charged Eubie. I see Mike as being a little white knight, walking up to Davida and saying, 'You want your shit done, lady, don't go to my *sister*, you go to *me*. . . .'" Decker wagged his finger in the air. "Wait a minute, I just remembered something. I'm trying to think of the exact words. I think they were: *You got my sister involved, you fuckhead!*"

"Whose words?"

"What Mike Ness said to Eubie Jeffers. *You got my* sister involved, *you fuckhead!* Margie, don't you *see* it? That implies that Eubie roped Kelley into doing the dirty work. But the way Kelley tells it, she roped Eubie. We got a contradiction here."

The room went quiet. Decker stood and stuck his hands in his pockets.

"Let's play it like this, Margie. Mike screamed at Eubie: You got my sister involved. Then Eubie answered back something like: I couldn't do it myself, Mike. That means Mike asked Eubie for help. Then Eubie asked Kelley to help him."

"Why would Eubie help Mike?"

Decker thought a moment, then said, "Simple. Mike covered for Eubie the night of Lilah's rape. I see Ness as the middleman between Davida and Eubie. Who knows? Ness might have checked out the murder scene first before sending Eubie over. Maybe Ness even removed the guns. He left the hard part—the removal of the bodies—to Eubie." He paused.

"Why did Kelley Ness insist that she masterminded the plot and take the heat for Mike?"

"Well, she could be protecting Mike," Marge said. "Of course, that contradicts your theory of Mike as the protective older brother."

Decker said, "So then the question is: Why did Mike *allow* his sister to take the heat?"

Marge said, "It seems to me, if Mike Ness was willing to let his sister take the heat for him, she must be protecting him against something big. Now I find this annual under a floorboard. . . ." She paused. "Maybe we should stop looking for dirt on Kelley and start hunting for info about Mike. Something Davida had on *him*!"

"Okay," Decker said. "He's two years older than Kelley. That would have made him a senior."

"I skimmed the seniors," Marge said. "He wasn't there at first glance. You give it a whirl."

Decker checked and didn't find his picture in the graduating roster. He leafed through the list until he came to the final page—Wendy Wyster, Jackie Zallero, Mark Zipp. . . .

Then a column of names; seniors whose pictures were not shown. Decker ran the tip of his finger down the column. "Here he is, Marge. Michael—" He stopped himself, then stared at the name. "Holy shit, that's *Michelle* Ness."

Marge peered at the page. "Must be a misprint."

Decker turned back to Denise's inscription to Kelley.

I know this has been the most trying of trying times for you and for Mitchy, *too.*

Mitchy.

And then things began to click: The pretty face, the surprisingly bony frame, the defined muscles without the bulk, even the ballet lessons. Who in heartland America gave their *son* ballet lessons?

"Marge, I don't think that's a misprint. I think Mike Ness is or was a girl."

"What!"

"He's pretty. You said it yourself—"

"Yeah, but Pete—"

"Androgynous looking—"

"Pete—"

"Not physically prepossessing—"

"He's slight, but most smaller-than-average men look slight to me."

"He moves with grace—"

"He had ballet lessons."

"A boy taking ballet?"

"It happens sometimes. That's why we have Nureyevs and Baryshnikovs. Pete, the guy may be small but he's very masculine. The way he talks, the way he *swaggers.*"

"You're right, Marge. He isn't effeminate. But that still doesn't negate his size."

"He isn't *that* small."

"It ain't the height or even the muscles. Hell, he could take steroids and build up some biceps. It's his *frame.* He's *bony.*"

Marge thought about the first time she'd questioned Kelley about the sexual harassment suit against Mike Ness. *If you knew my brother, you'd know how inane the suit is.* Then she felt her eyes widen.

"Oh, my God!"

"What is it?"

"The hairs, Peter! The ones used to match against the semen found on Lilah's sheets. Buck found a bag of *female* hairs. He thought I fucked up. *I* thought I fucked up. Maybe I didn't. Maybe I just gave him *Mike's* hair and it was really *Michelle's* hair! *That* would explain the female banding. You can change your dick, but you can't change your DNA." Marge shook her head in amazement. "You can't make up stuff as weird as this."

"Ain't that the truth."

Decker picked up the phone, asked the operator the area code for Fountainville, then dialed local information, asking for the number of the hall of records. He hung up and punched in the number.

"Quarter to five," Decker said. "Think someone's still there?"

"Should be. But we're talking civil servants."

"Like us."

Marge socked him. Unlike Rina, his partner could do damage if she wanted to. A moment later the voice cut through the line. Decker said a silent thank you and identified himself. After being put on hold, being transferred from one department to another, he finally found a person who could help him. Miss Jones.

"Do you have the birth date of this Michelle Ness, Sergeant?"

"Just a sec." He turned to Marge. "Look through my stuff. Scott Oliver gave me a copy of Mike Ness's blank yellow sheet. To pull it, he must have had Ness's birth date. See if it's on the sheet."

Marge scavenged through Decker's illegible notes

and found the computer printout. "It's here. Six-one-sixty-five."

Decker gave the numbers to Miss Jones. She told him to hold for a moment.

"No guarantees he was born in Fountainville, Pete."

"It's a start."

"You know, Pete, if Mike was a Michelle, it would make sense for Kelley to protect him even for a low-grade felony. Imagine him going to jail. Wherever they put him, she'd *know* he was going to have mucho problems."

"Absolutely."

Marge smiled. "He is a nice-looking guy."

"Pretty."

"Yeah, he's pretty."

"Sergeant?" Miss Jones said.

Decker returned his attention to the phone. "Yes?"

"Sergeant, I don't have anything for a Michelle Ness. But we do have a Michael Ness born six-one-sixty-five. Would you like a copy of his birth certificate?"

Decker didn't answer.

"Sergeant?"

"Yeah, I'm here. Miss Jones, are you sure?"

"Yes, I'm sure."

"Is it possible for you to look at the birth certificate?"

"You mean right now?"

"Yes, right now."

"It'll take me a moment. It's on microfiche."

"I'll hold," Decker said.

Marge said, "You look like you just sucked on lemons."

"No Michelle Ness," Decker said, "only Michael."

Marge returned the sour look. "Well, that shoots that theory to hell. Damn, it would have been nice to discover something we could *use* to get to *Davida*. Why are you still on the phone?"

"I'm having her look up the birth certificate. I want her to tell me if it has the word *male* on it under sex."

"Thorough," Marge said.

"Always," Decker said.

Miss Jones came back on the line. "I have a Xerox copy of Mr. Ness's birth certificate. Would you like me to fax it to you?"

"In a moment. I need you to tell me one thing. Under sex of the baby, what does it say?"

"Sex?" She sounded confused. "It says *male* . . . *M*, actually."

Decker sighed. "You're sure?"

She laughed. "Of course I'm sure."

"The name on the birth certificate is Michael Ness?" Decker tried again.

"Yes, Michael Ness . . . Michael Steven Ness."

"Okay, thank you for your help, Miss Jones. I'm going to give you a fax number now." He recited the station house's number, thanked her again, and hung up.

"Mikey's a boy," Decker said. "It was probably a simple misprint. Should we call it a day, Detective?"

"Pete, how'd Kingston Merritt break into Lilah's inner safe?"

Decker said, "I know. Let's ask *Davida*."

They both laughed. Then the room fell silent for a moment until they both heard a key being inserted into the front door. Decker held his fingers to his lips. A moment later the door opened cautiously, then all the way. Mike Ness tiptoed inside, then stopped short, his eyes focused upon their faces.

Marge said, "*Surprise!* We're *still* here!"

"I'll come back later," Ness said.

Decker held up the yearbook. "Is this what you're looking for?"

Ness turned white.

❧ 33

Decker laid the album on the coffee table, watched Ness settle his gaze on the yearbook. He said, "How's it going, Mike?"

The blue eyes snapped up and focused on Decker's face.

Marge said, "Come in and take a load off."

Ness shut the door quietly. He was dressed in cutoff jeans, a pea-green muscle shirt, and Nikes. His legs were exposed and exhibited a fair amount of black hair. Long hair under his armpits as well. He took a gulp from a thermos, then wiped his wet mouth with his arm.

Nobody spoke for a moment.

Ness said, "Davida's lawyer already sprung Eubie and my sister on their own recognizance last night. Kell and Eubie were back at work this morning. That must mean you don't have anything substantial on them."

Decker waited.

Ness said, "As far as Davida goes . . ." He let out a soft laugh. "You think you have Freddy, don't you? Forget it, Sergeant. His balls are in Davida's pocket.

She'll coo him . . . and woo him . . . he'll come around. You wasted your time."

Marge said, "Everyone's a critic."

Ness said, "My sister's an A student without a record. If you can't make murder stick—and you won't be able to because she didn't kill anybody—what are we talking about? Two-year probation for obstruction of justice and evidence tampering . . . something like that."

"Are you asking my opinion?" Decker said.

"Yeah, I guess I am."

Decker said, "I can't answer for the legal system. Is there something on your mind, Mike?"

Ness's eyes went to the yearbook. "You need that thing?"

"It's evidence," Decker said.

"For what?"

Decker wasn't sure, but he didn't answer.

Ness looked down. "Look, Detective . . . all that book can do is further fuck up my already fucked-up life. Right now, you don't have a case. You may never *get* a case. But if you give me the annual, then maybe I'll give you a little lesson in theory."

Decker remained silent.

"You know, fill in a couple of blanks," Ness said. "Just as long as you know it's just my *opinion*. I don't care what you threaten me with, I'll never go against Davida."

"Why are you protecting her?" Marge said.

"It's not because of any loyalty or anything like that." Slowly, Ness walked over to the bar and poured himself a finger's worth of Chivas. "But you just can't go against Davida and come out a winner. If you can't beat 'em, et cetera, et cetera, et cetera."

"You have something on your mind, Mike?" Marge said.

"Not particularly." Ness sipped Scotch. "Look, you don't have anything against me. And you won't get anything against me as long as I stay mum about Davida. You want some information—rather, I should say, some of my words of wisdom, fine. If not . . . I'm out of here. As far as that goes"—he pointed to the album—"I can't force you not to show it to Lilah, but it would be nice if you didn't. It would probably cost me and Kelley our jobs. Lilah's kinda squeamish."

Decker picked up the yearbook and leafed through it. "Michelle Ness, huh?"

Ness paled but didn't answer. Decker felt his brain buzz. What was the big secret? Was he cross-dressed as a kid? Did his parents mutilate his genitals? Decker placed the album in his lap. "Mike, you want to make some conversation, it's your choice."

"Just as long as you know we're only talking in hypothetical terms. So what pearls would you like to fish from my wondrous brain?"

Marge said, "How'd Kingston Merritt get into Lilah's inner safe?"

"I'd say someone hid a high-tech camera inside Lilah's closet and taped her opening her safe."

"Your little *video* camera," Marge said.

"So *that's* why they call you a *detective*!"

"Can we dispense with cute remarks?" Decker said.

Ness blew out a mouthful of air. "I'm sorry. I get obnoxious when I'm nervous. I wouldn't think it was that camera exactly. But it was something similar—a basic hand-held camcorder which was modified—the motor quieted and hooked up to the ceiling fan in Lilah's closet. You know, so every time she'd close the closet door and turn on the light, the fan and the camera would kick in automatically. The fan noise blocked out the sound of the running motor."

"How long did it take you to tape the combinations?" Decker asked.

"Me, I couldn't tell you 'cause I don't do illegal things. But it might take a person an average of seven months—about twenty different shots and angles. Even then it would be hard to read the tapes real clearly. It might even take another month of fiddling with the dial before the person would finally hit the right combination. But that person would be real smart afterward and destroy all the tapes."

"Why didn't you just take the memoirs when you finally got the safe opened?" Marge asked.

"I never said I opened the safe—"

"Mike."

"I just suggested how an inner safe might be opened."

"So why wouldn't that person just take the contents of the safe after he had opened it?"

"You'd probably have to ask the Queen Bee on that one. She had real specific ways of how she wanted it handled. You know—one getting the combination, another distracting the victim by taking her out to dinner, and still another doing the actual theft. Miss Q-Bee would want as many people involved as possible. The more dirt she had on people, the better. Then she could use them and abuse them."

"What was the payoff?" Marge asked.

"Different strokes for different folks. For a doctor doing funny things with fetuses, it would be lots of money—much more than he could ever hope to get by doing Paps. For the weaker son, it would be *approval* from Mama and maybe a few spare bucks to keep him happy. With people like lowly little me, it would be blackmail. Maybe I wouldn't want certain things about my past made public to my boss—ruin my job and my sister's."

"How'd Davida get this?" Decker patted the yearbook.

Ness looked sick. "Shortly after I came here to visit, my sister's room was burglarized. Nothing but personal things were missing. Kelley thought it might have been a weirdo who works in the kitchen, a guy who had a crush on her. But she didn't want to make a big scene. She was new here and I can't tell you what this job meant to her. Things like independence . . . Anyway, she forgot about the burglary. Then I got this phone call from a person who I won't mention by name. Break-ins and personal stuff missing . . . see any parallels here, guys? The Q-Bee's M.O."

"Why would Davida break into *Kelley's* place and steal her *yearbook*?" Marge asked.

"Q-Bee probably wasn't *out* to steal the yearbook specifically. She was just looking for employee *dirt* in general. That's what Miss Bee did. Gather dirt against anybody she could." Ness's eyes went to the yearbook. "She got a direct *hit* on *me*. So I became one of her errand boys just like her sons. Only she expected *more* from me."

"You had an affair with her?" Marge asked.

"Why are you talking in the past tense?" Ness frowned. "What difference does it make anyway?"

"What happened with Kingston Merritt?" Marge asked.

Ness pushed hair out of his eyes. "I'd say someone miscalculated her errand boys. I don't know why anyone would want to use scum like *Russ, especially* when someone like me might have helped out." He paused. "She claimed she was trying to protect me. Maybe she was."

"So what happened after she sent Russ over to Kingston's office?" Marge asked.

"Who knows?" Ness said. "*I* wasn't there. Next thing I knew, someone suggested that I check out King's office." He took a deep breath and let it out slowly. "Russ and King . . . both of them were floating in blood. I've got a strong stomach, but it made . . . the smell . . . I got out of there as fast as I could."

"You got Eubie to take care of Russ's body?" Marge asked.

"Go reread Eubie and Kelley's statements," Ness said.

"Eubie agreed to help you out because he owed you, didn't he, Mike?" Decker said. "For covering for him the night of Lilah's rape."

"That wasn't the only time," Ness said. "You meet Eubie, you meet a guy with a perpetually runny nose and loose zipper. Lilah would have fired him a long time ago if I hadn't intervened."

"So why'd you do it?"

" 'Cause I'm a *jerk*, that's why."

"Did Davida put a hit out on her own son?" Marge asked.

"Well, Q-Bee is one cold-blooded reptile, but that's not her style." Ness shrugged. "She likes them alive so she can squeeze them dry. I think Davida's telling it true. I think they did shoot each other. But I really don't know, because I wasn't there."

"But you did check out Merritt's office."

Ness shrugged again. "Hey, what does it matter? I'm just talking theory, not fact."

"Two men were shot and no guns were found in Merritt's office, Mike," Decker said. "Happen to have any theories about the weapons?"

"Might make more sense to ask *what* are the weapons. And the answer might be they're sheet metal. Recycling is very good for the environment. Can we finish up and put a lid on this whole mess?"

"Mess is right," Marge said.

"Yeah, it's been a mess." Ness was quiet for a moment. "Not that it hasn't had its benefits. Once we established ground rules, Q-Bee's been all right. Did you know Davida wants to build her own spa . . . a much nicer one than VALCAN. We thought Palm Springs would be a good location."

"We?" Marge said.

"Kelley and I would be silent partners," Ness said. "Our expertise'll be our contribution to the partnership. We've almost got all the papers signed—a few more glitches to iron out and I've *finally* got a piece of the action. Kelley and I have learned a lot from Lilah. It was good that I came here. But it's time to go forward."

"You're going into competition with Lilah," Marge said.

Ness grinned. "I'm not going into competition with Lilah, Detective. *Davida* is." He looked at his watch again, then at the yearbook. "Can I have that?"

"Why was this so important to you, Mike?" Decker said. "You could have told Lilah that the name Michelle Ness was a misprint."

Ness's laugh was forced. "God, you didn't look closely, did you? Not like Davida did."

"What'd we miss?" Marge said.

Ness buried his hands in his face, then looked up. "What the hell. I'm beyond humiliation. Maybe you'll take pity on me."

The room was quiet.

"Mike Ness," he whispered. "AKA Michelle Ness—tennis team, volleyball team, softball team, basketball team, and . . . the *cheerleading* squad." He laughed softly. "I was a *cheerleader*. No chick on earth could jump as high as I could. It was all the hormones, you know."

"You were taking male hormones?" Marge said.

"Didn't have to take them, Detective, I was *born* with them. You look at my birth certificate, you'll see I'm a male."

"We know that."

"You know—" Ness laughed. "Man, you guys are dedicated. Now can I have the album?"

Decker said, "One more question, Mike—"

"I know the question. A variation on the old *who am I?* game. In this case, it's *what* am I?"

Decker was quiet. He watched Ness pour himself another Scotch. Comfortable in the room. Decker wondered how many times Davida had called him down here to do her bidding—sexual or otherwise. Ness took a big swallow of booze.

"I've got this condition called CAH—cortical adrenal hyperplasia. I'm missing this enzyme . . . a genetic screwup. Without this enzyme, the adrenal glands go nuts and pump out gallons of extra hormones—androgens."

He faced them, eyes hot with anger.

"Know what androgens do to fetuses? They turn little baby girls into little baby boys. Wasn't until I was a year and a half old that some doctor finally figured out my balls weren't gonna descend because I *had* no balls. In fact, I wasn't even a boy. I was a girl born with fused labia that looked like a scrotum and a clitoris as big as a dick. Got that way because my adrenals had been feeding me testosterone since I was conceived."

He took another sip of booze.

"The condition wasn't life-threatening. Matter of fact, my mom could have done nothing about it and just raised me as a boy. Other than the fact I'd be sterile and would wind up with a small dick—small but I could do the job—I could lead a pretty normal life.

"But *my* mom didn't want that. My chromosomes said I was a girl and Mom was a firm believer in God's plan. If God wanted me to be a boy, he would have made me a real boy. So Mom decided to turn me back into a girl. So . . . we moved to another neighborhood. After a year and a half of being Michael wearing overalls and playing with firemen, I suddenly became Michelle wearing dresses and playing with dolls. I remember being very confused."

He finished his drink and quickly poured another one.

"Let's see, I was on doca, cortisol, then one estrogen after another. My parents could have done corrective surgery right away, but Mom was a fanatic about things being perfect. Because I was so much *less* than perfect, she insisted on the best surgeon in the country, which cost a fortune. She and Dad decided to save up and do it right. Meanwhile, I'm a little girl with a bulge in my underwear. I learned real fast that private parts were kept *private*. The hormonal therapy did shrink my dick a little but I never looked like a real girl. I never, ever *felt* like a girl."

He gazed into his drink.

"I wanted to *die*. Only thing that kept me going was Kelley. God, I loved her. I was a monster and she was *perfect*. A perfect little girl with a perfect little body. She reacted like a little girl, too . . . something I could never get the hang of. Screaming when she saw spiders or worms." He raised his voice to a falsetto. " 'Mitchy, Mitchy, kill it, kill it!' "

He laughed.

"I was her insect henchman. Kell used to follow me around and sic me on whoever was giving her a hard time. Everyone knew Kelley's sister didn't take no shit."

He rubbed his hands over his face.

"Course everything got worse during adolescence. I stopped taking my meds regularly 'cause I hated the way they made me feel—soft and moody. Soon as I started skipping them, I started changing back—hairy legs, peach fuzz on my face, deeper voice. It was slow so people didn't notice real fast. What happened was I was turning into a real *ugly* girl. What made it a real nightmare was I started *liking* chicks. Gym was a sick joke—me looking at all those naked girls, getting hard under a towel. It was *hideous*."

The room was silent.

Ness said, "I didn't have a friend in the world except Kelley. I was a fucking *freak*. But man, I could do the splits like no chick alive." He laughed. "The *in*-girls were *furious* when I made cheerleader. Course they couldn't say it out loud. I wasn't only strong, but junkyard mean. Any girl gave me or my sister a hard time, I'd take care of them. They knew I meant business."

He let out a soft laugh.

"Their boyfriends would come after me and try to intimidate me—push me, poke me, yank my hair. Then I'd jump 'em and beat the *shit* out of 'em. The guys wouldn't really fight me because they thought I was a girl, spent all their energy trying to block my punches. By the time they realized I wasn't fighting like a girl, I'd done serious damage. They never dared to say anything—too embarrassing. Even *I* had my few moments in the sun."

He smiled again at the recollection.

"Eventually, everyone just left me alone. Life was never good, but at least it was calm. Then my wonderful parents knocked on my door one day and announced they'd saved enough money to get me a first-class surgery job."

His eyes made contact with Decker's.

"Know what *I* heard, Sergeant? We're gonna take you to a doctor and he's gonna cut off what little remains of your dick."

He shook his head fiercely.

"Uh-uh, no way, man! I had the unmitigated *nerve* to tell my parents that I wanted to be a boy—fuck the meds, fuck the surgery, fuck the senior prom—which infuriated my mom because she'd spent a hundred dollars on the gown.

"My wonderful, wonderful parents promptly told me they'd disown me if I went back to being a boy. So I did . . . and they did. Only one who stuck by me was Kelley. So they started getting on *her* case. Finally, they kicked her out of the house 'cause they were fighting so much. She was just seventeen and had no way to support herself. An A student and they wouldn't give her a red cent. *I* supported her. I got us an apartment and put her through college. All this crap raining down on me and my sister because my parents couldn't accept what *their* genetics had done to me."

Ness flicked his wrist and checked the time. He let out a lungful of air. "I gotta go . . . five o'clock yoga. I'm late."

Decker stood, then tossed Ness the album. Ness one-handed it and tucked it under his arm.

"I *told* you guys I didn't rape Lilah."

Decker didn't answer.

"Thank you," Ness said.

"You're welcome," Decker said.

Walking into the station house, Decker was philosophic. They'd found nothing at Davida's bungalow—

the memoirs were probably a lost cause—but at least he'd be home before Shabbat with time to spare. Hollander grunted and lifted his butt from the chair.

"You guys just missed Ms. Eversong."

"She's gone?" Marge said.

"'Bout twenty minutes ago. You guys want some coffee?"

Decker picked up his phone messages and began to sift through them. "Thanks, Mike. Coffee sounds great."

"They couldn't keep her longer than an *hour*?" Marge complained.

"You need a *reason* to detain someone, Marge," Hollander said. "What are we going to bag her on? Not reporting a crime?"

"What about Freddy?" she said to Decker. "We still have Freddy."

"Want to know what I think, Margie?" Decker said. "I think Ness is right. I think Freddy's going to recant. I think we're going to end up with less than what we started out with."

"So she's just going to walk?"

"'Fraid so," Hollander said. "And Morrison suspects she'll probably throw us a lawsuit for harassment. At least *this* time, it'll be a suit we can probably beat. You see him on the boob tube? I thought he came off okay. I didn't see you two, though."

"You didn't see my 'Hi, Mom'?" Marge asked.

"It's probably videotape on the editing floor," Decker said.

"Yeah, the story was just a couple of sound bytes," Hollander said. "With Davida released, it's yesterday's news."

"Where is Morrison?" Decker asked.

"Out." Hollander shrugged. "He did leave a message for you guys. On your desk, Rabbi."

Decker walked over to his spot in the squad room and picked up a plain white envelope resting on his desktop. He pulled out the contents and read the note to Marge.

"Burbank's prelim of the Merritt homicide jibes with Davida's account, but they'll do follow-up . . . Devonshire'll do follow-up on Donnally. . . . Lilah's assault ruled self-inflicted. . . . Davida's jewels have been recovered. . . . Charges dropped against Totes. Good job . . . time to move on."

"That's it?"

"It looks that way."

"That stinks!" Marge banged her fist against her desk. "*I'm* gonna follow up on this."

"Better be on your own time, Detective," Hollander said. "I took the liberty of giving you a new two-forty-one. Girl was attacked in the underground lot of a parking mall in daylight. She was checked out, sent home. I contacted her, started the initial paperwork. She's real scared and I had a problem with rapport. She jumped when I asked her if she wanted a female detective. You should probably interview her before the weekend starts. I'll take your two juvey cases in exchange."

Marge slumped down in her chair and placed her chin in her hands. Decker groaned and handed her a message slip.

"Just when I thought I was out of deep water," he said.

"Sun Valley Pres," Marge said. "Lilah must not

have been transferred yet. Are you going to call her back?"

"Do I have a choice?"

"You can put it off until Monday."

"Right. Then she'll croak over the weekend and I'll feel guilty for the rest of my life." He picked up Marge's phone and dialed the number on the slip. "I hate this."

Marge gently patted his back. "Ain't it a drag to have a conscience?"

Decker said, "Damn it, it's ringing. Maybe she'll hang up on me."

Lilah answered hello, her voice low and sultry. Decker felt his stomach tighten. "Lilah, it's Detective Sergeant—"

"My mother just phoned me not more than ten minutes ago! Do *you* know what she told me?"

"Lilah—"

"She told me you had her brought down to the station house for questioning!"

"Li—"

"She *told* me the press was crawling all over her. Snapping pictures of her inside a *police* car! She told me you were tearing her room apart."

"We had a warrant—"

"Looking for ways to *ruin* her—"

"Not at all—"

"That you were spreading *lies* about her!"

"I'm not spreading anything—"

"Lies about her, lies about *me*, lies about *Kingston*!"

"Lilah—"

"Then she said that you said that I had stolen her jewels. Did you say that, Peter?"

"Lilah—"

"I'd never seen her so furious! She was outraged! Screaming and ranting and raving!"

"It is not our intention to—"

"Don't give me that garbage! Are you out to ruin her good name?"

"We were—"

"Just hold on a second, Peter. I have a visitor."

Decker heard mumbling in the background.

"I've got to go now, Peter."

Her voice had turned treacly sweet.

"My dear brother John is here to visit me," Lilah purred. "My God, I haven't seen him in *ages*! He brought me orchids, the dear man."

So the *good* brother had come a-calling. Was he trying to clear his conscience for not visiting Lilah after she was supposedly raped or had Davida somehow roped this poor guy into the family as Kingston's replacement? The heck with it, Decker told himself. None of it was his business. "Have a nice visit, Lilah."

"You're turning Mother into a *basket* case, you know."

"It's unintentional," Decker said.

"That may be true, but that's what you're doing!" She suddenly giggled. "God, it's great to see the bitch suffer. *Do* keep up the good work, Peter!"

She hung up. And so did Decker.

🍃 34

No one was home but the table was set—starched white linen, bone china, sterling, and crystal stemware. In front of his place setting were two braided loaves of egg bread covered by a dark-blue velvet cloth embroidered with silver and gold thread. A table fit for a king but meant for him.

He took a quick shower, then shaved. When he came out, the house was still empty. Where was everyone?

He listened and heard yapping noises outside. He went out the back door and found Rina sitting on the patio. She was wearing a loose housedress and had mules on her feet. She was trying to comb out long strands of wet black hair and was meeting resistance. She muttered fiercely each time the teeth fought with a tangle. The boys were whooping it up on horseback. They shouted hellos to their stepfather, and Decker smiled and waved. Rina looked up.

"One day, I'm just going to chop it all off."

"Go ahead." Decker sat next to her and kissed her cheek. "I'll love you bald."

She attacked her tresses and didn't answer.

Decker said, "You look tired, darlin'. Hard day?"

"No, just another hot, *pregnant* day." She kissed Decker on the lips. "I promise I won't take it out on you."

"Hey, that's what I'm here for."

She loosened a snag and smiled victoriously. "You're home reasonably early."

"What can I do you for?"

"Nothing. Everything's under relative control." She put down the comb. "I saw your captain on the five o'clock news. He looked uptight."

"He probably was."

"Is Davida being charged with the murder?"

"Nope."

"Then why the hoopla?"

"It wasn't necessary. I told her I was going to bring her in for further questioning. Not that I really had much on her, but I just . . . I don't know. I wasn't going to let her get off easy. Then she got mad and called the press. So I called Morrison, who said he'd handle it. Big stories, big brass. It was fine with me."

"You don't feel usurped?"

"Not at all. I feel relieved to be rid of the bunch. I've got a brickload of current cases. It's not as if I'm lacking for work."

"Did you talk to Lilah?"

"I think she'll be fine." He paused. "I hope we won't hear from her again."

"It was a lousy week for you, wasn't it?"

"Yes, it was. Really *unsatisfying*. That's why I love horses. They're honest."

Rina kissed him. "I'm sorry."

"S'right. At least I earned my paycheck." He watched the boys and smiled. "They have the right idea."

"Go join them."

"Nah, I think I'd rather watch." He kissed his wife's cheek. "Rina, I promise I'll wallpaper the spare room this Sunday."

"Don't worry about it."

"I've got *nothing* else planned."

"Peter, I think it would be better if you painted it instead of wallpapered it."

"You spent seventeen bucks a roll on wallpaper. Now you want it *painted*?"

"It's going to be Cindy's room for the summer. Maybe lilac walls would go over better than pictures of Mickey and Minnie having a Sunday picnic."

"That's right. I haven't even thought about Cindy. Some father I am."

"You're a *wonderful* father, Peter. Cindy loves you, the boys love you, I love you. Try loving yourself, okay?"

Decker smiled. "What are we going to do if the baby comes early?"

"We can set up a crib in our room."

"You don't mind?"

"What's our choice? You can't build another room in two and a half months."

"Do you mind that Cindy is staying with us for the summer?"

"*Mind? Chabibi*, I wouldn't have it any other way. She's *family*!"

Family. After what Decker had seen this past week,

he had forgotten what real family was all about—things like love and nurturance instead of torment and jealousy. "You're a good kid, Rina."

"Just one of a kind." She got up. "As long as you're supervising, I think I'll go check on the food."

"Sure. Then go put your feet up and rest awhile, darlin'. I'll serve tonight."

Rina mussed his damp hair. "Thanks."

Decker watched her waddle to the house, waiting until she was inside before he broke into laughter. Click your heels together, Deck. There's no place like home.

A Little Something Extra from Faye

❧

Living in Los Angeles, we're influenced by regional cuisine as exemplified by Rina's southwestern meal in *False Prophet*. Here is her personal recipe for Salsa Chicken. She might serve this entree with wild rice and a fresh avocado-and-grapefruit salad.

Enjoy!

Faye Kellerman

Salsa Chicken

Serves 6

4   large tomatoes, coarsely chopped
1   small onion, finely chopped
1   small green pepper, seeded and diced
1   clove fresh minced garlic
2   tablespoons fresh lemon juice
2   tablespoons minced fresh coriander
2   teaspoons minced fresh parsley
½   teaspoon salt
½   teaspoon pepper
2   tablespoons flour
½   teaspoon garlic powder
½   teaspoon salt
½   teaspoon pepper
6   boneless chicken breasts (each ½ inch thick)
    Oil for frying
    Parsley sprigs and lemon slices for garnish

In a medium bowl, mix together the tomatoes, onion, green pepper, garlic, lemon juice, coriander, parsley, salt, and pepper. Set aside in refrigerator for at least two hours.

Preheat the oven to 350°F.

In a separate bowl, mix together the flour, garlic powder, salt, and pepper. Dredge the chicken in the dry mixture, then sauté in oil until the chicken turns slightly brown. Place the chicken in a shallow greased baking pan and bake for 30 minutes or until done to taste. Remove the chicken from the oven and place on a serving platter. Decorate with parsley sprigs and lemon slices. Serve hot with salsa on the side.